THE SPARTAN DAGGER

FORGE BOOKS BY NICHOLAS GUILD

Blood Ties
The Ironsmith

THE
SPARTAN
DAGGER

Nicholas Guild

FORGE

A TOM DOHERTY ASSOCIATES BOOK
NEW YORK

This is a work of fiction. All of the characters, organizations, and events portrayed in this novel are either products of the author's imagination or are used fictitiously.

THE SPARTAN DAGGER

Copyright © 2016 by Nicholas Guild

Map by Jennifer Hanover

A Forge Book
Published by Tom Doherty Associates
175 Fifth Avenue
New York, NY 10010

www.tor-forge.com

Forge® is a registered trademark of Macmillan Publishing Group, LLC.

The Library of Congress Cataloging-in-Publication Data is available upon request.

ISBN 978-0-7653-7651-0 (hardcover)
ISBN 978-1-4668-5138-2 (e-book)

Our books may be purchased in bulk for promotional, educational, or business use. Please contact your local bookseller or the Macmillan Corporate and Premium Sales Department at 1-800-221-7945, extension 5442, or by e-mail at MacmillanSpecialMarkets@macmillan.com.

First Edition: December 2016

Printed in the United States of America

0 9 8 7 6 5 4 3 2 1

This book is for my friend,
Bernard Klem

Donec gratus eram tibi
—Horace, *Odes* III, 8, 5

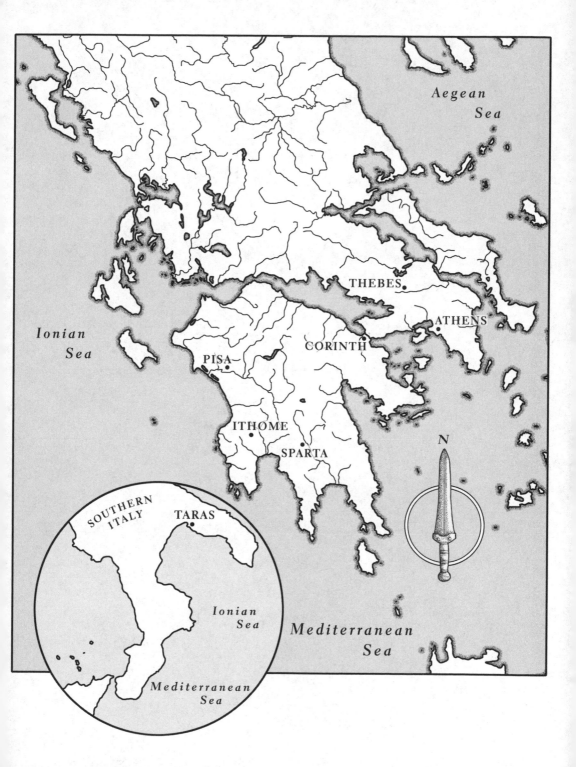

THE SPARTAN DAGGER

1

It was the coldest autumn anyone could remember. Eurytus sat in the shadow of a rock face, tapping the flat of his dagger against his knee as he cursed not the cold but the moonlight. He hadn't eaten in two days and the moon was as bright as a new gold coin. The night sky was nearly cloudless.

The valley beneath them seemed a stark landscape, full of hard lines and deep shadow. A faint wind blew across it, but the naked branches of its few scattered trees hardly stirred. In daylight it probably would have appeared a different place, but at night, in the tarnished moonlight, it was the land of the dead.

His brother Teleklos was asleep and untroubled by such reflections.

"Go out and wet your blades," their father had told them. "A warrior kills, without remorse or pity. Become warriors."

A quarter of a century before, their father had wet his blade in Helot blood. Eurytus thought him very like Teleklos in temperament, endowed with a warrior's perfect confidence. In his middle forties he was still tall and slim, broad shouldered and powerful. With his black hair and pale blue eyes, which both his sons had inherited, he had the face of a bird of prey.

"To have both of you selected for the *Krypteia* is an honor for our house. We have too many Helots as it is. When you need food, steal it. Plunder them, even of their lives, and prove your manhood."

The difficulty was that the Helots also seemed to know about the *Krypteia* and after dark they mostly kept indoors. It was rare to catch anyone on the roads at night and to venture into their villages might be to disappear forever.

Three days ago they had almost surprised a herdsman, but he saw them in time to save himself, scampering away like a rabbit but leaving behind a reed flute and his dinner bag. They had shared a small loaf of bread and a piece of goat cheese wrapped in leaves.

They had been on the march ever since, farther and farther south, hoping that, a day and a half's march from Sparta, the Helots might feel themselves safe.

Eurytus knew it might prove necessary to enter a village. They could not return home until they had each made a kill—better to die the worst death than to face the dishonor of failure. But the mere thought of venturing in among the Helots made his skin tingle with fear.

And his fear shamed him. Fear was unworthy of a Spartan and yet it would come, unbidden. To be torn apart by a mob of slaves . . .

At the ceremony it had seemed so simple. The Elders together had offered sacrifice of a kid at the shrine of Artemis and declared the annual war against the conquered peoples, thus absolving of blood guilt any who killed a slave—who was, in any case, the property of the state—and the ten young men who would go out in pairs to accomplish the rite had been selected from among the best of those who had just finished their military training. Eurytus, described by his instructors as the perfect soldier, brave, disciplined, and cunning, had known he was certain of a place, and Teleklos had been almost as deserving.

"You will enjoy yourselves," their father had said as Eurytus and Teleklos set out. "It is no different from a hunting party, except that you kill men instead of deer or wild boar—and, trust me, wild boar are more dangerous than the Helots. They are slaves in their souls."

So they had each been given a dagger and a leather bag full of water and had been sent off south over the hills.

But Eurytus knew this would be no deer hunt. Even a slave will fight for his life. And one man, or even two, cannot prevail against twenty, not armed with a blade no longer than a crow's wing.

The *Krypteia* was a test of stealth, no less than of courage. Hence the name: the Hidden. One concealed oneself during the day, for to be discovered was to hazard death, and at night one stole food and killed.

"We will have to go into a village," Teleklos announced, now apparently awake.

"It is a serious risk."

"Nevertheless, we have to eat. And when should a Spartan be afraid of risk?"

Teleklos grinned, as if issuing a challenge—and what else could it be?

In the moonlight Eurytus could see his face clearly. It was like seeing his own reflection.

They were twins, in appearance as alike as two halves of the same apple yet, like the halves of an apple, not quite identical. The difference was a reflection of their temperaments, which were at odds. Eurytus had long recognized a streak of madness in his brother. Teleklos was not as gifted in intellect, but he was recklessly brave. Aside from skill with weapons, it was the only virtue he thought a Spartan needed. He was born to be a hero, yet would never command troops in battle.

They were near a road, really more of a footpath, a pale streak running north and south between two villages. The brothers had positioned themselves so that they had a clear view of its length, a distance a man might walk in little more than an hour.

"We will wait until the moon is directly overhead," Eurytus said finally. "If no one has come along by then, at least we can be sure the villagers will be deep asleep."

"They are asleep already. They sleep like cattle." Teleklos laughed quietly. "They *are* cattle."

When Eurytus didn't respond, Teleklos apparently felt encouraged.

"It will be easy," he went on. "We go into a hut, we kill everyone there before they have a chance to cry out. We steal some food, and then it's home again."

"Have you ever been inside a Helot village?"

"No." Teleklos shook his head. "And neither have you."

"True. But I have wit enough to realize that I have no idea what we might find there. The Helots are poor. Even from the outside we can see that their huts are small. For all we know, they probably sleep like dogs in a kennel— parents, grandparents, little children, uncles, cousins . . . There might be ten or twelve in one room, covering the floor like rushes. We can't kill that many without someone living long enough to raise an alarm. We will wait."

"I'm hungry now."

"Nevertheless, we will wait."

This was met with sullen silence. Brave as he was, Teleklos had never learned to defy his brother. Instead, he hunched his shoulders and went back to sleep.

Let him sleep, Eurytus thought.

"I'm hungry now."

It had been exactly the same when they were eleven years old and their military instructors decided that the boys were becoming sluggish.

"A Spartan should be strong enough to fight on an empty belly," one of them had announced. "Too much food is turning you into women. Corinthians can be women. Athenians can be women and no one notices the difference. But Spartans have to be men. Learn to do with less."

After five or six days the boys learned they could not "do with less." Some tried to run away, to return to their parents, which, of course, was impossible. A few just curled up on the ground and couldn't be roused.

Teleklos's solution was more drastic—he wanted to attack the instructors' mess in the midst of their evening meal.

"Don't be a fool," Eurytus had told him. "What can you achieve except a sound thrashing and perhaps even expulsion? Then, if you're not a Spartan anymore, what are you?"

"I'm hungry."

"Wait."

"I'm hungry now!"

"Wait until tonight and we'll steal some food."

"How will we do that?"

"I'll think of something."

It was summer and the training was entirely out of doors—even Homer was taught under the shade of an olive tree. The boys slept on the bare ground. Cooking was done over pits dug in the earth and filled with coals. The larder was in a tent to keep the flies off.

Of course the instructors pitched their tents all around it, so one had to be quiet.

In the darkest part of the night, Eurytus nudged Teleklos awake.

"Let's go."

There was a sliver of moon, so they had just enough light to find their way. The night air was thick with cold and Eurytus was shivering—but more from sheer excitement, he suspected. It was like war except, probably, without the threat of death. He had no idea what the punishment might be for stealing food, but it would be bad.

The tent was secured to the ground with pegs. It was no more than a matter to prying one loose and slithering in beneath the flap.

Once inside, they could smell bread.

"We take two loaves and we leave," Eurytus said, his voice hardly more than a whisper.

"And some beer and cheese."

"Teleklos, listen to me—"

But it was already too late. Where only a few pale slivers of light came in through the tent seams around the roof, Teleklos was stumbling among shelves of jars that might have held anything from wine to cooking oil. Almost immediately one of the shelves collapsed with a crash.

And then Teleklos began cursing loudly because a jar had landed edge down on his bare foot.

Eurytus could already hear a murmur of alarm from the instructors' tents. They had hardly a moment before they would be discovered, and someone would have to take the blame.

But perhaps not both.

Ever since they were six years old, keeping Teleklos out of trouble had seemed to be half the business of Eurytus's life. Whatever punishment was about to be visited upon them, Teleklos was so rash that he would make it ten times worse for himself. It was necessary to get him out of there.

Eurytus felt around on a table and found a heavy butcher's knife. He used it to cut a large rent in the back of the tent and practically kicked Teleklos out through it.

"Hide yourself," he whispered tensely. "Better yet, go back to bed. Get away from here."

Once Teleklos was gone, Eurytus sat down in the dark, awaiting the inevitable, his heart clenching with fear.

The instructors were not pleased. Eurytus was whipped on the soles of his feet until they ran with blood and then they were wrapped in vinegar-soaked rags. It was a fortnight before he could walk.

He had endured his punishment without crying out.

When he had recovered, he took Teleklos out into the woods and thrashed him. Teleklos did not even attempt to defend himself—he knew he deserved it.

"I was punished for being caught," Eurytus told him. "You have been punished for being stupid. Next time, listen."

It was advice Teleklos had heeded through all the years that followed.

"And next time I'll go steal food on my own."

And he did, always bringing it back to share with his brother. And he was never caught again.

So, hungry or not, Teleklos would listen and they would not go into a Helot village unless they had to.

Perhaps half an hour later Eurytus jarred him awake.

"Look down there."

Eurytus was pointing toward the northern village, where a tiny rectangle of light had appeared.

"Someone has opened a door," he said softly, as if afraid that someone, perhaps a thousand paces distant, might hear him.

"Whoever it is probably only wants to come outside to piss," his brother answered, sounding annoyed.

"Who would trouble to light a lamp for that?"

The light seemed to flicker, suggesting that perhaps someone—perhaps more than one—was passing in front of or through the doorway. Then, suddenly, the light collapsed.

And all at once Teleklos became as alert as a hunting dog.

"There is movement," he announced, with a low rumble of laughter. "Two—no three. They are walking toward the road."

"A family, do you think?"

Eurytus stared into the distance, seeing nothing. But he was prepared to take Teleklos's word. Teleklos had the eyes of a hawk.

"Two adults, one a head taller than the other. And a third not quite as tall as either."

"That sounds like a family."

"If it is, I claim the woman." Teleklos grinned. He had a taste for that sort of thing.

"As you wish. But then you kill the child as well. I will take the man."

※ ※

Uncle Neleus was dead. Protos could see the grief in his father's face, the way his teeth drew away from his lips and the flesh around his eyes appeared to thicken. Uncle Neleus had been his father's brother, his elder by two years. For himself, Protos had been astonished by just the naked fact of death. At fourteen he knew well that people died, just as he knew that the gods lived on Mount Olympus. But his uncle's death had shocked him, no less than if a swan had waddled in through the doorway and then transformed itself into Father Zeus.

Eventually he supposed he would grieve, like his father, for he had been fond of Uncle Neleus, who could tell wonderful stories. But not quite yet. He still had to recover from the surprise.

His mother and Aunt Nausicaa were weeping. Uncle Neleus had been sick for almost a month—no one seemed to know what from—but perhaps they had not expected him to die. Cousin Mantios, having run the whole way from his village, had entered their house late that afternoon to tell Father he had best come at once if he wished to see his brother alive. Mantios was the same age as Protos, but Protos was almost a span taller.

And now Protos, his father and mother stood outside in the darkness.

"Let us go home," his father said. "For these few hours he belongs to his wife and children. We shall return in the morning and his sons and I will dig my brother's grave."

His father smiled, but his kind, triangular eyes were sad. He put his hand on Protos's shoulder and looked up into the night sky.

His father was his hero and model. His father knew everything and could do everything, and in every word and action he was quietly, unobtrusively noble. It was from him that Protos had inherited his height, just as his wheat-colored hair was from his mother.

The path out to the main road was narrow so they walked single file, his father first, then Protos, then his mother. A year ago, Protos would have been last. But he was nearing manhood now. When they reached the road he would walk beside his father, who might describe to him the burial rites that would take place the next day. His father was his teacher now. His father was the best man alive.

The moon was huge and directly over their heads. Except for the depth of their shadows, it might have been day.

The moon was a goddess named Selana. She had whelped many children and when she was big like this it meant she was near her travail. Perhaps her pains were upon her and made her wrathful, for the full moon was said to be a dangerous time.

They had just reached the end of the path when his father stopped, putting his hand on Protos's shoulder. Two men were standing by the edge of the road. Suddenly, like wicked spirits, they were simply there.

In an instant the moon, with supernal mercilessness, revealed everything. The two men were strangers and, stranger still, precisely alike. And in their hands they held knives.

"Protos! Antheia!" Father shouted. "Run! Save yourselves!"

Mother screamed—it was like no sound he had ever heard. She turned and fled. Protos could not understand what was happening.

"Run, Protos! Now!"

Death suddenly felt so close. Protos ran like a startled deer.

Sixty paces from the road the ground became a wilderness of rock, trees, and brush. No one ever went there except small boys who wished to play. There was no other reason to go there. Beyond were only the hills and beyond them the barren mountains.

Just at the edge, before Protos plunged into that trackless waste, he heard something that made him stop. It was like a sob, cut brutally off. He turned and looked back. What he saw would live in his memory until he was dust.

His father was on the ground, curled up like a newborn, his hand clutching at his guts, his legs kicking strengthlessly. Even at that distance, Protos could see the bright blood welling out between his fingers.

And his mother was on her knees. Protos did not have to hear her words to know she was begging for her life. One of the two strangers had her by the hair, his knife raised.

"Teleklos, stop toying with the woman," his companion shouted. "Get the boy before we have the whole village down on us."

With a stroke the man called Teleklos cut Mother's throat. Protos saw a spray of blood and then she fell over sideways and lay twitching on the earth as she died.

"The boy, Teleklos!"

Protos did not wait. He ran, jumping over rocks and fallen trees, hardly conscious of the sharp little stones that tore at his feet. He headed into the deepest undergrowth, hoping to find a hiding place.

But even as he ran he knew flight was hopeless. There were two of them and soon they would both be upon him. And they were men while he was only a boy. They would run him down quickly enough.

He might hope to escape only one. One he might be able to evade. So he would have to do something about the one who was nearer. Teleklos—somehow knowing his name rendered him less terrible.

So it was Teleklos he had to stop. The means were everywhere around him.

"My son Protos can kill a crow at fifty paces," Father had once bragged to a neighbor. "Give him a pebble no larger than a grape, and he'll knock its eye out."

"Not a very practical skill for a farmer," the neighbor had responded, and then laughed.

"Here, boy, show me what you can do," he went on, picking up a small stone and tossing it to Protos. "Hit that fence post over there and I'll give you a swallow of my beer."

Protos had been eight years old, and it was the first time he had ever tasted beer.

"No one can choose the gifts he is born with," his father had told him once. But this one might now be the means of saving his life.

Even as he ran Protos searched the ground and at last he found it—a stone, almost perfectly round, about half the size of his fist. He ducked low and scooped it up and kept on running.

His pursuer was no more than forty paces behind and closing the distance. Protos struck off to the left, ran about fifteen paces, and hid himself within the shadow of a tree.

He had only to wait. He could feel the pulse beating in his neck. It was as if his heart had somehow become trapped in his throat.

Just there the ground was fairly open. Teleklos stopped and looked about him, no doubt wondering where his quarry had disappeared to. This opportunity would last no longer than an instant.

Protos made his throw. As the stone glided away under the first two fingers of his right hand, he had no doubts.

Perhaps Teleklos saw something, or heard something, because in the last instant he turned his head. The stone caught him on the outer end of his left eyebrow. He pitched over as if struck dead.

But he was not dead. Protos made his approach slowly and by the time he found the man's knife lying in the grass—still stained with Mother's blood—Teleklos had begun to groan.

Protos weighed the knife in his hand. He tested the blade and it was very sharp. Suddenly he knew he was going to kill this man.

He wanted him to be awake, to know what was happening to him. It would have been the easy thing to slit his throat while he lay unconscious, but it wasn't enough. It would not appease the hatred he felt.

He sat down on the ground beside Teleklos's head, gathering up the Spartan's long hair in his hand. By then he had come to understand that these men were Spartans—who else would ambush innocent people to kill them for sport?

He let the knife blade rest on the bridge of the Spartan's nose, allowing it to split the skin until blood welled out and flooded the man's eye sockets.

Teleklos regained consciousness with a start.

"Don't struggle," Protos almost whispered. "Lie still. If you move I'll dig the eyes out of your head."

With visible effort, Teleklos became still. He was panting for breath.

Good, Protos thought. *Let him be afraid, as my mother was afraid.*

"I can't see." Teleklos made as if to touch his face, but a touch of the knife stopped him. "Who are you?"

"I am your death."

"Are you the boy?"

"Yes. You killed my mother, and for that you will die."

He pressed the point of the knife against the Spartan's throat.

"You can't kill me," Teleklos said, in a voice that was no more than a strangled whisper. "You're only a slave."

In answer, Protos drove the blade into the Spartan's neck until he hit bone. Then he gave the knife a sharp twist. Blood spattered his face.

For a moment Teleklos jerked about like a fish on a riverbank. And then he was still.

"Teleklos!"

Having killed once, Protos suddenly found he had no courage left. All he wanted was to flee.

The moon, merciful at last, stepped behind a cloud and the world went dark. Protos did not run but crept along, working back toward the road. His pursuer would probably expect him to escape danger by fleeing from it, so he would do just the opposite.

In the next instant the air was split with a scream of anguish. Brother had found brother. Protos was perhaps a hundred paces distant, but he could hear the sobbing. For some reason he could not have explained, the sound filled him with remorse.

By then he had gained the road, where he found his parents' corpses lying in the dirt. Their eyes were open and their blood seemed black in the faltering moonlight.

And remorse died.

He headed east, into the hills.

But he quickly sensed he was not alone. Sometimes, if the wind died away, he would stop and hear the faint sound of sandals scraping against the stony ground. The brother had not been fooled by his doubling back. Somehow, even in the darkness, he was tracking him.

Once, lying on his belly behind a thistle bush, Protos saw him at a distance, watched him hunting over the ground.

He was clever, this one—subtle, where Teleklos had been bumbling and obvious. If he and not his brother had first set out after him, Protos suspected he would have been dead these two hours.

What was he looking for? Footprints?

Protos decided to stay off the paths and try to use the rock face. It would be harder, but he might live to dawn.

Finally, when his strength had all but left him, he found a cave, small enough that he had to crawl inside on his hands and knees. He reached out and pulled some brush over the mouth, hoping that would be enough to keep it hidden.

And he still had Teleklos's knife. If the other one came in after him, Protos would see to it that he never crawled out again.

It was only in the cave, when he was still and his heart was no longer racing with fear, that he realized how cold the night was. He wondered if he might freeze to death before morning. It gave him a certain satisfaction to reflect that then surely the Spartan would never find him.

"BOY!"

It could have been coming from anywhere—it sounded almost as if he was standing directly in front of the cave.

"You cut my brother's throat, and I promise I will not rest until I see you crucified over his grave. Do you hear me, boy? I know you are here somewhere. I am Eurytus, son of Dienekes, and I have taken a vow over my brother's corpse that I will see you die. You will die hard, and you will pray to the gods for death long before it comes. I will find you, boy!"

Protos waited, hardly daring to breathe. Fear sharpens the senses, and a ferret could not have climbed out of his burrow without him hearing it. But there was nothing. Eurytus, son of Dienekes, had been announcing that he had given up. He would be back, but not tonight.

Protos never closed his eyes. Fear and grief kept him awake—and the cold. Yet somehow that night, in the chill, black solitude of a mountain cave, the child died and the man was born.

2

An hour before sunset, Eurytus was standing before the entrance of his father's house, beating the door with his clenched fist.

At last the door opened. Dienckes at first looked merely annoyed, but when he saw his son the expression on his face changed. Even then he was prepared for bad news.

"Teleklos is dead," Eurytus announced breathlessly. "We ambushed a Helot family. We killed the parents but the boy escaped. Teleklos went after him."

He looked down at the threshold, suddenly unable to find the words to describe what had happened.

Dienekes was one of the Ephors, five men elected by the Spartan Assembly of Citizens and second only to the two kings in power. Thus his reaction to the news of his son's death was not that of a private man. Eurytus could not tell whether he was more stricken with grief or simple embarrassment.

"Are you telling me he was killed chasing down a Helot boy?"

"Yes."

"*One* boy?"

"Yes."

There were still people in the street, although most were women and slaves. Dienekes cast his eyes about, and suddenly it seemed to occur to him that he might be about to learn things he wouldn't wish his neighbors to know.

"Come in," he said quietly. "You must tell me everything."

The inside of the house was small and reflected the Spartan abhorrence of display. Its few sticks of furniture were unpainted wood. Eurytus and his brother had been taken from here to begin their military training when they were seven. Now, with their mother long dead, the house might have belonged to a stranger. Their father almost was a stranger. Eurytus did not even know if he loved him.

Father and son sat on two stools before the kitchen fire, their knees nearly touching. There was no one else in the house, not even a servant. Eurytus hadn't eaten in three days and had been on the march for the last fourteen hours. His emotions were raw and he was almost fainting with fatigue and hunger. But he held himself erect and did not as much as glance at the cooking pot. A Spartan did not show weakness.

"Why are you crying?" his mother had asked. It was almost his earliest memory.

"Teleklos hit me. It hurts."

"In Sparta even a woman would be ashamed to weep over a little pain. Pain is nothing. Do you want to be a child forever?"

"No."

"Then learn to overcome weakness. Be a Spartan."

"And now tell me," his father murmured, almost as if asking a favor. "Tell me exactly how your brother died."

It was the request Eurytus had been dreading. Walking alone through the night, he had gradually awakened to the blunt truth that his brother was no more. He had seen Teleklos's corpse and had felt the sharp stab of grief, but it was hours before he discovered his own terrible aloneness. His brother had been careless and rash, and even a little mad, but he had been like a second self. They had done everything together. They had been inseparable. And now Teleklos was consigned to the inaccessible past. He was gone. It was unimaginable.

Their father, however, was concerned not with feelings, but with facts. His feelings, his state of mind, Eurytus could never have explained, not even to himself. But the facts he could just manage. And it was also a point of honor to describe everything exactly as he had seen it.

"He was lying on the ground when I found him," he began, feeling the awful weight of each word. "There was a narrow wound in his throat."

"Go on."

"His eye sockets were full of blood, but that was from a cut across the bridge of his nose—I think the boy only wanted to wake him up."

"Wake him up?"

"I saw a cut just above his left eye. The boy must have hit him with something. I think the boy wanted him awake while he died."

"And so he cut his throat?"

"Yes—I think with Teleklos's own dagger, since I didn't find it."

Dienekes shook his head. He seemed incredulous.

"My son," he began, as if adding up a list of numbers, "my son, a Spartan warrior, lies dead on the ground because he allowed himself to be outwitted and overwhelmed by a Helot slave boy. The boy kills him with his own weapon and then disappears like a ghost."

He rested his hands on his knees and stared into the fire, seeming to contemplate the scope of the disaster.

"And now Teleklos, through his blundering, has left us with a not inconsiderable problem," he went on at last, turning his eyes back to Eurytus. "We must find this boy and kill him. The Helots must never be allowed to think that one of them can spill Spartan blood without having visited upon him the most terrible revenge."

It occurred to Eurytus, simply as a fugitive thought, that the boy had just witnessed the slaughter of his parents, that he had killed Teleklos to save his own life. What would he, Eurytus, son of Dienekes, have done in his place? Exactly the same.

"They are not like us," his father said, as if he could read his son's mind. "We are the masters. They are slaves. They have no rights, not even the right to their lives. We must kill this boy and crucify his corpse in front of his village, where his neighbors can watch the flesh rot off his bones. We must do this, or one day they will rise up and murder us all."

Of course, his father was right. It felt better not having to think of this boy as someone like himself. The Helots were a conquered people. Centuries ago they had yielded up to the swords of the Spartans their freedom and their right to be thought of as men.

But still, Eurytus kept remembering the Helot father, who had stood his ground. He had made no attempt to escape, had almost dared them to kill him. He had been prepared to lose his own life in order to give his wife and son a chance to live.

If manhood was courage—and the Spartan prided themselves on courage above all else—then that Helot had been a man.

"I take it you attempted to find this boy," his father said.

"Yes. I tracked him up into the hills, but there he would know every hiding place. And I had to get away before the villagers discovered what had happened. If I had four good men I could go back and find him."

"If he is still there."

Eurytus smiled. "He is a slave boy. He has probably never been more than two hours' walk from his village. He won't wander far."

Dienekes appeared to consider this.

"Yes. Five of you should be enough to overawe the villagers, and they will give him up rather than risk a massacre. They will need to be experienced men, and you will be one of them, but you will not lead them."

He peered into his son's face, waiting for a reaction that did not come. Then he nodded, as if satisfied.

"It is no criticism of you, Eurytus. But this will be cruel work and will require men who know how it is done."

Then his expression changed as his thoughts seemed to take him somewhere else.

"Did you bury your brother?"

"The ritual three handfuls of earth to hide him from the sight of the gods—there was no time for anything more. We can retrieve his body when we go back."

"No. He deserves no honors." Dienekes's eyes narrowed. "Let him rot where he fell."

※ ※

Protos crawled out of his cave at first light. An hour of cautious scouting convinced him that Eurytus, son of Dienekes, was gone, and the exertion worked the cold out of his bones. Eventually he found a small grove, where he could sit with his back against a tree trunk and consider his situation.

He could not go back to his village. He could not even bury his parents, who were probably still lying dead in the road. He had killed a Spartan and if he asked anyone for help he would be calling down destruction upon them all.

He was utterly alone and full of grief. His father, the wisest and best of men, lay murdered, and his mother, that gentle, sweet soul . . .

Suddenly Protos began to weep. He sobbed uncontrollably, helpless against the sense of desolation that engulfed him. He wanted to be with his parents, even in death—even if death was extinction.

At last, as the spasm released its hold on him, he began to feel ashamed. What would his father have thought, seeing him like this? His father, he was sure, would never have surrendered to despair.

To survive was a duty, not least to his dead parents. Only the means were in question.

His attention kept coming back to the knife, his new possession. He had killed the one called Teleklos and now the knife was his. He had never seen anything like it.

For one thing, it was made of a gray metal he thought was probably iron. Iron was supposed to be harder and stronger than bronze, and Helots were forbidden, upon pain of death, to forge it or even to possess it. All their tools, even plowshares, had to be made of copper or bronze.

And it was beautiful in its way. It was a weapon with but one purpose. It was designed to kill.

His mother had a knife—somehow it was impossible to believe she was dead—a clumsy little bronze thing with a blade no longer than one's little finger that his father had had to recast three times. She used it to cut up vegetables.

The Helots were forbidden to possess weapons.

But this thing was perfectly balanced and its blade was sharpened on both edges. Protos kept weighing it in his hand, holding it loosely by the hilt. It felt almost as if it were part of him.

Was a knife so different from a stone? A knife would tumble end over end through the air, but might it be possible to control its flight so that it struck its target point first?

He thought it worth a test. He stood up and measured off ten paces from the tree against which he had been sitting. Aiming for a place on the trunk, no larger than a clenched fist, where the bark had peeled away along three sides and seemed ready to fall at a touch, he grasped the knife by the blade and threw it.

It flew through the air with a sound like the beating of wings and buried its point in the trunk. A fragment of bark floated to the ground.

He practiced for perhaps an hour, by the end of which he knew the knife would obey his will no less than would his own hand.

Then it occurred to him that he was hungry.

After a morning of wandering, he came across a juniper tree still loaded with berries. These were edible but bitter. A few handfuls were all he could stand.

He noticed deer droppings around the base of the tree. Perhaps they liked the berries. Perhaps they only ate the leaves.

But deer suggested the possibility of meat.

Protos's experience of meat was confined to the few yearly festivals, when a goat or a lamb might be roasted over an open fire. For the rest he ate bread and beans and the vegetables from his mother's kitchen garden. He wasn't sure one could eat deer meat, but he had to eat something.

It took him until the middle of the afternoon to track a doe, about half grown. Protos kept downwind of it and got to within about twenty-five paces—an older, more experienced animal would never have allowed him so close.

At such a distance he had no idea if the throw was even possible. The doe was facing away but at an angle. It was grazing and seemed totally occupied with that. Protos aimed for the neck.

The knife dropped down like a falcon on a rabbit. In the last instant the doe raised its head. Perhaps it had heard something. The point caught it about a span below its left ear and sank in almost to the hilt.

At first the doe seemed merely startled and turned as if ready to bound away. Then it took a step and stumbled. It rested for a moment on its knees and blood began pouring down its neck. Then slowly it collapsed.

Protos experienced a flush of triumph. He would butcher off a hind-quarter and then set about the awkward and time-consuming business of starting a fire.

❧❦

Outside the city of Larissa, many days' journey from where Protos was thinking about a supper of roast deer, a woman sat on the ground, leaning against the wheel of a wagon that had been drawn up beside the Pineios River. She wore a black shirt, so short it hardly reached her hips but with sleeves that covered her arms, and a long green skirt, dress that clearly marked her as a foreigner, although from where was indeterminable. In fact, she dressed thus because she found Greece chilly and cared very little what people thought of her.

She had long black hair and a complexion that made one think of a bronze idol, and she just missed being beautiful. Instead, her mouth and particularly her eyes, could you have seen them, suggested a sensual nature, as if she could answer every longing of a man's flesh.

Beside her on the ground was a pottery cup, its bottom still wet with beer into which had been mixed a powder made from the dried berries of a plant that grew wild all over the Greek mainland but was shunned even by animals.

The woman was asleep or, more accurately, in a trance, for she saw things through her closed eyes that made the world in which most people lived seem a dismal, gray place, little more than a foretaste of death.

Her dreams might wander in different directions, but their beginnings were always the same. She was in Egypt, where she had been born, in the city called Naukratis on the western branch of the Nile's delta. The name was Greek and meant "mistress of the sea," for Naukratis was a trading port established by Greeks centuries before. She lived in a Greek house located in the Egyptian quarter of the city. She was a slave in that house, as had been her mother before her. She was fourteen years old then.

The man who owned the house was a Greek, but he preferred to live among Egyptians because he had a taste for luxury, which the Greek merchant colony frowned upon, and because the Egyptians were more tolerant of his vices.

She was his daughter but more important, his slave—his property, and thus no different from any other of the women in his house. And she had reached an age when her body was not without its attractions.

It was late into the night and he had sent his other slaves away. He lay on a couch, eating greedily out of little golden bowls. From time to time he held up his right hand and expected her to lick his fingers clean. Then he would touch her breasts and sometimes the cleft between her legs and then go on with his meal.

He was well into middle age and fat, with a black beard that grew in little tufts, as if pieces of it had been plucked out. His face was greasy and he smelled like river mud.

She loathed his body. He had taken her virginity more than a year before, so her loathing was of an intimate nature.

Tonight she was his cup bearer, bringing the wine to his lips, leaving his food-smeared hands free to clutch at her. In another half hour, when he was sufficiently drunk, he would expect her to reach under his tunic and caress his genitals until he was hard enough to enter her.

But tonight she would avoid that horror. Tonight she had put something in his wine, a slow-acting poison that would first reduce him to helplessness and then strangle him as his lungs lost the power to draw in air.

Already his movements were heavy, as if his arms were becoming leaden. After a few minutes he tried to sit up, and then collapsed.

"Too much wine," he said, slurring the words. He tried to laugh, but it tailed off into a hoarse gurgle. By then he knew something was very wrong. "Khryseis, what is happening to me?"

"My name is not Khryseis. Khryseis is a Greek name. I am Nubit."

Nubit leaned down and whispered into his ear. In her dream she could not hear what she was saying, but she could see his face and that was better. His face was racked with terror.

The priests, both Egyptian and Greek, taught that the gods sent dreams to great criminals as punishment for their wickedness. Either the priests were foolish or their gods were, for Nubit never tired of her dream. She had poisoned her father, a vast impiety, but in her own mind she had merely rendered justice to her mother, whom her father had kicked to death for the sin of being clumsy with his bathwater. The laws of Egypt did not recognize killing one's slave as a crime. Nubit did not recognize killing her father as a crime.

Yet she was an outlaw in Egypt. In Egypt she would have been fed to the crocodiles. She could never return to Egypt. She never wanted to.

The dream always drifted away when her father's face became rigid with death and then dissolved into broken pieces of light.

And then, tonight, gradually the light gathered again and became a mountain meadow, a place Nubit had never seen before. It was so beautiful and quiet she wanted to weep.

But suddenly she heard a strange sound, a fluttering, like a flock of birds rising in panic. And then something struck her. She felt the blow, but there was no pain.

And she was awake. She opened her eyes and saw the remains of her campfire and heard the soft murmur of the river.

She was not dead. It took her a moment to realize that she was alive and unhurt. The blade had not killed her.

It had killed the doe.

She could see it now in memory—if one can truly *remember* the events of a dream, things that never really happened. She saw the doe, with a dagger buried up to the hilt in its neck. She saw the doe stagger and fall.

Someone came and pulled the blade free. It was a man. She knew because she could see his hands as he held the dagger. She saw the dagger through his eyes and felt with his heart, and the sight of the gray iron blade filled her with a strange pleasure.

And she knew that Earth, the Mother of All Life, had sent her an omen.

3

Eurytus marched south in company with four men who were unknown to him, even by sight. They all had the look of hardened veterans. All were without pity or mercy—they talked about the task ahead as if it were a holiday excursion, and perhaps to them it was. War, real war, doubtless had that effect. The *Krypteia*, by comparison, must have seemed a lark.

The leader was named Pantites. At thirty he had reached the compulsory marriage age and had already left the soldiers' mess to establish his own household. He was old enough to have participated some seven years before in the massacre of an entire village, retribution for the death of an Ephor whom the headman had struck and killed. He had told the story on the march from Sparta and affected not to remember the headman's motives, but perhaps he had never known. It had been no part of his business to know and, like a good soldier, he doubtless hadn't cared.

A good soldier understood only his duty and his duty tonight was to capture a boy, by any means necessary.

"The trick is to make them understand that we would as soon kill them as not," he explained. "Once they understand we are prepared to spill as much blood as necessary, they will tell us everything they know.

"The boy may even be still hiding with his relatives. You say you know which house he came out of?"

"Yes," Eurytus answered. He was a little intimidated by Pantites and thus felt a need for his approval. "The door opened and we were attracted by the light."

"Then we will know where to start."

Pantites laughed. He carried many scars, including one from a sword thrust through his left cheekbone, which had sufficiently paralyzed the muscles on that side to leave him with a permanent sneer. When he laughed his face assumed an expression of almost demonic cruelty.

"We will wait another half hour, by which time the family will have assembled for dinner, and we can have them all in the net at once. I hope the woman is a decent cook."

His comrades joined him in his laughter at the jest, even Eurytus, who had killed his first man less than two days ago on this very spot and thus had not yet grown hardened to butchery.

"Someone must know where he's hiding," his father had said. "They may not even know that he's killed a Spartan, but it makes no difference. You will squeeze them until they give him up. Justice has nothing to do with it."

What they planned was both right and necessary—Eurytus understood that. Yet suppose they didn't find the boy in the house. Suppose no one knew where he was. Then they would probably end by killing the whole family. He dreaded such an act, even though he understood that there would be no other choice, and, interpreting his dread as cowardice, he felt deeply ashamed of it.

They waited on the road, sharing some wine from a flask one of them had brought.

Eventually there was a flicker of light from the doorway, then another. People were entering the house.

"Time to pay them a visit."

※ ※

The house, Eurytus noted, was of mud brick worn smooth by decades of wind and rain. It was small, with an outside perimeter no greater than five paces by six, a place to eat and get in out of the weather, nothing more. Slaves did not build on a lavish scale.

The door was of thin wooden boards and would have yielded to a kick, but even that was unnecessary. The latch string had been left out. Pantites had merely to pull it and the door swung open of its own.

The inside was so bare and comfortless that Eurytus was reminded of a horse stall. A hearth fire burned fitfully. Pushed up against the walls were a few sleeping pads made from woven reeds. The family sat around a small table, eating off wooden trenchers. They all turned to see who had come in. At first their expressions registered nothing more than surprise.

There was a woman, somewhere between thirty and forty, two boys and a girl. The boys were just on the threshold of manhood—one even had a few tufts of wheat-colored beard—and the girl could not have been more than six or seven. They stared at the five armed soldiers lined up abreast between them and the door.

Pantites looked from one to the next, as if they were wooden figurines, and then turned to Eurytus.

"Is he here?" he asked.

"No." Eurytus shook his head. "No. Both of these boys are older, and heavier. He is not here."

Then Pantites turned to the woman, who by this time had become visibly afraid.

"Where is your husband?"

The woman needed to stretch her neck before she could answer. She looked like she was trying to clear some obstruction from her throat.

"Dead," she answered. "He died night before last. We buried him yesterday morning."

Pantites looked confused. "What did he die of, woman?"

"We don't know. He was sick and he died. We buried him."

They seemed at an impasse, and then Eurytus put his hand on Pantites's arm to attract his attention.

"Did anyone visit you the night your husband died?" Eurytus asked. He even smiled at the woman.

Because by then she had realized what this was about.

"Who would visit?" she asked

The woman had not a Spartan's talent for lying.

"A man and a woman, and a boy of about fourteen." Eurytus allowed his smile to broaden a little. "It would be best if you told the truth."

"My husband's brother, his wife and son." She nodded stiffly. "They were found dead on the road yesterday."

"The father and the mother, yes. But not the son."

"No. Not the son."

"Where is he?"

"We have not seen him since he left this house with his parents."

"She's lying," Pantites growled. "Maron, take off the little girl's head."

Maron smiled, as if he had received a favor. He was tall and unpleasantly thin, with arms that seemed too long for his body. He stepped around the table, grabbed the girl by the hair and drew his sword. She raised her arm, perhaps to fend off the blow, but it did her no good. Maron's sword severed her hand at the wrist and cut straight through her neck. Her body slumped to the floor and was still twitching wildly and gushing blood through the neck as Maron set her head on the table in front of her mother.

For what felt like a very long time there was no sound except the mother's screams. They just went on and on as she clutched at the table, staring at her daughter's severed head.

Finally Pantites seemed to grow bored. He stepped forward, picked up the head and threw it into the hearth fire, where the girl's hair burst into flames.

"Be quiet!" he shouted, and slapped the woman across the face. It had the desired effect because she instantly stopped screaming. "You have two sons left. We will kill both of them, one after the other, and then we will kill you if you do not tell us the truth. Where is the boy?"

"I swear to you," the woman sobbed. "We have not seen him. We thought he must be dead too. I swear this. I swear!"

Pantites wandered over to where the elder of the two boys was sitting, a heavyset lad of about sixteen who seemed merely perplexed by all this. Pantites picked up the boy's trencher and began eating, shoveling food into his mouth with a piece of broken bread.

When he had satisfied his hunger he drew his sword.

"And now you'll learn something useful," he said, looking straight at Eurytus. "I'll show you how to gut someone so that he dies slowly."

He patted the elder son on the head, then took a step back and kicked him hard enough to knock him off the bench. Then, as soon as the boy was down, he put his foot on his chest and used the point of the sword to slit his chest muscles, just inside either shoulder, so that he could not use his arms.

Next he pierced the abdomen and drove the sword straight across from side to side, cutting open the liver and the stomach and severing the intestines. The boy would bleed to death, but he might survive for perhaps a quarter of an hour and he would be in agony.

The mother began screaming again. She climbed over the bench and threw herself on her dying son, sobbing and stroking his hair, covering herself with his blood.

"These people know nothing," Eurytus said. "The woman is telling the truth."

Pantites nodded agreement.

"Then let's finish this business." He looked about him, as if taking a count of his men. "Does anyone want the woman before we kill her?"

Maron pulled her away from her son, who by then was showing no signs of life, and with his sword cut away her tunic. She offered no resistance as each of the Spartans raped her, one after the other, bending her over the table. She seemed hardly to know what was happening to her.

Only Eurytus held back.

"Not to your taste, eh?" Pantites said as he readjusted his loincloth. "Well, she's a bit messy by now. I'll finish with her and you take care of the other boy."

Eurytus thought it possible he had never hated anyone as much as, at that moment, he hated Pantites. The man was an animal.

"A certain level of brutality is a precondition of rule," his father had told him. "The basis of our power over the subject peoples is the dread in which they hold us."

But somehow it had never occurred to Dienekes's son that "a certain level of brutality" would translate into butchering children before their mother's eyes and then raping the mother.

It was horrible. And that he saw it as such struck him as evidence of his own unworthiness. A Spartan should be beyond such weakness.

"You take care of the other boy."

Eurytus knew precisely what was expected of him and knew there was no way of evading it. He could not escape being a party to this.

The younger son was huddled in a corner, perhaps hoping that these terrifying strangers might have forgotten him. His eyes were filled with fear as Eurytus approached.

"Stand up, boy. Let's not make this any harder than it needs to be."

The boy stood up, his legs trembling, but gradually he gained sufficient control of himself to assume an attitude almost of defiance.

"You will never catch Protos," he said. "You will never catch him."

"Is that his name?"

"You will never catch him," the boy repeated.

Let him die with honor, Eurytus thought. *He is braver than I am.*

A quick stroke up under the rib cage pierced the boy's heart.

Instantly the boy collapsed. He coughed once and a spray of blood came out of his mouth. Then he lay still, with his eyes open.

"Very well," said Pantites, loud enough to address the entire room. He was wiping blood from his sword with the woman's torn tunic. "Let's get these corpses outside. It was a waste of time after all, but we might as well stay here tonight. At least we'll be in out of the cold."

They opened the door and pulled the bodies outside, dragging them by their legs. The floor was only hard-packed earth and soon it was criss-crossed with bloody smears.

The thought came unbidden into Eurytus's mind that these people would be under the gods' eyes for only this one night. The corpses of the man and woman he and Teleklos had killed two nights ago were no longer lying in the road. Their neighbors, it seemed, had found them and given them burial. Or burned them.

Eurytus realized with a slight shock that he had no idea what the Helots did with their dead. Until this moment it would not have occurred to him to wonder, as if they were merely animals, with no thought but for their own blind appetites.

However, it seemed that even slaves were human. These four, likewise, once the Spartans were gone and the villagers crept out of hiding, would find their decent way into eternity.

But his own brother was still lying in the open, the stinking prey of scavengers. It was a hard judgment on a brother and a son. But that too was part of being a Spartan.

"Line them up near the door as a warning to the neighbors to mind their own business," Pantites ordered. "And, Maron, get that girl's head out of the fire. It's beginning to stink."

He turned to Eurytus. "What was the boy saying? Anything useful?"

"No. Only a name."

※ ※

That night Protos came down from the hills, directing his steps to the village where his uncle had lived. He had no thought of food or of spending the night in a warm room. He knew there was no safety or comfort for him in the village. He only wanted a few words with his aunt Nausicaa, to know where his father and mother were buried that he might pay them the homage of a few tears.

And he wanted to hear if the Spartans had come back.

He knew that they lived to the north—whether five hours away or five days, he had no inkling. The Spartans came and went like a streak of frosty weather.

Once a year fifteen or twenty of them would come into the village with their whips. Everyone would have to line up and bare their backs, even the women and children, and the Spartans would scourge them to remind them that they were slaves.

While the Spartans worked their whips, the very air would turn red with blood. Every year a few of the old people would die of it.

Protos had merely to touch the scars on his back to know what the Spartans were like.

And he knew they would be coming back. The brother he had not killed, Eurytus, son of Dienekes, had told him as much.

He met no one on the road and the outskirts of the village were deserted. It was not that late. People would have finished their suppers and be visiting neighbors. Men would be standing about, drinking beer together and talking about the harvest. A few children would still be up and playing in the twilight.

But all was quiet. The doors of people's houses were shut and he saw no slivers of light coming out through the shuttered windows. The village was like a place deserted.

People were staying inside, with their doors bolted and the latch strings pulled in.

He was perhaps thirty paces from Uncle Neleus's house when he caught the scent of blood.

That door was open a few fingers width and light was streaming out—from this house and no other. He could hear men's voices coming from inside.

Then he found the corpses. Aunt Nausicaa, naked with a great tear below her right breast. The boys, Abrax and Mantios, his particular friend. And little Antheia, named for his own mother, headless and with her left hand missing.

The emotion that swept through him like a cold wind was at first bewildering. It bore no resemblance to what he had felt seeing his parents murdered. That had been grief and terror. This was something else. This almost choked him. This was rage.

And the men who had done all this were inside, laughing.

He still had Teleklos's knife. For a wild moment he thought of rushing through the door and killing at least one or two before they cut him down.

But that would be stupid. Better to wait.

Tomorrow, doubtless, they would begin hunting for him. Let them.

❧❦

The five Spartans were walking up the path from the village to the road, Pantites and Eurytus together in the lead, discussing how the boy Protos might be hiding himself, when suddenly they saw him.

He was standing on top of a large boulder, perhaps two hundred paces up the hill. He must have wanted to be seen. When they stopped to stare at him, he even waved.

"Is that him?" Pantites asked.

"It's hard to be certain at this distance, but . . ." Eurytus narrowed his eyes to slits as he tried to focus. "But yes, I think so."

Almost immediately the boy turned his back on them and literally dropped out of sight.

"Then we'll spread out and do a thorough search. Poke your javelins in every crevice. There are probably a hundred places up there he could hide himself, and doubtless he knows every one of them.

"Spread out, spread out. He can't be allowed to escape around us."

❧ ❧

Concealed in the shadow of a tree, Protos watched the man who was anchoring the southern end of the search pattern. The Spartans were almost halfway up the hill by then and their line had widened until they could no longer see one another.

This man didn't appear to be enjoying himself. Probably he was bored, since he didn't seem to be paying close attention to what he was doing—he passed within fifteen paces of where Protos was standing and never noticed him. It was probably a tedious business for him, chasing down a runaway slave boy.

When Protos judged the distance was right, he stepped into the light.

"Good morning."

At the sound, the man began to turn . . .

The knife caught him in the throat. He tumbled over backward and he was dead by the time Protos pulled the blade free and wiped it clean on the Spartan's tunic.

That was one. He had seen four of them and Eurytus, son of Dienekes. This one, and the other three, could die like this, crushed in an instant, like swatted flies. But that would not be enough for Eurytus. Eurytus, he would save for last. Eurytus must understand that the hunted had become the hunter. Let him stare into the face of death. Let him see it coming, the way Mother and Father had. It was not enough for him just to perish.

He searched the body and found a small leather bag containing a piece of flint and three silver coins. There was also the man's sword and a throwing stick with an iron point. These were weapons about which Protos knew nothing, but he hoped they would soon reveal their secrets.

Surprisingly he felt no fear, only a kind of exhilaration. Even before he had shown himself to them, he had known what they would do. What would any hunter do? And in doing it they had yielded him the initiative.

The throwing stick looked an obvious business. Protos decided he would try it out—take a few practice throws and then use it to kill the next Spartan. But what interested him more was the sword. It had a blade no more than a cubit in length and was as well balanced as Teleklos's knife. One had to grant that the Spartans genuinely understood weapons. With its greater weight the sword would probably throw more accurately and with deadlier effect.

It had a good, sharp blade as well. Protos used it to hack off the dead Spartan's head.

❧ ❦

Eurytus was no more than thirty paces from the top of the hill, and no one had yet found the boy. For a while they had all been calling back and forth, but gradually the calls had died away.

He kept remembering the boy back at the house, the younger son who had faced death with such courage.

"You will never catch him," the boy had said, as if that constituted his revenge. Eurytus was beginning to wonder if it might be true.

"Eurytus, son of Dienekes! Raise your eyes!"

Eurytus was startled by the nearness of the sound. He looked up and saw the boy Protos sitting on the very crest of the hill.

Suddenly the boy laughed and stood up. In his right hand was something which he threw so that it rolled down the hill until it came to rest almost at Eurytus' feet.

It was Pantites's head. His eyes were open and even in death his face still had its sneering expression.

Then another came sailing through the air, then another and another. The heads of all four of his companions, Spartan warriors of proven valor and skill, lay before him in the grass.

A boy had killed them, a slave boy with a stolen knife. Eurytus felt his guts clenching with fear.

"And now, Eurytus, son of Dienekes, what are you going to do about it?"

The boy laughed again—the boy in whom Death seemed to abide like a second soul—and then Eurytus saw him reach down to the ground to fetch a javelin. He buried the point in the ground next to his right foot.

"I could have killed you any time in the past quarter of an hour," he said, as if stating the obvious. "I could have killed you, and you would never have known, no more than if Zeus had struck you with a thunderbolt. But after what you did last night I decided that such a death would be too easy. My father and mother weren't enough. You had to kill my aunt and cousins. You have stripped me of my whole family. My cousin Antheia was only six years old!"

He was in a rage, this slave boy, and his rage was terrible to behold. He was not a boy now. He seemed hardly human. Eurytus could not remember a time when he had felt such appalling terror.

And then, suddenly, the rage passed, and the slave boy smiled. He raised his right arm and his hand held a dagger—Teleklos's dagger.

"Come up and kill me, Eurytus, son of Dienekes," he shouted. "I swear I will use no weapon except this, with which I cut your brother's throat."

They stood facing each other, and Eurytus knew with perfect certainty that to accept this challenge was to embrace death. Honor demanded that he accept, but he dared not.

For a moment he could not bring himself to speak. His tongue seemed frozen in his mouth. He couldn't just run away.

And then he remembered that this ferocious slave boy was, after all, only that. In one's dealings with a slave, honor played no part.

"You think I would accord you the courtesy of a duel? A Spartan does not duel with a slave."

His voice, he knew, had a desperate quality, a quaver of fear he could not suppress. He heard it, and he knew Protos heard it. He was deceiving no one.

He turned on his heel and started back down the hill, forcing himself not to run. He knew he could never tell any living soul what had happened this day. He would have to invent some lie for his father.

"You are a coward, Eurytus, son of Dienekes," the boy shouted after him. "How will you explain to your mother why you are not honorably dead? All the days of your life you will remember how you quailed in fear before a slave boy. You chose shame over death, but nonetheless death will find you. One day, Eurytus, son of Dienekes, I will bury your brother's knife in your bowels."

4

Eurytus stood beside Myles, the military governor of the southern district of Laconia, who was tall, broad, and possessed of a florid complexion. In all, having just pushed past his middle forties, he was a ferocious-looking man.

Eurytus had first met him two days before.

Today they were on a flat stretch of ground, perhaps ten paces in width, on the hills overlooking two of the villages within the governor's command. At their feet were the headless corpses of four of the men Dienekes had sent to avenge his son.

The bodies had been found over a wide area and collected together.

"Tell me again what happened," Myles said.

"We saw him a few hundred paces up the hill. He wanted to be seen—he even waved to us. Then he disappeared, like a ghost. We spread out to search for him. Eventually I found the bodies, but I never found him. I think no one will find him."

"Did you look?"

"Of course I looked!"

"Then why, I wonder, are you alive when they are dead?"

"I have no idea!"

For just an instant Myles glanced at him, and from that one glance Eurytus could tell that the man knew he was lying.

Myles shook his head.

"Five Spartans, four of them hardened veterans, go searching for a Helot boy and he manages to kill four of them. It defies possibility."

"Are you suggesting that I killed them?"

"No." Myles turned his eyes to Eurytus's face. He seemed to be looking for something. "No, I believe your slave boy killed them. That much I do believe."

The corpses were lying on their backs. Myles pointed with his foot to the closest one, whom Eurytus could identify by his long arms as Maron.

"Now, this one was killed with a dagger—presumably your brother's. The slave boy obligingly trimmed his head off a little higher up, so you can still see the wound. It would be instructive to discover how the others died. Perhaps you would be good enough to strip off their tunics."

These men had been dead for four days, so it was not appetizing work, but eventually Eurytus had the three corpses naked to the waist.

"Well, that is interesting," Myles said. "As you can see, this one was also killed from the front, and with a dagger. But these two took it in the back— that is obvious from the way the skin is frayed around the wound. One died from a javelin, but the other, I'm not quite sure."

Myles smiled at Eurytus.

"I'd like to see his back. Would you mind?"

Eurytus took the corpse by the arm and rolled it over.

"By the gods," Myles said under his breath. "Today is a day of wonders."

He knelt down for a closer look.

"This one was killed with a sword—who was he, by the way?"

"Pantites."

"Pantites." Myles nodded, as if his worst fears had been confirmed. "I knew him. The man was no rabbit.

"But look at this."

He pointed to a wound, almost three finger widths wide, just above the right shoulder blade.

"That was done with a sword—and, if you recall, the exit wound was just under the right nipple.

"Now, even assuming this slave boy could have crept up on Pantites from behind, which by itself is next to incredible, how could he have managed such a downward angle to his stroke? Is he a giant, this boy?"

"No. He is probably tall for his age, but nothing remarkable."

"Then how would he have done that with a sword?" Myles tilted his head a little to one side, as if something had just occurred to him. "Except, of course, if he threw it."

He stood up and laughed, apparently out of sheer incredulity.

"It is almost impossible—and yet that is the way it must have happened."

A soldier approached. His name was Amyklas, and he was Myles's second in command.

"Governor," he said, "we found the heads."

They were precisely where they had been the last time Eurytus had seen them, gathered together at the foot of a stretch of rising ground. He could have taken the governor's party to them immediately, but he lacked the courage.

Because, of course, the implication was clear.

"Now why do you suppose he did that?" Myles asked, directing the question to Eurytus. "The slave boy kills four men and cuts off their heads. Why? And why, when the bodies were scattered over so wide an area— probably he left them where they fell—why are the heads just here? What could his purpose have been?"

He regarded Eurytus in a way that suggested the riddle admitted to an easy solution. His purpose had been to terrify the one member of the punitive expedition whom he had left alive.

"I don't know," Eurytus answered, knowing that Myles knew he was lying, "any more than I know why he didn't kill me with the others. I don't know."

"Then probably we will never know. Unless we catch him. And even then probably not, for I don't suppose he'll allow us to take him alive."

So there it was. The secret was safe—that was what Myles was saying. Myles was his father's friend, so Eurytus's failure would never be revealed.

And it would not do to raise up among the Helots the legend of an avenger. That boy had to be found and killed, but in the meantime the story of what had happened on this hillside must remain a secret.

"What shall we do with the bodies, Governor?"

Amyklas was seeking instructions.

"Strip the corpses—leave nothing that could identify them as Spartans. Then find some cave to hide them and seal it up with stones." He turned to Amyklas and smiled. "The Helots have brought forth a champion, my friend. But they must never be allowed to know it."

❧❧

Perhaps he had made a mistake not to kill Eurytus, son of Dienekes, when he first saw him trudging up that hill. Protos wondered if he hadn't been too self-indulgent in his revenge. He had expected Eurytus to fight. Weren't the Spartans warriors? Instead, Eurytus had run away.

In a way, however, seeing him run—shaming him—had been even

better than killing him. And Protos would kill him one day. He had promised himself that.

But to have shamed him, to have stripped him of his self-conceit, was delicious.

How would he explain coming home and leaving his four comrades dead on a hillside? What lies would he tell? The Spartans, Protos had heard, gloried in their valor. They were cruel—hardly even human—but they were brave.

But not Eurytus, son of Dienekes. Not now.

Still, it might have been a mistake, for Protos soon discovered that he was once more being hunted. If he had killed Eurytus, he might have had a little more time.

And now he was alone. His family was dead, and he was being hunted. He could not even return to his own village, to be among his own people, for if he sought refuge with them he would call down upon them the most terrible revenge. The Spartans would likely massacre them all. It was not as if they did not do such things.

He was utterly alone. He was afraid, but fear was not the worst of it. He felt desolate. What had he done, what impiety could he could have committed that heaven had visited this fate upon him? How had he sinned? The bright gods had turned their faces from him, and he did not know why. Life had become a bitter mystery.

The Spartans were sending out patrols of five or six men, who stayed together. Protos could not fight so many. All he could do was hide.

He did not want to kill these men, to remind the Spartans of his existence. He wanted to be left alone.

But they seemed determined to find him. And eventually they would succeed.

But they could not be allowed to succeed. His father had stood his ground, had sacrificed his life that his wife and son might have some chance of escape. And thus to survive had become a duty he owed to his father's ghost.

Time to move on, to find someplace beyond the Spartans' reach.

Time to move on.

The mountains, which ran north and south, were a barren and desolate place. In the hills one might occasionally encounter a shepherd, but in the mountains he would be utterly alone. There would be no one who could betray him.

He could not trust to the plain, so he would have to go north or south.

And he had heard there was nothing to the south except the sea. Since he was not a fish, if he went south he would be trapped.

So it would have to be the mountains.

They might be hoping, perhaps even expecting him to go south. He would be easier to find then. And it might not occur to them that he would risk venturing into the Spartan homeland.

So he would go south for three or four days, laying an easy trail for them to follow—the Spartans seemed to be good trackers—then he would try to drop from view for a while. Then he would head north.

The Spartans were to the north, but somewhere beyond them had to be a place where their power did not reach. It was perhaps a slim chance, but it was the only one he had.

For three days he traveled south. He built campfires in the mornings and afternoon, leaving them to burn themselves out so that the smoke would tell the Spartans where he had been. In late afternoon he would head higher up into the mountains and try to find a cave in which to spend the night. Once he had to sleep in the open. The cold wind was almost unbearable.

Occasionally he could spot the scouting parties after him. Sometimes there would be five or six men, or they would break off to follow different trails. They never seemed to tire and they never stopped.

On the afternoon of the third day, he came to a river. It was wide and lazy. He swam across and left his footprints going into the rocky hillside. Then he doubled back over stony ground that would bear no trace of him and got back into the water. He let the river carry him for almost an hour, just floating along, clutching a piece of driftwood to which he had tied his weapons with his loincloth.

And then he got out and headed north into the mountains. He walked all through the night, staying within a few hundred paces of the ridge, guided by the stars and the waning moonlight.

Near morning he followed a trail down to where trees provided more cover. He found a grove of poplars and fell asleep.

He lived as best he could on berries and seeds and wild garlic. Once, when he was almost mad with hunger, he wounded a wild boar when he threw his sword at it and spent two hours tracking its blood spore. He ate part of the shoulder raw and left the rest for the crows.

At twilight of his third day going north he spotted the smoke from a campfire. He made his approach under the cover of darkness and discovered two men in Spartan dress. He sat concealed under the shadow of a tree and listened to their conversation over dinner.

"We'll never catch him."

"Why not? We have as good a chance as anybody."

"How many teams have they sent out? And what if he isn't heading north at all? He's probably going south—he's a Helot, so he'll run away from us. None of us has a very good chance. The slave patrols will probably find him wandering around in some fishing village on the coast, wondering why the land stopped."

They both laughed.

"Yes, but if we did catch him . . ."

"Yes. We'd be heroes. It's nice to dream."

Protos was faced with a choice. He could slip past or he could kill them. To evade them was the safer choice, but they had food and warm clothing. And they were Spartans. He decided to kill them.

He waited for an hour after they had gone to sleep. Then he walked into camp with a sword in one hand and his knife in the other, ready to strike at the first one who stirred.

Neither woke up. Protos stood over them, watching them as they lay asleep in their cloaks. His heart was empty of pity. He was trying to decide which was closer to his own size. He wanted to kill that one with the least blood spilled because he wanted his clothes.

Finally he made his choice. The other one died when Teleklos's knife went through his breastbone and into his heart—he flopped about a little but hardly made a sound. Then Protos prodded his partner awake and, when he began to sit up, gave him a sharp smack in the face with the flat of his sword. Resistance was at an end.

Protos stripped him naked and then killed him with the sword before he even had time to plead for his life.

Then Protos threw himself on their food packs like the starving man he almost was. It had been agony to watch them eating.

He found a flask of wine. He no idea what it was and the taste of it was not encouraging, but it flowed through his veins like lightning. In a short time he was drunk. He knew what being drunk was. During the festivals he had seen men drunk on beer.

His head was swimming. He wrapped himself in one of the Spartan's cloaks and went to sleep. In the morning he would worry about what to do with the bodies.

✣✣

The morning came, and with it a headache. Protos had never before experienced a headache and thought it possible he might be dying.

He sat on the ground beside the cold remains of the campfire, staring at the two dead men, wondering if the gods were punishing him for the crime of murder. It didn't seem fair. He had so far killed seven Spartans, but they had killed six of his family and would kill him if he ever gave them the chance. He killed to stay alive. These people had made murder into a sport. The world could not help but be better off without them.

He ate some bread washed down with water and began to feel less like his head was full of cinders. Perhaps the gods had thought better of it and lifted their curse.

He began to examine his loot.

Between them the Spartans had two swords, three javelins, food enough to last them about five days, flints, a hatchet, two small stone cubes with various unintelligible signs drawn on the sides, about four cubits of heavy twine, a small cooking pot, a couple of iron trenchers, and their clothes.

Protos tried on their sandals, but they were either too large or he simply wasn't used to wearing them because he tripped with almost every step.

He wrapped the weapons and the hatchet in one of the cloaks and bound it tight with the twine. The small items would go in his leather pouch. There was too much food for him to carry so he took half of it.

The corpses he dragged off into the woods. It might be many days before those two were missed.

5

"No one has the least idea where he is," Myles said to Dienekes, setting down the cup of his host's rather indifferent Sicilian wine and shaking his head as if at an intractable mystery. "Yesterday a patrol found the corpses of a two-man search team that hadn't reported in. The estimate is they had been dead about a week. He probably killed them for their supplies."

"You mean to tell me he's living off his pursuers?"

"So it would seem."

They were in the tiny enclosed garden of Dienekes's house, which was as lightless as a tomb. Dienekes was a widower and his slaves tended to leave things undone.

"How is Eurytus taking all this?" Myles asked.

At first Dienekes merely shrugged.

"I packed him off with a diplomatic mission to Macedon," he said finally, "if only so he would have time to take hold of himself."

"I'm sure it's been unsettling for him."

"He's a Spartan. He should be beyond being unsettled."

Dienekes was almost shouting, then he caught himself.

"The way things are going," he went on, his voice even, "perhaps we should send a diplomatic mission to this boy Protos and sue for peace."

He laughed, somewhat hysterically, and then rested his forehead in his right hand.

"We'll find him yet," Myles answered quietly. "And then we'll kill him."

"You think so? No one has ever even seen him except Eurytus—no one, that is, who's still alive. He could be out in the street right now and we'd never know."

In fact, Protos was in a Helot village about three-quarters of an hour north of Sparta. He was pretending to look for a nonexistent brother named Mantios, but his real purpose was to seek information about whether he would be safer going west or north.

"And they sent you looking for him? You are hardly more than a boy."

Protos was drinking a cup of beer with a farmer named Georgikos, in front of the farmer's door. Even a poor man can show hospitality to a stranger.

"I am the only son left, and my father is ill. There was no choice."

Georgikos, a squat man of about forty and very hairy everywhere except the top of his head, was suspicious, or at least curious, but there was no harm in him. Protos, who was using his dead cousin's name, was clearly not a Spartan spy.

"He might have gone over the mountains to Messenia," Georgikos said, in a way that implied he wasn't convinced that the runaway might not be Protos himself. "The Spartans control it but indirectly. From there he might go anywhere."

Protos thanked him and rose to depart, but Georgikos waved him back down.

"Perhaps you should spend the night here," he said, "My wife can make you up a bed. The patrols have been active just lately."

※ ※

A slave's day usually began a few hours before dawn, and by then Protos was on his way west. He avoided the roads and walked away from the rising sun, and by early afternoon he had reached the foothills of the western mountains.

Being a fugitive was beginning to seem almost pleasant. Georgikos's wife had made him up a food bundle that would probably last three days and had actually been embarrassed when Protos forced on her one of the silver coins he had taken off a Spartan's body. He had had no idea of its value and probably neither had she. Money was almost unknown among the Helots.

For the rest, Protos enjoyed the exercise and had become less and less afraid of his enemies. He had discovered that they were mortal and soon he hoped he would escape them entirely.

Someday, he told himself, when his pursuers had forgotten about him, he would come back and kill Eurytus, son of Dienekes, but that day would not be soon.

Someday, when they had forgotten all about him, he would have his revenge.

The idea gave him no pleasure. It merely reminded him that his mother and father were dead.

Why had his parents been taken from him? Why? What sort of people were these, who made a game of murder?

He would kill them all if he could. They had filled his life with torment.

It hardly crossed his mind what he might do with his life if ever he got beyond the Spartans' reach. Once or twice it had occurred to him that he might become a soldier, but that was no more than a fleeting idea.

On the whole, it seemed best not to think about the future—or the past. Surviving through one day at a time was goal enough.

By twilight he had climbed halfway up to a saddle between two mountains and he decided to stop for the night. He found a small shelf of land, reasonably level and concealed behind a curtain of ragged boulders, so he spread out his cloak and decided to find out what the farmer's wife had provided for his dinner. He was pleased to discover that her concern for his welfare had extended to a small jar of beer. By the time he had drunk half of it he felt sleepy.

That night he dreamed he was back in his own village, walking beside his father. Then, suddenly, as happens in dreams, they were outside the village, in the wheat fields.

His father reached down to caress the grain heads with his hand.

"It will be a good harvest this year," he said.

His hand, when he drew it back, was covered in blood.

Protos woke up with a start. For the rest of the night, he hardly dared close his eyes.

The next morning, well before noon, he crested the mountain range and, for the first time in his life, beheld the sea. It was far away, just a dark smudge against the horizon, but it glistened in the sunlight so that it seemed a living thing.

This mountain range, he had been informed, was the boundary between Laconia, the Spartan homeland, and Messenia, where the danger might be less immediate.

By early afternoon he was down on the plain. Almost immediately he encountered a village, very like the one in which he had been born.

The place was perhaps two hundred paces from one side to the other and as he walked through it, carrying his bundle, the few people he met regarded him with ill-concealed suspicion. It was almost the end of harvesttime, so most would be off working in the fields. Almost everyone Protos saw was either very young or very old, and they made a wretched sight.

If anything, these people seemed poorer than the Helots in Laconia. Even the dogs looked like they were starving.

One old man was leaning against the side of a house, seemingly unable to catch his breath, with no attention for anything except his own distress. He wore nothing but a loincloth and his arms and legs were wretchedly thin. The skin over his ribs was stretched so tight it seemed ready to crack. He was obviously unfit for any work, so perhaps his relatives had been forced to stop feeding him. Or perhaps he had taken that decision himself.

Everyone back in Protos's village had said this would be the best harvest in five years. How much worse could it be here, only a few days away? And yet everyone he saw looked desperate, as if they did not know how they would survive. Why?

Why, except the Spartans—or whoever did their bidding here in Messenia.

Protos realized that he had learned something, and the world had become a few shades darker for that knowledge. He had begun this journey with a very specific grievance, the murder of his family, and now the list of victims was growing longer and longer. Famine in the midst of plenty was not an accident.

He did not linger. He was glad to be away from the place.

That night he slept in a field, and the next morning he reached the sea.

It rolled up onto the pebbled shore in swells and the sound of it was hushed and mournful, like thunder at a vast distance. White birds coasted about in the faint wind. Protos stood in the water up to his knees and it pulled at him as if trying to gain possession.

The sea was not as cold as the rivers inland and its water was bitter to the taste. It reflected the sun so intensely that it hurt his eyes.

The world could be a beautiful place.

He walked along the shore for perhaps an hour, until he came to a finger of land that jutted like a wall out into the surging water.

On its other side he was surprised to find what he thought must be a town. To a village boy it seemed vast.

He opened the pouch that dangled from his belt and counted out his collection of coins. He had eleven, all of them silver. In this place, he suspected, he would need money.

The town had a harbor. About three hundred paces from shore he saw some sort of natural breakwater where the waves seemed to lose their force and turn to white foam. The harbor was full of what Protos concluded must be ships. He had heard stories about how the heroes of his race had sailed away in ships to fight long-ago wars.

He wished Mantios could have been there with him—how he would have enjoyed it! Mantios had always dreamed of being a warrior, an adventurer like the heroes of the stories his father told. He would have loved these ships.

But Mantios was dead, butchered like a sheep. He would never grow up to be anything. He would always be fourteen years old and live only in the memories of his friend and cousin. Why? It made no sense.

And suddenly he found himself wondering if that was manhood, the recognition that life adhered to no pattern—that the whole of human existence was something in which words like "justice" and "mercy" had no meaning.

The Spartans must hate their lives. The world they had made for themselves was such a savage place. Yet apparently they did not. They seemed to feel comfortable enough with their brutality.

But when he recalled his own father, Protos felt ashamed to think such thoughts. His father had been wise, wiser and better than the Spartans could even imagine being. He had made of his life something loving and noble, and in the end he had laid it down with courage.

※※

He came across a building by the docks where a few men sat around on benches eating what smelled like lentils wrapped in flat bread. They drank beer out of wooden cups and averted their eyes when Protos came through the open doorway.

He sat down in a corner and was approached by a fat man, apparently the proprietor, who wore the sleeves of his tunic rolled up to the armpits.

"What can I bring you, boy?"

Protos opened his hand. One of his silver coins rested in the center of the palm.

"A cup of your beer and some information," he said quietly. "I will drink the beer and then trouble you no more, and I will leave the coin."

The proprietor nodded and brought him a cup of beer, then sat down beside him.

"What do you wish to know?" he asked.

"First of all, what is this coin and what is it worth?"

The proprietor seemed to consider the matter. His mind, it appeared, was as ponderous as his body, but at last he nodded.

"That there, my young lord, is an Athenian drachma, and it would buy

you a decent meal, with wine, and a bed in any tavern, plus the tavern master's
wife to share it with you."

He laughed, as if he had made a rare jest.

"That there is five or six days' wages for most men. I won't ask you where
you got it."

"You are wise."

Protos detected a flicker of fear in the proprietor's eyes, but then he
smiled.

"What else do you want to know?"

"I want to know what place this is, and who rules it. I want to know if
I shall be left in peace here."

The proprietor's answer turned out to be complicated and not encouraging.

"Our lords of Messenia fought two terrible wars against the Spartans and
lost them both," he said. "They learned their lesson when the Spartans finally chopped their heads off. Since before my grandfather's day, we might as
well *be* in Sparta. They make life terrible hard for common folk. The country
people are bound to the land as slaves and can hardly keep themselves alive."

He said a lot more besides, but the essence was that Messenia was no
more than a province of Laconia and was plundered accordingly.

"You being on your own," he asked finally, "what is it you mean to do?"

"I thought I might become a soldier."

"Not here, boy." The proprietor shook his head and laughed. "Not here.
Except for the local lads they leave here to keep the peace, the only soldiers we ever see are Spartans, and with them you have to be born to it."

"What is north of here?"

This required another lengthy consideration.

"Arkadia, maybe," the proprietor answered, with the air of one who bore
unwelcome news. "It's a poor place and full of mountains, they say. And
they bow down to the Spartans just like we do."

Protos finished the last of his beer and stood up.

"Thank you," he said, and opened his hand so that the proprietor could
take his drachma.

❧ ❦

He had walked about an hour north of the town, the name of which he
never learned, when he became aware that he was being followed. He
turned and saw four men on horses, perhaps three hundred paces behind.

They were dressed alike and wore helmets, which meant they were soldiers of some kind, but they weren't Spartans—Spartans would have been wearing body armor, or at least leather corselets. Spartans would have made a more impressive appearance. These men were Helots like himself, but, as the proprietor had suggested, they were the dogs the Spartans had let out of their kennel. They licked their masters' hands and oppressed their own people

Protos understood their business at once. The proprietor had sold him out.

It was such a rare jest Protos almost laughed. He had trusted the man. How could he have been such a simpleton?

He was surprised at his own calm. He was frightened, but he was in control of himself. These men were merely another problem that perhaps he could somehow solve.

He knew he would gain nothing by running.

One man would have been simple—one man would be dead before he came within fifty paces—but four, and four on horseback, was not so simple. He would have to let them come in close enough that their horses would give them no advantage and he didn't want to injure the horses. He had nothing against the horses.

They were probably slave hunters, so they meant his death. Runaways were subject to immediate execution, and these men were paid a bounty for the heads they carried back with them.

So, if he wanted to live, he would have to kill them all. If one escaped he would have twenty more after him before he was two hours older.

But killing all of them didn't seem possible.

When they were only a hundred or so paces away, he set his bundle down on the ground and untied the knot that held it together. He reached under the fold of the cloak and grasped his knife by the point, holding it against his arm so that the riders would not see it.

When they were about ten paces away, the horsemen came to a halt. Then one of them rode forward another five paces.

"How does a slave boy like you come to possess a silver drachma?" he asked, in a tone that suggested he already knew the answer. "I know a slave when I see one, even if he's dressed up in a linen tunic. Whose throat did you cut to get the money?"

Protos shrugged his shoulders and smiled.

"I know not what you mean, Lord. In my life I have never even seen a silver drachma."

The horseman urged his mount a few paces closer—he was insultingly sure of himself.

"The tavern keeper says otherwise," he announced, shaking his head as if in disappointment. "He showed us the coin. If you were prepared to give that one to him, you must have others. You are a thief, boy."

There was no easy way out. So be it. Instead of fear Protos felt rage. *If I am to die, I will take some of these with me. . . .*

He took a step and then another. He extended his left arm in supplication. "My lord—"

The sentence was never finished. He grabbed the horseman's arm to pull him off balance and, letting the knife slip down into his right hand, drove the point in just below the man's rib cage.

It was the work of an instant. The man hardly even knew what had happened to him. Protos twisted the blade and yanked it free, then reached forward with his left hand and pulled him off his horse.

The next sound he heard was the whine of swords being drawn from their metal scabbards.

He would keep the knife, he decided. He wouldn't risk a throw. He might have a chance at one of them before . . .

He waited.

The soldiers spread out around him so that they had him encircled, but they had not yet rushed in for the kill.

Why was he still alive?

"Drop the blade, boy. You're worth a good deal of money alive, but after this we're not taking any risks. Drop the blade or we'll kill you now."

The man directly in front of him smiled.

"Drop the blade, boy," he repeated. "Or you won't live to find out what awaits you in Sparta."

It was a bitter moment, as bitter as death itself, for the choice had come down to a quick end this instant or execution in Sparta, and he knew what that would be like. But while he was alive there was at least some hope.

Protos opened his hand and the knife fell to the ground.

"That's a good boy."

The man smiled again and then seemed to lose interest.

"Rasdos, throw Kabaisos over his horse and let's start back to the garrison. It'll be dark soon."

They gathered up Protos's weapons in his Spartan cloak, tied his hands behind his back, and led him along by a rope around his neck. To amuse themselves, they would sometimes goad their horses into a trot, forcing Protos to run to keep up—it was almost a relief, in that the struggle to keep from tripping and being dragged along the ground drove away thought.

6

The "garrison," he soon saw, was a two-room brick building with a walled yard and a stable in the back. It was on the outskirts of the town and Protos guessed he must have passed it earlier that day without noticing it.

In the backyard there was an iron cage, about three cubits to the side. They locked Protos in and left him alone.

After about an hour the men assembled at a table and benches in the yard for their evening meal. There were five of them, and with their helmets and uniform cloaks stripped off they looked like exactly what they were—peasants, no different from himself. They had power only because they had thrown in their lot with the Spartans.

The meal was brought by the proprietor of the same establishment where Protos had unwisely stopped for refreshment and information. He glanced toward the cage and frowned, and then, after setting out food and drink for the soldiers, accompanied by the customary banter, he came over and held out a small jar of beer, which Protos was just able to squeeze between the bars.

"I'm sorry," he said, with an anxious little shake of his head, "but I had no choice. I have to report all strangers or they'll put me out of business— or worse."

"I won't hold a grudge," Protos told him, breaking the seal on the jar and then raising it in salute.

"They tell me you killed Kabaisos," the proprietor whispered, and then glanced back over his shoulder to see if any of the soldiers had heard. "Well, you did everyone a favor. He wasn't well liked, not even by his own men."

"So he was in charge here?"

The proprietor nodded.

"I have to go now," he said, straightening up. "Good luck."

From the expression on his face, he seemed to regard any luck at all as the remotest of possibilities.

Protos sat back in his cage, drinking his beer and listening to the soldiers' conversation over dinner. They were discussing how they should punish him for killing Kabaisos.

"What difference does it make?" said the man who had spoken to him on the road, whose name was Galaisos and who seemed to be in charge now. "They'll probably crucify him as soon as he gets to Sparta. Isn't that enough?"

"But first he has to answer for Kabaisos."

"Why? Was he a particular friend of yours?"

Everyone laughed.

"Still, he was one of us. We owe it to him."

Galaisos shook his head.

"Then we have a problem. Kabaisos showed me the letter, and apparently this boy killed an Ephor's son. Sparta wants him in prime condition— they want to keep all the fun for themselves."

"But that doesn't mean we can't bruise him a little."

For a long moment Galaisos said nothing. He seemed to be considering the matter.

"I'll send a courier to Sparta," he said finally. "One man. We're already shorthanded and it would take three of us to guard him for the journey— according to the letter this boy has already killed seven men, and you saw what a neat job he did on Kabaisos, so let the Spartans take the risks.

"So it's three days to Sparta and then three days back, then another three days to transport the prisoner. That would give him nine days to heal up—plenty of time. But we'll have to be careful. I won't be happy if one of you gets carried away and breaks something."

"We'll be good."

So it was settled that the after-dinner entertainment would be giving "the slave boy" a sound thrashing with some barrel staves from the trash heap.

"Now remember, don't touch his head," Galaisos warned.

The beating lasted about half an hour. They formed a circle around Protos and drove him back and forth like a ball in a child's game. After a time, when there was hardly a spot below his neck that wasn't bruised, he lost all courage and began screaming every time they hit him. He couldn't help himself. His tormenters thought this was wonderfully funny and made a sort of contest out of it—who could make the slave boy scream the loudest.

Eventually he collapsed, but the beating didn't stop. He lay on the ground, curled up in a ball, sobbing with pain.

They dragged him to his feet, and the beating went on. By the time they decided that Kabaisos had been sufficiently avenged, Protos was bleeding from places where his skin had split open. To fall down was agony. At last they allowed him to crawl back into his cage on knees that were soft with blood.

Then they all went to bed.

Sometime after midnight a cold rain blew in from the sea. Protos was drenched and shivering. There was no way he could sit or lie down without weeping from the pain.

"Bright Apollo, who turns aside suffering," he prayed, his voice no more than a whisper. "Show me mercy. Draw your bow and send me the arrow of death."

But, instead of death, dawn came, and with it a cup of water and a plate of wretched food—it was dark brown and lumpy and Protos had no idea what it was.

"You're as purple as a grape," the one called Rasdos told him cheerfully. "But you'll be fine by the time you get to Sparta. In Sparta they'll crucify you. Do you know what that's like? They'll nail you to a tree and leave you there until you rot. If they feel merciful they'll lash you halfway to death first, just so you'll die sooner. But I don't think anyone will believe you deserve mercy. A strong boy like you might take a week to die, a week in which every breath you draw will be torture."

Protos said nothing. There was a limit, he had discovered, to what anyone can suffer, beyond which even fear loses its power. Death was only a word, and the future could hold no horrors greater than he had already endured. He drank the water and forced himself to eat the food, and promised himself vengeance.

❦

Nubit had spent a profitable month in Trachis, but there were signs that she had overstayed her welcome. The people of northern Greece were primitive and superstitious, and they had a dread of witches. In her travels, Nubit had developed a refined sense of the public mood, and so she had packed up her wagon and departed the city before any unpleasant situation had a chance to develop.

On the first night of her journey south she camped by the Euboean Gulf, just outside a village where she was able to buy a fresh turbot for her dinner. She built a fire on the sandy bluff just above the shore, cut up the fish and fried it in oil. Afterward she sat outside for a long time, listening to the waves break over the rocky beach and drinking beer.

There was a powder mixed in with the beer, and when she felt it beginning to take hold she crawled into her wagon and surrendered herself to her visions.

She lay on her back, staring up at the wagon cover. The wooden bows that held it up looked like the ribs of some monster that had swallowed her whole. She fell asleep, lying in the belly of the beast.

But they were not ribs surrounding her, but rather the iron bars of a cage. She was in the most agonizing pain—yet it was not her pain, but another's. Around three sides of the cage dogs were barking, yapping frantically, a sound almost like laughter. That other whose pain she felt was crouched, bleeding and torn. He watched the dogs in silence, waiting his time, knowing that his time would come.

That other was a wolf, gray like the sky at dusk. He watched in hatred. Nubit could feel his hatred as something chill and silent.

The dogs barked their challenge. They threw themselves at the bars of the cage, as if to break them down. Did they not know? Could they not see? The cage protected not the wolf but them. When he came out, his vengeance would be terrible.

The wolf was alone now, and from one instant to the next it was bitterly cold. Nubit woke up with a start and found herself listening to a sound that she eventually recognized as rain pelting against the wagon cover, and she no longer felt the cold.

The cold belonged only to the wolf.

※ ※

Protos remained as the "guest" of the garrison for seven days. On the second day he was taken violently ill, running a fever so high that they were forced to bring him inside and wrap him in blankets. He was lucid enough to hear their conversation, and they were very worried because the reward for his capture alive was a thousand drachmas, but if he died he was merely another dead slave.

By the fourth day the fever had broken. After that Protos willed himself to get better. He would need to be strong.

On the seventh day the courier returned, and with him were two soldiers from Sparta. They had brought an extra horse for their prisoner.

By then Protos had been returned to his cage, and the Spartans came out to look at him.

"He's just a skinny boy," one of them said—he was the elder of the two and he studied Protos with appraising, pitiless eyes. "I had expected a monster with claws."

Protos stayed huddled in the back, his arms wrapped about his knees, trying to look as helpless as possible.

"Hey! Boy!" the other, younger man shouted at him. He looked in his early twenties and was heavy with muscle, and he had a fool's face. "Are you a killer?"

The only response they received was a faint wail as Protos buried his face in his arms. He couldn't let them see the hatred in his eyes.

"He won't be any trouble," the younger one said as they went back inside.

They weren't to leave until the next morning, so that night the garrison hosted a small celebration. Protos could hear the laughter. A cold fog had come in from the sea and he was shivering.

"Let the cold seep into my heart," he murmured to himself. "I will have need of it."

❧❦

They left at dawn. Protos's hands were tied in front so that he could hold on to the horse's mane to keep from falling off. He fell off anyway, within two hundred paces of the garrison. He made it look very convincing. His warders cursed him and put him back on his horse.

There had been six or seven horses in Protos's village, shared for plowing among thirty families. Every farm boy learned how to ride. If these two Spartans had lived a little closer to the soil that fed them, they would have known as much.

The third time he fell off, badly scraping his shoulder on a rock, it wouldn't have occurred to them to doubt. Protos could see it in the older one's face. He was annoyed. They were dealing with a child, someone as harmless as an infant. They were growing careless, and the moment would come.

It was going to work. Protos could feel it—it was going to work.

The older one, who was helping him to his feet, turned to ask his companion to catch the horse. It was a brief exchange, lasting only an instant, but for that instant he was turned away from Protos. The man's sword was hanging from his belt, not a cubit from his prisoner's eager grasp.

The moment was now.

Protos lunged for the hilt. There was enough play in the rope around his wrists for him to take it in both hands. He pulled it from the scabbard and with a fast, fluid motion drove the point into the guard's right side.

The guard seemed more surprised than anything else. He grunted and turned to look at his attacker, his eyes going wide. Protos yanked the sword free and was about to strike again, but the guard collapsed to his knees and then over on his face.

That left only one. Thank the gods, that one was a fool.

"And, yes, I am a killer," Protos shouted. "So run or fight, Spartan. Those are the only choices."

It was a challenge Protos knew this brute could never refuse.

They were only about ten paces apart. The Spartan goaded his horse forward, but in that distance the animal couldn't gather momentum. The instant it was upon him, Protos slapped the horse across its nose with the flat of his sword, making it stumble and veer away. Then he swung the blade up at the rider, but as he did he felt a sword point skitter over his ribs and his own sword was yanked violently out of his grasp.

I'm dead, he thought to himself. *He'll finish me now.*

But the Spartan seemed in no hurry, even to turn around. It was strange. . . .

And then the horse stopped, seemingly of its own accord, and the rider slumped to one side and fell to the ground. He lay facedown, the point of a sword sticking out through his back.

Then Protos understood. It had all happened so quickly. He had made his kill without realizing it, and it was the horse, stumbling to get away from him, that yanked the sword out of his hands.

The Spartan had only grazed him. The wound to his side was painful and messy but was otherwise just a cut in the skin. He took a few strips of cloth from one of the dead men's tunics and bandaged it up so that it no longer bled, then he sat down to rest.

He was alive and, for the moment, he was safe, yet he hardly felt anything. It was as if those few frantic moments of battle had left him drained.

And then, gradually, as if coming out of a trance, he could feel the blood pounding through his veins as fear and relief fought each other. He felt his heart would burst. He had survived after all. It was like a miracle. He knew exactly what he had done, but *that* he had done it seemed unaccountable.

Protos looked at the two corpses stretched out on the ground. These enemies were dead.

But not all of them.

He still had bruises all over his body, although they were beginning to turn from blue to brown. The night they had beaten him they had all been drunk. Sober, they might have been more careful, but as it was they had almost killed him.

He told himself that it was stupid and dangerous and gained him nothing, but he already knew that he was going back to the garrison. Those men had beaten and starved him, had sold him to the Spartans. They were worse than the Spartans because they betrayed their own. He was going back.

So now it became a question of tactics. Protos had no illusions that he could survive against all five at once, so he would have to divide them off from one another. He tried to remember every detail of daily life within those brick walls.

Of course, he himself had been inside for only two nights, and for most of that time he had been too feverish to pay much attention. But he did remember that there had always been a free bed for him. Probably they all had women in the town. Perhaps they took nights off in some sort of rotation.

So the best time was perhaps two hours after sunset, when a few would be absent and the rest deep in wine.

When he was first captured they had taken everything from him. His weapons and tools, wrapped in his Spartan cloak, his guards had intended to bring back to Sparta with him, so those he had again. But his few coins the garrison soldiers had divided among themselves. He searched the bodies of his two warders, but they had nothing—why would a Spartan need money when the whole world was his to plunder?

So it would be up to the garrison to make good his loss.

For the last seven days he had slept hardly at all. He tethered one of the horses and took the bridles off the others and let them go, so that they wandered away into the open countryside. There was no road, and he hadn't seen so much as a village since leaving the town. He would leave the two Spartans to rot where they lay—there was no danger of their being discovered. Then he found himself a piece of slightly rising ground and stretched out on the grass to rest and perhaps to sleep.

❧ ❧

He awakened with a start. Above him in the clear night sky he could see only three stars, which meant that it was a little past sunset. Plenty of time.

An hour later he was on the outskirts of the town. He tied his horse's reins to a tree where, if he didn't come back, someone would be sure to find it.

No light seeped out from beneath the garrison door, but they would not be asleep at this hour. They would be out in the yard, celebrating the thousand drachmas that would be their reward for turning their prisoner over to be crucified.

When Protos had first been brought in, they had entered the garrison through a stable. He remembered it opened onto an alley. There was also a door that led into the stables from the yard. Both entrances were left unlocked, since soldiers stood in no danger of thieves.

Protos waited in the shadows of the barn, knowing this was where the men came to relieve themselves.

He did not have to wait long. Someone opened the door from the yard, singing a song about a donkey and a tavern master's daughter. The singer kept interrupting his performance to laugh. He had left the door open, so he would have to be killed silently.

The singer went into one of the empty stalls, faced the wall and lifted up the hem of his tunic. The song broke off in mid-phrase, since pissing apparently required his full attention.

He would have had just enough time to feel the point of a sword touching him on the back before it drove up under his rib cage to puncture a lung. He sank to his knees, gasping quietly. He rolled over and lived only long enough to recognize the man who had killed him—Protos could see it in his eyes.

It was a pity, Protos decided. The narrative of the song had just reached a highly interesting point, and now he would never hear the end.

Through the open door he could see two men in profile, sitting on either side of the table. One was laughing as the other told a story in a low voice. A brazier provided plenty of light. The distance was only ten or twelve paces.

Protos threw his Spartan knife and it caught the storyteller in the side of his throat. He fell off his bench with a jerk, as if snatched from behind.

The other man stopped laughing and simply stared. Protos was almost on him before he knew he was under attack.

Protos slapped him in the face with the flat of his sword. The man, whom Protos recognized as Galaisos, clapped his hands over his nose as blood went streaming down over his chin.

Protos kicked him off the bench and stood over him, the point of his sword balanced delicately just below his right eye.

"Remember me?" he asked pleasantly. "Now, this can go easy or hard. It's up to you. Where are the other two?"

It was a long moment before Galaisos could catch his breath to answer, and Protos had to let the sword point cut him a little.

"Gone whoring," Galaisos said finally.

"When will they be back?"

"Rasdos probably not until morning. He has a fisherman's widow he sleeps with. Pedanios sooner than that."

"Thank you. You're been most helpful."

He lifted the point of the sword away from Galaisos's eye, smiled, and then drove it into the man's chest. Galaisos heaved up for an instant and then was still.

As he watched Galaisos die, Protos became aware of a certain feeling of disappointment. He had been so looking forward to killing these men, but in the event he experienced no sense of triumph. He was already sick of his revenge, which was beginning to seem more like murder than justice.

But, once begun, it had to be carried through. He didn't know if there wasn't a larger town, with a bigger garrison, just a few hours away, and he needed time to disappear into the mountains before they learned what had happened here. He didn't dare leave any of these men alive.

He retrieved his knife and found a bucket of water in which to clean his weapons, drying them on a cloak he found hanging in the main room of the barrack.

He searched the room and discovered a small wooden box with several silver coins in it—the garrison treasury, he imagined. He poured its contents into his pouch.

He might be hours waiting here, he thought.

The lesson of the past several days had not been lost on him. There was no safety until he found a way to put himself beyond the reach of the Spartans. And where was that? These people seemed to own the world.

He would go north, he decided. Really, there was no choice. He had reached the sea, which was as far west as he could go. To the south and east was Laconia. It had to be north.

What was in the north? He had nothing except the tavern keeper's sketchy description, which was vague to the point of uselessness, and in fact he had no idea. Perhaps the Spartans really did own the whole world.

Perhaps even the hope of safety was an illusion. Then he would go on fighting and hiding for the rest of his short life.

As he fought against sleep, Protos found himself wondering again how he had come to this. Not even a month ago he had been a farm boy, living with his mother and father and perfectly happy. Now he was a fugitive with blood on his hands. Why had the gods visited this fate upon him? Or was life simply a journey without a goal? Nothing made sense.

He actually was asleep when he heard the door creak. A man entered from the street, walking with the loud, clumsy gait that meant he had been drinking. He never noticed Protos, who was sitting on a chair in a darkened corner. He merely walked blindly across the room and pushed open the door to the bedroom.

He did not close the bedroom door. Apparently he never noticed that the other beds were empty. In what seemed no time at all, Protos could hear him snoring.

It was better so. Let him die in his sleep and never know fear.

Protos walked into the bedroom, his sword in his hand.

❧ ❧

Protos had to admit to himself that in a brutal sort of way Rasdos was a handsome fellow. He was tall and strong and possessed of a glistening black beard, so perhaps the fisherman's widow didn't sleep with him only for the money. When he returned just at dawn he looked as if he had washed his face and eaten his breakfast and was ready for anything.

Except perhaps to walk in and find the Helot boy poised to receive him.

"What are you doing here?" he asked.

"Waiting for you."

Protos was leaning against the desk, holding his knife, as if weighing the point in the palm of his left hand.

"Where is everyone?"

"Don't worry. You'll be with them soon."

Protos shifted the knife so that his right hand closed around the side of the blade.

At this stage it seemed to occur to Rasdos that he might be in danger. He reached for his sword, but he was too late. With a movement almost too quick for human sight to follow, Protos threw the knife and it buried its point in Rasdos's heart.

❧ ❧

Protos retrieved his horse, which he would release as soon as he was near the mountains, and as he headed north out of the town, he saw the building where he had stopped for directions and a cup of beer that first day. He decided he would stop there again.

He was thirsty and he truly believed the proprietor had had no choice in what he had done. They were all under the hand of the Spartans. They were all slaves. He bore the man no ill will.

But it would be amusing.

He tied the horse's reins to a post and went inside. He sat at the same table as the first time, and when the proprietor saw him he dropped the jar of beer he was carrying. It smashed against the floor.

"Is it really you?"

"Yes, it's me." Protos placed a silver drachma on the table. "May I have a cup of your beer?"

The proprietor, looking faintly ill, hurried away to fetch it. When he came back and set it on the table he forgot himself enough to sit down opposite Protos.

"Did you escape?"

"Yes."

The proprietor glanced about as if he expected the room to be swarming with soldiers.

"This time I won't tell them that I saw you," he said, nodding his head vigorously.

"I know you won't." Protos smiled and took a sip of his beer. "There's no one left to tell."

7

On the ship to Pella in Macedon, Eurytus had kept to himself. He was the junior member of a delegation being sent to King Amyntas to negotiate an alliance against Olynthus, which would help give Sparta a presence in the north of Greece. It was an important mission, so his fellow passengers probably interpreted his reticence as modesty. In fact, it was a depression of spirit, for Eurytus regarded his life as in ruins.

At twenty, the fervent patriotism which had been drilled into him during his military training was unblemished. He had finished the best of his year. His instructors could not praise him enough for his valor, self-discipline, and intelligence. They saw great things ahead for him.

And indeed, all he wanted—all he had ever wanted—was to be a worthy servant of the state and to live up to the example set by his ancestors.

Yet on his first test, matched against a Helot slave boy, he had failed miserably. His father, who had arranged his current assignment, no doubt felt his failure as painfully as he did himself.

The Macedonians had a reputation for bravery, conviviality, and drunkenness. Eurytus felt sure he was not going to redeem himself at the banqueting table. What he longed for was a war.

And if he died fighting, then so be it. All that mattered was that he win back his honor.

But now he had to make himself agreeable to a herd of northern barbarians. And all because he had failed to accept the challenge of a slave boy.

❊❊

Upon arrival at the Macedonian capital, Eurytus found the nobles of that race more agreeable than he had anticipated. Lacking the discipline of the Spartans, they seemed to approach life with a childlike exuberance—at their banquets they became joyously drunk and fought mock battles riding on each other's shoulders and throwing food. Even sober, they spoke of war as if it were a game played for the sheer animal pleasure of it.

Within half a month he was an accepted partner of their revels, and the alliance was well on its way to being realized. There would be a war against Olynthus, and Eurytus could only hope he would somehow find a way to be part of it.

Then he received a letter from his father. Protos had been captured in Messenia and was being held in a cage at a place called Kyparissia. An escort had been dispatched to bring him back to Sparta.

It was perhaps the happiest moment of Eurytus's life.

❧ ❦

But even as Eurytus was reading of his capture, Protos had vanished into the Erymanthos mountains. The Spartans sent patrols out after him, which always returned without having found so much as a footprint. Sometimes Protos would sit in the shadow of an overhanging rock and watch the files of soldiers working their way up the narrow, rocky mountain trails. He left them alone and headed north.

After about a month the patrols ceased and Protos concluded that he had passed beyond Messenia into some other place.

When the winter began in earnest, he had to come down out of the mountains. After four days of aimless wandering, he found a city.

At first he had no idea what it was. From a distance all he could see was a wall, which was certainly three or four times the height of a man and extended for some distance before terminating at either end in a sharp line. Who would build a wall like that, and to what purpose? That this might be some sort of human settlement did not at first occur to him.

But then he noticed the roads—or, more accurately, the people and carts moving over what he had to assume were roads. Their movements began or ended at opposite ends of the wall, but the traffic on the eastern side was greater than on the western.

An hour's walk revealed to Protos that what he had first seen was merely the south side of a gigantic stone rectangle. He also discovered a gate through which people entered and left whatever was enclosed within the wall.

He decided to investigate.

Nothing could have prepared him for what he found. The space within the walls was filled with buildings, most of wood but many of stone, and narrow, crowded paths hardly wide enough for a farm cart. Never had Protos experienced such a crush of people. The crowds consisted mainly of the poor, and the poor were the same everywhere, but here and there among them were men and even a few women with embroidered tunics and robes of dyed wool. Some wore thin bands of shiny metal on their arms.

The sound of their mingled voices was inhuman and the smell, compounded of sweat, garbage, and excrement, was overpowering.

What a place! Why would anyone choose to be here?

Yet for all the confusion and squalor, it was comforting to be once more in the presence of men. Protos had not spoken so much as a word to another human being in almost two months. In all that time, men and those his enemies, had been something observed from a distance, and only now did he understand how lonely he had been.

Perhaps he could stay in this place for a time—provided he really had moved beyond the reach of the Spartans.

With his Spartan knife in his belt and carrying his parcel of weapons, he walked through the city for several hours, eventually discovering a second gate and concluding, in the end, that this place was essentially a village, except vastly bigger.

He quickly realized he could buy food here—apparently, he could buy just about anything. He bought a piece of flatbread wrapped around a few strips of meat. It was not terrible. He had eaten much worse. What he wanted next was somewhere to sleep out of the cold.

The people spoke a tongue not very different from the Doric with which Protos had grown up, so he had no difficulty making his wants known. He bought a cup of beer at a stall and inquired where he might find a place for the night. The woman behind the counter, who was thin and elderly, seemed to resent the question, but at last she pointed to a door across the way.

"They serve food there," she said, "and for an obol they'll give you dinner and a place to sleep by the fire."

"What is an obol?"

The woman looked at him as if she judged him to be simpleminded and then told him that an obol was the sixth part of a drachma. At that rate he would have food and lodging until the summer. He thanked her and crossed the street.

※ ※

The proprietor of Protos's new lodging was a man named Kephalos who appeared to be in his late fifties and was, by his own account, a restless soul who in his youth had traveled as far east as Persia and as far west as the island of Sicily and had at last, through the exercise of his considerable personal charm, won the heart of the former owner's widow. That lady had now been dead for three years, and her praises were ever on Kephalos's tongue, although now and then he offered a hint that the marriage had not been perfectly blissful.

He was so impressed with Protos's willingness to pay in advance—and in Athenian silver—that he instructed one of his two servant women, and she the one who seemed to be occupying the place of his late wife, to heat up water so that "the young Lord Protos" could wash off the dust of his long journey. While they waited, Kephalos treated him to a cup of beer and entertained him with a history of his adventures.

"Ah, my boy, the vicissitudes of chance put a man's feet on strange paths," he said, patting Protos on the arm and then refilling his cup. "I had thought to be a great merchant prince, and now it seems likely I will end my days here, in this carbuncle on the backside of Greece, offering to visitors like yourself such conveniences as my poor establishment can boast. But you will never hear me complain. No, never."

"Then you were not born here?"

Kephalos was a large man, tall and built on a generous scale, but the most impressive thing about him, the thing Protos would always remember, was his head. It might have been the head on a painted idol. The eyes, nose, and mouth all seemed too large for the face and suggested a personality at once avaricious, cunning, and sentimental.

At the moment he was smiling, as if Protos had guessed his secret.

"No, my boy, I was born and bred in Corinth, although my mother was from Salamis—that is an island, and island women are always longing after strange places and forbidden men. She led my father a miserable existence, and I suppose I inherited my lascivious and footloose nature from her.

"Corinth—now there is a city, beautiful and rich. Would that I had never left her!"

"Is it bigger than . . . what did you say the name of this place was?"

"Elis, lad. The rectum of creation. Paugh!"

Protos had never met anyone quite like Kephalos, and it was amusing to listen to his stories and his descriptions of life in what he liked to call his "unloved final resting place."

"Yes, boy, Corinth is immensely bigger. Corinth is the wonder of the world, but this place is merely an overcrowded farming village. The airs they give themselves! And now they have provoked some sort of quarrel with Sparta. It is all the most unblemished madness."

Interrupted only by Protos's bath, their conversation lasted well into the evening, when at last the servant woman, whose name was Gulas, came to drag Kephalos off to bed.

The accommodations offered by his new friend were not quite all that Protos had hoped for, since space on the floor was let out to an assortment of travelers, day laborers, and beggars crowded together like dogs in a kennel. By midnight the hearth fire had burned itself down to a few embers, and the room was drafty. There was such a cacophony of snoring that the impression was of a continuous earthquake. It was not particularly restful.

❧❦

Protos had only a few days to experience the charms of city life before his landlord summoned him aside one evening, just as he was finishing his dinner.

"Rumors have reached us of a Spartan army crossing the border with Arkadia, which means that they are no more than a day or two from Elis. Doubtless their object is to settle certain political disputes, but their presence may make it uncomfortable for others as well.

"Gulas noted the scars on your back when you washed yourself. I make no inquiries, but it struck me that you might wish to avoid our visitors from Laconia."

"Your warning is timely, Master Kephalos, and the act of a friend. I will gather my things."

"If anyone should ask after you, I will say that I threw you out for lewd behavior." Kephalos smiled and winked and put his hand on Protos's shoulder. "But there is time for yet one more cup of beer before you go . . ."

❧❦

So. Even this place was not beyond the reach of his enemies. Was there nowhere he could rest his head and feel safe? It appeared not.

Protos left at twilight. At the city gates he found himself pushing his way through a flood of terrified humanity. People from the surrounding villages were eager to get within the walls before the dreaded Spartans arrived.

Kephalos had advised that he head north and, when he reached the sea, take a ship to the mainland of Greece. But Protos's instinct told him to head east into Arkadia, which he had been informed was mountainous and sparsely populated. Besides, he was in no hurry to get away. He was frankly curious.

He had had no contact with the Spartans except as individuals. He had never seen this army that all seemed so to fear—in fact, he had never seen any army. So he decided he would stay in the vicinity and watch how things developed.

If he was condemned to spend the rest of his short life fighting them, he thought it might be wise to learn a little more about the Spartans.

There were forests east of Elis and within half an hour's walk. Protos bedded down there for the night, and the next morning found a tree that towered over those around it. He climbed it and discovered, as he expected, that he had a clear view of Elis's eastern gate.

For a slight consideration, Kephalos had provided him with a leather bag full of food, and even a jar of beer. It was enough, he thought, to last about three days. He hung the bag and his parcel of weapons from the great tree's branches, and descended to explore his surroundings. In an emergency he might need an escape route.

That evening the Spartans arrived. They established their camp to the southwest of his lookout, an elaborate process that took them all night. Their slaves worked by torchlight and Protos, sitting in his tree, could look down into the interior of the stockade.

His best guess was that, excluding their Helot labor force, there were only about two hundred of them.

The next day they were quiet. They sent out a few mounted patrols that rode a circuit around the city walls, but these seemed to serve no purpose except to intimidate the Elisians.

On the morning of the third day, the Spartans left their stockade and formed two squares, ten men wide by ten deep. In perfect order they marched to within five *stadioi* of Elis's main gate, where they stood chanting something. Protos could not make out the words, but he assumed it was a challenge to battle.

It seemed strange. War was a thing he knew about only from Uncle Neleus's stories and he thought of it as a series of duels between heroes—Achilleos against Hektor, Menelaus against Paris—this clearly would be nothing like that.

Within a quarter of an hour the city gate opened and the Elisian soldiers marched out and arranged themselves into squares like the Spartans. They made five squares, which meant that their force was over twice as great as Sparta's. The Spartans, it appeared, had come on a fool's errand. Surely the Elisians would win.

But what happened defeated all expectation. As soon as the two armies began moving toward each other Protos could see how different they were. The Spartan squares were tight and precise. Their advance was that of a single object, the men who formed each square so integrated into it they seemed almost to disappear as individuals. It was like watching an animated building stone.

The Elisian squares, by contrast, were simply men who had arranged themselves into a given pattern. As they advanced, their lines wobbled, the rear struggling to keep up with the front.

The battle began when men within the Elisian squares threw javelins at the Spartans, but almost instantly the Spartans raised their shields, forming a kind of roof over themselves. If any of the javelins found their mark, Protos couldn't see it.

And when the enemies collided the Elisians might as well have been attacking a stone wall. The Spartans advanced and the Elisian lines held, then buckled, then collapsed, becoming once more individual men trying to escape being run over by the inhumanly efficient Spartan squares.

And that was how it ended. The Elisians simply ran away, leaving the Spartans in possession of the field. The battle had lasted no longer than three-quarters of an hour. Two hundred men had defeated five hundred as easily as a stone crushes an egg.

And men had been killed. The battlefield was strewn with Elisian dead—and even, here and there, the odd Spartan.

So this was war. Over the past few months, Protos had become intimate with death, but this . . .

Farmers organized for planting and the harvest. City people, it seemed, organized only to slaughter one another. How many had fallen today? Eighty? A hundred? What dispute had Elis and Sparta to settle that was worth so many lives?

It was madness. And the Spartans, who excelled at killing because they centered their lives around it, were the maddest people on earth.

There was nothing more to see. The city of Elis would have to work out whatever peace they could with the Spartans, but that would not take place on the battlefield.

Protos gathered up his food bag and weapons and slid down the tree. Before him now was Arkadia, and probably a hard winter, but he would find a way to survive. The mountains were without mercy, but men were worse.

And he felt he had learned something: in strength there was always some core of weakness.

8

Nubit had had a tiring day. Her voice was hoarse from trying to draw an audience. Since breakfast she had told six fortunes and sold eight or nine of her love potions—she couldn't even remember. Making money in Argos was like squeezing water from a turnip. As usual, the only places where she could find space to put on her performances were the steps leading up to temples, and the city magistrates were beginning to watch her. By mid-afternoon she had decided it was time to move on.

By sundown she was already a few hours east of the city. Her wagon was parked in the trees near some nameless creek and her horse was hobbled and eating its dinner. Her own was simmering over a small fire. She knew she needed food because she felt weak, but what she really wanted was to rest her head against a wagon wheel and take refuge in her dreams.

She would poison her father all over again in that ecstatic vision, which over the years had acquired great intensity of detail. She would watch the life ebb out of his eyes, and then, when he had faded away, the Divine One, the Great Mother, would fill her soul with things seen and unseen, would open her to the future and the past so that she would become the mere vessel of that final truth, which was the Goddess's most precious gift.

What people called the world was a shadow. Her dreams were truth. This Nubit believed. And when she died, she believed she would be gathered into that truth and live there forever.

But the shadow world held every living soul in its chains. She had to work to earn bread that turned stale in a day and fish that stank until she fried them stiff in oil and garlic.

She had known no home since leaving Egypt, and "home" was an idea that held little charm for her. Nubit had fled Egypt on the first ship outward bound, selling her father's gold dishes to pay for her passage. She had landed in Greece, in the city of Athens, with nothing but a few pouches of herbs and the wisdom she had learned from her mother.

Mother—not the Goddess but the poor, fragile woman who had died coughing up blood from her ruptured guts. Nubit knew almost nothing of her mother's personal history—only that she had not been born into slavery but was the daughter of a farmer in Upper Egypt. Her mother's father, it seemed, had lived in fear of his wife because she had an unpredictable temper and could raise the spirits of the dead. Apparently he did not wish to live in thrall to another witch and so, when his wife died, he sold their daughter to a slave trader.

"You will not wear out your life under the yoke," her mother had told Nubit. "Another fate awaits you when you have the courage to seize it."

And so she had taught her daughter what the world in its folly called witchcraft.

Had her mother been a little wiser she would herself have poisoned Nubit's father, that wicked man, and they could have fled together.

Had she lacked wisdom or courage? Or had she stood in such dread of the gods that she shrank from the act?

The gods were children—or the inventions of men. Only the Divine One was real, and She cared nothing for the priests' catalog of sins. For Her there was only life and struggle.

The sun had been down an hour. Nubit's campfire seemed the only light in the world and her cooking pot hung over it from an iron tripod. Today she had decided to treat herself and at the temple of Hera had bought the hindquarters of a lamb, sacrificed only that morning, she had been told, by a rich merchant celebrating the birth of a grandchild—there had also been a pig, but Nubit was too thoroughly an Egyptian to touch it. So tonight she would celebrate along with the merchant and enjoy a stew of lamb and foxtail millet.

Nubit was sitting with her back against a wagon wheel and had not yet even tasted her beer when she heard a twig snap somewhere out in the darkness. The knife she had used to cut up the hindquarter of lamb was on the ground beside her, so she hid it under the folds of her skirt.

Suddenly a man stepped into the circle of light from her fire. He stood directly across from her, illuminated by the flames. He carried a long bundle wrapped in a cloak she recognized from the pattern as of Spartan weave, but the man himself wore only a loincloth and his feet were bare. He was slender but strongly muscled and, for all the tufts of beard that grew on his cheeks and chin, very young.

"I would be most grateful if you could allow me to sit and warm myself by your fire, Lady," he said. "I intend you no harm."

She noticed the way his eyes glanced away from the cooking pot. He was hungry—she could see that in his face—but too proud to beg. And he was not a thief.

"Sit down then, boy. Supper will be ready in half an hour. I will be glad of the company."

"I thank you."

Nubit almost had to force a cup of beer on him and it was amusing to watch the way he would allow himself only tiny sips. He would not permit himself to appear hungry or thirsty, or even cold. It was a chill night and he was almost naked, but he would submit to no weakness.

She leaned forward to stir the contents of the cooking pot.

"You have traveled far?" she asked, careful not to look at him directly.

He seemed to consider the question for a moment, and then he shook his head.

"I hardly know," he said. "I have wandered. What is this place?"

"We are perhaps two hours from the city of Argos."

"Is that a Spartan city?"

"No, boy. Argos is Sparta's dog, but you are safe enough."

"What makes you think—"

"That you are a runaway?" Nubit glanced at him and laughed, suggesting that he must be a simpleton if he needed to ask. "Unless I am mistaken, those are weapons you have wrapped in that Spartan cloak. I am told that the Spartans are severe on their male children. Did you flee from home?"

"I have no home." It was said without self-pity, merely as a fact.

"How long have you been on your travels?"

He seemed to consider the question for a moment.

"I started in the autumn, and there have been two winters since."

"And now it is the spring." She nodded. "So it has been a year and a half, more or less."

Nubit was about to ask him where he had been but then decided it was probably wiser to let the matter drop.

"The stew is ready," she said. "I will fetch us a couple of bowls and some bread."

"Then, when you get up, be careful not to cut yourself on that knife you have concealed under your skirt."

This made her laugh.

The stew was good, and if the lamb was a little stringy the boy did not complain. He ate slowly, seeming to savor every mouthful.

"Why do you say that Argos is Sparta's dog?" he asked at one point, as if he had been brooding on that question all during the meal.

"Because the Argives are too weak to resist the Spartans and so have perforce become their allies—rather like a virgin who marries a man because she fears otherwise he will rape her. Besides, it was a joke. Argos was the name of Odysseus's dog."

"Is this Odysseus some friend of yours?"

"No."

Nubit struggled not to smile. It was hard to imagine a Greek who had never heard of Odysseus.

He was only a boy, she told herself. Yet he seemed to have left childhood far behind. There was nothing of awkwardness about him. His every movement was possessed of economy and grace. He was courteous, but that seemed a natural rather than an acquired quality.

Still, he seemed to know nothing about the world except, obviously, how to survive in it.

"I am like you," she said finally, after the silence between them appeared likely to grow permanent. "I have no home except the journey."

"Then you are not like me." He smiled, signaling he meant no disrespect. "A journey implies a plan."

"We all have a plan—or there is a plan for us. Even if you go wherever the breath of the world blows you, there is still a direction behind it."

"The only direction I would follow is the one away from death, but I cannot guess which way that is."

"But so far you have managed to follow it."

He could but shrug, and smile again.

She began to say something else, but he held up his hand to silence her. At first she was on the verge of being offended but then realized he was listening to some sound she could not hear.

"Someone is coming," he said quietly.

"If that is the case, then it would be better if you were not here."

He nodded, picking up his bundle as he rose from the ground. An instant later he had disappeared into the woods as soundlessly as a shadow.

He is only a boy, she thought to herself. *And no doubt a fugitive. He cannot be blamed for being afraid.*

And yet she could not dismiss her disappointment.

But she was not afraid, she told herself. It was too early to be afraid. And if she showed fear she surrendered every advantage. She must not be afraid.

Nubit knew, at least in general terms, what to expect. This was no more than some man who had seen her on the road and come to amuse himself. She would smile at him as if she had been waiting all evening just for him, and if she was very lucky he would accept the cup of beer she would offer him, in which case he would wake up sometime tomorrow afternoon, alone and naked by a cold campfire.

If she was less lucky he would rape her, and she would be wise enough not to fight him. For a woman traveling alone rape took on the character of a natural disaster, like breaking a wheel in the middle of a snowstorm.

But if she was truly unlucky he would beat her and then rape her. There were such men in the world, and at a lonely campsite in the middle of a wilderness, what was there to stop him from killing her?

Although she might not die. She probably wouldn't die. She would lift her skirt and try as best she could to protect her head.

Once, when she was seventeen, a man in Epirus had beaten her and left her for dead. He broke her cheekbone—to this day her face hurt in cold weather—and it was two months before she could take a deep breath without pain.

Then she remembered her knife. Perhaps she would be able to frighten him off with that.

In the first few seconds after the boy had gone, Nubit took his beer cup and used the tip of her middle finger to paint the inside with a cream from a small copper pot in her medicine bag. Then she refilled her own cup and sat down to wait.

She could hear the crackling in the underbrush now. He was almost upon her.

By the Mouse God's navel, there were two of them.

The knife would do her no good. If she cut one the other would seize her, and then they would surely kill her. The knife must be forgotten.

So she stayed on the ground and put on her wanton's face to meet them. "Good evening, my lords."

She raised her beer cup in salute and smiled. She even winked at them. Inside she was trembling like grass in the wind, but they must not see her fear. Her fear would only embolden them.

They were big louts, farmers probably. They wore ragged tunics that did nothing to hide their permanently dirty knees. They looked enough alike to suggest that they might be of the same blood. Their black beards were greasy tangles and Nubit could see from their glassy, staring eyes that they were already drunk.

A clod with a skin full of wine was the worst. No woman living, no matter what she did to encourage him, would succeed in stiffening his limp manhood, and he would likely beat her almost to death just to soothe his wounded vanity.

But if they had been drinking, perhaps they would like more. Perhaps she could arrange a comfortable nap for them.

She drained off her beer cup and pretended to sigh with satisfaction.

"Would your honors care to taste a drop of my beer? I brew it myself and it is strong." She laughed, as lasciviously as any tavern harlot. "I like strong men and strong beer."

At last one of them grinned, but not, it seemed, at her little jest. They might not even have heard her.

"We saw you in the marketplace today," he said, almost as if he had detected her in a crime. "We watched you do your tricks with sparks and green smoke, but what we liked best was the way your tits looked through your gauzy little costume. No Greek woman would let her nipples show like that. I told my brother here that you were likely a foreign woman."

"My lord is wise. I am from Egypt."

"Egypt! I have heard of Egypt. They say that all Egyptian women are witches and whores."

"Then, my lord, drink a little of a whore's beer and be merry," she exclaimed, filling the boy's cup from her jar and holding it up like an offering. Her voice sounded a trifle hysterical, even to herself. "Come, drink, and I will show you some of my magic the marketplace never saw!"

The other one stepped forward and with a swat knocked the cup from her hand.

"We don't want your beer, whore." And then he turned to his brother. "Come along, Zantheos, let's get on with it."

Zantheos touched him on the arm, as one might quiet a child.

"Yes, I know. But there's no harm if we have a little sport with her first."

But his brother was not to be appeased. He reached down and grasped the front of Nubit's tunic, pulling at her as if he meant to strangle her in it.

"Give us the money, whore! People gave you silver coins—we saw them!"

He threw her down on the ground and raised his fist as if to strike her. And then . . .

And then something strange happened. He seemed to stiffen and when he opened his mouth, perhaps to speak, blood poured out between his lips. He collapsed to his knees and stared into Nubit's face with astonishment.

Then she understood. There was a dagger buried up to the hilt in his neck. He was as good as dead.

The expression in his eyes reminded Nubit of her father as he had looked while she watched him die.

And then the boy stepped calmly out into the circle of light. With his foot he pushed at the man so that he collapsed on his side, truly dead now.

The boy was carrying a sword in his right hand.

Zantheos needed to see no more. He let out a cry and turned to run.

The boy deftly tossed his sword into the air and then caught it by the blade. Zantheos had gone no more than five or six steps when the boy threw his sword. With a faint sound, like a cough, the point caught Zantheos high up on his back, and he stumbled and fell. For a moment he seemed to rest on his elbows and then he sank to the earth. After that he never moved.

The boy pulled his dagger free from the nameless brother's throat. Then he straightened up and regarded Zantheos's motionless form with an expression of faint perplexity. Then his face cleared and he turned to Nubit.

"I had best bury these two," he said calmly. "Someone might come looking for them, and it would be better if they disappeared. Have you a shovel?"

Nubit stared at him, bewildered. He had just killed two men, and now he was asking for a shovel.

"You killed them," she said, with a kind of awe. "Why? It was not your quarrel."

"You have been kind to me and they would have hurt you. It *was* my quarrel." He turned his head a little, his eyes still on her face. He seemed to be waiting for something. Then he seemed to decide that he had waited long enough. "Have you a shovel?" he repeated.

The dagger was still in his hand. She could not take her eyes from it.

"A shovel—yes. Strapped to the other side of the wagon."

"Then I will fetch it."

"Give me your dagger and I will clean it for you."

This suggestion seemed to amuse him. "Is that what you call it?" he asked, and then, without waiting for an answer, drove the point into the ground at Nubit's feet and went to retrieve the shovel.

When he found it he came back and grabbed the nameless brother's foot, clenching the ankle in the crook of his arm.

"I'll take them a little way into the woods," he said. "No one will ever find them."

"Thank you," she said, still feeling overwhelmed by what she had just witnessed. "I think it almost certain that you saved my life tonight." And then, "Where did you ever learn to kill like that?"

He smiled. "It's only a matter of practice," he said. And then he dragged the corpse off into the darkness.

When he was no longer there, Nubit's attention was drawn back to his dagger. She stared at it for a moment and then grasped the hilt and pulled it free from the ground. Blood still glistened on the upper half of the blade.

She fetched a cloth and a pan of water from her barrel and sat down to clean it—first with water, then with a handful of sandy earth, then with water again. Then she dried it thoroughly.

When she was finished she held the dagger in her two hands, the point resting delicately against her left palm.

And then she remembered the dream.

The hunter holding his dagger in his hands, just the way her hands held it now. The sound like the flutter of birds' wings was the dagger flying through the air. It struck the doe in the neck and the doe had sunk to the ground and died, just as Zantheos's brother had died.

It was the same dagger. The dagger she had seen in her dream—it was the same one.

How long ago was that? A year, at least. Longer.

He had thrown the dagger and then a sword. Both times the point had found its target unerringly. How many men could do such a thing?

And now the Divine Mother had sent him to her, to save her life.

She stood up, for suddenly she felt the need to be busy. She unhooked her cooking pot from the tripod—they wouldn't want any more food tonight—and went to fetch an armful of wood for the fire. Then she climbed into the wagon and took out a little wooden stool and her largest cauldron, the one she used for her laundry, hooking the cauldron to the tripod. Then she filled it with water.

When she came to rest again she felt an urge to laugh, but she did not want the boy to hear her so the laugh came out as a kind of gasp.

It was more than an hour before the boy came back, and he was as dirty as she had expected.

"Sit down," she said, as if this were a nightly ritual with them. She pointed to the stool. "I have prepared a bath for you and I will wash you myself.

If you are going to sleep with me in the wagon tonight, I would prefer it if you did not stink of blood."

He sat down on the stool, as docile as a child, and she undid his loin-cloth for him. Then she poured warm water over his head. She was scrubbing his arm with a cloth before she spoke again.

"Tomorrow, when we are well away from this place, I expect you to tell me everything. Then we can decide how to get you free from whatever this trouble of yours might be.

"By the way, what is your name?"

"Protos."

"How did your parents happen to call you that?"

"I was the first child and, as it turned out, the only. I think they hoped for others, so they called me 'first.'"

Nubit nodded her head, a gesture he could not have seen with his face turned away.

"They did well to name you thus. The word also means 'destined.'"

9

They slept that night in the wagon, covered by a single blanket. Nubit pillowed her head against the inside of his arm and her hand rested against his chest.

"You can touch me," she told him, "wherever you wish. But be careful not to hurt me."

"I don't want to hurt you."

"I know."

It was clear that he had never been with a woman before. This man, who only a few hours before had killed twice, was afraid of her.

"Here—let me show you," she said, taking his hand in hers and guiding it to her breast. She crept a little closer to him, so that their legs touched, and began nibbling at his lips with tentative little kisses.

It was a new experience for her to have a lover who treated her body as if she were the only woman in the world.

But he had doubtless been born close to the earth, and no farm boy grows up utterly innocent of the commerce between the sexes. He needed only a little guidance, a nudge or a word here and there, and he did well enough—more than well enough.

When he first entered her he shuddered to his climax nearly at once. She was disappointed, but then she found he was still hard.

Yes, of course. He was very young. His stamina, as it turned out, was almost boundless. He seemed ready to go on forever.

But not quite forever. And even when it was all over he kept touching her. He would slide the tips of his fingers over her shoulders or down the small of her back. It was delicious.

After he had been dead asleep for perhaps a quarter of an hour, she found that the insides of her thighs were still trembling.

The next morning she slept late. When she awoke she discovered he was gone, and she was seized with panic until she heard the sounds of someone moving about outside.

He was relighting the campfire, using an ax to shave thin strips of kindling from a stick. She lifted up the flap of the tent and watched him. The sight of him, the deft little movements of his hands, filled her with an unfamiliar pleasure.

"I have a clutch of eggs," she said quietly, "and there is still some of the lamb remaining. I can cook them for your breakfast."

His back was to her, but of course he had known she was watching. He was striking a piece of flint against the ax head to cause a spark. He seemed absorbed in his task, as if he hadn't heard her.

"I can't remember if I have ever eaten an egg."

He turned his head and smiled at her. It was a cold morning, but he was naked. Strangely, it was the first time she had noticed how scarred his back was.

"Come back to the wagon," she said, her voice almost hoarse, for her desire was suddenly urgent. "The fire can wait. I cannot."

❧❦

They sat before the fire, wrapped in his Spartan cloak, eating eggs and little pieces of lamb out of an iron pan. They made a kind of game of it. Protos would scoop the food up with the edge of his dagger and feed it to her. Nubit could not recall a time when she had felt so innocently happy.

But finally it was time to remember that survival was a serious matter.

"Those marks on your back," she said. "You have been scourged."

"More than once."

"So you have been either a soldier or a slave, and I think you are too young ever to have been a soldier."

"I was born in Laconia," he answered. "I am a Helot. Once a year the Spartans whip us to remind us that we are slaves."

"I have heard they are hard masters. And so you ran away."

"One night they murdered my parents—they were only amusing themselves. They would have murdered me, but I ran. One of them came after me and I killed him. This is his knife."

He held the dagger up before her eyes and then stabbed the earth with it. He was only cleaning the blade, yet Nubit felt her heart grow cold.

"You killed a Spartan?" She could hardly believe such a thing was possible.

"Yes. They die as easily as other men. One day I will go back and kill his brother. I would kill them all if I could."

"And you have been running ever since?"

"Yes."

"And you are still alive." She shook her head in astonishment. "Have they been hunting you?"

"Yes—they even caught me once." He smiled, as if the recollection pleased him. "They put me in an iron cage, but I escaped."

For a moment Nubit felt as if her heart had stopped. *They put me in an iron cage.* She remembered her dream of the wolf in a cage, and the laughing dogs taunting him.

"What happened to the men who captured you?"

"They are all dead."

"You killed them?"

"Yes."

"How long ago was that?"

"A long time." He pulled his knife from the ground and inspected the blade. "It was during that first autumn."

Yes. The time fit. And now the wolf of her dream was sitting beside her, cleaning his knife against the dew-laden grass.

"And now? Do they still hunt you?"

He shook his head. "Lately I have been in the mountains. I haven't seen a soldier, Spartan or otherwise, in several months." He laughed. "Perhaps by now they think I am dead."

"You have done very well."

It was an astonishing story, but she knew how it would have to end. Even he knew it. They would find him—someone would betray him—and they would have their vengeance. All of the Greek states in this part of the world were afraid of the Spartans. Every man's hand would be against him.

Unless, of course . . .

"We have to get you out of the Peloponnese," she announced.

"What is the Peloponnese?"

※ ※

Nubit was astonished by the things he did not know. She took a stick and drew him a rough map in the dirt.

"All of this," she told him, "This is the Peloponnese. Sparta controls most of it, and it is surrounded by water, except for a narrow bridge of land which connects it to the rest of Greece." She pointed with her stick. "Here is the city of Corinth. I have heard rumors that Corinth is on bad terms with the Spartans right now. We have only to go there and you will be safe."

She smiled, and touched his arm.

"I was going to Corinth anyway. Corinth is rich."

"I can walk north to the sea and then east," he said. "It will be safer for you alone."

"Was it safer for me alone last night? No, you will ride with me. Besides, if the Spartans are looking for you they will expect a man alone, not a man traveling with a woman."

She patted him on the knee and then let her hand wander up to caress his scrotum.

"The Goddess sent you to me for a reason."

❧❦

The road between Argos and Corinth was crowded. It was a paved road and the noise of the wagon wheels clattering over cobblestones only intensified Protos's sense of being enfolded in a great mob. He found it unsettling.

"Wait until we get to Corinth," Nubit said, smiling slyly. "In the marketplace you cannot extend your arm without touching someone."

He leaned toward her and kissed her on the neck. "The only one there I will want to touch is you."

It amused Nubit to hear him say such things—and he said them often enough—but she warned herself not to trust them.

Not that the boy was a deceiver. He was merely very young. He had discovered the pleasures of sex only the night before and probably imagined himself enthralled by love. Besides, he had been alone for a long time, during a period of life when it was hard to be alone. Nubit had only to remember her first year in Greece, and the bitterness with which she had missed her mother, to imagine what her young lover must feel.

He was a man in so many ways that it was sometimes difficult to recall that, really, he was hardly more than a child. Nubit was a full ten years older—a fact she knew she must school herself to remember. And she had become, in a sense, his mother as well as the woman in whom he spent his seed. Eventually, when he no longer needed a mother, he would look elsewhere.

But for the moment it was ecstasy. When he touched her he made her body ache with longing—and he was always touching her.

She would have to find something to distract him, if only to prevent them from making an exhibition of themselves.

"Why don't I teach you how to manage the horse," she said suddenly. "Here."

She gave him the reins and threaded them through his fingers, taking pleasure in the touch of his hands, which were strong and calloused but still wonderfully clever.

In the end she taught him nothing. He managed the horse as if he had been born to it.

"You have done this before." Nubit glared at him in a parody of anger.

"No. But I have ridden horses and this is no different. Besides, your mare is very tractable."

She laughed and let her arm drape over his left shoulder, her hand dangling down so that her fingertips touched his chest.

"You could do nearly anything," she said suddenly, for the idea had just then come into her head, like a revelation. "You could be a blacksmith or a stonemason. You could build ships. What would you like to do?"

"Become a soldier and make war on Sparta."

He said it calmly, dispassionately, but the words conveyed perfect conviction. No doubt he had asked and answered this question for himself long ago.

Glancing at her, he smiled, as if he had decided to be a boy again. And then he turned his eyes back to the road.

"What will you do when we reach Corinth?" he asked. "Will you build a ship or . . . ?"

"I will do magic."

For a long moment he said nothing, and then at last he shook his head.

"You are a sorceress?"

"I am an entertainer. I read fortunes. I make small objects disappear and then pull them out of people's ears. I sell love potions."

"Is it magic? I have never known anyone who could do magic."

"Most of it is illusion—tricks to separate fools from their money. But some of it is real. The real things I do not show off in the marketplace."

"What are the real things?"

"Sometimes, in dreams, I see the future. And the love potions work. I have a powder that will make a man's phallus as hard as stone, and he will have to labor over his woman almost to exhaustion before he can unburden himself of his seed."

"Can I have some?"

She shook her head in amusement. "You don't need it."

"Where did you learn all this?"

"From my mother."

She turned her face away. Suddenly she was close to tears, and he seemed to understand. For a long time they followed the road in silence.

"Why are you helping me?" he asked finally.

"Because you saved my life. Because you pleasure my body. And because until you came—as I knew you would come—I had not realized how lonely I was."

"And those are the only reasons?"

"No. But they will do for now."

❧❧

When they camped that night the walls of Corinth were no more than a gray line in the distance. They entered the city at first light to avoid the worst of the crowds and stood in the marketplace to watch the sun rise over the temple of Apollo, which stood like a mountain of white marble atop a stairway more than twice a man's height. It was all columns and straight lines, beautiful and vast, a place where only a god could feel quite at home.

And there were temples everywhere, and porches with stairways fifty paces wide. The marble gleamed like water.

"I never guessed that men could build such a place," Protos said, with undisguised awe. "I knew a man once who told me that Corinth was the wonder of the world, and now I know he spoke the truth. I might have thought these to be the creations of the bright gods themselves."

"They are only temples and they are the work of men. But you are right to be amazed. Corinth is the largest, richest city in Greece."

By then the marketplace had begun to fill with people. Many were elegantly dressed in fine linen garments held together by jeweled clasps. Here and there Protos saw men with long, plaited beards, wearing brightly colored wool robes that reached almost to the paving stones, or whose faces were dark brown or even black.

"Corinth is a trading city," Nubit explained. "Trade is the source of its wealth, and thus there are people here from all the corners of the world. See that one?" She pointed to a man with a shaved head and heavy black lines painted around his eyes. "He is an Egyptian, as much a stranger here as I am."

Protos could only shake his head in wonder.

Nubit laughed and took his hand in both of her own to kiss it. Love was the gods' curse on a woman, but at that moment she didn't care. Life—this moment—suddenly seemed so perfect.

"We will stay a month and we will make so much money you might strain yourself lifting the bags of silver.

"By the way, speaking of money, have you any?"

"Yes." Protos smiled, as if afraid his answer might have sounded too abrupt. "My enemies have been generous to me."

"Then we should buy you some new clothes, lest you be taken for a beggar. Besides, it is safer if you conceal the scars on your back."

10

<hr/>

Eurytus had also gone out to see the wonders of the Corinthian market-place, having arrived only the day before. He had been on garrison duty in Thebes, which was both uninteresting and disagreeable. Spartan troops held the acropolis to support the oligarchy they had imposed on the Thebans but were so universally hated that they could hardly venture into the city without being insulted in some way—once a citizen had "accidentally" spilled a cup of beer down the front of Eurytus's tunic so that he seemed to have pissed himself.

Thus he had been looking forward to returning home when he received a letter from his father suggesting they meet in Corinth, where Dienekes was part of a diplomatic mission to explore the possibilities of reviving the old alliance against the northern cities.

Eurytus did not find Corinth to his taste. The city, with its beautiful buildings and unimaginable wealth, was like an expensive harlot, the very antithesis of everything a Spartan was taught from childhood to respect.

Moreover, Eurytus had realized that his father obviously was planning a diplomatic career for him. First Macedonia, then Thebes and now Corinth. Eurytus suspected that his sojourn among the Corinthians would probably be of some duration.

It made a certain sense. On both his father's and his mother's side Eurytus was connected to the small number of families that controlled Sparta. Besides the two royal lines, there were eight or ten such families, generally descended from some half-legendary hero. In Sparta, family prestige was the key to power, and prestige was proportional to the number of distinguished men, paradigms of courage and patriotism, one could number among one's forefathers.

And, of course, one had to be seen as embodying in one's own person the martial glory of one's ancestors. The Spartans were soldiers, and what they looked for in their leaders were a soldier's virtues.

And that, as Eurytus keenly understood, was his problem. Who trusts a soldier who has been outmaneuvered and outfought by a slave boy? At least Pantites and the others were excused by the convenient circumstance of being dead—death in combat made up for every failing, even that of dying at the hands of a beardless child.

But Eurytus had come back from that disastrous adventure alive. It was difficult to explain.

It was even more difficult to live with. A thousand times he wished he had answered the boy Protos's challenge and gone up that hill to an honorable death—he was a trained warrior, the best of his year, and yet somehow it never occurred to him that he might have survived the encounter. In Thebes he had actually hoped the city would rise in revolt so that he could be torn apart by the mob and at least die fighting.

What he wanted, what he yearned for, was a good war. If he survived he would be washed clean of his shame, and if he died . . . Well, how was his life now better than death?

Diplomacy was the work of old men, men like his father, who had already proven themselves. Sparta was not a place where any man could rise to greatness except through the sword.

His father had been surprisingly understanding the night Eurytus arrived in Corinth, which only made him feel worse. Some rich pro-Sparta merchant had made available to them a large house that backed up to the gulf, and the two of them sat within hearing of the lapping water to share a jar of Sicilian wine.

"Your peasant boy has left us a trail of corpses to follow," Dienekes told him. "Seven in Laconia, eight more in Messenia—these are simply the ones we can be sure of—at least six in Arkadia. It reached the point where Arkadian soldiers refused to go into the mountains looking for him. It is almost an honor that you managed to survive."

But Eurytus could only shake his head.

"He let me live," he said, feeling that he owed his father, if not the truth, at least something that approached it. "I am sure of it. He spared me for some reason of his own."

"Then I am thankful." Dienekes managed a tense smile. "With your brother dead the future of our house rests with you."

"I have no future, Father. He has seen to that."

Dienekes shrugged.

"I would have said so immediately after, but not now. It is clear that this boy is—"

"His name is Protos, Father."

Their cups were nearly empty, so Dienekes refilled them, implying that a Helot's name could hardly be thought to matter.

"This Protos, then, is clearly very formidable, but so is a bull in a pasture. He has an innate mastery of weapons, which is a skill some are born with, no different in kind from being able to balance an egg on the tip of one's nose. He is no Spartan."

"Perhaps not, but he is not a coward and he is also very far from being a buffoon. He knew what we would do before we did ourselves. He showed himself to us, Father. He stood on a rock and waved to us to attract our attention. He used himself to bait a trap and Pantites and the rest of us walked straight into it. And now they are all dead and I am alive only until he decides to kill me."

"You make me ashamed of you, Eurytus." Dienekes seemed unable to meet his son's gaze, so instead he stared out at the dark waters of the gulf. "It is unlike a Spartan to be so afraid of death."

"Believe me, Father, I would embrace death at his hands, if only to free myself from my shame. What I fear is not death but the disaster I have unwittingly unleashed."

"Now you are talking nonsense. It has been months since there has been any word of him. He is probably dead. He probably froze, or starved to death."

"You think so?" Eurytus found it hard to believe that anything, even the pitiless Arkadian winter, could kill Protos, whom he suspected of being not quite human. "I suppose one can hope it's true."

❦ ❦

Eventually his father had gotten around to the real subject of their discussion. Another war with Athens and the northern states was inevitable, and Corinth was the fulcrum on which the balance of power would depend. For one thing, Corinth controlled the land route out of the Peloponnese, so she would have to be wooed into an alliance or conquered, and conquering her might prove expensive. Corinth had an excellent army, composed primarily of mercenaries, and her navy was second only to Athens's. Sparta would win but might be so exhausted that she would be forced to sue Athens for peace.

"Besides, her interests naturally incline her to us," Dienekes explained.

"The Corinthians are traders and the Athenians are their only real competition. Probably all merchants regard us as uncouth rustics because we don't perfume our beards or eat off silver dishes, but the main fact for them is that we don't threaten their commercial interests. Thus they will be inclined to buy us off with military cooperation and help overcoming the inevitable Athenian embargo."

"And what is to be my part in all this?"

"To be charming, with just a hint of menace." Dienekes made a gesture with his right hand, languidly stirring the air. "I have in mind a series of banquets for the leading citizens. No doubt you will be an object of some interest, since they rarely see a Spartan under forty. You will ingratiate yourself with the younger men. Become their friend and confidant. Find out what they are thinking—and what their fathers are thinking—and report it all to me."

"So I am to go brothel crawling with a crowd of wastrels who paint their fingernails?"

"The whores of Corinth are famous throughout Greece. Most men your age would envy you."

There was a terrace at the back of the house and they sat on a wide stairway that led down to a gravel beach. The only light was from a sliver of moon, so it was impossible for them to read each other's expressions. Dienekes sat with his elbows resting on his knees, and then suddenly he straightened up.

"It will only be for a few months," he said. "And then I promise you a posting where you will see blood spilled. I know what is in your mind, my son. You imagine you have something to prove. Do this one thing for me and I promise you will have your chance to prove it."

❧❧

"I saw him," Protos said. "He was in the marketplace."

Nubit turned her head to look at him as he stood beside the horse, which was tethered a little distance away from the wagon. He was stroking its muzzle.

He had announced his discovery almost as a piece of indifferent news, but they had been in Corinth together for more than a month, which was long enough for her to understand the dark currents that flowed through his soul.

It was not good news. It was only with difficulty that she could spare any attention for her cooking pot.

"You are sure?" she asked finally.

"He was wearing a Spartan cloak and carrying a sword—when do Corinthians carry swords? Besides, his is a face I will know on my deathbed."

"Did he see you?"

"No." Protos shook his head. "I am quite sure. He never glanced in my direction."

"And how did it feel to see him again?"

"Feel?"

Protos had continued stroking the horse's muzzle, but suddenly his hand became still and Nubit realized that in his mind he was in some hidden place, alone with his anguish and his terrible wrath.

Then he looked at her and smiled.

"I hardly know what I felt. I can't describe it, even to myself."

"So what will you do? Will you kill him?"

"I haven't decided."

During their month in Corinth, Nubit had made almost as much money as she had hoped. Perhaps it was time to move on.

"If you kill him in Corinth, it will be murder."

"It will be justice, though I cut his throat under his mother's eyes."

"The city magistrate will not think so."

"I will not be caught."

"Then you plan to kill him?"

He did not answer. He sat down beside her and for a long time simply stared into the flames. Nubit had grown accustomed to these silences and kept her peace.

Finally, when their dinner could be left to itself, she brought him a cup of beer and crouched behind him, resting her hands on his shoulders.

"Eurytus, son of Dienekes, killed my father," he said at last. "My father was a better man than I will ever be."

"I think you are already a good man."

He reached back and put his hand over hers, but he still did not look at her.

"My father never killed anyone."

That night he lay with his back to her and she held him in her arms as he wept. Since that first morning he had never spoken of the things that had befallen him. He seemed almost to have forgotten his loss and his vengeance. But tonight, when he said "I saw him," Nubit had not had to ask whom he meant.

And now, in the darkness, he was once more the boy who had seen his parents murdered and he sobbed out his grief. He was still too young to be ashamed of the anguish that tore at him or of allowing himself to be comforted. For these few hours he was no woman's lover and Nubit cradled him in her arms.

⚜ ⚜

The more Eurytus saw how the rest of the world was governed, the more he admired the Spartan constitution, which was based on balanced power and a community free from faction.

Its two kings, each descended from a separate royal line, were essentially military leaders whose prestige was accordingly based on success in war. Below them were the five Ephors, chosen for single one-year terms by an assembly of citizens whose only business in life was soldiering. And beyond them all were the Elders, a self-selecting body of men noted for their wisdom and all over the age of military service. The kings could be either rivals or colleagues, depending on temperament and circumstance, but they were necessarily checks each other's ambition. The Ephors, of whom Eurytus's father had been one, could stand against either or both kings, provided only that they held together. And the Elders, although they rarely interfered in policy questions, had sufficient prestige to curb any government. Disputes that could not be settled any other way were referred to the assembly for a yes-or-no vote. It was an orderly, conservative system that had worked well for four hundred years. Men competed for glory and honor, not for power or money, which Spartans rightfully disdained.

His time in Macedon had convinced Eurytus of the weakness of conventional monarchies. In Macedon kings were said to be descended from Hercules and, in theory, had no check on their power. Yet every other reign seemed to end in assassination.

One night, when the old man was deep in his wine, King Amyntas, the ruler of Macedon, had told him the ghastly story of his family.

"We have had a great harvesting of kings," he said, laughing, his arm across Eurytus's shoulder. "It started with Alketas, who was my grandfather's uncle. Everyone has a right to get drunk at night and forget his troubles, but Alketas started drinking wine as soon as he got out of bed. He was never sober, never. So my grandfather, Archelaus, killed him, along with two or three other inconvenient relatives, so that his father—my great-grandfather—could rule in his place."

"And what happened to him?"

"My great-grandfather? Oh, he died in his bed." Amyntas waved his hand, as if he found the recollection distasteful. "And then my grandfather, Archelaus, who was a great man, succeeded him and reigned for fourteen glorious years. Then he was assassinated."

"Why?"

"You have heard of the playwright Euripides?"

"Yes, of course. He's famous."

Amyntus reached up and patted Eurytus on the face, as if to say, *Clever boy.*

"Well, Euripides was staying at court as my grandfather's guest, and a fellow named Decamnichos insulted Euripedes—said he smelled bad, or something like that—and my grandfather allowed Euripides to flog him as punishment. So Decamnichos killed him—my grandfather, not Euripides—while he was out hunting.

"Then things went to the dogs. All my uncles—there were three of them—were idiots, especially the last one. I killed him, and that's how I got to be king. It had to be done."

The old man shook his head, as if over the mournful necessity of the thing.

Yes, Eurytus thought, *better to have two kings than one.*

Corinth was even worse. Corinth was supposedly an oligarchy, but the Elders were chosen from within the merchant guilds and did their bidding. Corinth was a city ruled by money, and thus a man of wealth might hold no public office and be nonetheless immensely influential in affairs of state.

Such a man was Ornytion, who virtually controlled Corinthian trade with western Italy and whose son, Thoas, was rapidly becoming Eurytus's intimate friend. Thoas was of a profligate disposition and his purse was of course very deep, so it was an expensive business keeping up with him. But he was also indiscreet, particularly when he was enjoying his wine, an almost nightly occurrence, and his information had so far proved reliable, so Eurytus's father made no difficulties about his son's frequent requests for money.

It was an amusing enough life, being the companion of Thoas's revels. Last night they had visited a famous brothel not more than thirty paces from the temple of Hera. The owner, a fat, fair-haired woman of about sixty, greeted Thoas with a hug and several kisses, as if he were a favorite son, but they both still had to pay the admission price of two mina of silver— enough to keep a farmer and his family for half the year.

For the first hour or so, it was always a race between the attractions of the wine jar and those of whatever whore Thoas had picked out for himself.

He liked to take his time with women—"the preliminaries are always the most amusing phase, don't you agree?"—but he found it difficult to pace his drinking accordingly, so some enticing little creature would as often as not find all her skills applied in vain.

As that hour wore on, however, his garrulousness invariably increased, and Eurytus had only to remain tolerably sober and keep his ears open.

"I wish my father wouldn't leave me so short of money when he goes on his travels. It's very irritating. He goes off to Athens and doesn't even tell me, and I'm supposed to look after myself with the measly twenty thousand drachmas that his clerk doles out to me as if it was all the money in the world. He'll be gone for two months—two months, mind you!—and I'm supposed to scrape by on twenty thousand drachmas."

They were in the steam room, and Eurytus was lying facedown on a marble slab while a girl with eyes like a cat was rubbing oil into his back with her breasts. He was enjoying her attentions so much that it was a moment before the significance of what he was hearing dawned on him.

"I thought your father hated the Athenians," he had just presence of mind to interject.

"And so he does, but he loves money—or, rather, he loves *making* money. It's astonishing how little conception he seems to have of what money is actually *for*."

But he has you for that, Eurytus thought. And then, out loud, "How is he going to make money off the Athenians?"

"Oh, it isn't the Athenians. It's something to do with Thebes."

By this time Thoas was half asleep and, besides, if he had ever known what his father's journey had to do with Thebes, he had certainly forgotten. The details of business and politics bored him.

A moment later he was snoring and Eurytus felt free to turn his attention to the little cat-eyed whore.

"Your body is beautiful!" she announced, indicating with a nudge that it was time for him to turn over onto his back. "I don't think I have ever seen a man blessed with such physical perfection."

"I am a Spartan," he told her. "We are soldiers, not merchants."

"A Spartan!" She seemed all amazement. "I have heard that the Spartans are such ferocious lovers that they keep their women in a permanent state of ecstasy!"

By this time she had him straddled and with a gentle undulation of her hips was bringing his manhood to a proper state of readiness.

Corinth was an education of sorts, but only an idiot yields to the flattery of harlots. In any case, Eurytus was learning a good deal about the pleasures of the flesh.

Yet a life spent in wine shops and brothels cannot help but have a weakening effect on one's soul. It was otherwise difficult for him to account to himself for something which occurred about a month after his arrival in Corinth.

It was almost the middle of the afternoon, but Eurytus had not found his bed until nearly sunrise and thus had awakened with a throbbing head. A breakfast of cold porridge and water had helped but little and he finally had to resort to restoring himself with wine diluted four parts to three. As he drank it he cursed Thoas for a soft, witless profligate, but only in a whisper—any louder sound would have been agony.

All he wanted, he told himself, was to return to the sober discipline of a soldier's life. He hated drunkenness and vice. He hated the excesses of wealth. He estimated he would be a good six months recovering his strength.

But all he could think about was the pretty little cat-eyed whore last night who had been so cunningly skillful in loosening his seed.

If he stayed in Corinth another six months he was quite sure he would be ruined for life.

Today, however, he had an errand. Thoas had organized a boating party for that evening and the gulf could turn unexpectedly cold at night. Eurytus had grown a little ashamed of his old Spartan cloak and had decided to buy a new one, something a shade more fashionable.

The marketplace was crowded, which perhaps explained why he never noticed that he was being followed.

Eurytus was standing in front of a fruit seller's booth, trying to decide if a slice of melon would take away the lingering heaviness in his head. The fruit seller might even be able to provide him with a cup of wine, since in Corinth almost every stall that sold food also kept a skin of wine cooling for thirsty customers.

He had almost decided he would rather have a bunch of purple grapes when he felt a pointed object resting lightly against his back, just over the right kidney.

"If you attempt to call for help you'll be dead before you utter a sound," a voice murmured close to his ear—a voice that spoke with a familiar Doric accent. "There's a wine shop across the way. We can sit in the shade like old friends. But if you run you won't make five paces. Turn around and look at me."

Slowly—very slowly—Eurytus did as he was told. The man he saw was at first unknown to him, a tall youth with a wheat-colored beard, dressed in a dark blue tunic that just reached his knees. The face was young but had a man's hardness about it, and his eyes were a cold, pitiless blue.

And then Eurytus looked down and saw the dagger. His bowels turned to water.

Protos the Helot, no longer a boy, smiled at him.

"Let's go sit down, Eurytus, son of Dienekes. Keep your hands where I can see them. Move."

The wine shop was no more than ten paces distant, but it felt the longest journey Eurytus had ever taken.

He was wearing a sword. All he had to do was draw it. But he knew that would be madness. His brother's dagger would be buried in his heart before his sword ever cleared the scabbard.

They sat at a small round table beneath the shop's striped awning. Protos held up a silver coin pinched between the thumb and first finger of his left hand—his right hand was out of sight. He set the coin down on the table.

"This should see us clear," he said. "I'm only a slave and know nothing about wine, so you order for both of us."

The proprietor came and Eurytus tried to speak but discovered that he couldn't utter a sound. The proprietor made a suggestion. Eurytus had no idea what the man had said but nodded stiffly.

Finally, when they were alone again, he found his voice.

"You have changed," he said, without believing it. He remembered the boy on the hilltop, and the heads sailing through the air to roll almost to his feet. The boy had not been a boy even then. "I recognized the dagger before I did you."

"You, on the other hand, look exactly the same." Protos smiled, as if at some private irony. "Tell me, since Spartan mothers always tell their sons to come home with their shields or on them, how did you explain to yours that you happened to survive?"

"My mother died when I was fifteen."

"Do you expect me to pity you?"

"Under the circumstances, no."

It was as well that at that moment their wine came, a jug and two glazed pottery cups on a wooden tray. Protos pointed to the silver coin, which the proprietor swept into his hand with a smile and a nod and a few hardly audible words.

Using his left hand, Protos filled the cups and set one before Eurytus.

"You could have bought fifty jars of wine with that coin," Eurytus said as he picked up his cup. "It was an Athenian drachma."

"I know. I took it off one of your comrades who had no further use for it. I've been saving it for a special occasion."

"There is nothing special about this occasion, unless you are going to kill me."

"That's still undecided." Protos lifted his cup to his nose, sniffed it and set it back down on the table. "I suppose one has to be born to wealth before one can develop a taste for this stuff. I myself prefer beer or even water."

"Then what is special?"

"About what?" The Helot's eyes flashed with mischief. "Oh, you mean the occasion? It has to do with knowing you. I didn't want you to be merely a name. Revenge should be more intimate than that, don't you agree?"

"I am a Spartan, which is all you need to know. There *is* nothing more to know."

"So was your brother, and yet you are not he. He was a dolt and you are something else. Would you like to know what his last words were? 'You can't kill me,' he said. 'You're only a slave.' I'll wager you led him around by the nose from the time you were old enough to talk. Tell me something. Did he choose my mother as his victim, or was it merely chance?"

Their eyes met, and Eurytus had the appalling sense that this slave genuinely understood him—understood him as no other person had in the whole of his life. It was like being transparent.

He shook his head, simply to rid himself of the sensation.

"Yes." It felt impossible to lie. "He was . . . perhaps a little peculiar about women."

"Then I'm glad I killed him. I've rid the world of a monster. But of course I'm forgetting that the Spartans put a great value on cruelty."

"We put a value on courage."

"I don't think of murdering a defenseless woman as particularly courageous."

There was nothing Eurytus could say—nothing he dared say. If he disagreed, if he defended his brother's act, he might be bleeding out his life before he finished the sentence.

And, indeed, he did not disagree. From Protos's point of view, Teleklos *had* been a monster.

And it was unpleasant to find that point of view so inescapable.

Beyond their little oasis of shade, in the frantic marketplace of Corinth, men and women were hurried along by their errands of pleasure or business, unmindful of vengeance and guilt. They were concerned merely with living.

Or perhaps not. Eurytus found himself wondering if perhaps their lives, too, were stained with secret crimes, blighted by failures of will and courage, dark with dread. Would death be a welcoming embrace for them as well?

"If it is your will to kill me, then do it," Eurytus said, almost spitting out the words. Never had he hated anyone as he hated this slave. "I am a Spartan, and you will not hear me begging for my life. Do it! Now!"

"Did my father beg for his life?"

"No," Eurytus replied, his heart suddenly cold and quiet. "He died without a word."

"And for that answer, Eurytus, son of Dienekes, I will let you keep your life—at least for today."

Protos's right hand came into sight from beneath the table, clutching Teleklos's dagger. He set it down next to his wine cup and then seemed to forget its existence.

"Go now," he continued. "Go away, and perhaps you can convince yourself that none of this ever happened."

Eurytus got up. He stood there for a moment—it was insulting that the man did not even trouble to look at him—then he began to walk away. His knees felt as if they would give way beneath him so that his entire attention had to be focused on not falling down.

Once he turned and looked back. Protos was still seated there, apparently lost in some private musing.

Finally Eurytus came to an alleyway, where he could command a little privacy. He bent over and retched. By the time the fit was over, his face was bathed in sweat. He looked down at the little pool of his own vomit, stained red from the wine so that it looked like blood.

He felt ashamed to be alive.

11

+⟫•⟪+

They had agreed they would meet at the first marker stone on the road west from Corinth, so that was where Nubit was waiting with her wagon and horse when she saw Protos striding up the road.

He climbed up beside her on the driver's seat, kissed her on the lips and took the reins in his right hand.

"You seem remarkably pleased with yourself," she said as he kissed her again, but this time on the neck. "Did you kill him then?"

"No. Instead we drank wine together and talked."

"So you have become great friends now?"

"No." Protos shook his head, apparently having taken her little jest seriously. "I will still kill him one day, if only to quiet my father's ghost, but I understand him now. Killing this one man will not be enough."

He seemed indisposed to continue the subject for he became playful. He joked and bit at her earlobe and reached under her shirt to fondle her breasts. He seemed very happy.

That night they made camp on a bluff overlooking the sea. To celebrate their prosperous visit to Corinth, Nubit had bought a freshly killed lamb and was cooking it on a spit over an open fire. They drank beer and Protos became a little drunk after the second cup, the effect of which was that he became amorous. This was not displeasing, for Protos was very sweet in his ardor.

"You are the most beautiful woman in the world," he said, letting his hand wander up the inside of her leg.

"You have seen very little of the world," she answered, laughing.

"I have seen you. That is enough."

He tried to gather her in his arms, which of course meant that she could no longer turn the spit.

"The lamb will burn."

"Let it burn."

"You will not be so indifferent when you wake up tomorrow with an empty belly." She kissed him and let him taste her tongue before she pulled away. "Here, take the handle—*you* turn the spit. It will give you something to do."

His response was somewhere between laughter and grumbling, but he took the handle.

"You are a good boy," she said, kissing him again.

"You have said that I am a man."

It seemed he fancied himself insulted, so she took off her shirt so that he could see her breasts.

"Tonight, provided you don't drink too much beer, you will be a man. But right now you are a boy and can only look."

"Then tell me at least that you love me."

"I love you," she answered, more than a little surprised at her own passion and frankness. She really did love him. She had never loved any man the way she loved Protos, and she knew she never would again.

She moved closer to him so that he could touch her.

But his mind suddenly was elsewhere. Even as he reached up to caress her nipple, he was thinking of something else.

"Eurytus would have been a good enough sort of man if he hadn't been born a Spartan," he said, as much to himself as to her. "His soul is like metal from the forge that has been beaten into a certain shape—and now he can imagine no other. He thinks it glorious to die at the hands of an enemy and conquest is the only purpose in life he can understand. I am glad I am a Helot and not a Spartan. We may be slaves, but we are still human."

"Then you like him?"

"No. He is the man who killed my father for sport. But if he weren't a Spartan he wouldn't have done it. His brother might still have killed my mother, but Eurytus is not like his brother. I wonder what the Spartans do to their children to make them into murderers."

The lamb was soon ready and they filled their bellies with it and bread and beer. After a while Nubit hid the beer jug because she did not want Protos's desire to lose its edge. She needn't have worried.

They took a blanket from the wagon and spread it out on the soft, sandy soil of the bluff. They could see the gulf, and the moonlight made the crests of the waves shine like silver. It was as if they were alone together in a world that knew neither evil nor death.

It was a warm night and they made love until they were spent and then wrapped themselves in the blanket and fell asleep.

The next morning at breakfast, Protos seemed thoughtful.

"Where do we go from here?" he asked.

"Megara is the closest city," Nubit answered, studying him out of the corner of her eye. She sensed that the question was not idle. "Then we can either strike east to Athens or north to Plataea and Thebes."

"What are these places like?"

Nubit could only shrug, it seemed such an odd question.

"Megara is a trading city, allied to Sparta. We will spend a few weeks there and you will find that enough to exhaust its charms. Athens, of course, is Athens, one of the greatest cities in the world. She is not so grand now as she was, but she is still beautiful and rich."

"What of the other two?"

"Plataea was destroyed in the great war between Athens and Sparta. They have rebuilt it, but it is an overgrown farming village. Thebes sided with Sparta and then rebelled, and the Spartans have occupied its acropolis—it would be a good place for you to stay away from."

※ ※

Megara was less beautiful than Corinth, but Protos, whose experience of cities was restricted, was not prepared to be critical. Corinth had seemed a city fit for gods to live in, but Megara was also beautiful, at least in its great public squares, and would probably do perfectly well for men.

Sheep and horses and cattle, bushels of wheat and crates of ducks, chickens, grapes, figs, and melons—the docksides were like overcrowded farmyards and smelled of several distinct varieties of animal droppings. For a boy brought up close to the land it was all comfortingly familiar.

And, if one kept one's ears open, Megara was an education in what for Protos was both a new word and a new idea: politics.

Everything had to be a decision. It was astonishing the number of things people found to argue about. It hadn't been that way in his village, where life was governed by the whims of the Spartans, tradition, and the seasons of the year.

In the spring you sowed the grain. In the autumn you harvested it. You married the bride your parents chose for you. There were few quarrels, since your relations with your neighbors and even the members of your own family were guided by the central, inescapable fact that you all had to work together to survive. Peace was maintained by necessity. Life was hard but at the same time simple.

Apparently, different rules applied in the cities. It was a wonder anything got done.

Megara, for instance, was a democracy—also a new word—which meant that all men with the property qualifications for citizenship met in an assembly and there decided all public questions. But some men, it was known, spoke with the backing of the great merchant houses, and the motions they put forward usually carried.

Megara was divided in her relations with other cities. Corinth was cordially hated, Sparta was feared, and Athens was both a rival and a model—everyone admired Athens and no one had a good word for any individual Athenian. Megara had fought with Sparta in the great war against Athens and was still formally her ally, but there were grumblings of resentment that Megara had not received her fair share of the spoils.

In democracies, apparently, politics were an obsession. Protos began frequenting the wine shops near the ports, where merchant sailors brought the news from every part of the Greek world, and the doings of its great men were the common gossip. Protos drank only beer, and very little of that, and thus, being largely ignored, was free to listen.

"What do you mean you'll pay me when the Thebans pay you? Did I sell two hundred head of cattle to the Thebans? No. I sold them to you. You aren't going to wiggle out of paying me my four hundred and seventy drachma."

"The Thebans always pay. You'll have your money in another two months."

"The Thebans have got a Spartan army sitting in their acropolis. The city is seething with rebellion—the gods know what could happen in two months. Borrow the money, but pay me now!"

"How am I supposed to borrow four hundred and seventy drachma? Credit is tight because everybody thinks there might be a war by next year."

"And they're probably right! Find the money."

The small merchants, who struck Protos as sensible people, didn't like war because war was bad for trade. Therefore, they didn't like the Spartans, whom they regarded as a gang of unworldly hooligans who never took into account the fact that other people had to make a living.

"Listen to what I'm telling you. Thebes is the lid on the jar. Break that seal and war could spill all over Greece. Then we'll have the Persians back."

"The Spartans will keep their foot on Thebes. They're good at that sort of thing."

"The Spartans should have known not to step on a coiled snake."

❦❦

"If there is a war against Sparta, I want to be part of it," Protos tried explaining to Nubit. "It isn't enough to kill two Spartans who went off to hunt Helots because their Elders told them to—because they had been told it was a rite of manhood. Eurytus and his brother are less to blame than the men who sent them. Sparta itself is to blame. I want to hurt these people until they no longer have the strength to send their sons out to do murder."

He couldn't be sure Nubit was listening. She sat on the ground with her back up against a wagon wheel, drinking beer. Sometimes she put something in it, something that gave her strange dreams. After a while he took the cup from her unresisting hand and saw that the beer was clouded. It would be another few hours before she was coherent enough to follow a conversation.

He sat down beside her and put his arm over her shoulders. It seemed unlikely she even knew he was there, but it was a cool evening and he wanted her to be comfortable. And perhaps she at least would know that she was not alone, and perhaps then her dreams would be pleasant.

Her eyes were closed and she was snoring lightly. Her head rolled toward him until it rested on his chest.

"This stuff is slowly killing me," she had told him once. "My mother warned me about that."

"Then why do you do this to yourself?"

"Because the world of my dreams is more beautiful than the world as it is. Because I would know the future even as I dread it."

Nubit's dreams were something he did not pretend to understand. She had faith in them and she was wise, and that was enough for him.

And besides, he loved her.

Even he understood that he had been alone for so long that he would have loved anyone who showed him a little kindness, and he loved her body with all the ardent lust of early manhood. But there was more than that. She was his friend.

So he sat beside her as she dreamed. Sometimes she muttered indistinctly, which perhaps meant she knew he was with her.

Finally he got up and fetched a blanket from the wagon with which to cover her, because it was time to build the fire. Nubit would be hungry when she woke and he had brought back a beef shank from the stockyards. He had watched the cow being slaughtered, so he knew it was fresh.

When she awoke, the shank was nicely roasted, so he cut off a piece and brought it to her. She ate as if she were starving, then she had a cup of beer—he poured it himself to be certain it was just beer—then she wanted bread and more meat.

For half an hour she had no attention for anything except food and drink. Finally she lay down on her back, holding her belly in her two hands.

"If you climbed on me now I would probably split open," she said. Then she laughed. "But do it anyway."

When all her appetites were sated, she sat before the fire with Protos's head cradled in her lap. Her fingers played with his beard, which meant that she was thinking.

"Much has been revealed to me," she said finally. "For now, I will tell you only what you need to know."

"And what is that?"

"That you must go to Thebes."

"Alone?"

"No. I will come with you. I will guide your steps, Protos, my darling, for as long as I live. And when I am dead my ghost will watch over you."

"Are you going to die?"

"We are all going to die. I not until you no longer need me, you not for many, many years. Do not fear. I will not die before you are tired of me."

"Then you will live forever, for I will never be tired of you."

This made her laugh, in part because it reminded her how young he was and in part for the sheer pleasure of hearing him say it, and she bent forward to kiss him.

"So we must travel to Thebes," he went on. "What am I to find there?"

"A man. I do not know his name."

12

Sitting in the prow of a trireme that cut through the water like a knife through linen, facing backward so that he could watch the rhythmic movement of the three banks of oars, Eurytus could not help but admire the skill of the oarsmen. They were free men, working for wages, and they seemed as tireless as grindstones. Hour after hour they drove the ship forward, as fast as a trotting horse.

If he had turned his head, he could just have distinguished the Italian coastline, but it didn't tempt him. It seemed an inhospitable place, with few trees and wide, gray beaches.

At night they would pull in at some little village to buy supplies and to sleep, and for a few hours everyone had the pleasure of feeling the solid earth under him. Then, before dawn, it was back to the ship.

They would not make a real port for at least two days because they would follow the coast north and east for a day and a half. Then they would be in Taras.

Eurytus had been horribly sick for several days—it had been the same during the voyage to Macedon—but that didn't matter. The Spartans were not a seagoing race.

And he felt glad to be here because there would be fighting in Taras. The citizens, who were Dorian but only vaguely Spartan, were being pressed by their Italian neighbors, whom it was time to teach a lesson.

The day after his encounter with Protos, Eurytus had gone to his father and on his knees had begged Dienekes to send him into combat.

Of course, he did not tell him the real reason.

"I am growing soft in this city of brothels," he said. "It was amusing at first, but this is no life for a warrior. And Thoas is beginning to fill me with loathing. Please, Father, send me somewhere men fight."

It took three days to arrange, during which time Eurytus refused to leave his room, but he got his will.

"You have heard of Taras?" his father asked. "It is our colony in Italy. There was a time when the Ephors consented to allowing unmarried Spartan women to bear the children of free non-citizens—their offspring were called 'Sons of Virgins.' It was during the Messenian Wars and we needed soldiers. When the war was over, their citizenship was revoked. We packed them off to Italy, where their descendants prosper.

"They are having trouble now and these people are merchants, not soldiers. But they send us tribute every year and recognize Sparta as the mother city, so we have to help them.

"Will that serve?"

"Send me."

Anything to get out of Corinth.

The expedition was not to leave for a month and the marshaling point was the port city of Gytheion in the Gulf of Laconia, so Eurytus decided he would walk the whole distance, carrying his armor, to toughen himself up.

The first five days were agony, then he rested for a day and after that he was all right. By the time he reached the gulf he felt he was once more in fighting condition.

Six ships were needed to carry a force of three hundred Spartans to the port of Taras, from which they would march north to meet a Samnite army of unknown size. Eurytus knew nothing of the Samnites and didn't care. He only wanted to fight.

The Tarasians could supply no more than two hundred lightly armed troops, whom the Samnites had already driven from the field. There would be no cavalry.

"Then I suppose it will be up to us," a youth named Oibalos announced cheerfully. Like Eurytus, he had never seen combat.

Their phalanx commander, who was with them in the ship's prow, nodded, as one might respond to the prattling of a child.

"It's always up to us," he said.

❧❦

After they landed in Taras, they were marshaled on the docks and paraded through the city, where the citizens cheered them and threw flowers in their path. Some of the women rushed into their lines, offering them kisses and cups of wine. It was all very festive.

Once outside the city walls they had only to march for two hours to be beyond cultivated land. Southern Italy seemed to be almost a desert, full of rocks and barren hills.

Two hours before sunset the Spartans stopped and established their first base camp. They dug perimeter ditches and established guard posts on the bluffs nearby. They would sleep in their armor because they were in enemy territory.

Their phalanx commander, whose name was Charilaus, explained the situation.

"Our Tarasian brethren assure us that the closest Samnite town is a good two days from here, so if the Samnites do not offer battle before then we will devastate the town and then march on to the next. The choice we must force upon them is annihilation or war.

"Now the Sons of Virgins . . ." This was met with appreciative laughter. "The Sons of Virgins also assure us that the Samnites are not old women. I am prepared to take their word for it. But they are savages and will fight like savages, and they will die like savages. Victory is not in question. We will conquer as we always do. But some of us will never leave this place.

"I speak now to the young men. You are doubtless afraid, although perhaps you would never admit it, even to yourselves. But fear is not a disgrace. Fear sharpens the senses and thus may save your life. The point is to remember that avoiding death is not the object. Victory is the object. The only thing that ennobles any man's life is his willingness to give it up for his country. If you die with your honor unblemished, your friends will remember you as a brave man, a Spartan."

He dismissed them to their beds or to guard duty.

"It was a good speech," Oibalos said, taking off his sandals as he prepared to wrap himself in his cloak. His black eyes were wide and shiny with an exultation that was the next thing to fear. "It makes one proud."

Eurytus merely pointed to the unstrapped sandal lying on the ground.

"Put it back on," he said. "If there is a night attack you might not have time."

"Oh, yes."

❧ ❦

The next day, just before the middle of the afternoon, they found themselves among cultivated fields again. The wheat was already sprouting and farmers, with their mattocks on their shoulders, stared at them as they passed. Whether these were Samnites or subject peoples it was impossible to say.

An hour later they encountered a substantial village. The position was judged to be defensible, so they made camp.

A road running north began immediately outside the village. It passed through open country, with a line of hills far to the east. The ground was mostly flat. It looked the ideal place for a battle.

The Samnites must have thought so too, because by dawn scouts sent out on the village plow horses were reporting movement just beyond where the northern end of the road disappeared into some falling ground.

"It's perfect." Charilaus glanced at Eurytus, who happened to be standing beside him, and his face broke into a savage grin. "They've probably been on the march for three or four hours already, and they'll have almost as far again to cover before they reach us. They'll be tired and we'll be fresh."

His optimism was undiminished, even when he saw the Samnite host spreading out over the plain. They were probably close to eight hundred strong.

"The thicker the grain, the easier to scythe."

By the second hour of daylight the Spartan order of battle was in place. They were organized into three phalanxes of a hundred men each, one in front and two behind. The Tarasians were on the left, the unlucky side. The Spartan commanders expected them to break and run after the first shock, but no one cared. They were merely a distraction. By then the Samnites would be fully engaged.

Up close, the Samnite warriors were impressive. They were big men and their helmets were decorated with horns and feathers. Javelins seemed to be their chief weapon. Some were heavily armored and some wore nothing except greaves to protect their legs from the edges of their massive, oval shields.

Eurytus had an excellent view of them, since he had been posted to the front rank of the forward phalanx. It was the position of maximum danger and to be placed there was considered a great honor, but everyone knew that it was bad tactics to risk one's best fighters in the front rank.

Oibalos was to his left. It was a cool morning, but Oibalos was sweating heavily. He was clearly terrified.

Perhaps they both were considered expendable.

As he studied this tiresome youth and waited for the Samnites to nerve themselves up for the first charge, Eurytus was pleased to find that he was not afraid. He was excited, but excitement was not fear. He would not disgrace himself.

He had allowed this business with the Helot boy to prey on his mind.

He preferred to think of him simply as "the Helot boy," without a name or a history, merely a runaway slave who had, no doubt, treacherously killed a number of good men. He was not a warrior. He was a murderer.

But he did not want to think about the Helot boy now. To think about him was to surrender to fear and Eurytus, at this moment, needed to be brave. He was a Spartan. In half an hour he might be a dead Spartan, but living or dead he would have regained his honor.

Thus he did not resent Charilaus's placing him in the front rank. He was grateful.

The lines of the two armies were no more than a few hundred paces apart. The Samnites were beginning their war cry and the sound was enough to make the grass tremble. They waved their spears in the air. They appeared consumed with defiance. It would not be long now.

"I never thought there would be so many," Oibalos said, just loud enough to be heard. "I never thought—"

"Many or few does not matter," Eurytus shouted. "One Spartan is worth five warriors from anywhere else on earth. If there were twice as many we would still outnumber them."

A cheer burst forth through the phalanx—a hundred men with one voice. And Eurytus felt welling up in him a rage no different from exultation.

At that moment the Samnites began their charge.

It was beautiful to watch. The first hundred paces were consumed at a trot, then a slow, loping pace, then finally, over the last forty paces, a dead run.

The sky grew black with javelins. The Spartans raised their shields, but some not quite quickly enough. A Samnite point went into Oibalos's neck, just below the jaw, snatching him backward into the waiting arms of Death.

Almost at once another man stepped forward to fill the gap. Oibalos's shield did not even touch the ground.

Eurytus hardly noticed. Death was everywhere except in his own heart. Knowing he could be killed in the next instant, he felt immortal. War was glorious, and his own life was subsumed in the struggle for Sparta's inevitable victory.

Their javelins gone, the Samnite's drew their swords, with blades as long as a man's arm. But the front rank of the first phalanx dropped to one knee and lowered the points of their spears.

The Samnites could do nothing. Some of them rushed the Spartan line only to be impaled. Others provided targets for the bowmen a few rows behind the front rank. A few broke through, but with their long swords they were too hemmed in and were easy kills for the short swords of the Spartans.

The Samnites made a second charge, perhaps only a hundred paces behind the first, and their javelins killed many—some even of their own. Eurytus saw men dropping all around him.

Sometime in this melee he felt a tug, as if he had been punched in the arm. He glanced down and saw that he had taken a Samnite javelin, its iron tip jammed into his left shoulder muscle. He reached up and pulled it free. He felt neither pain nor fear, merely impatience. The wound was only a distraction.

Then he discovered he could no longer hold up his shield.

It didn't matter. His body was a shield for the man behind him. It didn't matter if he was killed. All that mattered was that he keep his place in the front line and fight on.

He would make the Samnites pay for every drop of his blood.

And the line held. Even a third charge could not break it, so the Samnites gave up and poured around the left side of the phalanx to the easier pickings of the Tarasian troops, who hardly even tried to stand their ground. They fled. The Samnites thought they had won, but instead they had stepped into the waiting trap.

Three Spartan phalanxes converged on them and the Samnites were caught beneath the millstone. After that the battle was little more than a massacre.

By an hour past noon perhaps as many as five hundred Samnites lay dead on the field. The survivors fled. The victors did not pursue them.

The Spartans suffered forty-four men dead and a like number wounded. One of these was Eurytus, who was still in the front rank to watch the last Samnite warrior drop his shield and run.

He was panting for breath, and he could hardly work the fingers of his left hand. His left arm and even his leg were coated in blood. None of that mattered. Only victory mattered.

The Spartans dug a long trench and buried their dead while physicians from Taras attended to the wounded. Eurytus's wound was sewn closed with a hair taken from a horse's tail. He endured the procedure with such fortitude that anyone watching would have assumed his shoulder was numb.

When it was over he took a cup of wine and then turned his attention to his wound. The scar would be large and that pleased him.

"You did well today," Charilaus told him. "You fought bravely."

"I was no braver than anyone else," was Eurytus's answer. He felt almost insulted that he should be singled out for praise.

"Not everyone was wounded, and you fought on with your shoulder laid open like a side of beef."

"I did my duty."

"Yes, you did."

Charilaus seemed to lose interest and his gaze drifted over the field, still covered with so many corpses.

"I too was wounded in my first battle," he said finally. "A trifling thing— an arrow in the foot. But once it has happened, you lose your fear of it. It teaches you that pain is nothing. A good battle is one you can hobble away from."

"What happens now?"

Charilaus seemed to find the question amusing.

"We wait through tomorrow, and if by then the Samnites haven't sent envoys we march north and destroy everything in our path. But they have suffered a major defeat. I think they will do the reasonable thing and sue for peace."

They took over the village for the night, chasing the inhabitants away with whips. A guard was posted, but nobody was worried that the Samnites would risk another attack. Eurytus seized the opportunity to become very drunk.

"Your war is over," Charilaus had told him. "You will spend a few days in Taras, just until your wound seals, and then you will take the first ship home. You will carry my letter to King Agesilaus announcing our victory and commending those who fought exceptionally well in their first battle. Your name will be among them."

So Eurytus was well pleased with himself as he lay on a farmer's bed in a nameless village somewhere in southern Italy. His wound had stopped hurting, for he had grown drunk enough to reach that state of agreeable numbness in which all one's little cares and grievances recede to a picturesque distance. Presently he would fall asleep and perhaps this once he would not dream of those heads falling through the air to roll to his feet.

13

"See? That is Thebes."

Nubit pointed toward the top of a low hill that, at a distance of half a day's ride and in the smoldering light of sunset, appeared no more than a dark smudge. It might as easily have been an outcropping of lifeless rock as a city.

"And there I will find a man . . . ," Protos said tentatively.

"You will know him for a patch of white in his beard and a scar on his left arm. And take your dagger with you."

"Am I to kill this man?"

"No." Nubit shook her head. "This man, whoever he is, is not your enemy. But take the dagger."

They were at the edge of a wide, shallow valley, dotted here and there by villages. The ground was golden with wheat.

"Let us pull over and stay here for the night," she went on. "We will drink beer and make merry and you will climb on my belly. I have need of you tonight, Protos, my darling boy, for you are standing on the edge of a new life, one in which we will not always be together."

❧

The next day, an hour past noon, they closed up the wagon and tethered the horse, about fifty paces from the main city gate. Then Protos was sent on his errand and Nubit flattered and bribed the watch to see to it that thieves stayed away from her wagon. Alone, she made her way to the marketplace to entertain and cozen the people of Thebes.

Protos wandered about, studying men's faces, looking for a man with a shock of white in his beard and a scarred left arm.

At Nubit's insistence, he carried his knife, now hanging from his belt in a stiff scabbard she had made from some old harness leather. It made him feel conspicuous, since almost no one in Thebes seemed to be armed.

At least in the public squares, it appeared an ancient city, a city of small stone buildings, so smoothed by time that they hardly seemed the work of men's hands. The streets were uncrowded and the citizens gifted with a natural, unforced courtesy. They reminded Protos of the people in his home village.

Yet none of the men he saw had a patch of white in his beard.

By the middle of the afternoon he had all but decided that there could be nothing to Nubit's dreams. It seemed he was on a fool's errand. The stuff she put in her beer conjured up pictures out of nothing. It was all nonsense.

Tired of the streets, Protos went up on the city wall. From there he could see most of the great public squares, as well as the athletic fields outside the gates. He would spend one more hour at this and then he would go back to the wagon for his dinner and to tell Nubit it appeared she would have to put up with his caresses a little longer.

The people in the squares were the same ones he had been studying all afternoon. He was sick of looking at them.

On one of the athletic fields about a hundred young men were playing some unintelligible game with leather shields and poles of wood. What were they doing? It seemed some sort of shoving match.

Their progress was being observed by a few people standing idly about. One of them, a man who appeared to be in the middle of life, happened to turn so that Protos could see his face.

His hair and beard were black, but on the left side, at the chin—at such a distance it was hard to be sure—appeared what might have been a patch of white.

Very well, then, perhaps it wasn't all nonsense. Protos took the stone stairway that ended almost at the main gate and started walking down toward the field.

The man he had seen from the wall really did have a white patch in his beard. He was standing a little distance from the others, watching the progress of the mysterious game.

Protos was no more than twenty paces away when someone stepped in his path and held up a hand to stop him.

"This is a private sports club," the man said. He looked a year or two older than Protos, but he was shorter by half a head and dressed in a white tunic that might have just come from the loom. His hair and beard were beautifully curled and he seemed to think they provided all the authority he might need. "You can't come here."

Protos shook his head in sheer impatience and pointed to the man with the white patch, who by then had turned his head away.

"Does that man have a scar on his left arm?"

The young man seemed not to understand the question, so finally Protos repeated it.

"Does that man have a scar on his left arm—yes or no?"

"Yes. That is Epaminondas."

There were a number of other people at the edges of the athletic field, mostly young men, uniformly well dressed and elegant. Protos sensed that his plain linen tunic, and the fact that he looked like what he was, a peasant boy from Laconia, was the reason for his exclusion. This sport was only for rich people.

At one corner of the field, standing alone, was one of these, a handsome youth with a shining black beard who held a parcel of some kind under his arm. He paid no attention to the game. His eyes never left the man now identified as Epaminondas.

Finally he laid the parcel on the ground and knelt down to unwrap it. When he stood up there was a sword in his hand.

Protos knew at once what was about to happen.

The man who was attempting to send him off reached up to push at Protos's shoulder.

"I said you can't—"

He never got to finish his sentence. Protos brushed his arm away, took a step toward him and drove an elbow into his stomach.

Even as the man sank to his knees, grunting like a woman in labor, Protos had slipped his knife from its scabbard.

For a second he watched as the youth with the sword began to run, a cry of rage breaking from his lips.

Epaminondas turned his head in surprise. From the expression on his face it was clear he knew he was about to be murdered.

It couldn't be allowed to happen. Protos knew instantly that he had not been sent here to watch this man die. He grasped the knife by the blade, took an instant to fix his target and threw.

Like a bird of prey the knife rose through the air and then seemed to swoop down, its point catching the assassin in the back of his neck.

The youth staggered for an instant, but his momentum kept him going for another few steps. Blood was gushing from his throat, and by then he was close enough to his intended victim that some of it spattered Epaminondas's face.

But Protos had only a fleeting glimpse of this. Almost as soon as he had made his throw, two or three young men wrestled him to the ground and started pounding him with their fists.

"We have the assassin!" one of them shouted. "We have him!"

"Stop! Stop at once!"

Epaminondas, still wiping the blood from his eyes, came trotting over.

"You fools! The assassin is there!" he said, in a voice like a growl. "This man saved my life."

He stood over Protos, who was almost doubled up with pain from the beating he had received.

"Did *you* throw that knife?" he asked, staring at Protos as he struggled to sit up.

"Yes."

"But at him, is that right? Not at me?"

A wave of his arm indicated the corpse still staining the grass with its blood.

Protos balanced his elbows on his knees and shook his head the way a dog shakes off water. Then he looked up at Epaminondas, angry in spite of himself.

"If it had not been him, old man, you would not now be alive to ask such foolish questions."

Epaminondas crouched down beside him, obviously still excited from his brush with death. He peered into Protos's face.

"I have been a warrior since my youth," he said breathlessly. "I have never seen anyone make such a throw. Until now, I would have said it couldn't be done. Who *are* you?"

"Someone who wants his knife back."

❦❦

They walked back together to Epaminondas's house, which would have sheltered at least four Helot families but which its owner insisted on referring to as "humble." Protos was shown into the garden, an enclosed space measuring perhaps eight paces square, a third covered with a stone floor and the rest gravel. Flowering vines climbed trellises along almost the whole of the outer wall. He was alone for a moment, until Epaminondas came back bearing two cups and a jug on a bronze tray.

"I keep no servant," he said, setting the tray down on a small round table. "I can't afford one and, besides, this way there is one less person in a position to betray me. Please, be seated."

The jug, thankfully, contained beer.

"As you can see," Epaminondas went on, with his left hand gesturing toward their surroundings, "I am not a rich man, but you have done me a great service today and you may claim any reward which it is within my power to grant. What would you have of me?"

"I cannot know that until I know you."

"That is a cryptic answer," his host replied with a smile.

Protos could only shrug. "You are no less in the dark than I am myself. All I know is that I was sent to find you."

"By whom?"

"By a woman who has dreams."

Epaminondas's eyes narrowed as, apparently, he considered this answer. There was no way of telling whether he believed it or not.

"Is there any chance this woman is connected to the Spartans?" he asked finally.

"None. If she were she would already have sold me to them."

"Which, of course, raises the interesting question of who you might be."

For a moment Protos gave the impression he had not heard. A small bird perched among the vines. He watched it until it flew away.

"How do you stand with the Spartans?" he then asked, keeping his face expressionless.

"They or their friends undoubtedly sent the man you killed today."

Protos nodded.

"You seem a man wise enough to seek an understanding of his enemies." He allowed himself to smile. "Have you ever heard of a custom of theirs called the *Krypteia*?"

"Yes." The expression on Epaminondas's face suddenly changed. "By the gods, you weren't . . . ?"

"They wet their blades on my father and mother. I ran. One of them followed and I killed him. A few days later, they came back for me and killed the rest of my family, four in all, simply to discover my whereabouts. My aunt and her children had no idea where I was, but they killed them anyway. I killed all of their party except one. Someday I will kill him too."

"You are a Helot, then?"

"Yes."

"How old are you, my son?"

"Sixteen this summer."

Epaminondas shook his head, in evident disbelief at what he was now obliged to believe.

"Then perhaps I should tell you a story . . ."

❦

"In the great war against Athens, Thebes was on the Spartan side." Epaminondas made a dismissive gesture with his left hand, as if waving the fact away. "Athens threatened our supremacy in Boeotia, and thus on the principle that the enemy of one's enemy is one's friend we allied ourselves with Sparta. That was the beginning of my own military career. I was with the Theban infantry and it was there I got this." He pointed to the scar on his left arm. "I was fighting to save a friend and in the end the Spartan King Agesipolis saved us both."

He smiled, as if to invite an appreciation of life's ironies.

"But after the war Sparta seemed intent on turning her old allies into subjects. In our case she protected a number of cities we wished to control. Finally there was a war, followed by an indecisive peace. Some three years ago, the Spartans seized our acropolis and have maintained a garrison there ever since. At the same time they installed a government favorable to themselves and drove many of my friends into exile. We have become, in effect, an occupied city."

"But they did not drive you out."

The implied question was obvious. Protos smiled to indicate he meant no offense.

"No, they did not," Epaminondas answered, returning the smile. "I am a philosopher, so of course they consider me half mad. Besides, they imagine I am too poor to be a threat to them."

"Are they right?"

Epaminondas merely shook his head. It was time to change the subject.

"I saw them fight once," Protos continued. "At Elis. They rolled over the Elisians. It was beautiful to watch, but they have a weakness."

"And what would that be?" Epaminondas seemed amused.

"To attain such perfect discipline I imagine they are subjected to endless drills. At Elis they were like sleepwalkers. They hardly paid any attention to the enemy—they probably felt they didn't have to. They just did what they have probably been doing for as long as anyone can remember, and it gave them victory. But if someone came at them in a way they didn't expect, I think they wouldn't know how to respond."

Epaminondas hardly seemed to be listening. Then, suddenly, he tilted his head to one side.

"This was at Elis, you say?"

"Yes. They defeated a force more than twice their size."

It occurred to Protos that he probably sounded like a fool, so he asked another question.

"Those men out on the athletic field—what game were they playing?"

"The game of war."

⁕⁕

Epaminondas had an invitation to dinner and asked Protos to come with him, but Protos declined. After all, he was only a peasant with a knife and he remembered the relish with which those young men, whom he now understood to be involved with Epaminondas in some sort of conspiracy, had beaten him. He would not be thus humbled again.

But the conspiracy itself was not without interest.

"You would join us? You have not been in Thebes even for a whole day and you would risk so much for her?"

"Not for Thebes, but to weaken Sparta." Protos grinned—he couldn't help himself. "The enemy of my enemy is my friend."

This made Epaminondas laugh, for just an instant. Then he was serious again.

"The risks for you are not to be despised," he said.

"I am used to taking risks. I have put my head into the lion's mouth before."

"Tell me."

So Protos told him. He gave him a complete history of everything that had happened since that first night, when his parents were murdered, stopping short of his arrival at Nubit's encampment. He had decided that, for the time being, Epaminondas and his friends did not need to hear about Nubit.

"And this thing you do with your dagger, this throwing. Can you teach others to do it?"

But Protos could only shake his head. "I don't even know myself how I do it."

"Then it is from the gods."

✹✹

Nubit's first afternoon in Thebes had proved a success. Her love potions had sold well and the crowds had been delighted when she conjured up the ghost of Cadmus in a cloud of purple smoke. Half of them really believed they had seen him.

Tomorrow her audience would be larger—the Thebans seemed so bored, they would believe anything and buy anything for the sake of a little entertainment.

It was almost dark by the time she returned to the wagon. Protos was nowhere about, but that might only mean that he had found what he was looking for. She fed the horse and then poured herself a cup of beer, drinking it slowly as she fed kindling to the struggling campfire.

By the time the contents of the cooking pot had begun to simmer, and Protos still had not turned up, she began to worry. After all, he was a Helot slave in a Spartan-occupied city. And he was still only a boy.

What if he never came back? What if he simply wandered away some day? How then would she find the courage to go on living?

She loved him. The thought of losing him filled her with panic. That she loved him was the gods' curse upon her.

And then suddenly he was there, standing on the other side of the campfire. He knelt down and sniffed at the pot and looked at her and smiled in a way that made her guts melt.

"I will never doubt you again," he said.

14

"I found the man in your dream," he told her. "And you were wise to tell me to carry my knife because someone tried to kill him. If I had left the knife behind, this man would have been murdered in front of my eyes."

"And the assassin, you killed him?"

"Yes."

He sat beside her, cracking open a lamb bone for the marrow—he was very fond of marrow. The fact that he had killed a man only a few hours ago seemed to weigh on him not at all. It was incidental, mentioned only to demonstrate the wisdom of her advice.

"This man . . . What is his name again?"

"Epaminondas."

"This Epaminondas, is he important?"

"He is training troops to take back Thebes from the Spartans."

"Is he mad? How can he train troops under their very noses?"

"They choose to ignore him—at least, they have up until today." This made Protos laugh. "They, like you, think he is mad, a harmless eccentric whom they can crush when it suits them. They don't know that there is another part to his plan."

"And what is that?"

"I have no idea. I have some role in it, but I shall have to wait and see what it is."

"I begin to believe I have delivered you into the hands of a lunatic."

Protos's answer was to put his arm around her neck and draw her in for a kiss.

"They are all lunatics," he whispered into her ear. "These great men who only want to rule over others, they are all mad. If they weren't mad they would be farmers, like my father."

❧ ❧

The next morning Protos returned to Epaminondas's house, entering through a gate in the garden wall that he had been told would have the latch string out. He found its owner sitting at the same small round table, examining an object that he held in both hands. Each end was like a spindle, and in between was something flat and thin.

"Can you read?" Epaminondas asked.

"What is that?"

"Then I assume the answer is no." Epaminondas smiled and set the object down. "Come here and look at this."

Having looked at it, Protos understood it little better. Between the spindles were sheets of something, and these were covered with black marks.

"This is a poem by a man named Pindar. Do you know what a poem is?"

"A sort of story?"

"Close enough." Epaminondas nodded. "My grandfather once heard Pindar recite. This scroll is written in his own hand."

"What are these?" Protos pointed to the black marks.

"Letters. Each represents a sound, and when you put the sounds together you have words."

Epaminondas closed up the scroll and put it into a small linen bag. Then he sat quietly, his hands folded in his lap, peering into Protos's face.

"I think you are a clever boy," he said finally. "It would be useful if you learned to read."

"Why? So that I can read this Pindar?"

"No, my son. So that you can carry letters for me and know what they say. So that one day I can write letters to you and thus you may know my mind although I am not with you. Do you understand?"

"Yes." Protos shrugged. "At least, I think so."

"Good." Epaminondas stood up. "Let us walk down to the athletic field and see how our young soldiers are getting on."

❧ ❧

"How can anyone fight like that?"

From the edge of the field, Protos and Epaminondas watched men form up in squares to push at each other with shields and wooden poles. It seemed a bad parody of the way the Spartans fought. As warfare it was incomprehensible.

"I admit they don't appear to be very good at it," Epaminondas said,

smoothing down his beard with the palm of his left hand. "And your particular talents incline you another way, but I want you to at least have some
experience of more conventional ways of fighting."

"Why?"

"Because war is inevitable. Even assuming we can drive the Spartans
out of Thebes, they will come back at us, if only to maintain their prestige.
We may still be fighting them ten years from now."

He glanced at Protos, and there was that in his eyes which reminded
one of a predatory animal.

"So far you have killed Spartans individually and, granted, with considerable success. You must now learn how to kill them in the mass."

"What are they trying to do, shove each other to death?"

Epaminondas laughed.

"No. They are trying to crack open each other's lines. As long as men
fight as a unit, locked together in these formations, it is very difficult to kill
them. But when the formations break, the men in them become once more
individuals, individually fighting for their lives. And they die alone."

"To what *other* way do my talents incline me?"

Protos felt the weight of the older man's hand on his shoulder.

"All in due time. But for now, have you ever used a sword?"

"Yes."

"But you can't throw a sword."

"You can throw a Spartan sword."

Epaminondas shook his head, as if in bafflement. "Perhaps you would
care to learn how to fight with one without throwing it."

Here and there about the field were individuals and pairs of men exer-
cising with various weapons—javelins and swords and occasionally the long,
double-pointed spears used by horsemen. Epaminondas found one who
seemed wonderfully dexterous with a curved sword somewhat longer than
his arm. He was a man of about twenty, very neat and precise in his movements, with his black hair cut short and a beard that was little more than
an outline of his face. He looked at Protos with good-humored contempt.

"If you would be kind enough, Aegisthes, teach our young friend here
the elements."

Then, with a dismissive wave, Epaminondas wandered away.

Aegisthes waited until he was some forty paces distant and then turned
to his pupil.

"Well then, you fancy yourself a swordsman?" he asked, in a tone that
mocked the vanity of such an ambition. "And have you ever held a sword?"

When Protos didn't answer Aegisthes knelt down beside a wooden case that lay on the grass, opened it and took out a second sword, a duplicate of his.

"Here—take it," he said, offering it hilt first. "There."

Before Protos even had a proper grasp, with a twitch of his own sword Aegisthes swept it out of his hand. He grinned as Protos bent over to retrieve it.

"You see?" he said. "A sword is not for everyone. One must be born to it."

As one must be born to wealth, Protos thought. As if every attainment, every privilege, was the exclusive property of those whose fathers had never gathered in a harvest with their own hands. This one was like the Spartans—except, perhaps, that he didn't kill people for sport.

Perhaps we would see who was born to what.

After that they practiced thrust and parry, and gradually Protos developed a sense of the weapon. It began to feel right in his hand. The moves seemed obvious.

"And now defend yourself," Aegisthes announced. "Don't worry. I won't really hurt you."

Protos didn't worry. He found he could anticipate every attack—his opponent, he decided, was not wonderfully imaginative. Over and over again, Aegisthes tried to force him back, but Protos would not give ground.

Soon they had acquired a small audience. Perhaps twenty young men gathered around them.

And under their eyes Aegisthes apparently discovered that he had something to prove.

"And now you attack. Please, do not hold back. You will never touch me."

You will never touch me. The crowd murmured its approval. Protos clenched his teeth and tried to ignore them.

When he was nine years old, a bull had gotten loose in one of the village fields. It was harvest time and they had to get the bull out before it trampled all the wheat.

"It is only necessary to know what the bull will do," his father had said. He went over to where a few rails in the fence had fallen down, letting the bull out of its paddock. He pulled them out of the way and walked toward the bull. After attracting its attention, he ran back toward the opening in the fence. The bull charged after him. When he reached the fence, his father swerved to the side and the bull kept going in a straight line, back into its paddock. After a while it stopped, but by then it had forgotten all about

Father and lowered its head to graze on a clump of grass. Father repaired the fence and they went home.

It is only necessary to know what the bull will do. Protos decided that his father would have made a good swordsman.

He offered an obvious attack, which Aegisthes repelled almost without effort. After a few of these Aegisthes seemed to tire of defense and Protos backed away.

The crowd was enjoying their performance. Protos had the sense that they liked seeing the peasant boy taught a lesson.

After a little more of this, Protos closed the trap. He appeared to stumble and Aegisthes rushed in—but too close.

Protos stepped around him, putting his foot behind his opponent's and then, by simply straightening his leg, knocked him off balance.

Aegisthes went down, and when he recovered from his first surprise he saw Protos standing over him, the point of his sword not two fingers' width from his throat.

"You tripped me," Aegisthes exclaimed, his voice rasping with indignation. "That wasn't fair."

"You must forgive me, for I am only an untutored peasant boy. It hadn't occurred to me that all this was merely a game."

Protos buried the point of his sword in the ground half a span from Aegisthes's head and walked away. Behind him he could hear the crowd's applause. Might the gods curse them.

❧ ❧

"I had expected something like this," Epaminondas said, as if commenting on the outcome of a dogfight. "I am told there was much talk yesterday of a 'lucky throw'—you must not resent it, since it is difficult for any man to see beyond the prejudices of his own class. But now they know that it was not luck but an innate skill with weapons. Now they will respect you. Even Aegisthes will come around."

"I care very little what Aegisthes thinks."

Epaminondas put his hand on Protos's shoulder and laughed.

"You must learn, my young friend, not to make enemies unnecessarily. Right this moment Aegisthes resents you because you have made him look like a fool, but before long he will be telling the story of his defeat even with a touch of pride. Wait and see.

"But today I think it better if you do not return to the field."

Protos started to say something but Epaminondas waved his hand to forestall any response.

"It is not because of our young friends, but because our doings here are observed and reported to the Spartans. I suspect you have long enjoyed some notoriety with them and I would prefer they did not make the connection.

"Besides, I have work for you elsewhere . . ."

☙❧

"He wants me to go to Athens," Protos told Nubit. It was night and they were closed up in the wagon. She was naked to the waist and combing her black hair so that it seemed to glow in the faint light of an oil lamp.

"What is in Athens?" she asked, without looking at him.

It occurred to him, not for the first time, how beautiful her back was and how her skin was faultless, the color of new bronze. It was a moment before he remembered that she had asked a question.

"A man named Pelopidas," he answered. "He escaped from Thebes when the Spartans captured the city. Epaminondas gave me a letter for him."

"Let me see it."

The letter was concealed in a scroll, which he held out for her just above her left shoulder. When she took it he allowed his fingertips to trail down her back. It was a pleasure simply to touch her.

Suddenly Nubit laughed.

"Do you know what is in this scroll?" she asked. "It is a play by Aristophanes and it is very naughty."

"You can read it?"

"Yes, of course. I cannot read my own language, but Greek is simple. It has only twenty-four characters."

"What does the letter say?"

She unrolled the scroll. The letter was on a single sheet of papyrus, which she lifted out by the corners.

For a moment she was silent.

"It is about you," she said at last. "His opinion of you is interesting: 'I introduce to you the boy Protos, who seems to have lived several lifetimes in his sixteen years. Feel at liberty to trust him, for he has good reason to hate the Spartans. He is as agile as a scorpion and as deadly. I am sure you will find a use for him, but do not make the mistake of underestimating him. Although without what you or I would call education, he is highly intelligent and will doubtless find a way to learn the contents of this letter. Ask him to show you how he can throw a knife.'"

She put the letter back in the scroll, which she rolled up and slipped inside its linen bag.

"We should leave here in the morning," he said.

Nubit sighed and smiled at him.

"It is a great pity. Thebes would have earned us a good deal of money."

"Can you teach me to read?"

"Yes, of course. It will give us something to do during the journey."

She slipped out of her skirt and smothered the light from the oil lamp. In the darkness he felt her hand sliding gently up his thigh.

"But the lessons can wait until the morning," she said.

15

By wagon, the journey from Thebes to Athens took about two days. Protos's efforts to learn the Greek alphabet kept them entertained. They used Aristophanes's comedy as a teaching text—Nubit would point to a letter, name it and give the sound, and Protos would find the same letter in other lines. By the middle of the afternoon he had all twenty-four of them.

"Sigma, omega, mu, alpha. *SSS, OOO, MMM, AAA.*" He pronounced each letter, unconsciously lengthening the sound. "Body? Is that it? Is that what it means?"

"Yes. That is what it means."

On the second day Protos was still sounding out words, but the words gradually became sentences and sometimes he would be struck by some joke in the comedy and would laugh.

"You have learned everything there is to learn," Nubit told him. "After this, it is merely a matter of practice. Find books and read them. What would you like to read about?"

"The heroes of my race. We were the Achaeans before the Spartans turned us into slaves. My uncle told me many stories about them and a great war they fought to conquer a faraway city."

"Troy?"

"Yes. That was its name."

Nubit leaned back against the wagon seat that Protos might not see her smile.

"You can hear those stories in any wine shop," she told him. "There are people who earn their bread by reciting them for a few copper coins. They were written by a poet named Homer."

"Then I would like to read this Homer."

As the afternoon lengthened, they reached the outskirts of Athens. The countryside was beautiful and well watered, and there were many plane trees along the road to provide shade. Here and there they would see ruined houses, their shattered walls so weathered after a quarter of a century that they almost seemed part of the natural landscape.

"The Spartans did this," Nubit told him. "They spread destruction throughout Attica. They would have destroyed Athens itself, but in the end they decided not to. They said it was because of Athens's service during the war against Persia, but I think they had other motives."

"The Spartans are not a generous people."

He said nothing more, seeming to retreat inside himself, until an hour later when the walls of Athens came into sight.

"Epaminondas told me to go to the northern part of the city and find a house near the Acharnian Gate. We might as well find somewhere to camp, as it will be dark in an hour. This friend of his can wait until the morning."

"You sound angry. Why are you angry?"

The question seemed to surprise him. Perhaps it had not occurred to him that he was angry. But now he realized that he was.

"I am sent on this errand and told nothing," he said finally. "They are using me."

Nubit reached out and took the reins, as if in sheer exasperation at his stupidity.

"Of course they are using you, as you are using them. And of course there are things they don't tell you. They don't know you, so why should they trust you? And you will never be one of them. You are at best an ally, but only so long as your interests overlap with theirs. This is the world, Protos. Best get used to it."

"Is that what we are? Allies?"

They had reached a patch of shade under a plane tree, and she pulled in the reins.

"No, we are not allies. And do you know why?"

"Why?"

"Because I am on your side simply because it *is* your side."

❧❧

Having never overcome the habits of a farm boy, Protos was up two hours before dawn to set the breakfast fire. Nubit gave every indication of having made a happy adjustment to the luxury of sleeping in until breakfast was ready.

While the sky was still a pearl gray Protos was walking around the city wall, looking for the Acharnian Gate. Once inside it, he could hardly believe that this was a place where men lived. The buildings were larger than the temples in Corinth, and as beautiful. Many were faced with white marble and had columns supporting the awnings over their entrances.

He had been told to look for the third house on the right side of the street and to ask there for a man named Dexileos. Protos found the house easily enough but, standing in front of the door, it took him a moment to work up the courage to knock.

He felt as if he were stepping off a cliff. Whatever destiny awaited him on the other side of this door—and he had no idea what it might be, except that it would be dangerous—it would be irrevocable.

Perhaps it would be better to just walk away. He could go back to the wagon, and he and Nubit could live what might pass for normal lives.

But finally he did knock, and at first nothing happened. He was about to knock again when at last the door opened and a tall, heavy-looking man in a white gown that reached almost to his feet peered at him with evident suspicion.

"Go away, boy," he said, as if he had played this scene many times before. "We have no kitchen scraps for you. Go away before I call the watchman."

"Are you Dexileos?"

Evidently the question was not what he had expected, because the tall man stood silent for a moment and then looked questioningly into Protos's face.

"No, I am not the Lord Dexileos." It seemed a painful admission. "I am the chamberlain of his house."

"Then tell him he has a visitor, one who brings him news he will be interested to hear."

Protos held up the scroll, which was in his left hand.

One could almost watch the progression of ideas working their way through the tall man's mind. This was a peasant boy who couldn't even afford a pair of sandals. Yet he knew that the Lord Dexileos lived in this house and he was possessed of a scroll. How had he acquired the scroll? Had he stolen it? That was likely. Perhaps he thought to sell it to the Lord Dexileos.

Or perhaps, since the Lord Dexileos was a man who dabbled in politics, there was something more here than appeared.

"You may come in, boy. I will inquire if the Master is prepared to see you."

He brought Protos into a room that was empty except for a marble bench and a few tables. It was perhaps three times the size of the house where Protos had lived with his parents. The walls were painted with murals to make them seem like windows onto an ideal world.

"Sit there, boy," the chamberlain said, pointing to the marble bench.

"Does Dexileos live here all by himself?" Protos asked incredulously. It seemed appalling that one man should have so much.

"He lives here with his wife. Now sit down, boy, and wait quietly."

After perhaps a quarter of an hour the chamberlain returned, followed by an elderly man wrapped carelessly in a sheet. His white hair was a tangle. It was obvious he had just left his bed and wasn't pleased about it.

"Young man," he snapped, "have you any idea of the hour?"

"Are you Dexileos?" Protos asked, rising to his feet.

"Yes, I am Dexileos. What of it?

"Then please be good enough to tell Pelopidas that I have a message for him."

Dexileos's whole manner changed at once. He was no longer irritated at having been awakened at what, for him, was probably an early hour. He stared at Protos through narrowed eyes, seeming to weigh him by the pound.

"If I knew someone named Pelopidas . . . ," he began, and then paused. "If I knew such a man I would hardly trust him to a lad who speaks with a Doric accent and carries a Spartan dagger."

"Then tell Pelopidas, whom you may or may not know, that his friend Epaminondas inquires if he still suffers from his toothache."

Without a word, Dexileos turned on his heel and walked back the way he had come, his chamberlain trailing along behind him. Protos was left alone to continue his study of the wall paintings.

After a few minutes another man entered the room. He wore a simple soldier's tunic and looked almost as out of place in such surroundings as did Protos.

"I am Pelopidas," he said.

❧⸙

"Have you read this?" Pelopidas asked, holding up the letter.

"I know what it says."

They were sitting across from one another in a room off the reception hall, a room which might have been intended for just such discussions, since it was small and sparsely furnished and had a door which could be locked from the inside.

"Do you know what we are planning?"

"In the broadest possible terms, you mean to take your city back. The troops Epaminondas are training will probably be used to at least contain the Spartan garrison. Of course he didn't tell me your part."

"Why 'of course'?"

"Because he expected you to do that. And until you do, perhaps the less I know the better."

Pelopidas smiled. It was the smile of a clever man who had that instant become aware of an interesting fact.

"Young as you are, you force me to speak to you as an equal," he said, reaching for the jug on a table between them. There were two cups and he filled them with what looked like wine watered to one part in seven—it was not to make merry with but to quench one's thirst. "I have the sense that you have been forced to surrender your youth, that you are a man because you have no choice. I am not surprised that my friend Epaminondas was so impressed with you."

"Are you going to tell me your part in all this?"

For a moment, Pelopidas seemed somewhere else. He might not even have heard the question. And then his gaze returned to Protos's face and he once more smiled his crafty smile.

"I have a group of Theban exiles," he said, "all good men, and the Athenians have promised a force of their infantry. I have to deal with the government the Spartans have imposed on us and with the Spartans themselves. How would you do it?"

Protos tasted the wine, almost without noticing it. The problem had his full attention. It was a matter to which, in the last two days, he had given much thought.

"I would keep the Athenian infantry a day's march from Thebes, in case the Spartans are sending out scouts. I would infiltrate your own men back into the city, because surprise will be everything, and then join forces with Epaminondas's group and keep the Spartans contained in their garrison until the Athenians arrive. Their garrison is in the acropolis, if I remember."

"Yes."

"As difficult to escape from as to reach. If you control the city you can eventually starve them out."

"You have anticipated almost my every move." Pelopidas nodded his approval. He was enjoying this discussion. It was almost as if it were about the strategy of a game. "But there is one crucial detail left. What would you do about the existing government, the traitors?"

"Kill them. Kill them all."

❧ ❦

It was the middle of the afternoon before Protos left the house of Dexileos. He did not go back to the wagon but turned his steps to the marketplace, which was no more than a quarter of an hour's walk south. He expected Nubit to be there.

He found her on the steps leading up to the Porch of Zeus. A cloud of purple smoke drifted slowly down the stairs, which meant that she had been raising the ghost of some local hero, and she was flirting outrageously and simultaneously with several of the men in the small group that had gathered to watch her performance.

Protos stood some ten paces away, to the side and a little behind the crowd, where she would be unlikely to notice him, thinking how beautiful she was and how fascinating. Her audience loved her. They did not realize it yet, but she owned them. Nubit could persuade a wolf to lick her hand.

With every movement of her head, her hair swirled about her like a dark cloud. It was easy to imagine she possessed magical powers—she *was* magical. The sound of her voice, pitched lower than one expected and filled with throaty insinuation, was intoxicating. The music was so enchanting that one almost forgot the words.

And all this I must leave behind, he thought to himself. He tried to find consolation in the reflection that he was unlikely to live through the month and therefore his period of grieving would be short, but there was little comfort in the idea.

Yet he might survive. It was at least possible. And then perhaps . . .

In that instant she turned her head and saw him, and her eyes filled with something like dread.

He joined the crowd and worked his way to the front.

"Can you tell my fortune, witch?" he said, raising his voice, and she laughed her best harlot's laugh.

"What you have between your legs will make your fortune, young man. But come with me for a private word. For a silver coin I will reveal to you a glorious future."

They walked up the steps to the Porch and slipped behind one of its massive columns. The first moment they had a little privacy she grasped his hand in both of hers and squeezed it in a way that said she already knew the worst.

"I have to go away—"

"I know," she answered, cutting him off as if she could not bear to hear more. "I had a dream. But come back to the wagon, just for tonight."

"I dare not. Sparta doubtless has agents in Athens. They are probably watching the house I visited this morning. I have to disappear. Even these few moments are folly, but I couldn't go and not . . ."

"I know. Promise you will come back to me."

"If I live through this, I will come back."

"Then you must promise me to live."

"I'll make every effort."

It was a small enough jest, but they both laughed. And then the laughter died and she reached up to touch his face.

"I know you will come back," she said, as if she could will it to be true. "You have a talent for survival. We will see each other again."

And then she broke away and ran down the steps.

Even as he hurried down the broad, shaded walkway of the Porch, Protos could hear her voice and the laughter of the crowd.

16

"Have you ever heard of a man named Epaminondas?" Dienekes asked his son.

Eurytus had been home from Italy a mere five days and had been enjoying the glory that accrued to one who had been listed as having distinguished himself in battle. Therefore, since the question involved politics—and politics was not heroic—it was not entirely welcome.

But it also reflected his father's new attitude toward him, a respect that allowed them to speak to each other as equals.

"Yes, of course," he answered. "Although our enemy, he is a distinguished man, both as a soldier and as a scholar. I saw him once in Thebes."

"Yes. Well, as it happens an attempt was made on his life some six days ago—I got the letter this morning. Although they deny it, I suppose it was the work of those idiots we installed as a government. We will never know, of course, because the assassin was cut down just before he reached his intended victim."

They sat in Dienekes's garden, waiting for dinner. Dienekes refilled his son's cup, almost to the brim.

Eurytus stared at his wine for a moment, as if it were the harbinger of bad news, and then seemed to forget its existence.

"I assume, Father, that there is something more to this story. You are saving the best until last?"

Dienekes turned his attention to the door that led back into the house. He seemed to be hoping for some sort of rescue.

"As it happens," he said, still not quite facing his son, "the assassin was killed by a dagger, thrown, we are told, from a distance of some twenty paces. The blade caught him square in the neck, so that he died almost instantly. Further, we are told that the individual who performed this remarkable feat was quite young, no more than sixteen, and spoke with a Doric accent."

"Oh, no . . ."

Eurytus looked longingly at his wine cup, which he did not dare touch for fear of spilling its contents all over the table.

Dienekes nodded. "I am afraid, oh, yes."

"Protos."

"That struck me as the likeliest possibility."

Dienekes turned his gaze those few degrees that enabled him to look directly at his son.

"I left your brother's corpse to rot," he said, with the harshness of a man accusing himself. "I thought he was no true Spartan if he allowed himself to be ambushed and killed by that boy, but subsequent events have shown me that I misjudged Teleklos. Truly, this Helot boy is a natural warrior—it is very remarkable.

"Nevertheless, this recent intelligence from Thebes obliges us to make another attempt to capture or, better yet, kill this Protos."

"And you want me to aid in this?"

There was in Eurytus's eyes that resignation which was perhaps the best part of courage. He would go and hunt this his most fearful enemy, because honor demanded it.

"You are the only one living who has ever seen him," Dienekes said quietly. "Of course it was a few years ago, and his appearance may have changed. . . ."

"I saw him again in Corinth," Eurytus almost shouted. He looked at his father and smiled bitterly. "It was quite cordial—he bought me a cup of wine."

And then he told the whole story. It was the most terrible confession of his life, but he had no choice except to make it. He could not live this lie any longer.

Dienekes listened in silence, until it was clear his son had finished. He knew the storm was over when Eurytus lifted his wine cup, his hand steady, and took a sip.

"It must have been terrible for you," he said finally. "And I don't blame you, not for the things you did or did not do, nor for keeping them from me. The whole business is appalling, but that is all the more reason why we must find this Helot and put him to death. Will you go?"

"To Thebes? Yes."

Dienekes managed to smile.

"One thing," he said, and he leaned forward to put his hand on his son's arm. "This wicked boy—"

"He is no longer a boy, Father, and I doubt that he is wicked. He avenges his family, just as you or I would do."

"He is a slave!" Dienekes drew his hand back. "No more than a renegade slave. That is the only thing I fault you for, Eurytus, the obvious respect you have conceived for him. He is a Helot and therefore without honor or even the right to live. He deserves no respect.

"And he has cost me one son already. Be sure he does not cost me another."

❦❧

Dienekes's conversation with Eurytus left him feeling oddly unsettled. He was beginning to feel he knew his son hardly at all.

He was beginning to think the problem was that Eurytus had too much imagination.

Or perhaps he himself had too little. It was as if the two of them inhabited different worlds.

Eurytus, so recently commended for his courage in battle, was afraid of a slave. He did not fear death—he had faced death—so it had to be some quality in this Helot boy that Dienekes could not even begin to comprehend.

Boy and man, Eurytus had always been clever. His brother had been no match for him. Eurytus had always been the leader. His grandfather had been a man of vast intellect, a military commander and statesman, and in his spare moments a profound student of the poets, particularly of Homer. Eurytus was like him.

Dienekes admired his son as he had admired his father, but in the quiet of his own soul he believed that life was essentially a simple business. Intelligence, as a practical virtue, was indistinguishable from cunning and was a weapon no different from one's sword.

For the rest, it was possible to see too much. Imagination was a weakness if it led to doubt. Dienekes had always believed that doubt was the only true enemy. To be impervious to doubt was to be a true Spartan.

And something about this Helot boy had made Eurytus doubt himself.

Still, he was prepared to travel to Thebes and hunt the slave down. That was something. It was no small act of courage to face that which was more terrifying than death itself.

It was all a mystery. Dienekes decided he would finish what was left of the wine and try to forget all about it.

※ ※

The matter was considered of sufficient importance that Eurytus was supplied with a horse, which allowed him to make the journey from Sparta to Thebes in only three and a half days.

The first news he heard upon his arrival was that no one had seen or had any news of "the thrower" for nearly eight days. Protos had appeared at the athletic field the day after killing the assassin, had demonstrated that he was also a formidable swordsman and then vanished.

Eurytus's first reaction was disappointment. His reckoning with Protos was inevitable, and he wanted it, even if it meant his own death. The mere thought that he and Protos inhabited the same world was becoming intolerable.

His first conversation with the garrison commander was not reassuring.

"We have no one inside Epaminondas's group of followers," he said blandly, as if nothing else could be expected. "We do have our agents inside the city—the government is not *totally* without support—and a watch is kept on the leading members."

"Might one inquire why they aren't all simply arrested?"

Eurytus smiled pleasantly. For all that he was the son of a former Ephor, he didn't care to antagonize the commander, whose name was Listeus and whose family was politically important. He was also at least ten years Eurytus's senior and had the look of a hardened veteran. He seemed nettled.

"Citizens carry on military drills in every city in Greece," he said rather tartly. "What could be more natural than that Epaminondas, Thebes's most distinguished soldier, should conduct the training? The point is that if we move against him we only turn the city more against us. And if he tries any kind of demonstration against the government we will of course crush him."

They were standing on the acropolis, and another step would have taken them over a sheer drop of some thirty cubits. There was only one narrow path up and it was completely exposed. The position was impregnable.

And it was also a snare.

From their position they could see the east side of the city and the plains beyond. Thebes was a tangle of narrow streets, the scene of a thousand potential ambushes.

It struck Eurytus with perfect clarity that if they lost control of the city they would be trapped up here on the summit of a barren rock. They would have little chance of getting down or of fighting their way out.

So then, Epaminondas and his followers would take control of Thebes in a lightning strike, after which they could deal with the Spartan garrison at their leisure.

"Are you hearing anything, anything at all, about this one who dispatched your assassin?"

"He was not *our* assassin."

"Still, did he just disappear?"

"Yes. He just disappeared." Listeus shrugged. "Why? Is he of some importance?"

Eurytus, having decided that the garrison commander was a fool, did not enlighten him.

❧❧

In fact, Protos was less than three hours away, in the village of Leuctra, at a gathering of about forty Theban exiles to discuss their secret return to the city.

They met in the village's only wine shop, which really served only beer. For a consideration, and out of sympathy for the Theban cause, the owner had left and gone to spend the night with his late wife's brother. The shop was small, so, perhaps as an expression of democratic feeling, the tables and benches, which could have accommodated no more than twelve, had been pushed up against the walls and thirty young men were sitting on the floor.

The meeting was run by Pelopidas, who had already worked out his plan in detail and who was merely assigning men their various roles.

"There are only three tasks we have to accomplish," he told them. "We must liquidate the puppet government, after which the struggle will come down to Theban against Spartan and no man's loyalties will be divided. Then we must pen the Spartan garrison in the acropolis—and to be successful at that we must achieve complete surprise, which means there can be nothing to alert them, no disturbances in the streets. Then we must rally the citizens and have ourselves declared the legal government. By that time the Athenian force will be in place to help deal with any counter-measures the Spartans may take.

"But the first task, the crucial task, is to liquidate the oligarchy the Spartans have imposed on us. And for that Epaminondas has provided us with a young man whose special gifts uniquely qualify him for this work. My friends, I introduce to your notice Protos the Helot."

When Protos stood up, a murmur ran through his audience, all of whom had been making free with the proprietor's stock of beer.

He tried not to take their obvious resistence as a personal affront. Probably all of them were well born and he was a peasant. Beyond that, he was not a Theban.

"The oligarchs are holding a banquet in two days' time," Protos told them. "The task at hand will require ten men, nine and myself. We will enter the city around dusk, in small groups, twos and threes, disguised as courtesans."

There was an immediate uproar. "As women?" "What a disgraceful . . . !" "A slave's trick!" "It will never work."

"It will work!" Protos shouted, in a voice that commanded attention. "It will be made to work. It will work even if I have to go in there alone and kill them all myself."

"Are you really just a slave?" someone asked. The question was greeted with derisive laughter.

"Would you like to see the scars on my back?"

In the silence this reply produced, Pelopidas rose to his feet and put his hand on Protos's shoulder.

"I should make a few things clear," he announced quietly. "The first is that a mere twelve days ago, our young friend Protos here saved Epaminondas from an attempt on his life. The second is, after having killed the son of the Ephor Dienekes, he managed to elude or destroy his pursuers and escape from Laconia. I have looked into the matter and know for a fact that the Spartans made a considerable effort to find him, and yet here he is.

"Epaminondas vouches for him. Epaminondas sent him to us for this particular task. I suggest we listen to him with attention."

"It would be a disgrace to be captured dressed as a whore."

The man who spoke was in the front row, almost at Protos's feet. Yet Protos hardly glanced at him as he made his answer.

"Disgraced or not, if you are captured you will be just as dead. And I would have you consider the disgrace of allowing your city to remain under enemy occupation. Thebes is not my home, but in two days' time, with or without your assistance, I will risk my life to free her. However, do as you wish. I am only a runaway slave who knows nothing of what the gently born call honor."

There was a sullen silence, and then someone stood up.

"What do you say, my friends? Are we to be shamed by the courage of a slave? Tell us your plan, Protos, and I, for one, will be glad to follow you."

The youth who spoke was named Agenor, and he strode forward and took Protos by the hand. By that act the issue was settled.

Everyone volunteered.

"You will have to shave your beards off," Protos told them. "You would make very odd looking courtesans if you kept them."

"Whom will you choose, Protos? The bravest?"

But it was Pelopidas who answered. He was so delighted, it was as if he had been hoping for someone to ask that very question.

"No," he said, "the prettiest."

❧ ❦

When the nine were chosen, they went upstairs to where the proprietor had his bedroom and Protos used a piece of charcoal to draw a map of the banqueting hall on the floor. Pelopidas's spies had done their work well, so the drawing was accurate.

"It is in a private home in the eastern sector of the city," he told them. "The owner, who is one of the oligarchs, is of a lecherous disposition and thus precisely the sort who would hire 'entertainers' for the amusement of his guests.

"As you see, there are four doors into that room. We will have one man at each door to hold it against all comers and prevent any escapes. Aside from an elderly chamberlain, all the slaves in the house are women, so I don't expect any difficulties from that quarter."

"Six of us will deal with the banqueters. There will be thirty of them and they will be unarmed. It will be like killing sheep."

"Not very glorious," someone said.

"No, but dangerous. There are a thousand ways this business can go wrong."

He paused for a moment. An expression almost of pain crossed his face.

"It is one thing to kill a man in an equal fight," he began, "or one who means to kill you, or one who has wronged you in some fundamental way. It is another to kill when your enemy is helpless and unknown to you. I have done this, and those are the ones who haunt my dreams.

"We are on the verge of a fearful act—not a crime, since it is necessary, but not a deed we will ever be able to look back on with anything except shame. So if any of you feel that you cannot do it, that you may waver in your purpose, say so now and withdraw. I will never think the less of you. I will think only that you wished to save your soul."

⁂

The details were settled. Someone even suggested a couple of real courtesans who could apply their makeup. A supply of arms would be left for the men in the place where they would assemble, the house of a wealthy patriot. They would come under the city gates in curtained carriages so that the watchmen would have less of a look at them.

And on the morning of the attack they would shave off their beards. They would even shave their arms and knuckles. Women were already busy making their clothes.

In the meantime the ten of them would remain together. Protos wanted to know them better because, at the last moment, he would have to choose who would guard the doors and who would come inside the hall with him to do the slaughter.

How had it ever come to this? He was sixteen and he had already killed a man for every year of his life. How had the Fates come to spin this strange thread that defined his existence? He knew that when he entered that hall he would spill blood without hesitation or mercy, but not without remorse.

He saw the risks with painful clarity. The most probable outcome would be his own death, and he almost welcomed it. For what would the rest of his life be like if he lived to commit this deed? His soul was already burdened enough.

Yet, if he lived and triumphed, the Spartans would be driven from Thebes, which would probably be the beginning of the great war that might finally end Spartan power.

If. Probably. Might. He was offering up his life to a conjecture. All he could do was push against the door and hope it opened.

Was it even possible that one day no Helot would have to die so that a Spartan lad could find his manhood in ritual murder?

The world was a mad place when the road to his people's freedom led through a banqueting hall full of butchered aristocrats.

The ten slept in a deserted farmhouse outside of the village—all but Protos, who could not sleep. So he was outside, his back against a tree and a jar of beer in his hand, staring up at the waxing moon. In two days it would be full, just as it had been the night his parents had been murdered. It would be bad luck for someone.

17

Eurytus had already presented the garrison commander with a plan for bringing the Spartan forces down from the acropolis so that they could deploy, if necessary, within the city itself. But Listeus, who had his orders and, apparently, no imagination whatsoever, would not be budged without express authority from the Council of Oligarchs.

"Take the matter up with Laius," he said, smiling in a way that implied he already knew what the answer would be. "We have to preserve at least the illusion that Thebes governs itself."

Laius, the leading figure in the council, turned out to be a fat, indolent man of about sixty who was more concerned with his complexion than with matters of state. He received Eurytus while still in his bath.

He was lying in a huge marble tub, with four of his naked slave girls in attendance. The water was cloudy with oil and smelled like rancid violets.

"Ah, the Lord Eurytus," he exclaimed, holding up a hand for one of his women to dry before he offered it to his guest. "The famous son of a distinguished father, welcome. Word of your exploits in Italy has reached us even here, in this backwater of the world."

He laughed at his little joke, if that was what it was.

"You must forgive the informality of this reception, but I am required by my physicians to spend at least two hours every morning bathing—the hot wind in this region is so drying to the skin, you know. I'm sure you've felt it."

Eurytus was embarrassed as to what answer to make, since he had not even noticed the wind, when he observed that his host was now preoccupied with the condition of his left foot, which he was holding out of the water so that his toenails could be clipped.

"Be careful, Chloe," he shouted in a panicky, effeminate voice. "I'll have you whipped if you cut them too close again."

"My lord," Eurytus interjected, "there is a security problem I wished to discuss with you. . . ."

"Yes, certainly, in a moment, my lord."

Finally Laius was able to lower his foot back into the water. He sighed contentedly.

"I am at your disposal, my lord," he said, smiling the weary smile of one who lives only for pleasure.

"My lord, there are signs that Epaminondas is readying forces for—"

"Oh, Epaminondas!" Laius emitted a groan, as if his bowels were troubling him. "Excuse me, my lord, but I have known Epaminondas all his life, I knew his father, and he is a harmless crank, a philosopher, a Pythagorean, if it pleases you—'Number is the secret key to the universe.' What folly!"

"My lord, it is reliably reported that he is organizing an army under your very eyes."

"Epaminondas could not organize a visit to a brothel." Laius giggled, as if struck that instant by his own witticism.

"My lord, something is brewing." Eurytus put his foot on the rim of the bathtub and leaned forward, his face not even a cubit's length from Laius's. He was growing impatient with this fat sybarite. "If the worst should happen, and the democrats take control of Thebes, it will go hard if the entire Spartan garrison is trapped up in the acropolis. I beg permission to move perhaps thirty or forty men down into the city proper."

"Oh, by the gods, no." Laius shook his head so vigorously that water sprayed out from his hair in all directions. "It would be an invitation to rebellion. I won't have it, I tell you. You would be putting all our heads on the executioner's block."

"If I am right, my lord, your executioner is already sharpening his sword."

⁂

That night, Eurytus wrote a letter to his father, which would go out the next morning by special courier.

I wish to put down my thoughts for you, in case I do not live to relate them in person. It is my conviction that, whatever the outcome of this business with the Helot Protos, our disposition of forces within Thebes will prove to be hopelessly ineffective. I am certain that Epaminondas is planning an insurrection and that, under current circumstances, it will be successful. I have tried to persuade both the garrison commander and the Oligarch Laius to move a contingent of our soldiers into the city, but to no effect.

It is now up to you to persuade the kings and the Ephors to prepare countermeasures should Thebes rebel. Unless we can enforce our will here, we will be involving ourselves in a long and costly war.

My father, I plan to stay here until it is apparent whether my fears are justified. If the garrison perishes, I prefer to perish with it. You, I suspect, will have no trouble understanding my "reasons."

Would he? It was impossible to know. Eurytus could not help the suspicion that his father was too conventional a Spartan to really understand. How could he know what it was like to contemplate a future in which he would have no place? To him, Protos was simply a rebellious slave—he could never imagine what it had been to feel the man's hatred and contempt and, at the same time, to feel their justice—and their inevitable victory. In spite of his being a slave, or perhaps because of it, Protos was someone Eurytus found it impossible not to respect.

Yet Eurytus was as much a Spartan as his father. He could not help it. His every reflex was conditioned by the tradition to which he had been born. And that was why he hated Protos, who had forced upon him a state of soul more terrible even than cowardice. His fear he had at last overcome, but he could not so easily subdue his doubt.

❦❦

As she drove her wagon over the western road from Athens, Nubit's anguish was nothing so complicated, for she had dreamed of blood and fire.

That Protos was returning to Thebes she did not need her dreams to tell her. He had met a man in Thebes who had sent him to another man in Athens. These men were patriots—one had but to mention their names and anyone would tell you as much—so what could they want but the liberation of their city? And what could they want with a youth such as Protos except his skill in the taking of life?

The dreams merely warned her that the moment was now.

There were a hundred Spartan soldiers garrisoned in Thebes. A hundred Spartans was considered an invincible army. What chance had these patriots? They were planning their own immolation and they would somehow use Protos to start the fire.

What could she do? Nothing, probably. Protos could not be persuaded to leave these men to their self-selected destiny. He had pledged himself, even if he had never spoken the words, and he would not back away. It was not in him.

But she had to be there. She had to be in Thebes. To see him again. To share his fate. To hold his hand while he died. She knew not why. She simply knew she had to be there.

She drove through most of the night. The moon was so bright it might almost have been day. Then, when her horse stopped and would not go on, she pulled off the road and allowed herself three hours of sleep. By the midmorning she could see the walls of Thebes.

She reached the gates just after noon and only had self-possession enough to feed and tether her horse. In case it should somehow prove useful, she grabbed her magic bag and entered the city.

There were the usual crowds in the marketplace. People went calmly about their business. Nubit sat on the steps of the temple of Dionysus, watching them, amazed at their apparent indifference to the atmosphere of foreboding that she could feel as one does the first approaches of a thunderstorm.

"Out of the way, woman!"

She was almost kicked aside by an elegantly dressed man carrying a staff. In that first instant Nubit recognized him as a herald.

"No, wait," someone else said, his voice slightly raised. "It is the witch, is it not?"

The speaker was an old man, grotesquely fat, whose perfume she could smell even though he was three or four paces from her. He grinned with pleasure, as if encountering an old friend.

"I saw you raise the ghost of Cadmus! How long ago was that? Ten, fifteen days ago? I wanted to have my fortune told and then you disappeared. And here you are again!"

He went down a few steps below her, probably because it would have been uncomfortable for him to bend over. He held out his hand to her.

For a moment she could not have spoken, for across his palm, from the base of the little finger to the ball of the thumb, was a thick smear of blood.

She looked up into the man's face. He was amused. The men about him, his hangers-on, were smiling and talking among themselves.

At last she remembered that she was to tell a fortune and cradled the man's hand in her own. With the tip of her finger she touched the smear of blood. She could feel its wetness, but when she took her finger away and looked at it, there was nothing.

They had no hint of the truth, these men. The blood was for her eyes only.

Nubit forced herself to laugh.

"Your Honor will be blessed with a long life," she announced, covering the lie with a smile. "Your Honor will know prosperity all your days, and all men shall envy you."

"Well, I have already lived to old age," the man said with a laugh that came out as a faint, wheezing sound. "But it is something to be assured I will not die in the gutter."

He dropped a coin into her lap, but she hardly noticed.

"What is Your Honor's name? I would offer sacrifice for you."

"Why, woman, do you know nothing?" the herald asked. "This is Laius the Oligarch."

She watched them descending the stairs. At last, when they had disappeared into the crowd, she picked up the coin in her lap. It was an Athenian silver drachma. She turned it over and saw the figure of an owl on the back—the bird of death.

With a twitch of revulsion she cast it away from her. It skittered down the steps. A beggar stooped over and picked it up.

❧ ❧

At that moment Protos was having his cheeks rouged with the dregs from a wine cup. He was wearing a red wig and had shaved off his beard with his Spartan dagger, its blade polished with a whetstone until it would almost cut at a touch.

Protos was the last to be made up, but by then they all had false bosoms under their women's clothes and their arms and hands glittered with cheap jewelry. The men kept complimenting each other on their beauty and making lewd jests. The whole process was regarded as hilarious.

The prostitute who had applied their cosmetics and given them instruction in how to behave was a fervent patriot and had offered to spread her legs for any or all of them. A few availed themselves, but most were too frightened of what was coming.

Protos knew what was coming, had known for days, and his emotions had settled down to a dull, resigned despair.

As a last act of preparation, Protos tied his sheathed dagger to the inside of his left leg. He would be the only one who carried a weapon into the city.

"Familiar tools are best," he told them. He told them other things as well.

"When you kill a man, do not look him in the face. Avoid his eyes or you may hesitate—or, should you live through tonight, they may haunt you the rest of your days. Pay attention to his hands because he will try to defend himself, to push you or your sword away. Strike for the belly. The best is just under the rib cage and up, so that you catch his lungs or his heart. He may not die at once, but he will die soon enough and there will be no fight left in him. When you have struck, forget him and go on to the next. When they are all down, there will be time enough to finish off any who are left alive.

"Remember, do not look him in the eyes. His eyes will remind you that he is a man like you, and tonight they cannot be men, only targets."

In an hour they would separate and take three carriages into the city, coming from two different directions. It was time for final instructions.

"The carriages will arrive in intervals of a quarter of an hour. Leave the carriages behind as soon as you are out of sight of the main gate. We will assemble at the house of Kleitomachos—do all of you know the way there?"

There was a general murmur of assent.

"I do not, but I will follow one of you. The house of Laius is only one street away, so we will go in a body. It will be dark, so probably no one will be vexed to wonder why a crowd of courtesans are carrying swords."

It wasn't much of a jest, but they all laughed.

"Once inside, Nikomachus, Agenor, Crates and Aristides will hold the doors—no one in, no one out. The rest will come with me.

"When the work is done, we will return to the house of Kleitomachos to clean up and change into men's clothes. Then we will go wherever we can be useful."

18

Protos was in the first carriage, with three other men and a courtesan who would speak for them and flirt with the watch officers to distract them from looking too closely at the other passengers.

If something went wrong at the gate, Protos planned to kill the watch, take their weapons and go on directly to Laius's house with anyone who was willing or able to follow him. They would probably never reach it alive, and four men had no chance of killing thirty, not when the exits were unguarded, but he would die in the attempt.

Perhaps I was born to do this one thing, he told himself. *Perhaps every man's life is simply the path to some single purpose, and this is mine. Afterwards, what difference does it make if I die in the attempt?* He tried to believe that his own life didn't matter, even to himself, but thoughts of Nubit kept intruding, unbidden. She made life so sweet. . . .

But there was no turning back.

When they came within a hundred paces of the city gate, conversation inside the carriage died away. They rolled up to the guardhouse and the courtesan, whose name was Thorakis and who was very pretty, looked out the window and smiled. And they were waved through.

The driver stopped two streets past the main gate and they all climbed out.

"A kiss for luck, Protos."

Thorakis was standing a little behind him. As he looked around she threw her arms about his neck and kissed him on the mouth. Then she turned and ran away into the darkness.

"She likes you," said a youth named Xenias, who, even before his beard was shaved off, was pretty enough to be a girl.

The others laughed, but Protos held up his hand to command silence. In fact he was merely embarrassed.

It took them twenty minutes to reach the house of Kleitomachos.

The house was empty and the door unlocked. An oil lamp burned in one of the rooms off the reception hall and there they found clothes, tubs of water, washcloths, and, wrapped in a bedsheet, about twenty swords. There was even a large jar of wine, which no one touched.

The waiting was the hardest part. Except for this one room, the house was dark and deathly silent. The shadows and the quiet preyed on the mind.

After what seemed much more than a quarter of an hour, the second group arrived. Agenor was one of these and his glance skidded away when Protos looked at him.

"How did it go?" Protos asked.

"No difficulties. They let us through without a word."

"No one followed you?"

"No one."

By the time the third group arrived, everyone's nerves were drawn as tight as bowstrings. It was time to be moving.

"Pick your swords," Protos told them, "and remember, they're like women. Choose the one that loves you. Those of you who are coming inside with me, take two."

The house of Laius was indeed no farther away than a brief walk. Still, it was a strange experience to be out in public in women's clothes, carrying swords. Protos had two of them, plus the dagger still tied to his left leg. But at that hour, and in this part of the city, the streets were empty.

All of Laius's windows were illuminated and there were no soldiers in evidence.

The front door was locked.

This was a problem. If they broke it down they would alert the whole house. When did whores break down the barred entrances of their clients' houses?

And then the answer became apparent. Whores knocked.

Protos kicked at the base of the door with his sandaled foot—he still wasn't entirely used to the sandals and promised himself he would take this pair off as soon as he was inside. After a moment or two, an elderly chamberlain came to the door.

"Yes, madam? Are you expected?"

He did not live to realize his mistake. The point of Protos's sword was already probing his vitals. He opened his mouth, as if to protest, but all that came out was a gush of blood.

Protos shoved him out of the way. The man stumbled and then fell to the floor, where he lay on his chest, staring at his outstretched arm with lifeless eyes.

"Someone drag him out of sight, and bar the door."

The design of the main floor was exactly what they had been led to expect. A corridor swept around three sides of the banqueting hall, and there were four doors. All four were open.

"Those of you on the doors, close them as soon as the six of us are inside. If household slaves come near, just wave your swords at them and frighten them away. We don't want to kill anyone we aren't obliged to. Anyone tries to leave the hall, you know what to do.

"And remember, do not look at their eyes. Just kill them."

He did not have to fear being overheard, for the noise of the banqueting hall was like the throbbing of a bruise. The very walls seemed to shudder.

He glanced around at his men, as if to ask, *Is everyone ready?*

They were.

Protos reached down for the dagger tied to his leg. He switched weapons, so that the dagger was in his left hand and his sword in his right, then he tossed the sword into the air and caught it by the blade.

"And now we will offer them an entertainment they didn't count on. It's time."

He opened the door on the left side to the back of the hall—it was probably the door used by the kitchen slaves—and the six of them filed inside.

Their disguise seemed to be working. There was even a small cheer at their entrance.

In that first instant Protos saw everything, and he nearly choked on his rage. The guests lay about on couches, their heads wreathed with laurels and flowers. They were all old men. There were probably as many serving girls as guests and none of them could have been older than fourteen. Their duties, it was clear, extended beyond merely serving food and pouring wine.

In the middle of the hall, up on a table, a girl, from the look of her no more than eight or nine years old, was dancing naked to music she could not possibly have heard over the din of revelry. At least, she was trying to dance, but the guests closest to her kept grabbing at her legs and buttocks.

"Leave the girls alone," Protos said, just loud enough for his men to hear. "They should not suffer at our hands as well."

"And the musicians?"

"Them too."

Then they took off their wigs and showed their swords. Suddenly even the most inattentive of Laius's guests fell silent. A few notes from a flute sounded, and then the hall was still.

Protos had already settled on who would be the first to die. An obscenely fat old man who occupied a couch near the center of the room had his hand between the little dancing girl's legs. She, being quicker in apprehension than her admirer—or perhaps having less to occupy her attention— saw at once what was coming and with a scream jumped down from the table and hid under it. Protos threw his sword, and its point caught the old man square in the chest.

"Time to go to work," Protos announced, switching his dagger to his right hand.

What followed was as organized as a dance. The assassins spread out and made their way forward through the hall, hacking and stabbing as they went. The revelers in some instances attempted to rise from their couches, while others tried to hide under them. More than a few lay still, paralyzed with terror, waiting for a death they perhaps could not bring themselves to believe was upon them.

There were shouts and screams in several different octaves and the air grew thick with blood. Protos was as efficient and pitiless as a grindstone. He followed a course up the right side of the hall, each of his victims receiving a swift thrust up through the belly. Sometimes he had to drag them out from beneath their couches or tables to kill them.

"No, no!" they shouted. Some simply screamed. A few sobbed piteously. One man covered his face with a pillow and died without a sound. At the end Protos had no idea how many men he had killed.

And it did end. The dead were lying about in tangles and there was blood even on the walls. A few of the revelers still feebly showed signs of life, but they were quickly dispatched. Finally there was no one left to kill.

The six of them stood about, staring at one another. They were covered in gore, their chests heaving with an excitement that was close to panic.

For Protos it was over when he recognized a sound that kept nagging at him as the terrorized whimpering of the girls, most of whom were huddled together against the walls. Some were spattered with blood.

Suddenly he felt ashamed—not for the men he had killed but that these frightened children had been made to witness this slaughter.

"No one will hurt you," he told them. "Get out of here."

None moved. Probably they didn't dare.

"Open the doors!" he called out.

The doors opened—surprisingly, no one had attempted to escape that way—and the four men who had been guarding them stepped into the hall. Even they seemed appalled by what they saw.

Gradually the girls found the courage to stand, and then to slide along the walls until they could slip away.

Protos felt someone's eyes on him and turned his head to meet Agenor's stare. His expression was a reproach. Protos quickly glanced away.

"Time to leave," he said, in a louder voice than he intended.

Out in the street, ten men with swords, six of them covered up to their very eyes in blood, met not a soul on their way back to Kleitomachos's house. The houses they passed were all dark. It was as if the city knew that some convulsion was at hand.

Inside, the first thing all of them did was strip down to their loincloths. Even those who had not been inside the banqueting hall felt the need to wash themselves.

It was a ghastly business. The towels, which they dipped in the water, were soon saturated with blood. It was simply impossible to cleanse themselves of this night's business.

Finally, Protos broke the seal on the wine jar and dipped a cup inside. He hated wine, but at that moment he hated himself even more and he wanted to take the edge off his self-disgust.

They all drank. It wasn't long before they were all at least a little drunk. It was better than being sober—anything was better than the stark, clear memory of what they had seen and done.

Protos sat by himself, morosely sipping his wine, trying to understand why he felt so defeated. After all, they had carried out their assignment and they were all alive. The oligarchs were a gory heap of offal.

But somehow, after such a deed, it seemed a sin against the gods to be still breathing the pure night air. It was something, he reluctantly concluded, he would have to learn to live with.

Then, all at once, he felt the pressure of someone's hand on his arm. He turned and saw it was Agenor who sat beside him.

"Why did you leave me outside?" The tone of Agenor's voice was somewhere between anger and despair. "Why? Didn't you think I was good enough?"

At first, the only answer Protos could make was a cruel, joyless laugh.

"Is that what you think," he said finally, "that I took the best with me? It was not work for better men, but for worse. How old are you, Agenor?"

The question must have seemed like a challenge. "Nineteen. Why?"

"Then you are three years older than I. I had my youth taken from me the night my parents were murdered and I will never get it back. Now I am older than you, not in years but in the men I have killed—much older tonight than I was even yesterday.

"Perhaps it was weakness on my part, but you spoke up for me and I wanted to do you a kindness. For a while you may feel diminished because you were kept at the edges of this deed, but that will pass. And this is one stain you will not have to carry on your soul."

19

Finally it came time to leave. No one seemed to have any clear idea what was to happen next, so they decided to go to the house of Epaminondas in hopes that there might be someone there who could give them instructions.

Epaminondas lived in a different part of the city, so the walk there took a good half an hour. It was not very long before the cold night air cleared away the wine fumes and left Protos wishing for a warm corner in which to grow drunk again.

Epaminondas was not at home, but it took little imagination to discover where he might be. His house was only five streets from the base of the acropolis.

And at that distance anyone could see the fires burning.

❊❊

It was beautiful in its way. Epaminondas had had Laius's house watched, and as soon as Protos's men entered he ordered teams of archers posted all around the acropolis, with bonfires set to send a demonic light up the sheer rock faces. The Spartans had been caught asleep in their barracks and were now trapped.

"The secret of any good military operation is timing," Epaminondas told Protos as they watched the flames licking up into the sky. "They can't get down and I happen to know they have water for no more than another five days. The fact that the Spartans set an 'invincible' army in our midst is thus no longer a factor. They can come down on our terms or they can come down dead."

"What do you want me to do now?"

Epaminondas seemed surprised by the question. "Do? Find a place to sleep, I suppose. The next phase will be political. We shall call a meeting of the popular assembly and ask them to legitimize our seizure of power. Since, thanks to you, there is no alternative, the vote is strictly a formality, but once it is taken we will be the government of Thebes. Then we will deal with our friends in the acropolis and with any countermeasures the Spartans may intend. But for the moment your role in this drama is finished.

"By the way, someone was asking for you." He smiled. "A woman—rather attractive . . . foreign, I think."

❧❧

It did not take them very long to find each other.

At first, in the darkness, they clutched at one another, like exhausted swimmers grasping at a floating spar. Nubit was sobbing helplessly.

And then, suddenly, she stopped and pulled away.

"Phew! You stink of blood. Was one of them Laius the Oligarch?"

"Yes!" He was surprised, and then he wasn't. "You knew?"

She shook her head, dismissing the question.

"Come with me back to the wagon," she said. "You can tell me your adventures while I scrub you clean—like the night we met."

They walked through a silent city, which tomorrow would wake to find itself free, but for the moment neither of them cared. It was enough they were both alive.

❧❧

Eurytus was at the summit of the acropolis, standing at its extreme edge. Looking down at the spectacle below, his soul boiled with wrath. He had walked all the way around the perimeter and the garrison was sealed shut. It gave him no sense of triumph that everything he predicted had happened.

"Well, you were right," a voice said behind him.

He turned to find himself face-to-face with the garrison commander.

"Laius should have listened," Listeus said, almost smugly. "I'm sure he feels a fool."

"I doubt he feels any way about it at all. Surely he's dead by now."

Listeus seemed bewildered. The thought appeared never to have occurred to him.

"Would *you* risk a coup like this with an opposition government at your back?" Eurytus could almost pity him. "Would anyone? I think it likely all

of the oligarchs have already crossed over the Styx and are making themselves as comfortable as they can in whatever part of Tartarus the gods re-
serve for collaborators."

"Certainly that's a bit harsh."

"Is it?" Eurytus smiled pleasantly. He had almost the sense that he was
speaking to a child. "You suppose that because they were our villains their
treachery won't count against them? You imagine that Aiakos will judge
them as good men because they were on our side? Perhaps he was a
Spartan in his mortal life?"

They looked down at the base of the acropolis, where archers were
stretching their bows and smoothing out the feathers of their arrows. Those
men were looking up at them, measuring the distance and deciding on
the best angle of flight.

"How much rope do we have?" Eurytus asked, the way a man might
inquire about the price of a meal he was not sure he wanted.

"A few thousand cubits, I think." The commander shrugged, the question apparently striking him as meaningless. "A few spools in one of the
storage rooms. Why?"

Eurytus ignored him. He was attempting to calculate how quickly a
man might descend thirty cubits by rope and what his chances of survival
might be on the way down.

"We can escape," he said finally. "At least, a few of us can. It is possible.
We are Spartans, after all. We might be able to fight our way out of Thebes."

"Are you mad?"

Listeus shook his head, not so much in disagreement as in the conviction that there must have been something wrong with his hearing.

"What would you have done at Thermopylae, Commander? Meekly
surrendered?"

It was a tense moment. Men had fought to the death over lesser insults,
and Listeus was just on the edge of feeling the need to wet his sword. But
at last, as Eurytus had expected, caution got the better of him.

"You think you are Achilleos because you have been in one battle," the
commander said, almost between clenched teeth. "I have more wounds on
my body than you have fingers.

"Besides, there is no need. This is no Thermopylae." He smiled, in
something like triumph. "The Thebans are not fools. They will realize that
forcing us to fight and die invites a campaign of revenge. They may be
ready for something like this, which is no more than a clever stunt, but they

are not ready for war. After a day or two, we will be invited to walk out of here."

"That is precisely what we must prevent."

❧❧

When he had finished his conversation with Eurytus, the commander retired to his room, broke the seal on a jar of wine and sat down at his desk to drink it.

That boy was mad. He had fought one good battle and he was drunk with his own glory. He would get them all killed and for nothing.

It took two cups of very choice Pramnion wine before Listeus could regain his equilibrium.

By then he was prepared to concede that Eurytus was a clever lad and that his analysis of the situation, as far as it went, was probably correct. The Thebans were counting on Sparta to take a tolerant attitude toward this latest political reverse—after all, the Spartans had garrisoned Thebes and imposed an oligarchy favorable to themselves through a piece of trickery, and now the Thebans had given them a taste of their own dish. If the garrison was allowed to leave unharmed, Sparta would probably decide that recapturing a well-fortified city was not worth the effort.

Eurytus was the son of a former Ephor and knew a thing or two about the way these issues worked themselves out. Listeus was forced to agree with his assessment.

But then Eurytus had gone seriously off his head.

"Do you really not know what this little episode means?" Eurytus had almost shouted. "Do you not see what will be the inevitable result if Sparta does not crush this rebellion at once? Epaminondas will drive us out of central Greece. He is ambitious for his city and he is clever—and just possibly a better general than any we have. We must crush him now, while he is still weak, and if the garrison is destroyed Sparta will have no choice but to crush him. Is that not worth the lives of a hundred men? How many more than a hundred must die in the war that Epaminondas will visit upon us?"

The boy wished for death. Everyone knew that Eurytus had been a little peculiar since the death of his brother. Perhaps he felt responsible—that whole episode was as murky as a thundercloud.

Listeus regarded himself as a responsible officer. Certainly he was responsible for the lives of the men under his command, and if he could get them out of Thebes alive, he would. It was up to the kings and the Ephors to decide matters of peace and war, and it would be presumptuous to the point of treason for any officer under orders to attempt to force their hands.

When they got back to Sparta, he decided, he would report Eurytus's erratic behavior to the Ephors.

It wouldn't be any more than he deserved.

⁂

Protos was easy in his mind. After Nubit had washed him and squeezed his seed from him, he drank three cups of beer—Nubit had added a little something to the brew about which he knew nothing—and then slept for six hours. When he awoke he remembered everything that had happened the night before, but he remembered it the way he remembered the stories Uncle Neleus used to tell when he was a child. None of it touched him. They were the deeds of a mythically distant Protos who was someone else entirely from the Protos who slept in Nubit's arms. He was no more responsible for that man's acts than he was for Odysseus's blinding of the Cyclops. His conscience was not troubled.

The next morning he breakfasted on wheat porridge and a melon, and then he retired to the wagon where Nubit again comforted him with her body until he was ready to sleep again.

Nubit, he decided, was a wise woman who understood him better than he did himself. He loved Nubit and wished never to be parted from her.

At about an hour before sunset, while Protos was lying on the ground with his head in Nubit's lap, digesting his dinner, a messenger came.

"The boeotarch asks that the Lord Protos attend him at his house, this at the Lord Protos's earliest convenience."

The messenger was about eighteen, very much the man of fashion in an embroidered linen tunic that hardly reached to the middle of his thighs. From the way he looked at "the Lord Protos" he seemed to suspect he had come to the wrong place.

"I am Protos, but I am a Laconian peasant, not a lord. What is a boeo-tarch?"

The messenger stared at him as if Protos's ears were on backward.

"A commander of the army, a leader of the state—in this case the Lord Epaminondas."

"Oh. Well then, I will come."

The messenger insisted on accompanying him, even though Protos assured him he needn't trouble himself, that he knew the way.

"Ah, Protos." Pelopidas himself came to the door and took the young man's hand in both of his own. "The assembly has declared us liberators. Epaminondas, Gorgidas and I have all been elected boeotarchs, so we control the government. In his speech of acceptance Epaminondas described how you saved his life—he thought it tactful not to mention the oligarchs— and the assembly in its gratitude has voted you the rights of a citizen. Congratulations. You are a Theban."

They went into the garden, where they found Epaminondas.

"Did you tell him?" Epaminondas asked, looking at his friend. Pelopidas smiled and nodded.

The contrast between the two men could not have been more striking. Epaminondas was taller and broader and exhibited a certain calm grace, where Pelopidas was smaller, thin and quick in his movements. Epaminondas possessed the gravity of a philosopher, while Pelopidas was impetuous and full of jests.

"Well, there is other good news," Epaminondas continued. "Since citizenship in Thebes involves certain property requirements, we have arranged for you to take possession of a small house, lately owned by one of the previous government's supporters who found it convenient to flee after the assembly attainted him as a traitor. There is also a sizable reward of money."

For a long moment Protos made no reply—he seemed not to have heard. Except for the odd handful of silver coins, he had no experience of money and could not decide what it might mean for him. The house would be nice, if Nubit would consent to live in it.

"What will happen to the slave girls who belonged to Laius?" he asked finally.

"They will be sold, along with the rest of his estate." As he spoke, the expression on Epaminondas's face suggested a certain disappointment. "Why? Did one of them, or more than one, appeal to you?"

"If my reward is enough, I would like to buy them all and provide dowries sufficient to allow them to marry decent men, men who will not abuse them." Protos's eyes narrowed. "Remember, old man, I have been a slave myself."

Epaminondas and Pelopidas exchanged a glance. It was as if they had had a joke played on them and were prepared to laugh at their own discomfiture.

"I think something of the sort can be arranged," Pelopidas said, stroking his beard. "But, since you will have spent most of your prize money, we will be obliged to find you employment in the army, lest you starve."

"It was the greatest mistake the Spartans made," Gorgidas suddenly announced. He slapped the table with his hand, he found the situation so amusing. "They should have disbanded our army instead of merely forcing the officers to swear allegiance to the Council of Oligarchs, who, thanks to our young friend, are now all conveniently dead. It enabled them to come over to us with clear consciences."

Suddenly the air in the little enclosed garden seemed to grow chilly, and Protos began to think that these busy and important men might not have brought him here on the first day of their rule merely to congratulate him. There was something else.

"And there is another matter which has come to our attention . . ." Epaminondas picked up a stylus that had been lying on the table and rolled it between his first finger and thumb. "In the last few days someone, a Spartan, has been making inquiries about the man who saved me from an assassin. One must ask, why would a Spartan be curious about such a thing?"

"Does this inquisitive Spartan have a name?"

"Yes, actually, we have been able to identify him. His name is Eurytus. Is he known to you?"

"Eurytus, son of Dienekes?"

"Yes."

Protos found himself staring at the gate in the garden wall, wishing he could escape through it. The idea that Eurytus was here in Thebes . . .

"He is a little unfinished business of mine," he said, as if it were a matter of no importance. "One day I will kill him. What is he doing here?"

"It would seem, looking for you."

❦

It was a complicated story, having more to do with politics than revenge. The new government of Thebes had sent envoys to the Spartan garrison to negotiate the terms of their withdrawal, and there was a problem. While the commander was prepared to surrender the acropolis and leave the city on honorable terms, Eurytus apparently wanted to make a fight of it, and a few of the officers supported him. Eurytus must have been a man of considerable influence.

"Our sources tell us that he fought well in Italy," Pelopidas said, with a shrug. "And, since physical courage is almost the only virtue the Spartans recognize . . . But that, by itself, would not account for the deference paid him, so we assume he is well connected."

"His father was an Ephor and has remained close to King Agesilaus,"

Protos told them, and then his expression changed into a mirthless and rather cruel smile. "I have made something of a study of the family."

"Can he be stopped?" Epaminondas asked. The question was directed to Protos.

But how could he answer? Eurytus was up on the acropolis, surrounded by his fellow Spartans, as inaccessible as if he were on Mount Olympus.

Besides, what was the point of killing a man on the verge of suicide? Eurytus seemed to want a glorious death, a death in battle, which would both cheat Protos of his revenge and touch off a war with Sparta, which Thebes was not ready to fight.

But perhaps there was another way—a way to take from Eurytus what was more precious to him even than life.

Protos turned to his host and smiled.

"Possibly."

❦❦

The next morning a somewhat larger group of Theban envoys trudged up the narrow path to the acropolis. One was a youth with only a two-day-old stubble of wheat-colored beard. His dress was aristocratic, but oddly he wore no sandals. In compliance with diplomatic protocol, he carried no weapon.

The Thebans were met at the main gate by the garrison commander and five of his officers, among whom Eurytus was numbered.

Such meetings followed a pattern dictated by ancient custom. First the Thebans were shown into a large room in the citadel. The walls were bare stone and the windows high up and small. It had the look of a room that was never used except for ceremonial occasions.

Then wine was served and the antagonists mingled and conversed in the manner of old friends. This informal prologue to the formal discussions might last some time, for it gave each side a chance to assess the mood of the other and for the principals to exchange information out of their subordinates' hearing.

It was early in this phase that Eurytus felt someone's gaze on him. Turning his head, he immediately recognized the youth with the stubble of beard.

When their eyes met, Protos briefly turned his head toward the door and then walked off in that direction.

Eurytus experienced a momentary shudder of dread, and then it occurred to him that, if he had his way in the discussions with the Thebans, he was as good as dead anyway. What then had he to fear from Protos? Besides, he was curious.

Not far from the main gate was a stone stairway to the top of the wall, where Protos was standing, looking out over the Boeotian plain.

"Somehow I am not surprised to see you here," Eurytus said quietly as he took his place beside him.

"Why should you be? You knew I was here. You have been making inquiries."

Eurytus nodded, not sure that Protos would even notice.

"Did the Thebans send you? Have you thrown in your lot with them?"

"I care nothing for the Thebans," Protos answered, sounding almost bored. "I have my own reasons for being here."

"And what might those be?"

Protos ignored the question. He seemed totally absorbed in his survey of the plain.

"I hear you did well in Italy," he said at last. "You were wounded?"

"Yes. In the shoulder."

"And has it healed yet?"

"Not completely." Eurytus smiled. "But I can hold a sword."

"You will not need to hold a sword," Protos answered, still without looking his enemy in the face. "Your commander, it seems, has not your taste for martyrdom. You will march out of here with the rest of the garrison."

"That remains to be seen. If enough of the officers side with me, he will be shamed into making a fight of it."

"Then you will have to withdraw your opposition to surrender."

For a long moment neither man spoke.

"Why should I do that?"

Protos turned now to look at his enemy.

"The Thebans do not want war with Sparta—at least, not yet," he said. "But, as I said, I care nothing for the Thebans. Personally, I would welcome such a war. You too would welcome it, even though you would not live to fight in it.

"I know you are not afraid to die. But you will not die here, now, in this place. You will not die until I kill you. I will not allow it. And the time for that has not yet come."

Eurytus had no thought that the implied threat was idle. He could only wait, hardly breathing.

"You massacred my family," Protos went on, his voice seemingly empty of emotion. "I think, should you disappoint me in this, that I will feel compelled to return the compliment. I will go back to Laconia to pay a visit to your father, the respected former Ephor. Believe me, he will be found in a condition that will do little credit to his memory. And then I will attend upon the rest of them. It is, I know, a large family, so it will take some time. But in the end . . ."

"You would be caught."

"Would I?" Protos smiled, as if to say, *You of all people should know better than that.* "They are not expecting it, and there will be no one to warn them. You will be dead. And they will soon join you."

Eurytus could only stare. He could see the truth in Protos's face. He would actually do it—he was looking forward to doing it. The whole family butchered, one by one.

Protos resumed his contemplation of the view.

"However, I give you my word that if you depart from this city alive, if you do not force a massacre upon the Thebans, I will leave your family alone. This matter will remain between the two of us.

"You needn't make your decision now. I will know what it is from events."

And then he turned on his heel and made his way down the stairs. In a moment he had vanished.

❧❧

Two days later the Spartan garrison came down from the acropolis and marched out of the city. Protos watched as they passed out through the southern gate, but soldiers in their war helmets were anonymous. When they were gone he went up to the now deserted acropolis.

"You will not cheat me," he said, under his breath, as he searched room after room of the garrison. He found nothing—no suicide stretched out on the floor in a pool of blood.

"So you are alive, and the duel goes on."

20

The next day Protos and Nubit took possession of their new home. It was a two-story building of unfinished stone and, although they had yet to see it, they had been told that there was a small garden in the back. It was in a pleasant district, not far from the marketplace.

For perhaps a quarter of an hour they stood in the street, holding hands, looking at it.

"What will we do with the wagon?" Nubit asked finally.

"We will leave it at the depot used for the army supply wagons. And the cavalry will stable the horse—let her have a little company in her old age."

"And what of my things?"

"We will bring what we need here, although I don't imagine that will be much. I am told the house is already furnished, its previous owner having abandoned it in some haste."

He bent his head down to peer into her face.

"Is there something about all this that troubles you?"

"A little." She shrugged and put her arm around his back. "I haven't lived in a house since I was a girl. I have bad memories of those days."

"Will you ever tell me about them?"

"Someday."

They waited in silence for a moment, and then Protos said, "Perhaps we should go in."

He was reaching for the latch string when the door sprung open. A girl of about nine stood inside. When she saw Protos's face, her eyes widened in terror and she threw herself to the floor, reaching out in supplication to touch his feet.

"Get up," he commanded, taking her gently by the arm. "Get up. I won't hurt you."

The girl rose slowly to her feet. She did not know where to look, as she was still badly frightened.

"And what is this?" Nubit asked, a touch of jealousy in her voice.

"A slave—at least, a former slave." Protos smiled, suspecting that he looked very foolish. "She is from the household of Laius—he had a taste for girls on the threshold of womanhood, or even younger. His house was full of them. I bought them with my prize money, with the idea of giving them dowries and a new start at life. I didn't expect to find any of them here.

"This one is afraid because the last time she saw me I was covered in blood."

He peered into the girl's face, as if trying to recall it.

"Were you the dancer?" he asked.

"Yes, master . . ."

"Don't call me that."

"Master, I—"

"Don't call me 'master.' My name is Protos and this lady is Nubit. You should know that I, no different from you, was born a slave." He smiled once more. "I suppose you were judged too young for a husband. Are you the only one left?"

"No, m—no, my lord Protos. There are two others."

Two little girls, even younger than she—they could not have been older than seven or eight—appeared in the entrance to an adjoining room.

Nubit stepped forward and placed her hands on their shoulders, kneeling down as they huddled close to her. She remained so for a long moment, and when she stood there were tears in her eyes.

When she looked at Protos there was a hint of a smile on her face.

"How do I know you did not buy them for your own particular pleasure?" she asked.

Protos could only laugh. "Because I have you for that."

※ ※

They went through the ground floor room by room, and indeed the house was richly furnished. Many of the walls were painted with murals and there were cushioned chairs and chests with carved lids.

"In my village twelve families could have dwelt in this house," Protos announced almost grimly. "How do they expect us to live in such grandeur? We were happy enough in the wagon."

"I suspect you are on the verge of becoming an important man in Thebes. You will need this house."

"Now, for instance, what is this place for?"

They were standing in the middle of a room furnished with only a table and chair, one chest, and a rack containing perhaps half a hundred scrolls.

"This must have been the former owner's study," Nubit answered. She went to the table and turned over a sheet of papyrus to see what was written on it. "Yes, this is where he came to read and write letters. And see? You have inherited his library."

Protos took up one of the scrolls and unrolled it about a cubit. For a long moment he stood reading it, his lips moving as he formed the words.

"I know this story," he said finally. "It is one my uncle Neleus used to tell." He smiled, pleased with the discovery, and then rerolled the scroll and put it back.

They went upstairs and in the largest room found a real bed, with a wooden frame to keep the mattress, which was stuffed with wool, off the ground. Neither of them had ever slept on such a thing.

"Will both of us fit?" Nubit asked.

"It's wider than the floor of your wagon, and we never had any trouble there."

"But it slopes to the middle—see? We will roll into each other."

Protos picked up one corner of the mattress and saw it rested on a lattice of rope.

"The rope only needs to be tightened and that is easily done."

Then something seemed to occur to him and he dropped the mattress corner.

"Do you really mind about the girls?" he asked. "I promise you I had no idea of their coming here. And they are ridiculously young."

"They are only a few years younger than you are yourself."

She smiled, and then suddenly the smile collapsed and she turned her face away.

"I don't mind," she said, in a voice thick with unspent tears. "For a while at least they will be the daughters I have never had."

He wrapped his arms around her and kissed her on the back of the head. For a long time they stood like that, saying nothing.

❧❧

Since Nubit owned little, and Protos hardly anything at all, they were moved into the house in an afternoon. And after the experience of one night, Nubit decided she liked the new bed.

"It is almost like floating on water," she said, "and I enjoy the way it squeaks to the rhythm of your thrusting."

The girls did, however, present a few problems.

They had been trained as body slaves and seemed to imagine that their duties in this household would be much the same as in the old. They tended to wander about the house naked and kept repeating their little pantomime of sexual submission—the smile, the downcast eyes, the hand kissing—until Protos became so irritated that he actually chased them from the room.

After this they went in tears to "the lady Nubit," who explained the difficulty.

"The Lord Protos is not interested in your bodies," she told them. "Mine seems to content him. He goes to the public baths to clean himself. He does not require your assistance. As he has told you, he was born a slave. He does not want to own you. He expects you to make yourselves useful in the house until you are old enough to marry. If you wish to please him, pay heed to what I have said."

Of course, they had no idea of how to make themselves useful. They had been taught nothing except how to goad an old man's lust.

❧❦

Their new education began only a few mornings after Nubit and Protos took possession of their house. Nubit awakened the girls before dawn.

"We will go to the temple of Hestia and receive the sacred fire with which to light our hearth," she told them. "From today forward it will be our responsibility as women of the household to keep the hearth fire burning. Fire is sacred and this fire is the soul of our house. It will only be extinguished if a member of the household dies.

"In the place where I was born the goddess was called Maat, but she is the same whatever she is called and she is one of the oldest of the gods. She is the goddess of the hearth and of right order, in the state and in heaven as well as in the home, and because of her, women are more powerful than men, no matter what anyone may think. Men play at war and politics and imagine they govern the world, but they do not. A woman runs the home and this places her at the core of life, for we can get along without war and politics but not without food and shelter. Not without children, whom we, the women, raise up. Before men even notice children, we have made them into whatever they will be in this world, and thus the future is ours to create, both in our bodies and by our nurturing. Remember that."

They walked through the streets of Thebes, each with her burden. Galene, the eldest, carried a small iron pot into which they would receive coals from the altar fire, and the two younger, named Hemera and Eupraxia, carried a honey cake and a small jar of wine with which to make sacrifice to the goddess. Nubit had a box of kindling with which to keep the fire alive until they returned home.

The temple was a humble business, a rough, wooden structure housing nothing except the sacred fire, an altar bearing a statue of the goddess, no more than a cubit high, and a single elderly priestess. Nubit gave the priestess a silver drachma and received three living coals. The girls offered sacrifice, after which the priestess touched each of them on the lips, enjoining them to silence.

On the way home Galene carried the pot of coals while the two younger girls took turns feeding the fire, and, as conversation was forbidden, Nubit had nothing to do except think.

What was she doing with these girls? What had she to give them? What could she teach them? They had been brought up as slaves. What did they know of ordinary life? Was she any different? What did *she* know?

Only the witchcraft that her mother had taught her, along with a few of the more ordinary female accomplishments that she had picked up as she could from the other slave women in her father's house.

Her father. Had he been any different from Laius, the elderly, repulsive sybarite who had made these children the prisoner of his degenerate lust? It seemed not.

Perhaps, it occurred to Nubit, that was one thing she could offer these girls, whom she was already beginning to love. She could give them the gift of her understanding.

When they returned to the house they entered the kitchen through the garden door and Nubit made a little pile of kindling in the center of the cold hearth. Then, one at a time, she shook the coals out of the iron pot, letting them drop on the kindling.

"The one is Galene," she said quietly as the first coal fell and almost instantly the kindling came alight. "This one is Hemera, and this one is Eupraxia. And thus the three of you, as daughters of this house, take responsibility with me for keeping these flames alive, just as each of us is responsible to the others."

She turned and looked at them, and was surprised to discover that their eyes were wet with tears. She could feel her own eyes brimming, for her heart was full, and so, as an alternative to weeping, she embraced the three girls together.

❧❦

Five days after he moved into his house, Protos took a walk around the perimeter of Thebes. Like everyone else, he knew that the Spartans would attack. When and in what numbers were matters open to speculation, but that they would attack was not in question. Protos wanted a look at the city's defenses. He was astonished to discover that trenches were already being dug beyond the northern quarter.

The next day he received a summons from Epaminondas.

"The army is badly trained and demoralized," the boeotarch explained to him. "We cannot possibly meet a Spartan army in the field. We would be inviting a massacre."

He was sitting in his garden, which he seemed to prefer to the interior of his house, feeding bread crumbs to an assembly of small birds, who were sure enough of him to approach within a few hand spans of his feet. He seemed absorbed in the task.

At last the bread crumbs were exhausted and he rubbed his hands together to let the last of them drop to the ground. Then, when he turned his full attention to Protos, he shrugged and held up his empty hands, the way a man does when forced to admit to an unpalatable fact.

"Thus our strategy will of necessity be defensive. We can keep them out of the city—you have seen the earthworks and the stockades. That is about all we can hope for."

"Is there nothing else we can do?"

"Very little." Epaminondas smiled wanly. "They will doubtless ravage the countryside, but that can't be helped. The only victory left to us is to remain free and independent after they finally decide to go home."

"What would you have of me?"

"I would have you make them want to go home," he said, as if he were asking some trifling favor. "I want you to render their lives wretched with uncertainty. I want them to think they can't go outside at night to relieve themselves without risking death."

Protos suddenly wished that Epaminondas weren't quite so ascetic in his tastes and would offer him a cup of beer.

"I want you to train a small band of men, perhaps twenty or thirty, to teach them what you can of your cunning and your use of weapons. Deploy them as you see fit. I want you to harass the Spartans past bearing. Can you do that?"

Protos smiled, showing his teeth—the effect was savage. "Making a nuisance of myself is what I do best," he said.

"Good, then." Epaminondas rose to his feet. He seemed about to speak and then suddenly he became still, as if something else had occurred to him.

"Yours, Protos, is the least glorious and most dangerous part of war," he said at last. "The Greeks tend to see war, as you once said, as a kind of shoving match. Men come straight at one another, each trying to drive the other from the field. One looks one's enemy in the face and it is dishonorable to run away. Skirmishers rush in to strike and then flee, and then rush in again. This is not considered a respectable way to wage war, so the skirmisher is not held in much honor. Yet he puts himself at greater risk than the men in the front line of a phalanx.

"There will be no great battles this year, so yours will be the only war we can bring to the Spartans. I suspect you know the dangers better than I."

❦ ❦

The first sound Protos heard when he returned home was laughter. It was coming from the kitchen and was as high-pitched as the singing of birds.

As he attempted to enter the kitchen, Nubit pushed him back out through the open doorway.

"The girls have been learning how to make bread," she told him, in a voice that was hardly above a whisper. "Their first efforts have not been particularly successful. It is all a great joke, but it would shame them to have you witness their failure."

Protos put his hand on the back of Nubit's head and kissed her brow.

"It shall be as you say, Little Mother."

Then he went to the room that Nubit called his "library" and sat down. It was the only place in the house where he could be sure of being left alone. It was forbidden to the girls, and Nubit never came in except to clean. He needed to think.

Life had been simpler before he met Nubit. There had been survival and there had been killing his enemies—and survival was important simply because his existence was so irritating to the Spartans. His life had been dedicated to vengeance and thus was not his own. It hadn't mattered if he was cold or hungry. It hadn't mattered that in all probability he would soon be caught and killed. He simply hadn't cared very much.

And then he had stumbled into Nubit's campsite and she had given him shelter and her body and had wrapped his every moment in her warmth. To love someone—and, more important, to be loved—changed everything.

Now there was this house and the girls, Nubit's little daughters, who had made something come alive inside her. It was like having a family again, except without the shared history.

It was not that Protos was afraid of this new task Epaminondas had given him—well, yes, he was afraid, but fear was something he had lived with for so long that he barely noticed it. It was not fear of death so much as the consciousness that now there were things that death could take away from him.

Nevertheless, it would be amusing. Already, in imagination, he could see the astonished look on the face of a Spartan as he suddenly realized that he had just been killed.

It would be better if he could be left to hunt alone, but one man could never inflict the damage Epaminondas was counting on. So Protos would have to recruit his little army and then worry about their lives instead of merely his own.

Suddenly he felt tired. Their new bed was wonderful for making love, but it was too soft and sometimes he woke up with a backache. Perhaps not only the bed but he himself was becoming too soft.

He lay down on the floor and within a moment was asleep.

21

Almost as soon as the Spartans who had been garrisoned in Thebes returned home, the former Ephor Dienekes brought their commander up on charges of neglect of duty. He had his son's letter, written before Epaminondas's takeover, and Eurytus's predictions had all been realized. It was damning evidence.

Of course, the object of the proceeding was not simply to destroy Listeus. Dienekes's son had convinced him of the absolute necessity of a preventive war against Thebes, and the trial of the garrison commander provided an excellent platform for preaching that war. Further, Eurytus had been right where a senior officer had been wrong. Dienekes had come to realize that his son was more farsighted than he was himself, that he had the makings of a great man. He wanted the whole of Sparta to realize this too.

Unfortunately after the first day of the trial, by which time the outcome had become obvious, Listeus went home and fell on his sword.

"The point is that I read your letter in open court," Dienekes told his son over breakfast. They were eating outside, enjoying the morning air before the dead heat of the Laconian Plain set in. "Everyone heard it. And as for Listeus, he passed judgment on himself."

"The point is neither Listeus nor me," Eurytus answered with barely contained anger. "The point is the war. It has to be fought, and I have to be part of it. Can you arrange that?"

Dienekes let his gaze settle upon his son, the last of his line, and experienced a baffled tenderness that embarrassed him. He did not wish to love this young man, whom he hardly knew. His own father, he was quite sure, had never loved him, and that was as it should be. Properly considered, Eurytus was merely an extension of his family—a family that reached back into an almost mythic past and might, with the gods' indulgence, endure into an equally remote future. The family was what mattered, not any individual member. Not himself, not his son. Eurytus's desire to join the expedition against Thebes was both natural and commendable, and it filled his father with dread.

"Your shoulder is not yet completely healed," he said at last, as an alternative to saying what he felt.

"Father, I must be with the army when it invades Boeotia."

"Why?"

"Because *he* will be there."

Dienekes suddenly lost interest in his breakfast. The world in that instant seemed a cold and forbidding place—yes, once more this wretched slave. He poured himself a cup of wine and it required every fiber of his will to keep his hand from shaking.

"You mean the Helot?" he asked, careful not to look his son straight in the face.

"His name is Protos, Father. Learn to call him by his name, and to stop pretending that he is just some runaway. He is not that—not anymore."

"You know he is there? You saw him?"

At first, the only answer Dienekes received was bitter laughter.

"Yes, I saw him," Eurytus said, in the tone of one explaining the obvious. "He was part of the Theban delegation—he has come that far in the world. But for him I would now be rotting under freshly turned earth, worm-eaten and honorably dead. By the gods, how I hate him for that."

Eurytus noticed that his wine cup was empty, but rather than refill it he picked up his father's and drank it off.

"He offered me a bargain and I took it."

Whatever his son would say next, Dienekes was quite sure he did not want to hear it. He knew in his bones that this "bargain" between his son and a runaway slave was certain to destroy his peace of mind. He also knew there was no escape.

"He told me he would kill our whole family if the garrison made a fight of it."

"That is preposterous."

"Is it?" Eurytus smiled, as if he could not believe there could be such folly in the world. "Is it really? Do you remember what happened to the garrison at Kyparissia? When I heard he had been captured I thought I would die of joy. They had him in a cage. Yet he killed them all—*and* the two Spartans sent to retrieve him."

Dienekes shrugged. He was uncomfortable in his mind, for either his son was lying—which he did not believe—or he had only just missed death.

"The garrison at Kyparissia was only six men," he said, as if the mention of such a thing offended him. "I have killed many more than six men in my time."

"It was eight men, counting the Spartans, and those you killed did not have you in a cage. I tell you, Father, in his hands my poor brother's dagger has become the shears of Aptropos."

Eurytus laughed again, but this time his laughter sounded full of hysterical dread.

"Is that not even his name? Protos. 'Destined.'"

"There is nothing in a name, my son. Except a father's idle wish."

"Then his father, whom I killed, chose well. The gods help me, what have I unleashed on the race of the Spartans? But for Teleklos and me even now he would be tilling a field somewhere, with no enemies except the crows. It is enough to drive one mad."

※ ※

"You will have your wish," Dienekes told his son. "King Agesilaus will be in command of the Theban campaign, and you will serve as a staff officer under him. But the army will not leave for a few months yet, and I must own that I am worried about your state of mind."

"What about my state of mind?"

Eurytus had just returned from dinner at the soldiers' mess, to which he had recently been elected. He would sleep there tonight, but his father had sent around a message asking him to stop by for a cup of wine. He found him in his garden, wearing a cloak as it was a cold evening.

"I have been rereading the letter you wrote me from Thebes," Dienekes answered, with a gesture directing his son to sit down. There was no wine in evidence. "You know, while the two of you were growing up I always thought of Teleklos as the reckless one. Now I see that the streak of heedlessness was in both of you—or this business with the slave boy has affected you more deeply than either of us realized."

Eurytus was about to make an objection, but his father held up a hand to forestall him.

"A soldier must sometimes accept death as a sacrifice he makes to his country, but he does not embrace it as an escape. You are too little in love with life, my son. We are all servants of the state, but even a servant has his hours of recreation to teach him that the breath under his ribs is precious.

"In short, I have reached the conclusion that you need a woman and so, as you are still too young to marry, I have made other arrangements. Her name is Iphigenia and she is upstairs."

Dienekes rose out of his chair and arranged his cloak, careful not to look at his son. He was embarrassed—the way he had always been embarrassed by these matters of the flesh. The way he had been embarrassed in the presence of his wife, so that he was almost relieved when she died.

"And now I am going to call upon an old friend who, like me, is a widower and, like me, prefers to stay up late and drink too much wine. The girl, by the way, is a Helot, so you may do with her as you wish, but I would recommend that you be gentle, as she is very young."

❧❦

At the top of the stairs was a short corridor leading to the back of the house, and at its end was the room that Eurytus had shared with his brother when they were young children. He couldn't remember the last time he had been in that room.

He pushed the door open and at first saw nothing except the empty floor. When he stepped inside, he saw that a sleeping mat had been unrolled against the opposite corner and a girl was sitting on it, her arms wrapped around her legs and her head resting on her left knee. She indeed looked very young.

When she saw him she tried to smile, but the attempt was not a success. It was obvious that she was frightened.

Never in his life had Eurytus seen a creature as beautiful as she. Her hair, which she wore long, was the color of bronze and framed a child's face with enormous, brilliant blue eyes. One could lose oneself in those eyes, he thought. One could look into them forever.

He came over and knelt down beside her on the sleeping mat.

"I won't hurt you," he said. "I will never hurt you."

He touched her hair with the tips of his fingers and she seemed to relax. It was only then that he noticed that she was naked.

"You can't help but hurt me if you take my maidenhood." She smiled again, this time a trifle more convincingly. "But that is a small thing. I am not afraid of that."

"How did you come to be here?"

His question, more than any threat of pain, seemed to wring her heart. She closed her eyes for a moment, as if there were things she did not wish to see.

When she opened them again, they were full of pleading.

"My father and mother work on one of Lord Dienekes's estates," she said. "Ten days ago—I think it was ten, I can't be sure now—men came and took me away. When I was brought here, they told me I was to be a concubine. It was a word I had never heard before. I gather it means a woman who serves a man's body as a wife does, but who is not a wife. Is that so?"

"Yes."

"What will become of me?"

She was afraid. Doubtless she had been afraid every hour since she was taken from her parents. Eurytus cradled her face in his hands. In that moment all he wanted was to take her fear away.

"You will serve me," he said, "and I will protect you. No one will ever frighten you again."

She leaned forward and kissed his lips. Then she smiled. Her smile was beautiful and serene.

"Then come into me, and make me yours."

❦❦

The next day there was drill, which kept Eurytus out in the countryside until almost dark, and then there was the barracks dinner, which required his attendance. He sat at table, hardly even conscious of his surroundings, remembering every moment he had spent with Iphigenia.

Eurytus, you are a fool, he would think to himself, and then he would smile, because he did not care that he was a fool. Just this once, to be a fool was to be blessed.

Who could he compare with Iphigenia? There had been Meda, a Macedonian noblewoman and a widow, several years older than he, to whom he had lost his virginity, and there had been the whores of Corinth. There had been his mother, of course. But had he loved his mother? Would it have been possible to love his mother? *Be a Spartan*, she had been forever telling him. *Don't be weak*. He could remember only a few occasions when she had shown him any tenderness, and then, at the age of seven, he had begun his military training and had lost her forever.

There had never been anyone in his life like Iphigenia. She was a Helot and she had been frightened, and the Spartans had achieved their position in the world by frightening people, most particularly the Helots. But he had taken away her fear, had made her feel safe, and she had willingly, even gladly, yielded her body to him. And by that single act—by her trust in him—she had compelled him to love her.

But she was a Helot slave and he was a Spartan. Eventually he would have to marry a Spartan maiden—that was the law. Marriage was a duty to the state. No future that included Iphigenia was possible. All they had was the present, however long that would last.

And so he knew he was a fool to love her, but he couldn't help himself. He couldn't even bring himself to regret it.

Iphigenia had opened a vein of tenderness in him he hadn't known existed.

The next afternoon, when he knew his father would be out, he went back. Iphigenia was waiting for him in the old bedroom.

"I knew you would come back today," she told him, and her eyes said she was glad.

"Did I hurt you?" he asked. "Do you still feel it?"

"Only a little."

"Then I won't touch you today."

"Are you sure?" She seemed even a little disappointed. "I don't mind if it hurts a little."

"But I mind for you. Today, it's enough simply to be with you."

And then she smiled and touched his face, and that moment seemed worth any sacrifice.

The next few months were perhaps the happiest of Eurytus's life. Iphigenia was not only beautiful but gentle and sweet-natured, qualities that constantly surprised him, as if he were forever just discovering them. Merely to look at her was like receiving a gift.

There was, of course, no provision for women in the soldiers' mess, so she continued to live in Dienekes's house and Eurytus visited her there whenever he could.

Simply by being in it, she made his world a different place.

Duty, honor, courage—the values upon which his life had been built— what were they except debts he felt compelled to pay? To be a Spartan was to be constantly sacrificing oneself, to one's ancestors and descendants and to the nation. It was like dying, over and over again.

A Spartan was taught that pain was nothing, that death was nothing. Then what was life?

Being with Iphigenia was being alive, and life became both precious and one's own.

What did she feel? He knew it shouldn't matter to him, but it did. Did she care for him at all? She seemed to enjoy it when he made love to her— it was not a thing that women could counterfeit nearly as well as they imagined—and perhaps that was enough. And perhaps not. Sometimes, when he was away from her, the thought that she was merely his property tortured him. He could not own her heart. That could be his only if she gave it freely.

But when he was with her his doubts left him and he was happy.

※※

And his happiness extended even into the work of preparing for the campaign against Thebes and into his growing relationship with King Agesilaus, who was a close friend of his father, immensely popular and considered a brilliant commander.

In the early days he spent a fair amount of time in conversation with Agesilaus, who had many questions: What sort of man was Epaminondas? What were Thebes's fortifications like? How well watered was the land around the city? What was the general quality of the Theban army? What use did they make of cavalry? What was the attitude of the other cities of Boeotia?

For many of these Eurytus had no answers, but he made every effort to find them. He spoke to men old enough to remember the days when Thebes had been an ally. "Good enough soldiers, but not like us." "Cavalry? What use are cavalry?" No one had very distinct memories of Epaminondas.

"I am thrown back on my own impressions," Eurytus told the king. "And, my lord, they are no more than impressions. I have seen him but never spoken to him. It is to be remembered that our own people dismissed him as a crank philosopher, not even important enough to drive into exile. And yet right under our eyes, in a single night, he took the city back. After the murder of the oligarchs, their army swung behind him to a man. Now he is the idol of Thebes. I think it safe to say they see something in him that we missed."

They sat on a pair of camp stools on a wide, empty stretch of the Laconian plain. Three hundred paces away two phalanxes were engaged in a mock battle, and the king's attention never left them. He was approaching sixty and was the most powerful man in the state—even King Kleombrotus deferred to him—yet he appeared a modest soul, easily approachable and willing to listen to intelligent advice.

Perhaps the fact that he was lame had kept him humble. One leg was slightly shorter than the other and had been so from birth, but he had never allowed himself or anyone else to use his infirmity as an excuse.

Everyone who had known him as a child or as a young man loved and admired him. And thus, when his brother died and his nephew was set aside on the grounds of illegitimacy, Agesilaus succeeded to the Eurypontid throne in spite of the ancient prophecy warning against a "lame reign."

"And he massacred the government we installed, down to the last man," Agesilaus said, without taking his eyes from the mock battle. "The assassination of an entire government—how did he do it?"

"I am informed it was done by a team of men disguised as courtesans— the late Lord Laius had invited his fellow oligarchs to a banquet and the sordid reputation of these entertainments guaranteed that all would attend. The operation was conducted with great efficiency, as I would have expected from the man who led it. People who inspected the scene report that almost all the wounds would have resulted in near-instant death. The assassins were probably in and out in less than a quarter of an hour."

"You know the man who led it?"

"Oh, yes." Eurytus allowed himself a single syllable of laughter. "We are almost old friends. I spoke to him two days after the event, but he didn't mention it. Perhaps he didn't regard it as important."

For the first time in several minutes the king allowed himself to be distracted from the military exercises on the plain. He stared at his new staff officer in apparent disbelief.

"You spoke to him? Who is he?"

"He is a runaway slave named Protos. He murdered my brother— apparently he was offended that Teleklos had killed his mother. You see, my lord, he is no respecter of the social order. He seems unable to grasp that killing a slave woman is permissible but killing one of us is not."

"I believe I have heard something of this affair. . . ."

"Yes, my lord. And now he has allied himself with the Thebans. He frightens me even more than Epaminondas. Epaminondas only wants to drive us away. Protos would destroy us all. He is cunning and without pity, and he gives every evidence of being able to walk through walls. We will have trouble with him in Boeotia."

❧❦

At that precise moment, in Thebes, Protos was sitting in the garden behind his house, pouring a cup of beer for Agenor, who still appeared to nurse a sense of grievance against him.

"You do not have to prove to me or anyone else that you are brave," Protos told him. "You came with us—that was the part that took courage. What happened inside had nothing to do with courage—is a butcher courageous when he slaughters an ox? But if you want to kill the enemies of Thebes, I will give you your chance. And I will not think any the less of you if you refuse it."

"What are you proposing?"

"A war that is the very reverse of everything you have been taught to admire. An inglorious war. A war more dangerous than battle. A war in which courage must remain your own private concern, which makes it all the harder to sustain. Anyone can be brave in front of his friends. It is bitter to die alone."

He then described to Agenor the plan that Epaminondas had presented to him.

"It will not be like combat," he said in conclusion. "In combat you face an enemy on equal terms, where you both have an equal chance. The point here will be to create a situation in which your enemy has no chance at all. Your chief virtue must be not courage but cunning. You kill one man and then go on to the next. But if you miscalculate you die.

"You will have to learn to fight like a gutter rat. Like me. But I am only a runaway slave and have nothing to live up to. You must forget honor."

Protos studied his face, knowing that Agenor had already made up his mind. It occurred to him that Agenor did not have the look of a fighting man, that in better times he probably would have been happy as a scholar or an architect. His glittering black eyes were full of intelligence—and fear.

Agenor was one of those who had to be always remaking the decision to be brave. Other men were brave from habit or necessity—that was how Protos saw himself—and some were brave from sheer lack of imagination. But Agenor had to choose courage, with death ever a presence in his soul. And in that choice, precisely because it was so hard, he purchased for himself a nobility of spirit few men could boast.

"But at least the enemy is truly the enemy," Agenor said.

Protos nodded.

"Yes, he is truly the enemy. The memory of having killed him will not shame you—and if he kills you instead, you will not have to worry about even that."

It was a jest and he smiled, but the smile died quickly.

"Tell me something, Agenor. That night, why did you even want to go in there with us? What is it that you are so eager to prove?"

Agenor's expression belonged to a man who is being forced to admit to some terrible secret. For a long time he said nothing.

But Protos was prepared to wait.

"My father . . ." Agenor made a small but desperate movement of his left hand. "My father supported the Spartan occupation. He did business with the oligarchs. He profited . . ."

"I see." Protos, who, as he waited for the truth, had let his face assume a masklike blankness, merely shrugged. "But you are not your father, and his choice was not yours."

"No. I left with the exiles. My father died two years ago and I did not even return for his funeral."

"Then Fate compelled you to make an unenviable choice, but the fault was not yours."

Agenor smiled bitterly and shook his head.

"But it has never *felt* that way. Sometimes one's conscience demands atonement, even if the crime was another's."

Yes, that is true, Protos thought. Had it been any different with his parents' death? They were innocent and he was innocent, yet he had been forced to accept the burden of vengeance.

"Agenor, tell me the truth," he said. "Have you ever killed a man?"

"No."

"Well then, you will have yet a few months to learn how it is done. And when the Spartans come back I will take you out one dark night and we will see if you have the stomach for it. It is not a thing a man can know until he has done it. And then you can decide."

※ ※

Agenor was only the first. By the time he was ready to begin training, Protos had gathered nearly forty recruits. With luck, he thought, he might end with fifteen.

The first order he gave them was, "Take off your sandals."

They seemed mystified, but they took them off.

"Until this last year," he told them, "I never owned sandals. Now I have one pair, which at this moment is under my bed."

This produced a ripple of nervous laughter, which made Protos smile.

"When you go home tonight, try walking across a stone floor in sandals. Keep your ears open and you will be appalled by how much noise you make. Just the sandal slapping against your foot is enough to wake the dead. Besides, sandals teach you to walk the wrong way. Watch this."

They were on the same athletic field where Protos had first made himself known to the Thebans. He strode across the grass, his head back, his arms pumping, making a parody of a parade ground strut.

His audience found this very amusing.

"You laugh, but do you see what I was doing?" He looked from one to the next. They seemed mystified. "The heel touches the ground first, then the toes. Here—I will do it again."

This time no one laughed.

"A young child does not walk thus, nor do I, nor does anyone too poor to own sandals. It is a habit you acquire because you are no longer afraid of the ground. You don't have to think about stones or nettles or the odd scorpion because your sandals will protect you. So you stride along, forgetting to respect Mother Earth. Well, my friends, this is the last day in which you can afford to be so forgetful."

He sat down on the ground and held his left foot up for inspection.

"You see that? The sole of my foot is one great callus. I can sharpen my knife on the soles of my feet. And when I walk my head is forward, and my toes touch the ground first that I may feel my way. And I am as silent as death."

He stood up again and looked about him. The lesson was beginning to sink in.

"Today I will be your nursemaid and you will be back in your infancy. You will learn to walk all over again. And after today you will throw your sandals away."

They circled around the athletic field in a line, ten paces apart, and Protos walked with each of them, teaching them how to touch down with the balls of their feet, to feel for the earth with their toes and then let their heels down softly. This went on for four hours, until they were ready to collapse. Many complained bitterly about bruises and stone cuts, but Protos only laughed.

"Babies' feet are harder than yours. But be not afraid, for they will toughen fast enough."

He sent them home at sundown.

"Tonight soak your feet in brine. Tomorrow I will teach you to run."

The next morning only thirty returned. Protos was glad to see that Agenor was one of them.

And so it went, day after day. How to walk. How to run. How to hide yourself in shadow. How to use the wind to cover your approach. How to kill silently.

"And above all learn not to hurry. Hurry is the mother of error, who is the father of death."

At the end of a month he was down to twelve recruits. Agenor was still one of them.

And the next day outriders reported a large Spartan force, moving north.

22

Eurytus rode out ahead of King Agesilaus's army to have a look at Thebes. He had marched the whole distance from Sparta, for he disliked horses, but doubtless the enemy had patrols out, so reconnaissance required speed.

He stopped on a low hill where he would remain concealed in a grove of trees. The city was an hour's walk to the north, but he had no trouble making out the system of earthworks and stockades that surrounded it. Epaminondas had been busy.

Which meant he had no intention of offering battle. He would play the hedgehog to Sparta's wolf.

Epaminondas would be a fool to offer battle, and Epaminondas was not a fool. The shape and even the outcome of the campaign were thus decided from the first instant.

King Agesilaus had a thousand men at his back. A thousand Spartans could conquer the immortal gods—except, of course, if they refused to come out and fight.

So it would be a campaign against granaries and herds of cattle. They would ravage the land, bringing starvation to the peasantry in a vain effort to weaken the city. They would threaten the other cities of Boeotia to keep them from returning to their old alliances with Thebes.

It wouldn't work. None of it would work. Eurytus toyed with the idea of advising King Agesilaus to turn around and go home, but that wouldn't work either. The inevitable political consequences didn't bear thinking about.

Besides, Eurytus was not eager to return to Sparta. As a staff officer he was allowed to be accompanied by his concubine, and this campaign was the first opportunity he had ever had to sleep through the night with Iphigenia. It was wonderful. To drift off listening to her slow, steady breathing was a pleasure he could hardly have imagined. To see her moving around in his tent while she made his breakfast . . .

He loved her. He knew it was folly, but he was helpless against it.

And then there was Protos, who was not the sort to sit quietly behind the earthworks and wait for the Spartans to leave.

I care nothing for the Thebans, Protos had told him. *I have my own reasons* . . .

Luring him out was the easy part. A Spartan army would prove irresistible. The trick would be to catch him or, better, to kill him.

Eurytus couldn't help it. Protos was his enemy and he wanted him dead, preferably by Eurytus's own hand. But he did not want him taken back to Sparta as a prisoner and then crucified. In the beginning, yes, but not now. He could not have said why.

The Spartans made their first camp at the edge of the Boeotian plain. It was perhaps a two-hour walk south of Thebes and thus amounted to an open challenge. Epaminondas ignored it.

But Protos did not. He had studied every cubit of that ground with a hunter's eye. He knew every tree, every bush, every gully. He could have walked from Thebes to the outworks of the Spartan camp in daylight, and they would never have seen him.

But he went at night, taking Agenor with him. It was time for Agenor to wet his blade.

They left at sunset. If it was a two-hour walk for a man with nothing to hide, it was four hours for one who knew the smallest mistake would mean death. They were barefoot and went toe and heel, toe and heel, leaning forward, in places almost bent double. It was an exhausting journey, but Agenor never complained. Even during training, when his feet had bled, he had never complained.

When they were within sight of the Spartan stockade, they hid in a riverbed that had not held water in living memory and Protos explained how the thing would be done.

"You see the guards patrolling just inside the earthworks? There is a ditch we will have to climb out of without making a noise but which also offers good concealment. The stockade is probably about a hundred and fifty paces to the side and I would guess there are probably eight men, four going around in one direction and four in the other. Thus, for half the time, as two men approach each other they are in sight of one another. Thus each can protect the other."

"So we will wait until they are walking away from each other?"

"No. We will attack while they face one another. We will use their defense against them. We will wait until they are each about twenty paces from the corner of the stockade, then you will come up behind the man on the right and kill him.

"Won't the man on the left warn him?"

"No. He will be too busy giving your man something to look at. In that instant, when all your man can think about is what is happening before his eyes, you will kill him. You won't have to worry about my man giving the alarm—he will be fully occupied with dying.

"Your man won't hear you, so be quick rather than quiet. Just kill him. And remember, if he does not die you surely will. Do not think and do not hesitate. As soon as he is dead, you run like a rabbit. Follow the route we took, but run."

"What will you be doing?"

"Amusing myself."

❧❦

The perimeter was illuminated by torches. Iron stands to hold them had been set out every forty or so paces. The result was that the Spartan guards were visible and their attackers were not. Protos regarded this as a small gift from people who seemed to think war could be fought only on the battlefield.

But the first obstacle was the ditch. It was only a little deeper than a man was tall, but the earth dug from it was piled up on the far side. Thus one had to go down into the ditch and then climb up a hill of loose earth.

"Take the hill at an angle," he had told Agenor. "Don't try to go straight up. The hill is steep enough that you will be on your hands and knees, so use your swords—that is why we each brought two. Stab them into the earth and use them as handholds. And be quiet about it."

It was a dirty, slow, dangerous business, but eventually they both got to the top of the earthworks and, as Protos stared down at the guards, still walking their picket line, it was clear they had heard nothing.

Agenor was about a hundred paces down the earthworks, a distance at which Protos could just make out his head.

They waited as, at precisely the same instant, the guards each turned a corner of the stockade and began walking toward one another. Protos watched his man, counting the steps. One, two, three, four . . .

At twenty paces he began slithering down the hill. The distance between the earthworks and the walls of the stockade was no more than about twelve paces, and as he came down he rolled and crouched behind one of the torch stands.

The torches provided an extra advantage—they were so bright that everything directly behind them was almost invisible.

Protos waited just long enough to confirm that he had not been noticed, then he rose up, grasping his Spartan dagger by the blade, took an instant to judge the distance, and threw.

The guard hardly seemed to know what had happened to him. For a moment Protos wondered if he hadn't missed, and then he saw the dagger hilt sticking out of the back of the man's neck. The guard took a step, then another, and collapsed.

His colleague stopped for a moment, apparently trying to puzzle out what had happened. Protos stepped out from behind the torch stand to give him something to look at.

Protos raised his arm and waved at the guard—anything to keep him from noticing that Agenor was coming up fast behind him.

Agenor did it exactly the way he had been taught. With his left hand he reached around the man's neck and pulled sharply up on his jawbone. Then he brought the sword in his right hand around low and stabbed him just under the rib cage, driving the blade up.

The guard went briefly rigid before dropping first to his knees and then down on his face.

Agenor simply stood there, as if he couldn't believe what had just happened. He seemed frozen.

Protos broke into a run—there was no time for this nonsense—and when he reached Agenor he shoved him violently.

"Get out of here," he whispered through clenched teeth. "Go!"

That was enough. Agenor came back to life and started clawing his way back up the earthworks. In an instant he was gone.

Protos reached down and relieved the dead guard of his sword. He ran silently to the corner of the stockade and pressed himself against the wall, forcing himself to breathe slowly so that he could hear. He was listening for the next guard.

Soon enough, he heard the soft crunch of sandals against the stony earth. The guard turned the corner and found himself staring straight into

Protos's face. He was so surprised that he might never have felt the sword point sliding into his heart.

Protos did not wait. He pulled his sword free, turned and ran back the way he had come. There would be another guard rounding the opposite corner of the stockade, and he would see the bodies and raise the alarm.

Protos was perhaps fifty paces from him when the guard began to shout. Without breaking stride, he reached down and yanked his dagger free from the neck of the corpse that stretched across his path.

Apparently the guard who was shouting hadn't seen him yet. He turned his head and his eyes went wide with surprise. He was still struggling with his sword when Protos killed him.

Time to go home. Protos was over the earthworks and running for any cover he could find when he heard the Spartan alarm trumpet. It would take them most of a quarter of an hour to organize any response, and it would be interesting to see if they thought to send out search parties. He found a gully where he was safe from any immediate threat and threw himself down on the grass. At first all he could think about was catching his breath, but finally it occurred to him to notice how very dry the grass was.

When he heard enough shouting back and forth to indicate the Spartans were beyond their earthworks, Protos started on his way.

He found Agenor at the edge of the Theban earthworks, sitting on a log with his hands covering his face. Protos took him by the arm and shook him out of his trance.

"I failed," Agenor said, his voice full of self-reproach.

"You didn't fail. You were just awed by what you had done. It's always that way the first time. But it was a perfect kill."

"I didn't think it would be like that," Agenor went on—Protos couldn't be sure he was even listening. "I thought . . . I don't know what I thought."

"Don't worry about it now. We'll go back to my house and Nubit will have warm water to clean ourselves, and we will drink too much beer. In the morning it will seem like something from another life."

"Do you promise?"

"I promise."

❧❦

Eurytus stood outside the stockade wall, observing as twenty or thirty soldiers staggered around out beyond the earthworks, looking for some trace of a man or men who had long since vanished.

He cared nothing for their search, which was pointless. The only thing of any use would be to find out what had happened here.

To that end, Eurytus gave orders that no one except himself be allowed on the picket line. He wanted the scene undisturbed, which of course was not entirely possible, since he had not been the first to arrive.

Still, it might be enough. The four bodies were where they had fallen, and the ground was not quite so gravelly that it wouldn't take the impress of a foot.

Eurytus kept close to the earthworks as he walked over the picket line, trying to reconstruct the sequence of events. It wasn't long before he was sure this was the work of two men.

It stood to reason that the man who had raised the alarm, whose name was Bukelos and whose voice had been recognized by the watch, had been the last to die. So Bukelos had come upon three bodies and had then been killed himself. Of those three, the one at the very corner of the stockade could not have been killed if the other two were not already dead—they would have spotted the attacker and raised the alarm themselves.

Thus the question became, how did those two men die? From the positions of the bodies they were walking toward one another. One man couldn't have killed them both. It would have taken two men, working together with almost inhuman precision.

The guards passed each other several times an hour, day after day, so there were thousands of footprints along the picket line. The interesting ones were the prints of bare feet—Spartan soldiers wore sandals.

It was easy to trace where intruders had come over the earthworks, which showed clear evidence of having been disturbed. The prints left in that soft earth were of bare feet. They came down in two places and, by measuring the prints against his own foot, Eurytus concluded that one set was slightly larger than the other.

Small Foot had come over the earthworks, killed the man on what would have been to him the right side of the stockade, and gone back the way he had come. Big Foot's prints were everywhere.

There was a line of them between the man killed at the corner and Bukelos. From the length of the stride, Big Foot had been running. The distance was something like 130 paces.

Who in the world would have the testicles to charge a Spartan warrior, all alone and over so great a distance? The question answered itself.

"What happened here?"

It was the voice of the king. He was still in his night clothes, with only a cloak thrown over them. He glanced about like a man who could not bring himself to believe what he was seeing.

"Eurytus, what is going on?"

"My lord, we now know that we have two wars to fight—one against Thebes and the other against Protos the Helot." Eurytus could not quite suppress a bitter smile. "And Protos the Helot has drawn first blood."

23

The girls had been sent to bed early, but they never troubled to close the door to their room and Nubit could hear them whispering among themselves.

They were frightened. Protos had not joined them for supper and they had all seen the way his eyes seemed to flash and his jaw muscles worked as he waited to leave for what he described simply as "an appointment."

"He is like that night," Eupraxia said—no one could doubt what night she meant. "He has on his killing face."

It was something about him that they knew and Nubit did not. She had seen him kill the two men who had come to her wagon, but he had been perfectly calm about it, almost detached, perhaps because he had sensed no danger. He must have been someone else entirely the night he led the attack on the oligarchs.

Nubit kept remembering how, that first day in their new home, Galene had cowered in terror before him, clutching at his feet in supplication.

After an hour the girls were still awake. At last, Nubit went into their room and sat down on the floor.

"You must not be afraid of Protos," she said quietly. "You do him an injustice if you are afraid of him. He is like the dog you have raised from a puppy, who will lick your hand and put his head in your lap and never dream of hurting you, yet will growl at strangers. As you have seen, Protos is terrible against his enemies. But he loves you and will always protect you.

"Now go to sleep."

A quarter of an hour later she checked again and could hear the soft murmur of their breathing. They were asleep and their dreams were tranquil.

It was a strange life she was leading, she thought. She had daughters who were not her own and a man who belonged more to blind Fate than to her. She felt like the watchman who guarded another man's treasure. Nothing truly belonged to her.

And someday, she knew, it would all be taken away. The Great Mother had Her own purposes, which She kept from the eyes of poor, blind mortals. The truth of things could only be known when it was too late and no longer mattered.

It was well after midnight when Protos returned. He had Agenor with him. Nubit did not ask what they had been doing. They were both filthy, as if they had been playing in the mud, and she made them wait in the garden while she heated water with which they could clean themselves.

She brought them beer while they waited. Agenor was strangely distraught, as if some disaster had befallen him, so she smeared a few drops of opium around the inside of his cup and after a while he became placid.

"We shall have to lock the door," Nubit said, once Agenor was sufficiently drunk to be put unresistingly to bed in the spare room.

"Why?"

"To keep the girls out, you fool." She looked at Protos with playful scorn. "They are very curious about young men."

Protos considered the matter for a moment and then nodded, for it made perfect sense to him. "I suppose, growing up in the household of a fat, elderly lecher, they must wonder . . ."

"Precisely."

He laughed and slid his hand into the neck of her shirt, cupping it over her breast.

"Did you enjoy yourself tonight?" she asked, and kissed his wrist.

"I would not describe killing as a pleasure, but it has its satisfactions."

"Revenge?"

"Yes."

"And is it possible that some day you might include in your revenge some larger purpose?"

"Such as what?"

"You were a slave and are the child of slaves, and you can ask me that?"

She said no more of the matter, but took her clothes off and climbed into bed. They made love and afterward, as always, she fell promptly asleep.

Perhaps it was still the excitement of the raid or perhaps something else, but Protos found himself broad awake, his mind whirring like a beehive.

Some larger purpose. What did Nubit mean? She was a wise woman, wiser in some ways than any man. She never spoke without intention.

What did he care about? Nubit and his revenge. The girls, yes. Thebes, but distantly.

What did a man like Epaminondas care about? His city—the place and the people in it. He had been born in Thebes and loved it—apparently more than any woman, since he had never married.

What did a runaway slave have to compare with that? His family were all dead. He had no city, no country. Such allegiances were denied to slaves. Whom did they have, except each other?

Was that what Nubit had meant? What could he do for the Helots—particularly since he could never return to Laconia? Free them? That was impossible. It would be necessary first to destroy Sparta, and no one could do that. Sparta was like a lion and he was but one small thorn in its paw.

※ ※

But a thorn, if not fatal, could at least be very irritating. And to that end Protos spent the next four days wandering about in the great yellow grassland that was the Boeotian plain.

His twelve carefully trained fighters in what, among themselves, they had come to call "the little war," could not understand it. Protos had taken only one of them out for a single raid and then seemed to withdraw into himself. Occasionally one or two would go out and sit with him, but he hardly seemed to notice their presence. Otherwise, they rarely saw him.

Finally, around noon on the fourth day, Agenor came out, carrying a jar of beer. He found Protos perched on a rock about the size and shape of an overturned chariot, staring at the Spartan stockade.

Agenor broke the seal on the jar, took a swallow and handed the jar to Protos.

"What is in your mind?" he asked finally. "The men are restless."

Protos at first appeared not to have heard and then, with a little jerk of his head, he seemed to snatch himself back from whatever place his mind had been wandering.

He smiled.

"Yes, I suppose they are. What do you suggest I do about it?"

"Give them some way to torment the Spartans."

Protos nodded. "Very well. Bring them here, to this very spot, an hour before sunset, and we'll decide what to do."

We'll decide what to do. Agenor went trudging back to Thebes feeling little satisfied with the outcome of the conversation.

Protos, in his view, had never adjusted to being a commander. He was a good teacher and absolutely terrifying in a fight, but he seemed to resist assuming authority.

The men wanted him to lead. They wanted him to say, *Here is what each of you will do.* He could have said, *Let's go conquer the Underworld,* and they would gladly have followed him. They were in awe of him. But they wanted to hear orders.

Agenor suddenly remembered that Protos had kept the beer jar.

Nevertheless, Agenor hunted everyone up, and one hour before sunset they clustered around the chariot rock.

"Did anyone think to bring some beer?"

They all understood their leader, so several jars were available. Protos took one and sat contentedly drinking it while the others waited.

"Do you feel the wind?" he asked finally.

"What wind? Protos, there is no wind. What are you talking about?"

"Just wait."

Sure enough, in about a quarter of an hour the wind began to rise in the west.

"It comes down from the mountains every evening at this time," Protos said, his glance shifting from one face to another, as if searching for something. "One hardly feels it in the city because Thebes is built on high ground, but as the plain drops down the wind increases. If we were sitting even half an hour's walk south of here, we would find it stiff enough."

He reached down and ran his hand over the dry, brittle grass.

"Suppose we did something, let us say, half an hour before sunset—something that would provoke the Spartans into coming out in pursuit. Suppose we managed to lure them west, well away from their stockade. And then suppose a grassfire mysteriously ignited some twenty or thirty paces in front of them. What would be the result?"

No one answered.

"It happened once when I was seven," he went on, smiling at the recollection. "It was at harvesttime and a storm was coming. Everyone was eager to get as much of the grain in as possible before it rained. The wind was high. We all knew there wasn't much time.

"Then out of nowhere, there was a lightning strike in the middle of the field. I can remember the sound of it. I thought my head would split. It was the sort of thing that makes you believe in the gods' wrath.

"The lightning started a fire and the wind picked it up. You never saw anything travel faster than those flames. Three people were caught in the fire and burned to death. I saw the bodies—they were scorched black. Then, just as suddenly, the rains came, so we didn't lose our village, but while it lasted the fire was terrible to see."

They all maintained a perfect silence for perhaps as long as it would take to count to twenty, and then Agenor spoke.

"Would the fire burn down the Spartan stockade?"

"No." Protos shook his head. "The earthworks would protect it. I am thinking only of the soldiers who would come out in pursuit of us."

"The fire would have to be broad enough," someone said—it was a good sign; they had accepted the idea and were concerning themselves only with the specifics. "Otherwise they'll simply run around it."

"The fire will broaden as it travels." Protos closed his eyes for a moment, perhaps to enjoy the sight of it in his imagination. "But you are right. It will have to be fifty or sixty paces wide at the beginning."

"We'll have somehow to start it along its whole width at once."

"Then what would burn quickly enough?"

"Lamp oil?"

It was Agenor's suggestion. His black, intelligent eyes seemed to come alive.

"Then we know how to do it. All we need is to make them angry enough to come out after us." Protos shrugged. "I'll think of something."

❧❦

A Spartan solder named Kynortas was walking between rows of tents set up within the stockade. He was thirty-five years old, which meant that he had a wife and a house. After the barracks, he found marriage agreeable. His wife was not a beauty, but she was pleasant company and knew how to be entertaining. They had a three-year-old son and an infant daughter.

Thus, although war was a Spartan's purpose in life, Kynortas was not thrilled to be on campaign in Boeotia. He missed his family. He missed his house. He missed sleeping in a bed away from the stink of other men.

He was hungry. At home he ate when he felt like it. On campaign he ate on a schedule and there was no chance for even a morsel of bread until dusk, which wouldn't be for another hour.

He was just glancing at the stockade walls to see if the sun had disappeared behind them when his eyes caught a flicker of movement. There was no time for more than an instant of surprise before a javelin fell out of the clear sky and buried itself in his bowels. His knees gave way at once under the shock. He was facedown on the earth before the pain surged through him. Within minutes he had bled to death.

❦❦

A soldier sleeps when he can and Eurytus, knowing he would be on night exercises in a few hours, was taking a nap when he was awakened, either by the alarm trumpet or by Iphigenia sitting up beside him, he knew not which. He snatched away the cloth that covered his face and was on his feet in an instant.

"Stay here," he told her. "Whatever happens, you'll be safe here. Promise me?"

She nodded, staring at him with enormous, terrified eyes.

As soon as he had crawled out of his tent he could see that everyone was heading to the west wall of the stockade. There was a ladder to a sentry post at the top of the wall, and when Eurytus had climbed it and could look out his first reaction was simply a vast irritation. He was not surprised. He was not even angry. But this was too much.

For there was Protos, wearing nothing but a loincloth, his skin as shiny as bronze, standing on a small, grass-covered mound, with two javelin quivers holding about twenty apiece lying on the ground near his right foot. He was holding one of the javelins in his hand. He was laughing at them.

"Protos, stop this nonsense," Eurytus heard himself shout. Even in his own ears it seemed an idiotic thing to say.

Protos's only answer was a deep, deliberately comic bow.

"He's already killed two men," the watch officer said. "The first was luck—he threw a spear over the wall and hit some fellow who happened to be walking by. Then he killed one of mine."

The watch officer was seething with suppressed rage, but Eurytus hardly noticed. His eye was measuring the distance from the wall to where Protos had taken his stand.

"He threw it *over* the wall?"

"Yes."

The javelin was not Eurytus's weapon, so he could not be sure, but he would have wagered much that Protos was outside of effective range.

"Has anyone answered back?" he asked. "Has anyone even *tried* to hit him?"

"Yes. They all fell short."

"And they had the advantage of throwing from above. But he can throw over the wall."

All Eurytus could do was shrug. He decided that nothing about Protos would ever surprise him again.

"I've sent for an archer," the watch officer said.

There were moments when Eurytus almost believed the Spartans deserved to lose. An archer? Brilliant. Archers were trained for distance but not for accuracy. When one's target was a phalanx twenty men deep, what was gained by being able to hit a single man?

The archer came, the arrows in his quiver rattling with every step he took up the ladder, but while he was stringing his bow he suddenly pitched over dead, a javelin through his chest.

"I saw that coming," Protos shouted. "Eurytus, son of Dienekes, have the Spartans no one with any strength in his arm?"

Another javelin sailed in and killed the watch officer. He stood there staring at it, made helpless by disbelief, as it flew toward him and caught him at the base of the throat.

They had hardly cleared the two corpses away before the king came up the ladder. Everyone saluted.

"What is going on here?"

Instinctively, Eurytus turned to glance at Protos.

Because Protos had seen everything. He had seen the way everyone had come to attention. He was already winding himself up for a throw.

Eurytus did not wait. He hurled himself at the king, knocking him off his feet. They hit the wooden floor with a thud, which did not quite drown out a sound like a hammer hitting a nail.

Eurytus looked up and saw the javelin with its point buried in a support post, its shaft still quivering from the impact.

The king, of course, had understood nothing. From the way he struggled to free himself from his grasp, he probably thought Eurytus had tried to assassinate him.

Eurytus released him and climbed to his feet.

"You missed, Protos," he shouted, clutching the railing of the watch post. "You missed your mark!"

"There will be others, Eurytus, son of Dienekes," came the answer. "I can wait."

By then the king was sitting up. Someone helped him to his feet. He came over and stood beside Eurytus.

"I owe you my life," he said, putting a hand on Eurytus's shoulder.

"Best to get out of sight, my lord. He may try again."

The king followed his gaze to the man in a loincloth, standing on a mound perhaps a hundred paces beyond the stockade walls. He turned back to Eurytus, his eyes seeking some explanation.

"That is Protos the Helot, my lord."

"And whom have you denied me the honor of killing, Eurytus, son of Dienekes?" came the mocking question from the mound. "Is he one of your feckless generals? He looks a little old for the work."

This was too much for the king.

"I am Agesilaus, slave, of the Eurypontid Dynasty, King of Sparta, and I trace my ancestors back to the immortal gods!"

The two men stood looking at one another, the king quivering with rage, and then suddenly Protos made another low bow. When he straightened up again he was grinning.

"Then may they protect you, Agesilaus, for it appears you command an army of women, content to hide behind their stockade walls forever. Even a cornered rabbit will fight."

He took a step back and his body coiled for another throw. The javelin flew well over the stockade walls, but everyone in the watch post ducked.

Protos laughed. It was a loud, hearty sound filled with good-natured contempt, and it was more than the king's honor could bear.

"Send a patrol after that naked rogue," he almost screamed. "And cavalry. Send cavalrymen to chase him down. I want him nailed to the stockade wall before he's an hour older!"

"My lord . . ." Eurytus put his hand on the king's arm, but Agesilaus shook it off.

"Do it."

"My lord, I know him. It is a trap."

"Is the army of Sparta to tremble before a slave? *Do it!*"

❧ ❧

Protos knew that the stockade gates were in the north and south walls, so he had two men positioned well away from either side who could flash him a signal with a copper mirror when either was opened.

Predictably, it was the north gate, the one facing Thebes.

There would be foot soldiers, but anyone with eyes could see that there was a break in the earthworks in front of the north gate and a drawbridge over the ditch, so there might be horsemen as well. Epaminondas made his spies' reports accessible to Protos, so he knew the Spartan cavalry numbered no more than twenty. They were used principally as scouts, since the Spartans had never really grasped that horses could be used for anything else.

Protos didn't think the Spartans would waste many horsemen chasing down a slave. He hoped not, because he liked horses and he knew he might have to kill these.

Sure enough, to his left he saw dust kicked up by their hooves. The cavalry was heading northwest, the direction they would have to assume Protos would take to reach the safety of Thebes. He had no intention of disappointing them.

Protos picked up the quiver of javelins and stepped down from his mound into a ravine that ran generally north and south for perhaps seventy paces in either direction and would allow him to escape unseen. He went north. He had to deal with the horses first.

One of the advantages a mounted soldier had was height. From the back of a horse he could see much farther than a man on the ground. It was also a disadvantage because the rider himself was more visible.

It took no time to spot the cavalry. There were three of them, clustered together, looking about as if they had lost their way. The wind was already blowing west to east, so the horses never smelled Protos as he crept toward them.

At fifty paces the riders were easy marks—it was simply a question of whether he could kill all three before they spotted him and tried to run him down.

The first rider was in profile, so he made a smaller target but the horse's head wasn't in the way. He never saw the javelin that killed him.

Protos squatted down, trying to make himself invisible. The other two riders were shouting and yanking their horses' heads about as they searched for their attacker. Protos gave them a moment and then stood up, chose his target and threw.

A second man slumped forward and slid from his horse's neck to the ground.

The third man saw him and prepared to charge. The horse's head blocked Protos's throw—he would have to kill the horse.

He waited, letting the horse charge him, hoping he might somehow get a chance at the rider, but it was not to be. At the last possible moment he threw and the horse stumbled and went down.

The rider shot over the horse's neck and landed almost at Protos's feet. He didn't live long.

Protos shooed the two remaining horses into flight—let the Spartans see them coming back without their riders—then he went hunting.

❧❧

The last of the Spartan foot soldiers were making their way down the crumbling hill of dirt and into the ditch. The rest were spread out in a wide search pattern. At a range of forty paces, Protos picked out the closest man and threw.

It was almost too easy. He killed two more before they even realized where he was. Then three javelins came at him, but he simply stepped out of the way and their points were buried harmlessly in the dirt.

"You'll have to do better than that, friends," he shouted. Then he threw another javelin—he had only a few left—and a foot soldier pitched over dead, knocking the man behind him down.

Six or seven javelins came at him—probably out of pure vexation, someone even threw a sword—but with an instinct even he did not understand Protos glanced at their pattern in the air and knew where each would come down. He stepped to one side and their points sank into the earth all around him, enclosing him like a fence.

"Are you really Spartans?" he called, his hands over his head in a gesture of disbelief. "Really?"

After that they would have chased after him into the mouths of Kerberos. All he had to do was turn on his heel and run.

He let them gain on him. The closest was perhaps ten paces behind when a wall of fire erupted in front of him. Protos merely jumped through it and kept running.

His men waited on the other side, their swords drawn, but apparently none of the Spartans thought to follow him. Even above the roar of the fire, one could hear their screams.

24

"Once in Corinth, when I was very young, I saw a famous dancer," the king said—he was deep in wine and therefore disposed to be conversational. "She was a Persian woman, as nimble as a cat, and beautiful. . . . She was a slave, and her master had once refused an offer of five talents of pure gold from an Egyptian prince who wanted to marry her. When she danced it was like water flowing. I had never seen anything like her, and never expected to again.

"Yet, your Protos was not less graceful. Did you see what he did? Spears falling all around, and nothing could touch him.

"How many did we lose today, Eurytus?"

"Twenty-seven. Ten died at Protos's hand, the rest in the fire."

"It was a trap. You were right. I should have listened to you."

There was little enough honor in being right. There was little enough honor in having saved the king's life. What honor could there possibly be for anyone in such a humiliating defeat?

Eurytus had learned through experience that he did not have a head for wine. If he drank too much he would fall asleep, and it would not do to fall asleep in the presence of a king. Therefore he drank little and listened as King Agesilaus, his new patron, a man ready to acknowledge his wisdom and the deep personal obligation he owed him, described his awe of Protos the slave boy.

It was perhaps the bitterest moment of Eurytus's life.

They were in the king's tent, just the two of them. The king lay on his bed, staring up at nothing. A single oil lamp burned on a table beside his head. Eurytus sat on a stool, his elbows on his knees, his hands clapped around the lower part of his face. He would have preferred to be almost anywhere else, but the king, apparently, dreaded being alone. It was as if he was afraid that even here, in the center of his army, Protos might come for him.

For a long time, neither spoke.

"Worse even than the losses in men, he made us look ridiculous," the king said finally. "The most important asset an army or a nation can have is prestige. Our aura of invincibility is half our power. And now this boy . . ."

He reached for his wine cup and then frowned, discovering it was empty. Eurytus refilled it for him.

"He has to be stopped. We have to kill him. The best would be if we could capture him and put him to death in public."

"We will never capture him, my lord. He will fight to the death, but he will never surrender himself."

"Then he is a fanatic, eh?"

Eurytus could only smile. "No more or less than we would be, my lord, facing crucifixion."

"Yes—well, I suppose there is some truth in that." The king took a swallow of his wine. "What do you know about him?"

"Next to nothing." With his left hand Eurytus made a small gesture of helplessness. "I have spoken to him three times before today. I know that he prefers beer to wine. I know that it would be a terrible error to underestimate him."

For a long time Eurytus was silent. He felt empty.

Finally he looked at the king's face and discovered he was asleep. He was still holding his wine cup, so Eurytus gently took it from his unresisting hand.

Then he got up and wandered into the black night.

❧❧

When he returned to his tent, Eurytus found Iphigenia still awake.

"You were gone so long," she said. "I was afraid . . ."

She did not finish the sentence, leaving him to wonder exactly what she might have been afraid of. That he had been killed? It would be pleasant to think so.

But he could not entirely suppress the thought that it might have been something else she feared. What might she have heard of this affair? What might she have guessed?

"There was an attack. . . ." He shook his head. "Attack" was too strong a word. "There was an incident—a provocation. It was the bait for a trap, and several men were killed."

"Was it your enemies?"

It was an interesting choice of words. Not "*our* enemies" or "*the* enemy," but "*your.*" But then, Iphigenia could not be blamed if she did not side with the Spartans.

"There was only one enemy, and he is not a Theban."

Iphigenia said nothing. She was waiting, expectant. And suddenly Eurytus discovered that he wanted desperately to tell her about Protos the Helot. Perhaps then he would understand the story himself.

"There is a man I once wronged," he began—hardly knowing how to begin, except with the truth. "He is a Helot, like you. Now he fights for the Thebans, but only because they fight Sparta. He would destroy us if he could. I can't say I would have felt any different were I in his place."

"What did you do to him?"

"I murdered his father."

The word had just slipped out. It was the first time Eurytus had acknowledged, to himself or to anyone else, that he had done evil that night.

Somehow, this night, it was impossible to say anything else. It was impossible to lie.

"Then did he come to avenge himself?"

"Upon me in particular? No. He will someday, but until today I doubt he even knew I was here."

"But he knows now?"

"Yes. I spoke to him."

He smiled. She was so beautiful and she understood nothing of this strange story. How could she? How could anyone who was not bound up in it?

"What is his name?"

"Protos."

After a moment, Iphigenia looked away.

"I have heard him spoken of," she said.

Yes, she would have. Everyone knew that some of the Helots in camp spied for the Thebans, and the Helots probably thought of Protos as a hero.

It occurred to Eurytus that he would never be able to trust her again.

❧❦

A few mornings later, well before dawn, Protos rose from his bed and went down to the kitchen, where he rebuilt the hearth fire. By the time he had it properly ablaze, he could hear the sounds of bare feet on the stairs.

Galene stuck her head through the doorway, saw Protos and frowned.

"Go back to bed," she ordered, in a voice she had learned from Nubit. "We are making breakfast this morning."

One after the other, the three girls trooped into the kitchen in their night tunics. It was obvious from the expression on their faces that their plans had been laid in advance and they would brook no opposition.

"Very well, but you must promise me not to burn down the house."

His jest was not met with very good grace and he considered it wisest to retreat soundlessly up the stairs.

When he crawled back into bed, he discovered that Nubit was awake.

"They have been planning this for days," she said. "You will of course find everything delicious, no matter how it tastes. They will probably be another half an hour."

"Half an *hour*! In that time I will be starving to death."

"Then you will have less trouble feigning pleasure in your breakfast."

In the end some histrionic talent was required. Breakfast consisted of lentil porridge, with an interesting but perhaps over-liberal admixture of fennel, toasted bread the color of river mud, beer and pieces of lamb fried until they were as stiff as wood chips. To make matters worse, the portions were gigantic and the girls stood around the bed studying Protos's reaction to every bite.

He managed to convince Galene and Eupraxia of the meal's tastiness, but little Hemera, the baby, who had burnt the flatbread, was in tears.

"I like it this way," he told her. "My mother made it this way—brown and crisp."

"It's not brown, it's black."

"No, it isn't. It's just very brown."

"Really?"

"Really. I hate soggy flatbread."

When the girls had cleared away the trays and were back in the kitchen, Nubit leaned against Protos's shoulder and kissed him.

"You were very convincing," she murmured into his ear. "But you have condemned yourself to several months of burned flatbread."

"Eventually she will learn."

"Eventually."

"And for now she's stopped crying."

25

Since they could not breach the defenses of Thebes, the Spartans had settled on a policy of ravaging the countryside. They burned fields and houses and drove off cattle, and they met any resistance with their customary brutality.

"This is pointless," Eurytus told his king. "We have succeeded in nothing except making ourselves thoroughly hated. The peasants will have a hard winter, and who will they blame? Epaminondas? No, us. And we have done everything possible to intimidate the other cities of Boeotia, with no result except to persuade them that in us they and Thebes have a common enemy. In the end, none of this will be to our advantage."

"Then what would you recommend?"

King Agesilaus was sitting on his camp bed and, without the slightest hint of movement, his whole posture had suddenly become more alert, even expectant.

And in that moment Eurytus understood that the king was waiting to hear confirmed the conclusion he had already reached alone. It was an opportunity loaded with danger. The wrong response might force Agesilaus into some face-saving action that he would subsequently regret—and would know who to blame for it.

Eurytus paused and took a deep breath, letting it out slowly.

"It is time to go home," he said finally. "There is nothing to be gained here."

"And how do we counter the inevitable accusation of failure?"

Allowing himself a faint smile, Eurytus shook his head. By telling the truth, he had given the right answer.

"Through a slight shift of emphasis," he answered. It was going to be so easy now. "By their unwillingness to face us in open combat, we will say, the Thebans have proved both their weakness and their cowardice. That this does not happen to be true, since all they have really demonstrated is that they are not fools, we can mask it behind a threat to come back next year—and every succeeding year until they come out from behind their walls. But next year is a year away."

There was a tray with two pottery cups and a jar of wine on the table beside the king's bed. Agesilaus picked up the jar and filled both cups, handing one of them to Eurytus.

"It shall be as you suggest," he said quietly, and then raised his cup in salute. "My boy, you have an adder's cunning."

⁂

And so it was that, two days later, the Spartans simply left. They burned their stockade and took the road south.

The people of Thebes, whose army had never offered battle, rejoiced as if at a great victory. The celebration lasted for days.

And over the next few months Epaminondas and the army he had almost single-handedly brought back into existence marched around Boeotia, from city to city, in a not quite threatening display of power. But the point had been made and in every instance the result was the same: the Spartan-style oligarchy capitulated and was driven out, a democracy was established and the people rejoiced and voted to join the Boeotian confederacy.

These developments were watched from Sparta with growing uneasiness. The Thebans were rapidly gaining allies. Something had to be done. At the very least, Thebes had to be prevented from winning support outside of Boeotia.

It was for this reason that, shortly after Eurytus's return home, his father was selected as an ambassador to Athens. Eurytus agreed to accompany him.

"This whole situation could become quite awkward," Dienekes told his son at the start of their sea journey from Laconia. They were standing together at the stern, and Dienekes looked back at the receding coastline of Laconia with genuine regret. He hated ships. He was always miserably sick and he dreaded storms. But a ship was faster than the land route and they were in a hurry.

"The Thebans are easily defeated," he went on, "always provided, of course, that they can be persuaded to come out from behind their earthworks and fight. The whole of Boeotia is perhaps another matter. No one seems sure whether this new Boeotian League will hold together. In either case, we have to find some means of keeping Athens neutral."

"I don't think it will prove difficult. Why should they interfere while Thebes and Sparta tear at each other? We are both enemies of long standing."

His son, as usual, made very good sense.

"I agree in theory," Dienekes answered, carefully stressing the word "theory," "but they supported Epaminondas's insurrection with troops, and democracies are unpredictable creatures."

"They supported Epaminondas to force us out of the north. That done, their sympathy for Thebes doubtless evaporated."

It seemed so simple—perhaps it really was that simple. Dienekes was reminded of his father, who had possessed the same knack for reducing any problem to its essence. His father, he suspected, had despised him as a simpleton.

At least he had been spared a similar disappointment in his own son.

"Thus it becomes no more than a question of bribing the right politicians?"

Eurytus cocked his head faintly to one side, implying, *When was it ever not so?*

※ ※

That night there was a howling wind. Dienekes, alone in his cabin, found the noise unbearable. Finally he wrapped himself in his cloak and went up on deck.

"The gods favor us, my lord," the captain told him. The man's face was covered with spray and he was grinning like an idiot. "With a wind like this at our back, we'll be in Athens day after tomorrow."

The sound of the wind was like a woman screaming—like his wife in one of her rages—but Dienekes found it more tolerable here than in his cabin, where he couldn't help imagining the ship was about to be swamped. On deck it was merely wind, not the voice of Death.

Death. Perhaps what he heard was the ghost of his wife, calling to him. Nagging him.

Her father had been a famous commander and his father's closest friend. Dienekes had been old enough to have fought in the last year of the great war against Athens, and then there had been peace for almost ten years. A soldier cannot cover himself with glory in peacetime, but Aella had never been able to grasp something so obvious.

And by the time the Corinthian War had begun, and he had achieved everything anyone could have expected of him, their dislike for each other had settled into a habit.

And then she had died, had collapsed while walking home from a visit to her parents. The physicians had claimed she died of heart failure, but Dienekes had never believed that. Aella's heart was the least vulnerable thing about her.

At the time Dienekes had been forty. His friends had expected he would remarry, but it was not an experiment he cared to risk twice. There were always servant girls if one felt the need, and the peaceful quiet that had descended on his house was a continuing pleasure.

The boys had been given leave to come home and attend their mother's funeral rites. Weeping would have been unseemly, but, even so, Eurytus at least had appeared strangely unmoved.

Every year, on the anniversary of her death, Dienekes visited his wife's grave to offer a libation of wine. He wished her to rest quietly and to leave him in peace.

So the wind wasn't Aella's voice. It was merely wind.

There were times when he missed her, though. Dienekes had come to understand that the fact of a relationship can sometimes be more important than its character. It was possible to hate someone and, if the hatred occupied a central enough place in one's life, feel that person's death as a loss.

His wife had been harder on Eurytus than on Teleklos, perhaps sensing some weakness in him that needed buttressing. Perhaps she had been right. Perhaps, Dienekes suspected, she could have explained the change that had occurred in their son since that ghastly business of the Helot slave boy.

"Eurytus is like your father," she had told him once. "He is clever"— implying, of course, that in her husband that quality had skipped a generation. "You see how he manages his brother. Teleklos's weakness is that he lacks the imagination to be afraid of anything."

"Fearlessness is a virtue."

"Yes." She had smiled as she said it. "It is the virtue of fools."

What had she known about Eurytus that his father had missed? Dienekes, standing on the deck of a ship in the darkness and the howling wind, would have given much to know.

If ever there had been a perfect Spartan, it had been Eurytus the day he and his brother had headed south to wet their blades. What had that slave boy shown him about himself? What flaw?

Damn that Helot. He had killed one son and, perhaps, maimed the other's soul.

❧❦

"I had a wretched night," Dienekes told his son the next morning—the wind had died down to nothing and there was a thick fog. "I feel quite sick."

"Then put something in your stomach."

"Food? The thought of eating is nauseating."

Eurytus shook his head.

"Beer. I had two barrels brought aboard. Beer is very soothing. I intend to stay pleasantly drunk all the way to Athens."

"That is good advice," his father said, putting a hand on his son's shoulder. "You were always wise."

This made Eurytus laugh. Then suddenly his mood changed.

"Will there be another invasion of Boeotia?" he asked.

"Oh, yes." Dienekes shrugged, suggesting that he regarded the matter as beyond dispute. "King Kleombrotus is probably already drawing up his lists of officers."

"What does Kleombrotus think he's going to accomplish in Boeotia?"

"I don't know. Probably he thinks he can succeed where Agesilaus failed. There is inevitably a certain element of competition. . . ."

They were crossing the mouth of the Argolic Gulf and a seagull drifted by, almost close enough to touch, suggesting that, but for the fog, they were probably within sight of the island of Spetses. In an instant the bird was gone, but for a long moment neither man spoke, as if waiting for another glimpse of it.

In fact, it was convenient not to speak. Neither had a high opinion of Kleombrotus's capacities, but it wouldn't do to say so.

"I keep remembering when Epaminondas drove us out," Eurytus said at last. "On the way south we met Kleombrotus at the head of an army, and he declined to attack Thebes."

"Possibly he thought his force was inadequate."

"He had been sent to rescue us—how could his force have been inadequate? At that moment, when Thebes was isolated and Epaminondas was struggling to establish himself, what would it have taken? What makes him think he can do it now?"

Dienekes didn't answer, which meant, of course, that there was no answer. He wished Eurytus would change the subject.

"Father, you have been a member of the assembly for over twenty-five years. How many gather now as opposed to when you first took your seat?"

"Fewer. Perhaps four out of five."

Eurytus nodded, as if Dienekes had said something profoundly true.

"We can't field the armies we could during the war with Athens," he said. "The population is shrinking. We couldn't fight a major war without our allies. How long will it be before we have to start arming the Helots?"

Dienekes looked sidewise at his son.

"What are you suggesting?"

"I am suggesting that war with Thebes is probably unwinnable and certainly against our interests. We cannot take Thebes by force. We should stop trying and attempt to revive the old alliance—as equals."

"That policy would find no support, either with the Ephors or with the assembly. It is an admission of weakness."

Dienekes turned back to his contemplation of the fog-shrouded sea, feeling he had offered the final rebuttal.

"Father, sometimes . . ."

Eurytus leaned forward against the ship's railing. He seemed to feel the cold, even wrapped in his cloak. The expression on his face was despairing.

"We *are* weak—or soon will be." Eurytus pulled himself up straight, as if preparing for some test of will. "That is the point. We have to start adjusting our policies to accommodate the facts."

Dienekes said nothing. He could see the logic of his son's argument, but it was unpalatable. It seemed opposed to everything he had ever believed about being a Spartan, which meant that it couldn't be true. Still, it was true.

But it should not be true. To even think such things was a kind of cowardice. And suddenly Dienekes became convinced that the business with that damned Helot slave had somehow undermined his son's manhood. How else could he speak of such things?

That damned Helot. It was his fault.

※ ❦

As his ship nosed into the harbor at Piraeus, what Eurytus saw rising up from the shore was a city that, less than thirty years before, had been prostrate. A Spartan commander had merely to give the order and Athens would have been destroyed and its people led off into slavery.

Sparta had chosen mercy, and now Athens was rich and powerful again and in a position to interfere in Boeotia. Mercy, obviously, had been a mistake.

But no one could fail to be impressed by Athens's beauty, certainly not at this moment, while the lowering sun caressed her with its red glow. Athens was a city of marble, of porches and temples, where the wealthy lived in a splendor the gods might envy—which meant, of course, that its people were spending their wealth on display rather than on ships and soldiers. Luxury softened the moral fiber, rendering a nation weak and unreliable. Added to this were the vagaries of the political system.

Democracies are unpredictable creatures.

In Sparta a handful of wise and dependable men could sit around a table and, in the time it took to eat dinner, settle any question before them. Eurytus's father had been one of those men—and would be still, if the law did not limit the Ephors to one one-year term. His father was right to distrust a government in the hands of shopkeepers.

They were to stay at the house of one Xabrinos, an admirer of Sparta and a man of some indirect influence in the assembly. As soon as the ship docked Dienekes sent him a message by one of the runners who loafed around the pier. Within two hours Xabrinos arrived with servants to light the way, sedan chairs to save them the fatigue of walking and a cart for their luggage.

Father and son exchanged a furtive glance.

"We still retain the use of our limbs," Dienekes said, not without a faint suggestion of scorn. "Lead the way."

Xabrinos was a heavy, strengthless man of perhaps fifty, so he "led the way" by climbing into one of the sedan chairs. Dienekes walked beside him and the contrast between them was stark. Dienekes was in his middle fifties but still strong and agile. He carried his leather pack—his only "luggage"—on his back and the empty wagon trailed along behind.

"I have assembled a list of men whom I think it would be advantageous for you to meet." As he spoke, Xabrinos leaned out toward Dienekes, doubtless much to the annoyance of the two men carrying his chair, for they were hard-pressed to keep him from dumping himself into the street. "They represent a range of opinion on questions touching your concerns. My intention was to invite them all to dinner, if you would find that convenient."

"That is very thoughtful of you," Dienekes replied.

"Yes, well, it has been my experience that these informal contacts—"

"Precisely."

Eurytus, only a few steps behind, saw his father turn his face toward this fat Athenian and smile. It was a smile he had seen many times before, and it meant, *I have taken your measure.*

"And are any of those with inconvenient opinions amenable to persuasion?" Dienekes continued. "What is your opinion?"

"My opinion is that all politicians are amenable to persuasion," Xabrinos answered with a slight waggle of his head—Eurytus could not see his face, but his expression was easy to imagine. "What other motive would they have for becoming politicians?"

It occurred to Eurytus that there was a certain enviable simplicity to living among corrupt men.

"At any rate," Xabrinos went on, "I do hope the scale of entertainment necessary for these occasions will not offend too deeply against your Spartan simplicity."

He laughed, apparently without noticing that he laughed alone.

❧❦

They stopped before the doors of Xabrinos's house, a vast pile of white and green marble that resembled less the home of a private citizen than the palace of a Persian king. Only a voluptuary would want to live in such a place.

"How does one acquire such wealth?" Eurytus asked his father.

"Our friend did very well out of our occupation of Athens," Dienekes answered. "That is why he shows us such favor—that and my knowledge of certain circumstances which would earn him a cup of hemlock from any Athenian jury."

Dienekes smiled.

"We own him."

They were shown to their rooms, which were large and lavish and provided with every luxury.

"Enjoy yourself," Dienekes told his son. "Knowledge of the world is largely an acquaintance with its vices. Under certain circumstances—this being one of them—it is well not to be too strenuous in austerity. Our friend imagines he can control us by gratifying our appetites. It is best to let him think that."

A servant girl brought Eurytus his dinner on a tray. The wine was cold and dark. The girl was pretty, with an alluring smile, and she demonstrated no inclination to leave.

Iphigenia was back in Sparta. Eurytus decided to follow his father's advice.

26

That same day Epaminondas, whom Protos had not seen in two months, paid him a visit.

"Are you keeping busy?" he asked, smiling kindly—it was a smile, Protos had come to understand, which meant this was not entirely a social call.

"As well as I can without the Spartans on our doorstep." Protos returned the smile as he wondered where this was leading.

They were in the garden, the delights of which Protos had only recently had leisure to appreciate. He sat on the steps leading up to the kitchen and Epaminondas occupied a stone bench.

"This is a pleasant spot," Epaminondas said, glancing about him.

"Yes. The previous tenant appears to have understood how to make his life agreeable."

Epaminondas said nothing.

"Would you care for some beer?" Protos asked, conscious that he was only trying to fill in the silence.

Epaminondas shook his head. His silence continued for a long moment as he appeared to admire the flowering vines. As all who knew him understood, this was merely his way of introducing a change of subject.

"There is to be a peace conference in Athens," he said finally. "The Athenians are insisting. It will of course achieve nothing, and everyone knows it, but it will give us a chance to test the intentions of a few of our friends and enemies. Pelopidas is leaving tomorrow, and I was wondering if you would care to accompany him."

"To what purpose?"

"To advance your education in public affairs." Epaminondas turned his eyes to Protos and smiled one of his cryptic smiles. "You are rapidly becoming a person of importance in Thebes, and it is time you learned that in war not all battles are fought between armies. Pelopidas is an excellent soldier, but he is also a diplomat of considerable subtlety and skill. There is much he can teach you.

"Besides . . ." The smile broadened and became almost cruel. "Your presence in Athens will greatly annoy the Spartans.

"And, trust me, I will have other work for you when you return."

※ ※

"Your friend the Helot slave boy is coming," Dienekes announced to his son one morning over breakfast. "The Theban delegation left the day before yesterday. Apparently he is traveling with them."

Dienekes, who was fastidious at table, sliced a chunk from a green melon with all the precision of a surgeon cutting an arrowhead out of living flesh. When he raised his eyes from his task he seemed annoyed.

"I cannot imagine what they mean by numbering him among their party. It seems a deliberately insulting gesture."

"Perhaps you should send the Thebans a note," Eurytus answered, wishing the whole subject could be avoided. "I'm sure they'll be interested in your views on diplomatic etiquette."

Dienekes pushed his plate away and raised his eyes to the ceiling.

"Do I need to remind you that this slave killed your brother? Is it possible you've forgotten?"

"No, I have not forgotten. Neither has he."

"*His* memories do not concern me. A slave has no right to imagine himself wronged." Dienekes resumed his dissection of the melon. "I think perhaps it is time to bury him and his grievances in the same grave."

For a long moment Eurytus made no reply. He simply stared at his father, wondering if there was any possibility he could be serious.

Yes, it was possible.

"What are you proposing?" he asked finally. "Would you send armed men into the house of an Athenian citizen to settle a private quarrel? The Athenians are not wonderfully scrupulous, but that might be a little much even for them. Besides, I might remind *you* that Protos is no cooing dove. Possibly he would object."

"Then perhaps I'll have to think of something else."

"Such as what?"

Dienekes shrugged, as if the means were a trifling concern.

※ ※

People were murdered in Athens every day. Fathers who kept their sons on short allowances slipped and broke their skulls climbing the stairs to their own front doors. Inconvenient husbands fell desperately ill and died in agony. There were men in this city who made their livings arranging such misadventures.

Two hours after breakfast, Dienekes stepped into the rear garden of Xabrinos's house and held a private conversation with his host. It was unusual only in that he had not seen fit to inform his son.

But Eurytus's room happened to face the back of the house and Eurytus happened to step out onto the balcony, where he was concealed within the shadow of the awning. He watched the two men as they strolled along a gravel walkway lined with hedges high enough to conceal them at ground level. He could only just see their heads.

Eurytus acted as his father's confidential secretary and advisor, so for any meeting of business he would normally have been present. Dienekes had mentioned nothing about this.

Besides, he detested Xabrinos and normally avoided him whenever possible.

Now they were meeting in the garden, as furtively as a pair of lovers.

They were too far away for Eurytus to hear what they were saying, but it was obvious from their gestures—or, at least, from Xabrinos's gestures—that this was not a chance meeting. Something of importance was being discussed. Xabrinos bowed and grinned and seemed excessively confidential, the way a man might who is only too pleased to be granting a favor.

At last Dienekes turned away and began walking back toward the house. Eurytus could see his face now. He had the look of a man who has just forfeited his self-respect.

※ ※

That evening, before dinner, Eurytus stopped by his father's room that they might go down together. He found him sitting on his balcony, a jar of wine resting on the tiled floor and a cup, half full of a vintage that was almost black, on the small table beside him. Dienekes must have been drinking it undiluted, since there was no water in evidence.

Eurytus was almost upon him when his father's head jerked up, as if he had suddenly come awake. His son was greeted with a clumsy wave. Obviously, Dienekes had been indulging himself.

"Father, it is almost time."

For a long moment Dienekes seemed to consider this statement, and then he shook his head.

"Make my excuses," he said finally. "Tell our host that I am indisposed. Tell him I have diarrhea. Tell him anything you want."

"Is something wrong?"

"Wrong? No." Dienekes shook his head, as if he was trying to clear it. "No, I am just not in a mood for that fat rogue's company."

"Very well then, I will tell him that your wounds are bothering you."

This struck Dienekes as an excellent jest and he threw back his head and laughed.

"Yes, precisely. Excellent. Tell him that. And presently, when I have drunk enough that nothing at all bothers me, I shall go to bed."

In an instant he became quite serious again—almost morose.

"Eurytus," he said, looking up at his son with sad, shining eyes, "Athens is a pigsty."

"Yes, Father. I will see you in the morning."

"In the morning, yes."

※※

Xabrinos did not seem able to sit down to dinner unless he had thirty or forty guests to eat it with him, and that evening's banquet was well under way when Eurytus entered the hall.

The room was perhaps twenty paces by twenty-five and so crowded with tables and dining couches that servants had to be agile to thread their way among them. Against the far wall a small group of musicians were playing, a fact made apparent more by the movement of their instruments than by any sound that could be heard above the din of the revelers. The noise was terrible. People seemed able to converse only by shouting.

It wasn't a meal, Eurytus thought. It was a debauch. The air stank with the smell of spilled wine. And these were not men, howling and belching, throwing food and mindlessly laughing, but animals, soulless, sensual, and base.

Was this the sort of scene Protos had encountered that night in Thebes? If so, he had been right to kill them all.

Eurytus would have preferred to sit somewhere in the back, but his host wouldn't allow him to be thus slighted. Almost as soon as he had entered the room, a page was set to fetch him to the raised dais from which Xabrinos surveyed his turbulent guests.

"We can't have you off by yourself like that, my young friend. Come— sit here beside me. You and I haven't yet had an opportunity to become properly acquainted."

Eurytus took his place on the next couch, irritated and bored at the prospect of this man's company—from which there could be no polite escape, since Xabrinos generally continued his revels until he had to be carried off to bed.

A servant brought Eurytus a gold cup and filled it with wine from a silver pitcher, which he left behind on the table. Xabrinos was already very merry and apparently Eurytus was expected to catch up.

"You see my friends," his host said, accompanying the announcement with a sweeping gesture of his right arm. "Politicians, merchants who control trading empires any king might envy, moneylenders who among them probably own half the city. And all friends of Sparta. Their power and influence are at your bidding."

He turned his face to Eurytus and smiled as if it were all his own doing, as if these men, great as they were, were his creatures, and Eurytus remembered his father's words: *We own him.*

"And can I expect to see the Theban delegation on another evening?" Eurytus asked, returning, as best he could, Xabrinos's rather fatuous smile.

"We can invite them, if you and your father think it would be useful." Xabrinos, having missed the point entirely, seemed to give the question his serious attention. Quite suddenly, he laughed. "But we shall have to be quick about it, otherwise they won't come. They'll be in mourning."

The jest so amused him that it actually brought tears to his eyes. He reached out and touched Eurytus on the shoulder as he was seized with another fit of laughter.

"One of their number, at least, shall already have died of indigestion."

27

The rest of the banquet was agony. Finally, after two hours, Eurytus was able to get away on the excuse that he must see to his father. Instead, he went to his room, where he could be alone with the turmoil in his mind.

He told himself he did not care. Why should he care about the execution of a slave? It was not murder to kill a slave, no matter how it was done.

That was what he told himself, without finding himself quite able to believe it.

What stuck in his throat was the method. *One of their number, at least, shall already have died of indigestion.* Protos the Helot slave was to be poisoned, and poison was the weapon of the weak and the cowardly, of those who would not own their deeds and stood in terror of their victims.

What would they say at his funeral? *We now commit to the flames the body of our brother Protos, a brave man who died through treachery, murdered by the Spartans because not one of them had the bowels to face him in equal combat.*

And it would all be true. Dienekes might have the excuse of his age, but Eurytus knew that his father never would have contemplated such a step if Eurytus himself had had the courage to avenge their son and brother.

Eurytus paced about in his room, drinking wine cut three parts to four with water, hoping it would dull his conscience enough to allow him to sleep. It had the opposite effect, of throwing the problem into ever-sharper relief.

In the hours before dawn, when the darkness of the night sky is like death itself, Eurytus at last accepted the conclusion that his own soul would be forever stained if he allowed this deed to go forward. He had to stop it. It would mean a betrayal of his father, but that could not be helped.

At last he went to bed and slept until dawn.

❧❦

The Theban delegation did not arrive in Athens until the late afternoon. Finding out where they would be quartered presented no difficulty, since everyone seemed to know they would be the guests of one Dexileos, a great partisan of their cause. Dexileos's house was but a few streets away. Eurytus had only to wait.

It was an irksome business, skulking around in the shadows of buildings. He told himself that he was a traitor to his family, perhaps even to his country. He told himself that he should leave and let events follow their inevitable course. But he did not. In his heart he had come to believe that not only his own honor but the honor of his family was at stake, both the living and the dead. He entertained no great hopes of the afterlife, but he could feel his ancestors' eyes upon him, the gaze of men who had fought and died in Sparta's wars since the foundations of the race.

They would be his only witnesses, he hoped. If possible he would somehow slip into the house, have a word with Protos, whose secrecy he instinctively trusted, and disappear. He did not want any knowledge of this to come to his father.

In the end there was no trouble about entering the house. Porters were struggling with the baggage. Eurytus picked up a bundle and, once inside, inquired which room assigned to "the Lord Protos." He had merely to walk up the stairs.

❧❦

The room into which Dexileos's chamberlain showed him was like nothing Protos had ever seen. Everything seemed to be made of white marble—the floor, the walls, even the bed frame gleamed so brightly that it hurt one's eyes to look about.

He approached the bed, almost as if sneaking up on an enemy, and touched the footboard. It was cold. It really was marble. He prodded the mattress with the tips of his fingers and it offered almost no resistance. It would be like sleeping in a pool of water.

How did rich people stand it? he wondered. *Why would anyone want to live this way?*

About a quarter of an hour later the chamberlain returned with a cold dinner on a tray. He set the tray down on a table and poured a cup of wine.

"I'm sorry to trouble you," Protos said, "but I wonder if I might have some beer?"

"Beer?"

The chamberlain drew himself up to his full height—he was a tall man—and his nose wrinkled with distaste.

"Yes, beer." Protos shook his head. "I have no stomach for wine."

"I'll see if perhaps there isn't some in the servants' pantry," the chamberlain said, picking up the wine vessel and cup and returning them to the tray. He bowed with almost mocking servility.

At that moment another person appeared in the open doorway, possibly the last person Protos expected to see.

Eurytus was unarmed and dressed in a plain tunic. He was carrying a bundle, which he set down on the floor. When their eyes met he held a finger to his lips in token of silence.

A moment later the chamberlain backed out of the room, carrying the tray. He hardly seemed to notice that there was a third person in the room.

When he was gone, Eurytus pushed the door closed.

"Don't touch the food," he said quietly.

"Why?"

"Poison."

An instant later, in the hallway, there was a crash, as if a heavy object had been dropped. Alarmed, Protos pushed past Eurytus and opened his door. He saw the chamberlain stretched out on the floor, a few paces from the stairway. The tray was halfway beneath his chest and the wine vessel was overturned, its contents leaking out like fresh blood from a wound.

Protos stooped down and touched the side of the chamberlain's neck. He was dead.

When Protos rolled him over, a thin trickle of wine slipped from the corner of the man's mouth. He must have decided to drink off the contents of the cup he had poured.

Protos felt rather than saw Eurytus's presence behind him.

"It would appear you were right," he said, just above a whisper. "I think perhaps you had better tell me about this."

"Let's get this one out of sight first."

He had a point. There was nothing to be gained by raising the whole house. They each grabbed an arm and dragged the chamberlain's body back into Protos's room. Then they returned to the hallway and cleaned up the mess as best they could.

When they were finished, Eurytus picked up the wine vessel and sniffed it.

"I wouldn't care to drink wine that smelled like that," was all he said.

Protos made no answer. He was too occupied with adjusting to the fact that he had nearly been murdered.

When they were safely behind a closed door, with the chamberlain's corpse wrapped in a sheet, they sat down on two chairs, facing each other. For a moment neither spoke.

"I don't have to ask who wants me dead," Protos said finally. "I only wonder that you decided to warn me."

Eurytus smiled, which somehow made him look as if he had a bad taste in his mouth.

"Do you remember what you told me once?" he answered. "'You will not die until I kill you.' Perhaps I feel much the same."

Protos seemed to consider this and then shook his head

"I suppose that will have to satisfy me for an answer," he said. "But I have no intention of letting the matter rest here."

"I never imagined you would."

"Then what did you imagine?"

"That you might listen to reason." Eurytus glanced about the room as if noticing it for the first time. "This is Athens, and you can't carry on here as though you were on a battleground. There would be diplomatic repercussions that neither of us would find pleasant."

"So it's perfectly acceptable for your people to poison me, but I can't go after them with a sword, is that it?"

Eurytus nodded. And then he uttered a single syllable of voiceless laughter, as if he had just seen the point.

"More or less," he said finally. "Yes, something like that. A quiet murder is one thing, a blood feud is another. The point is to avoid embarrassing the Athenians."

"Still, someone tried to kill me. They have to learn that I won't sit still for that sort of thing."

"Granted."

"Then who pays the reckoning?" Protos shrugged, including his arms and hands in the gesture. "Who else is there in the Spartan delegation?"

"Only myself and my father."

"So your father arranged this. And I imagine you would be mightily offended if I took him to task for it—well, I suppose I owe you the small courtesy of leaving him alive."

It suddenly flashed through Eurytus's mind that, even before he had warned Protos, the chamberlain had already removed the wine. Thus, even if he had stayed away, Protos would have been spared, the chamberlain would have tasted the wine and died on the landing and Protos would have known everything. Perhaps, after all, the only thing he had accomplished was to save his father's life.

"I would appreciate that," was all he could bring himself to say. He felt like the victim of some grotesque joke.

"But your father did not personally poison the wine," Protos said, his eyes as cold as an adder's. "Someone arranged all this. I intend to find out who."

"An excellent idea." Eurytus's smile was a trifle less painful. "If you kill that person perhaps the Athenians will put up a statue to you for the service you have rendered the city."

And then something seemed to occur to him.

"Perhaps I could accompany you," he said.

"And why should I consent to that?"

"Because you do not know the principals in this little drama." Eurytus raised his eyebrows mockingly, as if he thought Protos a great simpleton. "Perhaps not even your poisoner knows—would *you* give your true name to such a person? You will need me if all he can provide is a description."

"That is a point."

※ ※

Once Protos understood Eurytus's need to conceal his involvement, they quickly agreed on what was necessary. Protos would find out what he could inside the house and they would meet again outside.

Eurytus left as anonymously as he had entered.

For a long moment, Protos simply sat in his room, staring at the shrouded corpse of the chamberlain. He had narrowly avoided death. A man whom half an hour ago he would have called his worst enemy was now his friend. Or at least his ally. Or what? He couldn't say. None of it made any sense.

But when had life made any sense? The world had gone mad that night when he was fourteen and had watched his parents die. Perhaps it would never be sane again.

When he went looking for Pelopidas, Protos took with him what was left in the wine vessel.

There was a room just off the downstairs reception hall. It was where Protos had spoken to Pelopidas the first time they met. It turned out to be a lucky guess.

The door was closed and did not yield to his touch, so Protos knocked.

After a moment it was opened perhaps three fingers' width by Dexileos. Beyond him Protos could see Pelopidas sitting on a chair.

"Your chamberlain is dead," Protos said quietly. "He died because I don't like wine."

The door opened and Dexileos stepped out of the way. Protos came inside and set the wine vessel on a table.

"I'm reasonably sure it's poisoned."

Dexileos picked up the wine vessel and held it to his nose.

"Aconite," he said. "And in considerable quantities. There's probably enough in this to kill half the district."

"Are you sure?" Pelopidas rose from his chair and came over to stand beside his friend, who smiled at him as if making a shamefully ludicrous admission.

"Everyone who plays at politics in this city lives in fear of being poisoned," he said. "One learns the basics."

"I want to know who prepared my dinner tray."

They both glanced at Protos, whose expression made it clear he was not prepared to be yielding.

Dexileos nodded, seemingly accepting the inevitable.

"Then we must ask my cook."

❦❦

The kitchen was a large, windowless room in the basement. It was crowded with tables arranged in no discernible pattern, most of them covered with pots and mixing bowls, vegetables of every description and joints of meat. Several ovens and open hearths raised the temperature high enough that the air was uncomfortable to breathe. There were servants everywhere. The majority were men but there were several women and even a few children.

At one end of the room, seated at a table with only a couple of waxed writing tablets on it, was a slender, white-haired man who in any other place might have been taken for a scribe or even a tutor of children. He rose to his feet in the presence of his master.

"Radanos, I would ask you a question," Dexileos began, placing his hand on the man's shoulder and thus marking him as an old and trusted servant. "Who prepared the tray that was sent up to Lord Protos this evening?"

"I did, my lord." Radanos blinked compulsively, the way a man might after he has been slapped in the face. "Was there anything amiss?"

Dexileos shook his head.

"And the wine?"

"That would be the wine steward, my lord. His name is Ludianos."

"And where will we find this Ludianos?"

"In the cellar, my lord." Radanos motioned to a trapdoor in the floor, no more than a few paces from where they stood. "He is doing an inventory this evening."

"And there is no one with him?'

"No, my lord. He is alone."

"Thank you, my friend," Dexileos answered, patting his shoulder as he might have a dog. "You have done nothing wrong, but we must have a word with the steward."

Radanos walked over to the trapdoor, put his hand through a ring and pulled it open. It must have been counterweighted because it moved quite easily in spite of its massive size.

Dexileos took a step forward, but Protos touched his arm to make him stop.

"This one is mine," he said, without apparent emotion.

He turned to the cook and smiled. "How large is the cellar?" he asked.

"It is full half the size of the kitchen," Radanos answered, with just a touch of pride.

"Nice to know," Protos answered, and turned to descend the ladder down into the wine cellar.

※·※

There was a ring on the inside of the trapdoor and Protos used it to pull the door closed. Then he waited a few minutes to give his eyes time to adjust to the darkness.

He could make out the vague shapes of things, rows and rows of heavy wooden shelves, all of them loaded with amphoras of wine, some of which were decorated. The smell of wine was heavy and sweet, making Protos wish the stuff tasted as good as it smelled—except that, were such the case, he would this minute be dead.

There was light coming from somewhere. Protos could see it flickering dimly on the ceiling. All he had to do was follow it.

The wine steward was standing in a narrow aisle, the shelves so close together he hardly had room to turn. He held a writing tablet. There was an oil lamp on a shelf at about chest height.

He was a slender man, middle-aged and going bald, so absorbed in his task that he did not even notice that he was no longer alone. The immediate impression he made was one of utter ordinariness. But murderers came in every conceivable type.

"Are you Ludianos?" Protos asked gently.

The wine steward started so violently that his feet almost left the floor, and Protos knew at once that his task was going to be easy.

"My name is Protos," he went on. "No doubt you are surprised to see me."

Ludianos's mouth opened wide, but no sound came out. Then it closed again with a violent snap.

"You poisoned the wine that was brought to my room this evening. I don't drink wine, so the chamberlain carried it away. He tasted it after he left me and I found him dead. He never even reached the stairway. I mean to find out everything you know about this affair. It will be vastly easier for you if you just tell me."

An empty wine amphora lay in the aisle. Protos fetched it and placed it on the floor upside down so that the steward would have somewhere to sit. He seemed to be having trouble with his knees.

At first all he did was weep. He put his head in his hands and sobbed. Out of a vague feeling of pity, Protos let him alone until the fit passed.

"I never meant to kill you," the steward said. "I was given a powder and told to put it in your drink. He told me it would make you too ill to attend a meeting tomorrow. He didn't want you there because you would make trouble for him. That was what he said. You would be ill for a few days and then you would get better."

"Well, the chamberlain won't get any better."

Protos had had plenty of time to consider how to proceed—the sobbing had gone on for almost a quarter of an hour—and he decided that the best way was to allow this man to tell the whole story and only at the end ask him the one important question. The "who" could wait.

"Why did you do it?"

"I have a lover," Ludianos answered. He shrugged and smiled lamely, as if to say, *Isn't it always so?* "He works in the dockyards as a porter. He is free and I am a slave, but I have a better life than he. He gambles and he has no talent for it. He is deeply in debt. The man who gave me the powder had bought my friend's debts. He said, as my friend could not pay, he would have his arms and legs broken, or I could do this thing for him."

"And you love your friend, so you said you would do it."

"Yes."

Protos nodded. He understood. Everyone must be loyal to something, or someone.

"How much is the debt?"

"Two hundred drachmas."

There had been a time, and not so long ago, when Protos did not even know what a drachma was. Two hundred drachmas, to ordinary people, free or slave, was a huge sum.

"Well, you will probably never see your friend again," Protos said, his voice soft as down, "but I can promise you that the man who set this trap for you will not live to pester him for the money. Give me his name and tell me where to find him, and he will be dead before morning."

"Yes, I will tell you." Ludianos, who had risked so much for love, swallowed hard. "What will happen to me?"

Protos shook his head.

"I know nothing about the laws of Athens," he said. "I can't give you an answer, but I will speak to your master."

"Thank you."

A few minutes later Protos climbed the ladder back up to the kitchen.

"Do you know what you need to know?" Pelopidas asked him.

"Yes." Protos turned to Dexileos. "What will happen to the steward?"

"The law is clear. A slave who commits murder either dies under the lash or is condemned to the galleys, which is worse."

"Then show a little mercy and offer him a cup of wine first."

28

Athens was a city that never went to bed. Many of the wine shops did not even open until the sun went down and this was especially true in the harbor district, outside the ancient walls.

Here the rich and the poor mixed indiscriminately. The streets were only hard-packed earth, and the buildings were mostly small and constructed of wood, but it was a place where anything could be bought or sold. A man who looked like a beggar might have concealed somewhere on his person a fortune in precious stones, or the promissory notes of a hundred wastrels the world thought rich, or little vials of powder that had been ground in places most people had never heard of and held the promise of paradise— at least for a few hours. Rich women came here to lie in the arms of muscular porters. The scions of great families came here to drink and whore.

And in the streets and hovels of the harbor district, murder was just another commodity.

"It was yesterday," Ludianos had said. "He summoned me to a place called the Blue Dolphin, where he seemed to be well known. His name was Phoneus."

"Can you describe him?"

"A dirty man. He smelled bad. He wore his hair as long as a woman's. He spoke Greek badly, so he must have been a foreigner. He had a scar across the bridge of his nose, as straight as if someone had cut him with a knife."

A little later, while Ludianos was still down in his cellar, trying to nerve himself to drink some of the wine he had prepared for his master's guest, Protos left Dexileos's house and began walking south. Within fifty paces Eurytus stepped out of the shadow of a building and fell in beside him.

"Did you find someone to answer your questions?"

"Oh, yes." He told Eurytus everything he had learned from the wine steward.

"My host has given me the key to the cellar of a building he happens to own. It is down by the docks and quite convenient. He was appalled that I proposed to enter such a den of crime alone." Protos laughed at the recollection. "I didn't inform him that I would have company."

"By the way . . ." He reached under his cloak and pulled out a sword, which he presented to Eurytus hilt-first. "A Spartan blade. Familiar weapons are best."

"A wise precaution. This Phoneus will doubtless have bodyguards."

"So much the worse for them."

❧ ❧

The Blue Dolphin was not hard to find. Despite its elegant name, it was the sort of place that catered to the poorest of the poor: day laborers, thieves, and prostitutes down on their luck. The floor was dirty and the air reeked of wine so stale it had gone putrid.

Protos was wearing his best tunic. He was a rich boy tonight, out of place and harmless. Under his cloak, hanging from his belt, he carried his Spartan dagger.

Eurytus kept a little ahead to avoid the impression that they were together. He stepped through the beaded curtain that served as a doorway. The proprietor, a greasy little man who was wiping a cup with a damp rag, never glanced at him.

There was another rattle of the beaded curtain and Protos came in.

"I was told to ask for a man named Phoneus," he told the proprietor, who looked him over very carefully and then silently indicated a table in a dark corner of an adjoining room.

Eurytus turned around and he and Protos exchanged a quick glance.

Even before they stepped into the next room, Eurytus noted two other men sitting at tables on either side of the entrance. Phoneus's watchdogs, tough boys from the docks. One of them moved and there was the sound of a sword point scraping against the tile floor.

At a table against the back wall was Phoneus himself, every bit as repulsive as Protos had been led to expect. The scar across his nose glistened in the smoky light from an oil lamp.

"I'll take the one on the right," Eurytus murmured. Protos nodded.

They went through the entrance, Protos just a little ahead. In a swift, smooth movement the man on his left probably never noticed, Protos reached beneath his cloak, drew the dagger and stabbed him in the throat.

The second man was scrambling to his feet when Eurytus's sword point went between his ribs, just below his left nipple. He subsided back into his seat and then, slowly, his head sank until it rested on the table. Neither man managed to make a sound.

"What! What are you . . ."

Phoneus began to stand up. He, too, began fumbling for the sword that hung from his belt, but he was obviously not a man accustomed to weapons and he was slow about it.

Protos stepped forward, tossing the dagger in the air and catching it by the blade. Using the hilt, he struck Phoneus on the side of the head. Phoneus collapsed instantly.

He wasn't a large man so Protos had no trouble carrying him slung over his left shoulder. Ludianos has been right about how bad he smelled.

Bearing his burden and still holding his dagger by the blade, Protos strode back out through the main room, past the astonished proprietor, who had no eyes for Eurytus.

"If you hope to die in bed, don't interfere," Eurytus growled

The proprietor merely waggled his head back and forth.

Apparently the sight of a man being carried unconscious over another man's shoulder was not so uncommon that anyone thought fit to notice. In that district people understood the wisdom of minding their own business.

※ ※

They were in a small room with stone walls and no windows. There was a single door, barred from the inside. The only light was from a torch stuck in a wall sconce. Phoneus was tied down to a chair. His arms were bound so tightly that, had he been conscious, he probably wouldn't have had any sensation in his hands.

Eurytus was standing behind the chair when Phoneus's head began to swing to one side, which meant that he was waking up.

About two paces in front of the chair, lying on the floor, was a dagger, which Eurytus recognized as having been his brother's.

Protos was beside the door, studying his prisoner without conveying the slightest impression of what he might feel.

"My name is Protos," he said, when Phoneus was finally able to raise his head. "You were hired to poison me but, as you can see, that didn't work out. Can you imagine why you are here?"

Eurytus stepped out from behind the chair, but Phoneus seemed hardly to notice him. His whole attention was focused on Protos.

"You want revenge?" Phoneus smiled—Eurytus noted that the smile was unpleasantly crooked. "Money is better. I am rich. You let me go, I give you money."

"I'm not interested in your money. I want to know who hired you to kill me."

"You think my customers give me names? A man comes to see me. He says, 'I have a problem with this person.' He gives me money and I never see him again."

Phoneus actually managed to laugh. Listening to him laugh was like listening as a pot begins to boil, in fits and starts, in random little eruptions of sound.

He stopped laughing when Protos picked the knife up from the floor.

"This is going to hurt."

Protos stamped down with his bare heel on the top of Phoneus's right foot, making him scream with pain. Then, with his left hand, he grabbed the loops of rope around Phoneus's ankles and pulled up until Phoneus almost went over backward in his chair.

Then, quite calmly, he inserted the point of the knife into the joint of Phoneus's right big toe and popped it off so that it rolled across the stone floor.

"Well, we can't have you bleeding to death," he said, and took the torch down from the wall sconce. He held the flame to the wound until he had burned it black.

All this time Phoneus was screaming. His screams were high-pitched, like bird calls.

Protos released the rope and Phoneus's feet slapped back down on the floor.

"I can go on like this all day and all night," Protos announced calmly. "I have plenty of time. I can cut your toes off one by one and then starting carving on your feet until there's nothing left but the bone. The choice is yours."

"You eat your own shit!" Phoneus was sobbing with pain and terror, but he was still defiant.

"As I said, the choice is yours."

They were at it for over a quarter of an hour before Phoneus reached the extremity of suffering, when he simply couldn't bear any more pain.

"Please, please, no more. Please!"

Protos grabbed his greasy, tangled hair and pulled back his head. Phoneus's eyes were pleading now. Resistance was at an end.

"Then tell me who hired you."

"I never knew his name."

"I believe you." Protos nodded reassuringly. "So tell me what you do know."

"He was tall and thin. He had red hair and his face was covered with freckles."

"That sounds like Gellios," Eurytus said. "He is my host's confidential servant."

"Don't hurt me anymore," Phoneus pleaded. "I've told you all I know. Don't hurt me."

"I'll try not to."

And Protos was as good as his word. The knife point slid down behind Phoneus's collarbone and pierced his heart.

❦❦

The night sky had just turned from black to gray as they reached the more fashionable quarters of the city. Dawn was no more than an hour away. They had hardly spoken since leaving the waterfront.

Protos carried something wrapped in his cloak. It was part of the compromise he and Eurytus had reached.

"I saw that you still have my brother's dagger," Eurytus said at last.

"It is no longer your brother's. Your brother has no need of it." Protos turned his head toward Eurytus. In the darkness it was impossible to read his expression. "But it is the knife he used to kill my mother, yes."

"You have become as hard as my brother ever was."

"I have become what you and your brother made me."

"I know that."

Protos slowed his pace and came to a halt, turning to his companion. The carriage of his body was itself almost a threat. Almost, but not quite.

"Eurytus, son of Dienekes," he began, "you have put me in your debt this night, and in a way I would not have expected. Know that I am grateful, but that it changes nothing."

"I know. For each of us the past is too heavy a burden."

Protos merely nodded.

"Then we both know that the next time we meet it must be as enemies. But know as well that I truly hope that meeting never occurs."

In the next instant he seemed to have vanished in the night.

Eurytus was in his room, taking off his sandals, before it struck him that the whole tenor of his life had changed. That was what Protos had meant—he could stop listening for the whisper of a drawn blade. He was no longer a condemned man who could only wait passively for the sentence of death to be carried out. Protos had given him back his life.

His very relief shamed him.

※ ※

The next afternoon a loud and insistent knocking was heard at the front door of Xabrinos's house. In response his chamberlain opened it, and what he saw standing before him on the top step was a tall young man, probably younger than twenty, carrying a covered wicker basket.

"I have a gift for your master," the young man said. "This is in fact the house of Xabrinos?"

"Who wishes to know?" the chamberlain answered, with the haughtiness that was one of the indispensable tools of his profession.

"A stranger." The young man set the basket down on the floor, just to the right of the doorway. "Tell him this is a present from a stranger."

"And does the stranger have a name?"

"I suspect the Lord Xabrinos will be able to work that out for himself."

The youth turned and walked away, as if he had forgotten the whole episode.

The chamberlain closed the door and stood staring at the wicker basket.

Perhaps out of idle curiosity, or perhaps because he regarded it as part of his duty, he reached down and lifted the cover from the basket. What he found inside, resting on a bed of straw, was a severed human head, the eyes open but already glazed over.

The chamberlain's reaction was immediate and involuntary and could be heard all over the house.

29

As Epaminondas had predicted, the conference was not a success. The participants—Sparta, Thebes, Athens, and, for some reason no one could identify, Thessalia—met at a succession of grand houses, talked a great deal, and achieved nothing toward establishing peace.

Their first meeting came close to being their last when Dienekes had to be restrained from protesting Protos's inclusion as a delegate from Thebes.

"I will not consent to treating on equal terms with a runaway slave," he shouted at Eurytus, who had almost had to drag him from the room. "It was in the most appalling taste for the Thebans to have brought him."

"And it was also in appalling taste to have attempted to poison him."

For a stunned moment Dienekes could only stare at his son.

"You knew?"

"Oh please, Father. By now everyone in Athens knows. It isn't every day one's host is presented with the severed head of a notorious murderer."

Dienekes seemed overwhelmed by this revelation, and Eurytus decided to make the most of his advantage.

"You don't have to speak to him," he went on, in a calm, even conciliatory tone of voice. "You don't even have to recognize his presence. Confine your remarks to Pelopidas and leave Protos to me."

Finally Dienekes consented, but he didn't speak more than ten or fifteen words the entire afternoon. He kept glancing at Protos, who sat at the opposing table grinning at him—with an occasional glance at Eurytus, as if to share the jest.

During one of the frequent breaks, when diplomacy was carried forward at a less formal level, Eurytus approached Protos, bringing him a cup of beer.

"I could ask that you stop tormenting my father," he said.

"Yes, you could." Protos took the cup and smiled. "You certainly could ask. However, since you seem to object to my killing him, I must take my revenge where I can."

After five days of talks it became clear that Sparta had no idea of relinquishing her war against Thebes, so the Theban delegation returned home.

"I think you should feel flattered," Epaminondas told Protos a few days after his return. "To be the object of an assassination attempt confers a certain distinction. They must be frightened if they attempt to murder you."

"It wasn't intended as a compliment. The motives, I suspect, were more personal."

Epaminondas seemed to consider this for a moment, and then he lifted his cup and took a swallow of beer. They were sitting in the garden of Protos's house, just at sunset.

"Then we must give them another reason to fear you," he said finally. "I want you to begin training troops."

"How can I train troops?" Protos laughed and shook his head. "I have never been a soldier."

"You could train them to do in battle what you and your friends did when yours was the only war we dared to fight. Do you know what a skirmisher is?"

"Of course. You taught me."

"Then skirmishers are what I would like you to train. The Spartans will be back one day—we learned that, at least, in Athens—and we will have real battles to fight on the plains of Boeotia."

"When would you like me to start?"

Thus did Protos, the slave boy from Laconia, become a ranking officer in the army of Thebes. He gathered his little band around him and made Agenor his second in command; Agenor let it be known that any soldier who desired an exciting and probably very short life should speak to him.

Then one afternoon, when the volunteers had been collected, a young man of seventeen strolled down to the training field. He wore a buff-colored tunic that reached to his knees and he carried no weapon except a Spartan dagger in a leather scabbard that hung from his belt.

Everyone else on the field wore the blue uniform of the Theban army. The youth seemed out of place. He stood at the edge of the field and looked about him, as if it was beginning to occur to him that he had lost his way. His blue eyes were wide and childlike and gave him an appearance of bewilderment, but he was merely taking in everything he saw, letting the impressions sort themselves out as they would.

Few of the soldiers noticed him, but one who did nudged the man standing beside him and smiled in derision.

"Run along, boy," he shouted. "We're busy here."

An officer heard him and was about to rebuke the soldier, when he glanced at the youth who, with a subtle gesture of his left hand, warned him to keep silent.

The youth himself seemed not to have heard and stepped onto the field as if uncertain that it would bear his weight.

The soldier sauntered over. "You heard me, boy," he said, loud enough for everyone to hear, and extended his arm to push the youth back in the direction from which he had come.

It was a mistake. With viperlike speed the youth grasped the soldier's thumb and twisted it, pulling him off balance. Then he kicked the soldier's right foot out from beneath him, sending him crashing to the ground.

Cursing, the soldier tried simultaneously to sit up and to draw his sword. He stopped when he saw the dagger in the youth's hand, its point not a finger's width from his throat.

"How do you think we should finish this conversation?" the youth asked quietly.

Several officers were running toward them.

"Protos, in the names of all the gods don't kill the bloody fool!" shouted one. His name was Labros, and he had been one of Protos's warriors.

Protos might not have heard. He looked at the soldier and smiled. "Answer the question," he said.

"I apologize." The soldier swallowed hard. "I . . ."

Protos took the dagger's point away from his throat and extended an arm to help the man up.

"Well, then—no hard feelings."

Labros was not so tolerant. He actually kicked the man as he was getting up.

"Babras, you idiot," he shouted. "Do you have any idea how close you came to death this day? This is Protos the Helot, who has killed more Spartans than you have fingers and toes. What sort of a fool picks a quarrel with a man he does not know?"

Babras the soldier stared up at Protos with frightened eyes.

"Let it go, Labros," Protos murmured, putting his hand on the officer's shoulder. "It was only a misunderstanding."

Then Protos turned his head and saw that every man on the training field was watching him.

"Take off your sandals," he shouted.

❧❧

"A skirmisher's war is between the lines of battle," he told them. "We are like the swarms of gnats that sometimes drive cattle to stampede, only there will be but few of us and many of them. We make the enemy understand that he is not safe behind his wall of shields. We kill their officers. We disrupt and weaken the Spartan phalanxes in any way we can. No man fights with his full attention when he knows that death, at any time and from any direction, may rain down upon him. We must make the Spartans, considered the best soldiers on earth, shake with terror.

"They also will have skirmishers, and you will have to fight them before you can attack the main body of their army. And you will fight all your battles on your feet. You must run like a firestorm if you wish to bring death to your enemies and live to rejoice in it. That is why you will learn to go barefoot. During King Agesilaus's last visit, Spartan skirmishers came hunting for me many times. They always wore sandals and they are all dead."

The hundred soldiers gathered on the training field to learn the skirmisher's art hung on Protos's every word. They had heard the stories. For them he was the living son of Death.

"You have been trained to admire the courage and honor of the soldier who faces his enemy and fights to the death. Your war will be nothing like that. Forget all that. A skirmisher, when the enemy concentrates against him, does the sensible thing and runs away. The enemy will give you many opportunities to kill him—learn to select your targets with care. If one is too dangerous, find another. When the battle is over the only thing that matters is how much you have disrupted and weakened the enemy. If the enemy hates you and calls you a coward, you can consider yourself a hero. But no one hates a corpse. If you have been careless enough to allow yourself to be killed, the only thing you are is dead.

"Thus the first thing you must learn is how to stay alive."

❧❧

He made it into a kind of game.

"You must never forget that the Spartans have javelins as well as we. Let it become a reflex for you to always be casting your eyes up, searching for the spear aimed just at you."

Protos ordered the iron points removed from fifty javelins and divided his hundred soldiers into pairs. Each man had a shield, but there was only one javelin per pair. They would hurl it back and forth, the first man trying to hit his partner while the second man learned to judge how close the javelin would come.

"Do not simply run away," he told them. "Let it fall within two paces of you."

After a week of this, Protos had the iron points put back on. "Now mistakes will be paid for in blood."

In the week that followed, only one man was wounded—he had his foot pinned to the ground and was sent home.

In another month the skirmishers were ready for war.

※ ※

"You will be eighteen this year," Nubit said one night, as Protos was drifting off to sleep. "What day were you born?"

"I don't know. In the summer."

"Just 'in the summer'? You don't know the day?"

"No. To a poor man or a slave, what difference can it make what day he was born? All I know is that my mother was too big with me to help with the planting that year."

"Then you must have been born in early summer, most likely in the month of Thargelion."

"I suppose so."

She was about to ask him something else when she noticed that he was asleep.

Nubit lay there, listening to his deep, even breathing, thinking that it was absurd not to know one's own birthday. She, too, had been born a slave, but she knew she had been born on the seventh day of the fourth month— how that would translate into any one of the various Greek calendars she had no idea.

What she wanted was to have a birthday celebration for Protos. She wanted to remind him that his life hadn't started with the murder of his parents, that he was a man like other men and not simply an impersonal instrument of vengeance. Most people liked him—many people loved him—

but he did not seem to like himself. Or perhaps it was that he didn't regard his own life, the life in which he was merely himself, as of any importance.

More than anything Nubit wanted to convince him that he was loved, that he was important to other people. As it was, he was prepared to risk anything—everything. Perhaps if he understood that his life was precious, if only to her, he might risk less.

Sometimes, without his ever knowing it, she would stand on the city wall and watch Protos and his skirmishers as they went through their drill. In its way it was beautiful. The target that Protos aimed at fell down. He ran like a deer and was as graceful as a dancer, and no man's weapon could touch him. It was as if he wore what the Greeks called a *halos*, the divine fire with which the gods cloaked their favored heroes.

But her visions tormented her.

She had stopped dreaming of her father's death. Now she dreamed of war, the clash of weapons and the screams of the dying. She saw Protos as weapons rained down upon him. She heard the Spartans beating their swords against their shields.

And every night her dreams ended the same way. She saw Protos walking away from her, his feet bare, carrying his weapons. And in the last instant he would stop and turn to look behind him, but he would not see her.

This was more terrible than war, because she knew he was leaving her forever.

From all these things the planning of Protos's birthday banquet was a release. It allowed her to think of him as simply another man, with his friends and his private pleasures, unburdened by the destiny that was his name.

The preparations were a deep secret. Nubit sent the girls out from house to house to issue the invitations—to all of his original irregulars and even Pelopidas and Epaminondas. All agreed to come.

The meal was to be lavish. Protos was paid as a ranking officer but, never having adjusted to the uses of money, he simply turned his salary over to Nubit and thought no more about it. The cook she hired complained bitterly about the limitations of their kitchen but at last decided his skills could rise above them. As recompense he was given a free hand in the purchasing of food and wine. He was scandalized to learn that the host would only drink beer.

"Beer is the drink of peasants," he announced.

Nubit only smiled.

Finally the day arrived. At two hours before sunset Nubit sent Hemera, the youngest of the girls, down to the drill field to tell Protos that he must come home early. Hemera was his favorite, if only because she was the baby. He would not refuse.

"Why?" Protos asked. "Why must I come?"

Hemera only kept her hold on the fingers of his right hand and looked up at him with her great brown eyes. She smiled. It was the unanswerable argument.

When he reached the house, Nubit, unsmiling, gave him strict instructions.

"Go to the back porch and wash yourself," she said. "I have heated water for you. Then go upstairs and change into your embroidered tunic. Your guests will be here in an hour."

"What guests? What is this about, Nubit?"

"Do as you are told."

It occurred to Protos, not for the first time, that Nubit would have done very well in the army. He went to the back porch.

The first to arrive was Agenor and then the other old fighters, some of whom, like Agenor, had been following Protos since the slaughter of the oligarchs. At sunset, Pelopidas and Epaminondas arrived together.

From the start the banquet was a success. Most of the men were from aristocratic families, but the triumph of democracy in Thebes, together with their association with Protos, had at least blurred their prejudices. Pelopidas and Epaminondas were a special case: both had been born to wealth and privilege but had given most of their money away and, in any case, were democratic politicians who could talk to anybody.

There were the customary humorous speeches in honor of the occasion, during one of which several of Protos's officers held up a foot to demonstrate that they had abandoned sandals. The girls were much admired for their beauty—probably the majority of those present still imagined they were Protos's concubines. Even the beer was good. It was one of those happy occasions when almost everyone knew everyone else and could therefore enjoy each other's company without constraint.

Pelopidas, who was under usual circumstances the most abstemious of men, had grown agreeably drunk and was entertaining Nubit with his story of the peace conference.

"Protos was almost solely responsible for the collapse of negotiations—him along with the fact that the Spartans never had the slightest interest in a peace treaty. He kept making faces at their ambassador. The poor man could hardly stand to be in the same room with him."

Nubit, who had already heard the story from Protos, appeared to find this hysterically amusing.

By the second hour, one of the officers had made Protos a serious offer to buy Eupraxia.

"She is not anyone's property, Ladamos, so you cannot buy her," Protos told him, with ponderous dignity. "Beyond that, she is too young for a husband."

It was amusing to watch Ladamos as he considered the matter. He couldn't keep his eyes from Eupraxia's face.

At the beginning of the third hour, a runner came with a message for Epaminondas, who read it and looked grave. He held a brief, whispered conversation with Pelopidas and then announced, "One of our outriders has reported that a Spartan army has made camp an hour's march the other side of Plataea. Pelopidas and I must leave. Perhaps, Protos, it would be as well if you and your lieutenant came with us."

The banquet was over.

30

In Epaminondas's garden, Protos and Agenor stood silently beside the out-side door while Epaminondas and Pelopidas studied a map they had spread before them. The only light was from an oil lamp on the table.

"By tomorrow midday they'll be on our doorstep again," Pelopidas an-nounced grimly, as if the fact fulfilled some sort of prophecy. "The ques-tion is, do we meet them tomorrow or do we wait?"

Epaminondas shook his head. "If we meet them tomorrow, we will have no idea what we will be facing."

Protos and Agenor exchanged a glance as the same thought came to both of them.

Someone should be watching the road tomorrow morning.

"But we have to meet them soon," Pelopidas, answered, with perhaps more heat than even he intended. "We can't spend another season hiding behind our earthworks. Our soldiers have to fight or they will lose heart. They have to learn that the Spartans are only men."

"True." Epaminondas scratched at the white patch in his beard, which had grown to cover most of his chin, and smiled. "A victory would also be useful."

Pelopidas turned to the two younger men standing beside the door.

"Protos, do you suppose you could arrange a victory for us?"

Protos struggled hard not to smile. Pelopidas knew as well as he that everything was at stake, and yet he could ask this question with the amused detachment of someone inquiring what might be available for breakfast.

"Agenor and I will have a look and let you know by tomorrow after-noon."

"That will be perfectly convenient."

❧❧

They rode straight through the night, and by first light they could see the smoke from the Spartan cooking fires. They found themselves a grove of trees from which they could observe the road north, tethered their horses out of sight in a nearby gully and waited.

"What are we looking for?" Agenor asked. He was understandably nervous—an army, particularly an army one has never seen, was always more terrible than individual soldiers, who, after all, were only men.

"First, numbers. Troops, equipment, cavalry. Next, officers. Who is in command? Is there anyone on his staff we know? Last, the baggage train, which will be followed by the Helot laborers. How many? Are there a lot of women? Will I see a familiar face?"

Agenor looked puzzled, which Protos chose to find amusing.

"Think of the numbers. If there are two thousand Spartans and only a hundred women—particularly after you discount the officers' whores— those women are going to be kept very busy. Plus, they have their regular work to do. How do you imagine they feel having eight or ten men a day wanting to crawl on their bellies? Of all slaves, women hate their masters the most."

"So you are thinking of spies?"

"Precisely."

"How will we be able to count the troops? There will be so many."

"The Spartans are always ready to meet the enemy and so they march in battle order, ten men wide and ten deep, with a space between each phalanx. It won't matter if the road is only wide enough for five; they will simply spill over the sides. Twenty phalanxes, two thousand men. You count the foot soldiers, I'll count the cavalry."

The sun was still bloodred on the eastern horizon when they heard the tramp of numberless feet, the squealing of wheels and the rattle of wagon chains—that chaotic blending of sounds which heralds an army on the march. They heard it a good quarter of an hour before they saw it.

"By the gods . . ."

It was something to behold, even from a distance of some seventy paces. The Spartans were considered the finest soldiers in the world, and they looked it. They marched with their lines perfectly dressed, their spears held firmly erect, and they were magnificent-looking men, with hard, brutal faces.

"They are not really human," Protos said, half under his breath. "They are machines for killing. That is their strength and their weakness."

Agenor risked a glance at his face, which was like stone.

"You really do hate them, don't you?"

"Keep counting," Protos snapped, and then, as a sort of apology, he laughed. "And yes, I do."

They counted thirty phalanxes—three thousand men—and sixty cavalry. There were remarkably few women in the baggage train.

And the Spartans had brought siege equipment.

"They aren't here just to pillage the countryside," Protos said. "With an army of three thousand, the Spartans probably imagine they could conquer Olympus. And with siege equipment they are forcing us to a choice. We can either fight them outside the walls or at the walls. Which would you choose?

"And it will be soon."

"How do you know?"

"Let's go. We have a report to make."

On the ride back, Protos was occupied with the challenge presented by so large an enemy force. He wanted to break their pride, which was perhaps possible. He wanted to destroy them, which was not. The Spartans were merely a problem to him now, and he focused on how the Theban army, which had never faced them in battle, could achieve something like a victory. Except in the abstract, he did not even hate them. And his mind was empty of fear.

Agenor asked him again, "How do you know?"

"Because they have so few cavalry. Sixty horsemen in an army of that size are hardly enough to carry messages back and forth. They won't be sending out scouts in any number, which means they don't care what we do. They have the initiative and they intend to take advantage of it."

Protos urged his horse to a canter and laughed.

"And that is why they left their whores at home."

"Then what can we do?"

"Do? We can take advantage of their mistakes. They've already made their first."

※ ※

They found Epaminondas and Pelopidas still in the garden. They might not have moved since the night before.

"Have you had anything to eat?" was the first question Epaminondas asked.

Pelopidas smiled in amusement at his friend and then, when Epaminondas had returned from the kitchen with a plate of meat and some beer, said, "Tell us what you saw."

Protos gave them the numbers and the two older men listened, hardly seeming to move. When the report was finished, Epaminondas merely shrugged.

"What do you think it means?" he asked.

"It means that they are here for blood," Protos answered. "It means that they will press for battle."

"And what would you do?"

Protos's grin was savage.

"I would give it to them—but on our terms. They do not have enough cavalry for reconnaissance. We could send a force out through the north gate and march them around to the east in a wide loop. With a little care, the Spartans would never know anything about it until you closed the trap on them."

"And then we take another force out through the south gate and challenge them?"

The two boeotarchs exchanged a glance, and Pelopidas nodded.

"It might work," he said. "Even if we only fight them to a draw."

"Yes, even then."

"How much time do we have?"

Epaminondas seemed to consider the question as he stared at the flowering vines that had almost taken over the outside wall of his garden.

"They will be here tonight," he said, touching his beard with the index finger of his left hand. "And tonight their slaves will build their stockade, so the commanders won't get any sleep. I would say it will be the day after tomorrow before they are ready to fight."

"Excellent," Pelopidas said—and Protos knew that he meant it. Pelopidas loved war the way a lecher loved women. "We will have an early dinner and then we will plan the destruction of the Spartans.

"By the way," he went on, turning to Protos, "did you recognize the commander?"

"No."

"Then it was probably Kleombrotus—they would not send out such a force except under the command of a king. It is lucky for us. Kleombrotus is less talented than Agesilaus."

❧❦

The next morning, while it was still dark, Protos left the city by the Proiti-des Gate and began surveying positions from which his skirmishers could block the Spartan scouting parties from access to the north. No commander would be fool enough to leave himself completely blind. Doubtless he would be keeping his eyes on the other cities of the Boeotian League, lest they attempt to send reinforcements, but it was obvious that Kleombrotus was not much concerned with Theban movements. Probably he thought that if he could keep Thebes isolated he had nothing to fear.

The job of the skirmishers would be to preserve that illusion at least for the next few days and to do that job they would have to know which routes the Spartan cavalry were likely to use as they probed north.

Protos knew that, should his skirmishers fail, the trap he envisioned would work the other way. Five hundred Theban foot soldiers would be marching into an ambush.

It took about three hours to discover that all the obvious paths north and east converged on two notches in a line of hills that were otherwise bad terrain for a man on horseback. A rider coming through those two points could easily be overwhelmed.

He would have his men in place by evening. And tomorrow he would discover if they had learned anything of what he had tried to teach them.

❦❦

To give them something to do, which she thought the best way to keep them from worrying, Nubit took the girls to the marketplace. She would buy a great deal of food she didn't need, since they were still living off the remains of Protos's birthday banquet, and would take a long time about it. The girls would complain about having to carry so much, and thus the normal pattern of life would reassert itself.

Last year, when the Spartans had first come, they had hardly noticed. This year the girls were older and no longer so preoccupied with the unfamiliar life they were living.

This year they were frightened.

If Protos had been home it might have been different, but he had disappeared with Pelopidas and Epaminondas. Without him in the house, the girls were prey to an irrational dread, as if the Spartans were already roaming the streets, searching for victims.

The marketplace was interesting. As always, it was a mirror of the city itself, reflecting its moods and caprices. Last year there had been virtual panic, with the price of bread rising tenfold the first day after the Spartan army was sighted. By that afternoon most of the stalls had been cleaned out—even though, in the end, the Spartans never attempted to lay siege to the city.

This time, with a far larger army less than two hours' march away, things were reasonably quiet. Prices were higher, but not by much, and there was no hysteria. People were afraid, as anyone would expect, but they had learned to trust their leaders.

"Epaminondas is an old fox," Nubit heard a butcher saying to a customer. "He'll think of something. He always does."

She almost laughed out loud when she heard the complaint of an old woman waiting to fill her jug from the public fountain: "What we need are a few more like Protos," she said. "If we had five more like him, the Spartans wouldn't dare to show their faces."

That was glory, Nubit thought. To be the hero of some toothless crone who had probably never rested eyes on Protos the Helot.

He was out there somewhere, preparing to take the gods alone knew what appalling risks. He could never hold back. It was as if he were daring the Fates to sever the thread of his life.

And Nubit could only wait, as women had waited for their men since the gods had created them. And that was why the gods had made women braver than men.

❧❧

Protos lay on a hillside, trying not to fall asleep. It was a warm afternoon, there was nothing to do, and he was sipping at the dregs of his beer jar.

As soon as it was dark, five Theban phalanxes would pass under the Borraiai Gate and begin their wide half-circle movement. They would march all night along a route that would eventually bring them westward into what would by then be the battlefield south of the city.

Kleombrotus did not want a siege—nobody wanted a siege. A siege could take months and the casualties on both sides would be horrendous.

He would want to tempt the Thebans into coming out from behind their fortifications, so he would not be present with his whole army. He would dangle perhaps a thousand men, perhaps even less, in front of the walls of Thebes, hoping Epaminondas might take the bait.

But that would be tomorrow. For now, Protos's battle was here, in the hills to the north, where he and his men must keep the Spartans blind.

And to do this he had issued orders he hated.

"Kill the horses too. We can't have riderless horses wandering back to the Spartan lines or they will know we are hiding something. Men and beasts must disappear together."

A lookout came scrambling down the hillside.

"We have a visitor."

Protos followed him back up the hill, where he looked south at a man on a fine black horse. The horse was being kept to walking pace. They waited through the next half hour as he approached.

"What a dandy! I'll bet he fancies himself."

And doubtless he did. The Spartans did not put much value on cavalry, so it was not a place for a young man with ambition. It was the place where influential fathers hid the sons who could not be trusted in the thick of battle, the place for parade-ground soldiers.

In a quarter of an hour he would be within javelin range. It was time to make a decision.

"Let him through," Protos said, and the signal worked its way down the line. It would be another three hours before the Thebans were ready to march, so there would be nothing for this wanderer to see.

"If he comes back in a great hurry, we'll know to kill him then."

At twilight they saw him again, coming south. His horse was still at a walk and he was drinking from a flask about the size of a clenched fist—no one would put water in so small a container, and from the way he sat his horse it was clear that the flask must be nearly empty.

This lout wouldn't be able to find an army unless he stumbled over it, Protos thought. *He hasn't seen a thing. All he's thinking about is his dinner.*

Protos gave the hand signal that meant "let him through" and the Spartan passed harmlessly within ten paces of his worst enemy.

"It is a pity about the wine," Ladamos said quietly, when there was no danger of being overheard. "I could have used a drop."

"That only means you have never tasted Spartan wine."

❧ ❧

They kept a watch through the night, but no one came. In the first gray light of dawn Protos gave the signal to move out. It was well known that the Spartans liked to begin a battle in the morning, that they considered it a lucky time, and Protos wanted at least a piece of this one.

They proceeded at a slow run, a pace that would eat up the distance and leave them nicely warmed up when they arrived. As they passed the eastern position they were joined by Agenor and his men.

"Did you have much to do?" Protos asked him.

"Only two." As he ran along beside Protos, Agenor shook his head. "They are so careless. It's almost insulting."

"At least it's an insult we will know how to answer."

By the time they arrived, the battle in front of Thebes was already two battles. Thus, where the opponents had initially been evenly matched, the surprise attack from the west had forced the Spartans to divert three phalanxes, leaving only five phalanxes to deal with the main Theban force, numbering eight hundred men, with Epaminondas leading from the front rank.

The Spartans were accustomed to triumphing over numerically superior armies, but this year the Thebans were not a frightened, disorganized rabble and the Spartans were only just managing to hold fast. This was not going to be the easy victory they had expected.

Protos and his fifty skirmishers threw themselves against the three hundred Spartans facing west, whose lines it was just possible they might be able to break.

In the skirmishers' war each man was alone and Protos forgot all about being a leader and gave himself over to the mad joy of battle. Soon he was having a glorious time. He killed five men that he was sure of and had the gratifying experience of watching the Spartans drag to safety inside their formation one of their commanders whom he had targeted.

"Did the big mean man frighten you little boys?" he shouted at them. "Then best you run along home to your mothers!"

This was answered with a cloud of javelins, which Protos danced through as if they were so many raindrops.

"Can't you do better than that? Or perhaps you expect your enemies to stand still for you!"

He wound up and threw, and his javelin killed a man on the left corner on the nearest Spartan phalanx.

"That's how it's done!"

But, even as he was tormenting them, Protos could see the north entrance to the Spartan stockade, where they were organizing another six phalanxes. He glanced at the front rank of the Theban formation and saw Pelopidas shouting something.

In battle, Pelopidas was impetuous and rashly brave, but it was clear that even he knew they could not yet hope to hold their own against a Spartan force of equal strength. An instant later the Thebans began to fall back.

Already the battle was inclining toward the Spartans, who would not be driven back. Pelopidas had seen that. It was time for a retreat in good order.

They had all known, from the beginning, that this was the most they could expect to achieve, and yet it was bitter. Protos had hoped to break at least one of the Spartan phalanxes. Reason had told him it was impossible, but reason had nothing to do with desire and he had wanted that small victory. If he had had another twenty men he thought he might have forced the enemy to withdraw, but as things were the discipline of the Spartan formations was destined to carry the day.

The fight went on almost to the city's main gate, where the Spartans were at last driven off by Theban archers behind the earthworks.

Although they had been driven from the field, once inside the walls the soldiers cheered, the citizens cheered; even Epaminondas, who had fought in the front line to the main force, cheered as if at a victory. And it had been a victory of sorts—they had proven that they could meet the greatest army in the world and not disgrace themselves.

"It was beautiful," Epaminondas exclaimed, with unphilosophical enthusiasm. "We bloodied them. For the very first time, we bloodied a Spartan army."

"But they're still out there," Protos said. He was as happy as everyone else, but life had forced him to be a realist.

"Yes, but that doesn't matter. We held our own against them." Epaminondas made a sweeping gesture with his right arm. "Next year we'll be as good as they are, and in three years we'll overmatch them. The trouble with the Spartans is that, unlike the rest of mankind, they learn nothing from experience.

"And you were right in your assessment, Protos. You have the makings of a general."

"Not in this war, old man." Protos shook his head, but he was flattered. "I'll leave that to you and Pelopidas."

※ ※

Nubit was among the crowd inside the main gate, and finally she managed to claw her way through to Protos. He was facing away from her, but she pulled on his sleeve.

She would always remember the look of delighted surprise on his face when he first recognized her.

"Where have you been these past days?" she asked, feigning an anger she did not feel.

"Where have I been, Little Mother?" He bent down and kissed her on the mouth. "Playing rough games with the big boys."

31

For three days and three nights Kleombrotus kept to his tent. He was consumed with sullen anger and he did not know whom to blame. The men had fought well, with courage and tenacity, as befitted Spartans. The men were not at fault.

Kleombrotus would have lived a happy man if his brother Agesipolis, who had preceded him as king, had not died of a fever. Kleombrotus was brave and stubborn, but he did not like being a king and the complexities of command made him anxious. He was not a politician. He was a soldier. He only wanted to fight.

Officially, the battle was a victory, since they had driven the Thebans from the field, but it did not feel like a victory and it had accomplished nothing. If it accomplished nothing it was not a victory, and if it was not a victory it was a defeat.

And if it was a defeat, someone must be to blame. Kleombrotus had the uneasy feeling it was himself.

On the third night following the battle, a man on horseback sought admission to the stockade. He was dressed like a Spartan and carried a letter to the king from the former Ephor Dienekes. Kleombrotus read it and ordered the messenger brought to him.

"You have seen the contents of this letter?" he asked.

"Yes, lord."

The king motioned to a stool. Eurytus sat down. A servant brought a tray with a wine jar and two pottery cups.

"Pour us some wine," the king said. "And tell me why your father is so eager for word about our campaign. He is a friend of my colleague King Agesilaus. Does he wish to see me embarrassed?"

The question was both naive and tactless. Eurytus was embarrassed for a reply.

"No true Spartan wishes to see Spartan arms embarrassed, my lord," he said finally. "Not for any reason. And my father is a true Spartan."

The king shrugged, and accepted a cup of wine.

"Then why?"

"Because his negotiations in Athens are not prospering. There is mounting hostility to Sparta, which is not necessarily pro-Theban and can only be fed if Thebes is successful in repelling us. Thus he is interested in your assessment."

The king drained his wine cup and held it out to be refilled.

It seemed likely the only assessment Eurytus would receive was a shrug.

During the moment of silence that followed, it occurred to Eurytus that King Kleombrotus was not a clever man. His every thought was reflected in his face, as if each one required a physical effort.

"During the battle, I saw something so remarkable I could hardly bring myself to believe it," the king said at last. "One of the Thebans, although not in their uniform, killed several of our men. He almost killed me. Of course, every one of his javelins was answered with many of ours, but they fell harmlessly around him, he hardly troubling to evade them. He seemed to think it was all a great jest. He mocked us sometimes, and his accent was Doric."

"I know the man you mean."

"Yes, I thought you might." The king sipped absentmindedly at his wine. "There are men in camp who were with the Lord Agesilaus last year—I believe you yourself were here."

Eurytus nodded.

"Well, they tell stories of a Theban they call the Barefoot One, who waged almost a single-handed war against us. I am wondering if the son of Dienekes might be able to tell me something about him."

"Tell you?" Eurytus threw back his head and laughed—even to him his laughter sounded slightly hysterical. "Only that he is the most dangerous man alive."

※ ※

"Ultimately, he is our worst enemy. Epaminondas and Pelopidas care for nothing except Thebes. It is not their object to destroy us but to preserve their city. Protos fights for them only because they fight us. If Thebes and

Sparta make peace, he will find another way to attack us. He will never stop."

"Then what would you suggest we do?"

"Offer Thebes terms of peace, and make it one of those terms that they turn Protos over to us. After all, he is a runaway slave."

The king seemed to consider this for a moment, and then he made a sound somewhere between a grunt and a laugh.

"It is hardly possible to offer Thebes terms of peace," he said. "One offers peace when one is winning, and that is not yet the case. At this moment I could not even offer a truce without its being interpreted as a sign of weakness.

"Besides, this Protos of yours . . . He is only one man."

※ ※

At first light Eurytus mounted his horse and began the journey back to Athens. He would report to his father that Kleombrotus had fought one engagement and driven the Thebans from the field. Whether this could be construed as a victory he would leave to others to decide.

His mood was black. The campaign against Thebes he regarded as self-defeating. The days when Sparta could expect to be the arbiter of Greece were over. Instead of frittering away her strength in wars against the other cities, she should solidify her control over the Peloponnesus.

Men like Kleombrotus—men like his own father—still believed in the great myth of Spartan invincibility. That by itself was a defeat.

32

The mere fact that Thebes had dared to take the field against Sparta, even if she had at last been forced to yield it, was seen as a victory not only by the Thebans but by the other cities of Boeotia. Graea, Koroneia, Thespiae, Hyettos, Orchomenus, and even Plataea sent soldiers to fight the Spartans. There followed a handful of bloody, inconclusive battles, and at last Kleombrotus's campaign ended with his withdrawal, a tacit acknowledgment of his inability to destroy the independence of Thebes.

Protos stood on the south wall, watching the Spartans as they formed ranks for the march south. Beside him was Agenor.

"It won't end here," Protos said. From his expression one would have thought he was glad of it. "It will go on and on for years. Kleombrotus and Agesilaus will toss command of these campaigns back and forth like boys playing with a wooden ball, and it will never stop until both sides are exhausted."

Agenor was appalled. "Surely they will grasp that this is fruitless," he said.

"No, never."

Protos shook his head and laughed. Yes, he was glad.

"I think they are all mad. I think it is something in the way they are raised that renders them incapable of grasping an uncomfortable fact, even when it is before their eyes. They lack the imagination to change, and so they will go on hammering at the same stone until the hammer breaks.

"But there will be intervals of peace. If there were not, men would quickly fall out of love with war. Wouldn't that be sad?"

❧❧

There was to be a banquet that same night, at the home of a ranking officer named Gaiomaxos, who happened to be rich, and Nubit had bought

Protos a new tunic, that he might not look like "a peasant with dung between his toes," as she put it.

"But I *am* a peasant with dung between my toes," he responded, mockingly.

"Then wash your feet and put on the new tunic anyway. And put on your sandals."

It had not been necessary to purchase new sandals because his one and only pair were under their bed, collecting dust.

"And mind you don't waste all your seed on the servant girls."

"Oh, I will be much too drunk for that."

She slapped him playfully and laughed.

The house of Gaiomaxos was less than a quarter of an hour's walk. The banquet was to be an affair for men only, which seemed to be the custom among well-born Greeks. Slavery had a leveling effect, and families in Protos's village had held their rare celebrations together, which struck him as at once more civilized and more amusing. Banquets in the houses of the rich tended to degenerate into drunken brawls from which guests often had to be carried home.

Tonight, however, those guests included the leaders of the Theban army, among them the boeotarchs Epaminondas and Pelopidas. It was unlikely that anyone would be willing to disgrace themselves in their company.

Protos had been surprised when he received the invitation. After all, he was only the leader of a thrown-together band of skirmishers, hardly a real soldier, and he barely knew Gaiomaxos by sight. Added to that, he was a low-born foreigner.

At Gaiomaxos's house he was seized with terror at the idea that he might have been the first to arrive. He decided to wait in the shadow of a building across the street until a few others turned up, but luck was against him.

"Protos, what are you doing skulking around down there? Come up and have a cup of that filthy beer you drink."

It was his host, standing at the top of the double stairway leading to his front door. Gaiomaxos was tall, about the same height as Protos, but built on a more substantial scale. His hair and beard were curly and black, and when he smiled he showed all his teeth in the manner of a growling dog. He was fearless in battle and had the reputation of being a good fellow.

"I'm glad you got here ahead of the mob," he went on, throwing an arm over Protos's shoulders. "It'll give us a few minutes to get acquainted. I've always wanted to tell you how much I enjoy watching you torment those Spartan clods. They hate you, you know—it's wonderful!"

Inside the door a servant girl appeared with a tray holding a single bronze cup. Protos suddenly found himself wondering if she was a slave. Yes, she must be a slave. What else could she be?

Gaiomaxos took the cup delicately between middle finger and thumb and offered it to Protos.

"Here. I hope this is to your taste."

It was beer.

"How did you know I preferred beer, or did you just assume . . ."

"It's one of the things one can't help knowing about you. Everyone in the army knows you hate wine. The brewers are thriving."

It was very good beer, Protos decided. He also decided to stop feeling self-conscious in front of this aristocrat, who apparently wanted nothing more than to be friendly.

The banqueting hall was large and filled with couches that seemed arranged in some hierarchical order. Protos instinctively drifted toward the back of the room.

"No, no. Come up here," Gaiomaxos almost shouted. "There will only be about twenty guests tonight and it's very informal. You don't want to be off by yourself."

Protos sat straight up on a couch two removed from the host, sipping his beer and feeling like a bumpkin.

There were two girls and an older man busy preparing the banqueting tables. Like good slaves, they had acquired the ability to seem invisible—there and not there at one and the same time. Except to one who had been a slave himself.

Protos watched them, wondering what their life was like in this great man's house. Did Gaiomaxos abuse them and force the girls to serve his bed? He seemed a decent sort of man, but who could say? Having almost limitless power over another human being was not calculated to bring out the best qualities in anyone's nature.

Probably most of the citizens of Thebes owned slaves and regarded that as the natural order of things. Except for those who worked in the mines or who wore out their short lives carrying stone for the great building projects, slaves in the city-states were vastly better off than the Helots of the Peloponnese, but they were still slaves. It was a fact that grated on Protos's soul, but there wasn't anything he could do about it. He had no power to change the world.

Neither Epaminondas nor Pelopidas owned any slaves, having long since freed those they had inherited. It was one more reason to love them.

Gradually other guests began to arrive and the atmosphere became even more convivial. Most of these were men Protos knew only by sight, if at all, but all of them seemed to know him. They talked to him with the familiarity of old friends. For the slave boy from Laconia, it was an odd experience.

After about an hour Epaminondas appeared and then, shortly thereafter, Pelopidas. They worked their way around the other guests and finally Epaminondas joined Protos on his couch.

"Are you enjoying yourself?" he asked.

"I will know that better when I know what I am doing here. Why did you arrange to have me invited?"

Epaminondas smiled quietly, as if some secret need had been answered.

"You are here to meet them, and they you," he answered. "I want you to begin to understand how important you have become."

A servant girl brought him a cup of wine. The cup had a wide brim and he handled it delicately, apparently worried about spilling it.

"The people need heroes," he went on, taking a sip. "Commanders think in terms of numbers, but the people in terms of individuals. That is probably because their sons, husbands and fathers are the ones doing the fighting and thus for them the war must assume a human face. You have become that face, I think as much for the Spartans as for us."

The noise of the banquet seemed to die away. The two of them were alone in a little pool of silence. Protos felt as if a sliver of ice had passed through his heart.

"And your purpose is what? To warn me?"

Epaminondas shrugged. "In a sense, perhaps. You should know that your life has achieved a significance that transcends your mere human self. This has benefits as well as dangers, for you and for Thebes."

Then he smiled his unreadable smile.

"I will tell you something which will tickle your vanity. Ten days ago I received a note from Kleombrotus, offering me a truce for six months. There was one condition, that I turn over to the Spartans a certain runaway slave." The smile broadened and then collapsed. "I refused, of course. Personal loyalty was comforted by that refusal—after all, you once saved my life, and you have been a useful servant of Thebes. But a leader is frequently obliged to ignore such considerations. I had two more compelling reasons.

The first is that I already knew from my spies that the Spartans were preparing to withdraw. The second is that, had I consented, I would have sacrificed my own political position. You are popular enough that the next time I appeared before the assembly I would have risked being stoned to death."

He put his hand on Protos's shoulder, as if to comfort him.

"An exaggeration, perhaps, but not much of one."

Protos felt the weight of that hand, and he was forced to admit to himself that he was frightened. In battle he was never afraid because his enemy was before his eyes and he understood everything that would happen. But in this man's world he felt lost.

"And where does all this leave me?" he asked.

"That is precisely the question we must settle."

Epaminondas took away his hand and picked up his wine cup. He ventured a sip and seemed lost in his assessment of it. Then his attention returned to Protos.

"We must decide how to make the best use of what you have become."

❧❦

When Protos came home he did not go to his bed. Nubit found him in the garden, sitting on a stone bench, drinking beer.

"Didn't you enjoy the banquet?" she asked.

He shrugged.

"Did they snub you, these aristocrats?"

"No. Everyone was very friendly."

"Then what is the matter?"

"I am the idol of Thebes," he said in a tone that suggested the thing was unaccountable and in rather poor taste. "I have become a hero. Did you know that?"

"I knew it long before the people of Thebes."

"Do you mock me?"

"No." She laughed briefly. "Never that."

Nubit stood behind him in the warm darkness and stroked his hair. He leaned his head back against her breast and closed his eyes.

"My father never killed anyone," he said finally. "What would he think if he could see me now? Where is the glory in killing?"

"You are brave. The glory lies not in the killing but in the courage needed to face death."

"Epaminondas wants me to accompany his diplomats on their missions. I am to be displayed like an exotic animal, with fangs and claws. He says I will win friends for the Theban cause. How am I to do that?"

"By being who you are."

And then she shook her head, implying that enough had been said on that subject. For a long moment neither of them spoke. And then Protos reached up and took her hand.

"I think I want to go to bed now," he said quietly.

"An excellent idea."

They were almost to the stone steps leading up to the kitchen when he stopped. He clutched Nubit's arm, looking baffled, almost afraid.

"Do I have to be this thing, a hero?" he asked.

Nubit looked up at the night sky, which was the color of jet and filled with stars. Overhead she saw the constellation that the Greeks called the Toiling Man and was associated with Herakles. It made her smile.

"Whether you will or no."

33

The same night sky was over Sparta when Eurytus received a summons from his father.

"You are twenty-five now," Dienekes told him. "It is time you married."

"I am still five years short of the mandatory age. Marriage can wait."

Dienekes studied his son's face: Eurytus had the look of a cornered animal. It was as he had feared.

"You are thinking of your slave girl," he said quietly. "I have made arrangements. She is to marry a free non-citizen, a presentable young man with ambition. She shall have a suitable dowry and they will go to live in one of the Italian colonies."

"And if I do not agree?"

"As I said, I have made the arrangements. It is not for you to agree or disagree. It is done."

They were in Dienekes's garden—it was not the sort of conversation to which Dienekes cared to have any witnesses—and both men were standing. The scene had all the makings of a quarrel.

"You knew it could not go on forever with Iphigenia," Dienekes continued, for he pitied his son. "You have always known it. You allowed yourself to grow too fond of her."

"It is not a mistake I will make again."

"No." Dienekes shook his head. "But you might find happiness with a wife. My friend Nykander has a granddaughter—"

"And doubtless there would be political and dynastic advantages to such a marriage," Eurytus interrupted. "Well, since you seem to have a taste for making arrangements, I leave it to you. It seems that one woman is as good as another."

With that, he turned on his heel and walked out of his father's garden.

His own father and he could not stand to look into the man's face—another instant and he might have struck him.

Out on the street he simply walked, without direction or purpose. He had no idea where he was or where he went. He was like a blind man, the world around him obliterated.

Finally he stopped. He felt exhausted, not from the exercise but from the black misery of his heart. He leaned against a building and covered his eyes with his hand.

Where was Iphigenia? Right now, this instant, where was she? Had she ever loved him? Even a little? Was she this moment in the arms of her ambitious, presentable new lover, soon to be her husband?

Against reason and judgment, Eurytus felt that she had betrayed him.

At the same time he knew that it wasn't her fault. She was a slave, at the absolute disposal of her master. What she might desire or feel didn't matter. Whether she would miss him out there in Italy, longing for his touch, or whether she experienced the new life opening before her as a release . . . no one, not even her new husband, would ever know.

And it was not his father's fault. This moment had been inevitable. By law and custom, as Eurytus knew perfectly well, he must marry. And by law and custom his bride must be a Spartan maiden.

His father had done him a service. A year from now it would have been all the harder to let Iphigenia go. Five years from now it might have been impossible.

In this moment, to lose her would not kill him, although he almost wished that it might.

❧❧

For the next several days his companions in the mess hardly knew what to make of Eurytus. He dutifully attended meals but always seemed to be elsewhere. He made no jests—he rarely spoke at all—and if anyone spoke to him he would smile wanly and ask him to repeat himself.

And he was drinking more wine than was quite seemly.

Had they known how he spent his mornings, his friends would have been even more concerned.

But no one did know because after breakfast Eurytus was nowhere to be found. He would take a horse and ride far into the countryside, with no companion except a jar of harsh Laconian wine, and find himself a patch of shade where he could watch the Eurotas River slide by and drink until he began to weep. After he had exhausted his grief he would take a nap under the trees and then a swim in the river. Thus he was able to get through the rest of the day without disgracing himself.

He never went near his father's house.

Eventually, he knew, even a broken heart will heal. Perhaps it will always carry the scars of its ordeal, but it will come to function serviceably enough. It will beat, even if has lost the capacity to feel.

Iphigenia was gone. She was in Italy, lying beneath her husband as he unburdened himself of his seed. Nothing would ever bring her back.

And Eurytus was soon to be the husband of a certain Helen.

He understood that this was necessary. It was the way Spartans had lived for hundreds of years. A Spartan must marry to propagate the race. This was the law, part of the discipline that had made them the best fighting men in the world and—briefly—masters of Greece. The difficulty lay not in understanding but in acceptance. He would do it because he was compelled to do it, although his wishes went another way.

But no one cared about his wishes.

Finally it struck Eurytus that he was just as much a slave as ever Iphigenia had been. And, where she was now free, he would be a slave to his last breath. His life belonged to the state.

But their recognition of that fact was what made the Spartans what they were. They served the gods, their ancestors, and their country. That was what ennobled their lives.

And liberation came only when they closed their eyes in death.

❧ ❧

Sparta, the Sparta in which Eurytus and his father lived, was a small place, really nothing more than a village where everyone knew everyone, or knew of them. Thus Eurytus was vaguely aware of a Helen, the granddaughter of Nykander. Her mother had died of a fever, brought on, so it was said, by the news that Helen's father had met his end fighting somewhere in Asia. The girl had devolved onto her grandparents.

Eurytus decided that he probably would have known her by sight, although he was almost sure he had never spoken to her. But that was about to change.

These things were arranged according to formulas of behavior that had proved their usefulness over the centuries. The Festival of Artemis was upon them and everyone would attend. Girls in saffron robes would dance through the streets—one would be Helen, who had just turned seventeen—and a kid would be sacrificed at the goddess's temple. There would be out-of-doors dining and a great mingling of families. And somehow—one never knew quite how—a "chance" meeting would be carefully arranged.

Thus it was that late one lovely afternoon, when the weather was perfect and Eurytus had already had a cup or two of wine, he found himself with his back against a tree, eating pieces of roasted ox in the company of a dark-haired, reasonably pretty girl who appeared, through her flimsy robes, to have a substantial and well-formed bosom.

What did they talk about? Eurytus ended up telling her about his Italian campaign. He even showed her the scar on his shoulder.

"Did it hurt?" she asked.

"Yes, but less than I expected. I'm told it's always that way. In battle one has no attention for pain."

Iphigenia had now been gone for five months and Helen did her best to be alluring. She almost climbed into his loincloth, and why not? There were as good as married already.

Finally, he reached out and cupped her left breast in his hand. It was almost a gesture of contempt. She didn't object. She seemed to be trying to give the impression she hadn't noticed.

No, he wouldn't mind opening this girl's legs. He was a man with a man's needs, and she would do for that. But he knew even then that he would never be able to love her.

❧❧

Two days later Eurytus visited Helen's grandfather and asked for her hand. The question of the dowry, his father had told him, had already been settled, so the call was a pure formality. He did not see Helen. By custom she was already his.

And late that night, when Nykander's house was dark, Eurytus returned on horseback to collect his bride for the act that would make her his wife.

It was a tradition, as inviolable as it was absurd, a hearkening back to the idea that the warrior stole whatever he wanted. A wedding had to take the form of an abduction.

So, after a few moments, Helen, dressed in men's clothes, came through the garden door, and he reached down to pick her up and place her before him on the horse.

When they had ridden far enough to be out of sight of Sparta, Eurytus climbed down from his horse and led it and his bride into the forest. There he spread his cloak on the ground for her.

He tried to make love to her, thinking that perhaps something would awaken between them if he kissed her and touched her the way he had Iphigenia, but she did not respond.

At last she whispered tensely, "Do it!"

They managed the thing. It seemed to give her no pleasure, and he was glad when it was over. They waited there for a while, sitting on his cloak, and then Eurytus stood up and helped her to her feet.

They rode back to Sparta and he left her beside her grandfather's garden door. Everything had happened precisely according to tradition. They had hardly exchanged a word.

※ ※

Protos was with Pelopidas, traveling around to the cities of the Boeotian League, and Nubit was at home, teaching the girls sums.

At first they couldn't see the point. They were as ignorant as swans and could hardly count the number of fingers they had on both hands, but finally Nubit was able to explain the matter in terms they could understand.

"Do you wish to be farmers' wives or the wives of porters and day laborers? Does your ambition extend no higher? I hope to see you married to merchants and men of skill, so that you can live comfortable lives and not die of exhaustion before you are forty. If you learn sums you will be able to help your husbands in their businesses.

"I intend to teach you to read as well."

"Read!" Galene shouted. "There are scribes for reading. What woman reads? It is unfeminine."

"I don't want to read," Hemera sobbed. "Numbers are hard enough."

But Nubit would not be moved.

"I can read," she answered them. "I taught Protos to read. It took him exactly two days to learn the alphabet and now he reads the Greek poets for pleasure—*and* he can write. Of course, it must be admitted that Protos is clever. There is not one man in ten who even knows the alphabet and not one in twenty who can scratch the characters of his own name. Your husbands, rich and prosperous as I hope they will be, probably won't know how to read, but it is by being wiser than her husband that a woman earns his respect. Come now, if Protos can learn this so can you. What a man can do a woman can do."

But first came counting.

The initial difficulty was to convince them that numbers extended above ten—in their minds, any number above ten was simply "many." So Nubit began by teaching them the names of the numbers up to twenty, then up to thirty, and so on. Within a few days they were counting everything—the number of stones in the kitchen fireplace, the number of trees that lined their street, the number of days in each month.

Then Nubit took her money bag out of hiding and poured the coins onto a table. She taught them the values of the coins and how to add them together. Since the coins came from many different cities, each with different values, the task of addition was complicated. Eupraxia proved particularly adept at working out equivalencies.

When all this was mastered, Nubit taught her daughters how to write numbers and, since the Greeks used the same characters for both numbers and letters, it provided a start to learning the alphabet.

These amusements lasted the better part of a month. Numbers came easier than letters, and reading continued to puzzle the girls, although Galene was making progress. Little Hemera would burst into tears at the mere sight of writing.

❧❧

Every five or six days, which was as often as he could bring himself to do it, Eurytus slipped in through the garden gate of Nykander's house to sneak upstairs and pay his addresses to his new wife.

Nykander was perfectly aware of his visits, would have regarded it as an offense against his family honor if they had not been paid, but the pretense of stealth had to be maintained.

When Eurytus opened her door, there was always an oil lamp alight on the floor beside Helen's bed. She would see him and, without a word, raise the edge of the bedsheet so that he could behold her naked body. She seemed to think that should be enticement enough.

After they were finished, she would fish a small jar of wine and a pair of cups from under her bed. Then they would enter into the conversational part of the visit, which after the briefest of times was wearisome enough to make Eurytus eager to leave.

When they had been married about three months, Helen began to complain that she had not yet become pregnant.

"If you would come more often, it might happen," she whispered.

Being with child, it seemed, would make up for everything, even her apparent indifference to the sexual act itself. The only thing she wanted from her husband was his seed.

"I come as often as I can. I have other duties."

This was greeted with a shrug of contempt.

And such was marriage, Eurytus thought to himself. It was a miracle the race of men did not simply dwindle into extinction.

※ ※

After being gone for a month, Protos returned one afternoon. The girls would hardly allow him to rinse his throat with a cup of beer before they insisted on demonstrating their accomplishments. He affected to be amazed but could not but notice that Hemera, the baby, held back.

When dinner was over he sat with her until bedtime, reading to her from one of his library of scrolls. It was an exciting story, but he would stop from time to time to point out the letters.

"You see this?" he asked. "This is 'alpha' and it looks like an ox's head, only backward. This is 'pi' and looks like a doorway."

"Do you think you can get her to learn?" Nubit asked him after they had gone to bed. "She is not as quick as the other two."

"She is young and afraid of failure. Remember the flatbread?"

Even in the darkness she knew he was smiling.

"Sometimes the trick is to teach a thing without seeming to teach at all," he went on as he rested his hand on her belly.

After they had made love, he fell asleep and Nubit lay awake, listening to his breathing.

She felt absurdly happy. She loved this man, who seemed to cherish her, was brave and clever and still would sit for hours teaching a little girl her letters. She had her three daughters, who appeared to have decided that the gods had corrected their mistake by giving them a mother. Her life seemed blessed.

Yet Nubit knew it was all an illusion. The girls would grow up and leave her for husbands and children. She would become someone from the past. Protos was a warrior who took ridiculous chances. Such happiness as hers came with the end clearly in sight.

She told herself that the present was enough. All she asked of the future was to see the girls well settled. Life itself had a time limit.

She closed her eyes and prayed to Mother Earth to delay her vengeance.

34

The war had dragged on inconclusively for seven years and both sides were sick of it. Even Protos was wearied of the stagnation. It seemed to him that no one was prepared to take any risks, that the battles had become like formal dances that decided nothing.

This was why Protos, Epaminondas and thirty other officers were waiting beside the ruined temple of Poseidon in Isthmia, where they would meet a similar contingent of Spartan officers and take possession of ten hostages who would act as guarantors of Sparta's good intentions.

Epaminondas and five of the Theban officers would travel on to Sparta to see if he could reach an agreement ending the war.

Protos sat on his horse, feeling the sea breezes from the Saronic Gulf and trying to imagine what his life would become if this war ended. He didn't want an agreement. He wanted a victory.

He felt uncomfortable in his army uniform. He particularly hated his helmet, which was of bronze and made it difficult to hear.

"You are twenty-five now," Epaminondas had told him. "You are an important officer and protocol demands that you wear the uniform. And I want the Spartans to see your face. They fear you, and your presence at the handover will remind them that Thebes will tolerate no nonsense."

Finally in the distance they saw a cloud of dust blowing from left to right. The Spartans were coming.

Half an hour later, just before sunset, the two groups faced each other and Epaminondas rode forward to shake hands with the senior Spartan officer, who turned out to be King Agesilaus himself.

"I thought we might as well talk on the way," he said, directing the remark to Epaminondas but speaking loud enough for everyone to hear. "It's a long ride. My grandson, by the way, is one of the hostages."

Epaminondas nodded. "That is an unlooked-for courtesy, my lord."

While this exchange was taking place, Protos studied the faces of the Spartan hostages. One was Eurytus.

Their eyes met and, after a pause, Eurytus nodded. Protos returned the greeting.

At last Epaminondas rode away with his Spartan escort, leaving behind ten Spartans, some of whom were less successful than others at concealing their dread. The Thebans closed around them and as a body they headed north.

Thebes was a good two days away, so they pitched camp that night on the broad plains an hour's ride west of Megara. They made a fire and dined on whatever provisions they carried in their packs.

As soldiers they bore their enemies no particular ill will, and soon the conversation turned general and Spartans and Thebans traded impressions of the battles in which they had fought. Seven years of war had left nearly everyone with a fund of stories.

On the ride the next morning the two sides mingled freely, having somehow become merely a group of men on a common journey. At one point Protos and Eurytus found themselves in proximity and, as if from a common impulse, drew their horses up beside one another.

"What are you doing here?" Protos asked. "Surely no one forced you to turn hostage."

"My father sits on the Council of Elders, so it was politic to volunteer. Besides, I was curious."

"About what?"

"About how things go with Thebes. About you. About whether peace is really possible."

"Whether peace is possible is not something you will find out in Thebes," Protos said. "I suspect you already know the answer."

"And what is that?"

For a long moment Protos said nothing. He simply stared ahead. And then he turned to Eurytus and smiled.

"Does Sparta want peace?" he asked.

"Yes." Eurytus nodded, but his yes sounded provisional. "It is a question of the terms."

"Then let me ask another question. Do *you* want peace?"

"Yes and no. This war is folly. We are bleeding each other white and to no purpose. It is madness to go on with it."

"That is the yes, so what is the no?"

"I am afraid of what you will do if there is peace."

This made Protos laugh.

"I have no idea what I will do," he said, shaking his head and grinning.

Eurytus pulled on his horse's bridle and dropped back among the other hostages. They did not speak again on the journey to Thebes. Perhaps Eurytus had decided that he had already said too much.

※ ※

The hostages were watched but otherwise treated as honored guests of the city. They lived with senior officers of the Theban army, and their presence caused a flurry of entertainments and banquets. They were all sons of important men and it was considered necessary that they return home with a positive impression of Thebes.

When the preliminary arrangements for the exchange were being drawn up, Pelopidas and Epaminondas had decided that none of the Spartans would board with Protos, since to do so might have proved politically embarrassing. After all, he was a runaway slave, and the Spartans might take it as an insult. The curious thing, however, was how many of them desired to meet him.

He had received an invitation to breakfast at the home of Gaiomaxos. Gaiomaxos probably wanted to talk about the peace conference, Protos decided, since everyone knew that Pelopidas regularly passed on to Protos the letters he received from Sparta.

But it wasn't diplomacy, at least not on that level, which was to be the topic of conversation. Gaiomaxos met him at the door.

"I have two young Spartans staying with me," he murmured, throwing an arm over Protos's shoulders as if to envelop him in some secret. "They're hardly more than boys, so don't eat them. They wouldn't stop pestering me until I invited you. I'm glad to see you're not armed."

"I could kill a Spartan with a toothpick, but I promise to be on my best behavior."

Gaiomaxos showed him into a small, sunny room where a breakfast of cold pheasant, millet broth, and beer was laid out on a low table. Two young men, dressed in Spartan uniform, were standing at what amounted to attention. Except for the hard physical perfection typical of Spartan youth, there was no particular resemblance between them, but Protos could not help but see in his mind the two brothers who had suddenly appeared on the road that autumn night when he was fourteen.

And then they did something to break the spell. They smiled and stepped forward, offering their hands.

"It is an honor," one said. "Four years ago at Tegyra you put a javelin through my father's thigh. He keeps the point as a souvenir and brags about the incident to anyone who will listen."

"I must have been off my mark that day. I usually aim for the heart."

Protos smiled to show he meant no insult.

Gaiomaxos had tactfully withdrawn. They sat about on couches. Protos did not touch the food, but he drank the beer.

They talked about the war, which Protos had been fighting for so long and which these youths were on the verge of entering. Like all soldiers, they were more concerned with tactics and the virtues and mistakes of various commanders than with the larger issues. It was a friendly discussion.

And then one of the young Spartans, whose name was Tyndareos, asked the perhaps inevitable question.

"My Lord Protos—"

"I am not a lord," Protos interrupted, without raising his voice. "I was born a slave and my name is simply Protos."

"Then, Protos, since you allow me that liberty I will take another and ask why you hate us so."

Protos took a sip of beer and set the cup down on the table with almost formal delicacy.

"I do not hate you," he said, giving each word exactly the same weight, "at least, not as individuals. I would not consent to be here, having breakfast, with men I hate. I hate the *idea* of Sparta. I hate what the Spartans have done with their power. I hate the slavery they have imposed on my people. The war I fight against them was forced on me—I was given the choice of fight or die. I chose to fight. I will not deny that revenge was also a motive, since the Spartans once did me a grave injury. You are of course familiar with a little ritual called the *Krypteia*?"

The two youths exchanged a glance, and then Tyndareos nodded.

"The *Krypteia* cost me my whole family." Protos smiled mirthlessly. "First my mother and father, and then all the rest. They were harmless people, innocent before the gods, yet they were killed—murdered—so that boys could think themselves men.

"But enough blood has been spilled to settle that account. Now I fight for the liberty of my people, and to achieve that I must cripple Sparta. Thus I fight for the Thebans."

"But you are a Helot."

"Yes." This was followed by a brief few syllables of laughter. "It is a fact of which I do not need to be reminded."

"And is not slavery the lot heaven has imposed on the Helots?"

For a moment Protos stared at the youth, whose name was Orestes and who seemed such a boy, although probably he was only four or five years younger than himself. And slowly his anger dissolved into something like pity.

"The Helots are the native people of the Peloponnese." For all the passion in his voice, he might have been explaining a problem in geometry. "You have read Homer so you know of the Achaeans. Achilles was an Achaean, as was Agamemnon, as was Menelaus, as was your namesake Orestes. The Achaeans lived in great cities while the Dorians were still wandering nomads. But then the Dorians invaded the Peloponnese and enslaved them. You would call it conquest. I would call it theft.

"Was this the will of heaven? Perhaps. And perhaps it is now the will of heaven that the Helots be free. In any case, whatever we may wish to believe, we have no choice but to act as if it is men and not the gods who shape the destiny of this world."

⁂

"Here, read this."

Pelopidas lay on a couch in his study. He had a headache—a sure sign things were going unfavorably at the peace conference—and his wife and children had been chased out of the house. Protos was his only companion.

"What does it say?"

"Read it for yourself." Pelopidas shot Protos an annoyed look. "Here, read it." He shook the scroll at Protos as if offering a bone to a dog. "Once in a while you should read something that wasn't written by your damned Euripides."

"Aeschylus. I don't much care for Euripides—although *Medea* wasn't terrible."

"Just another damned Athenian. Here, read what Epaminondas has to say."

Protos took the scroll and opened it.

"'It appears we have a treaty, although I doubt it will hold even until the ink is dry. The Athenians, who count for nothing, are hungry for peace, and the Spartans know they need a breathing space and for that very reason are too full of injured pride to care. I suspect the whole business will fall apart over some niggling detail.'"

"That was written ten days ago. I expect to see the bonfire lit any hour now."

Indeed that very night the watchmen reported a point of light on the summit of the southern hills. That was how the signal was to be passed, all the way from Sparta, one bonfire after another in a line winding north. It meant that Epaminondas was on his way home.

❦❦

The temple of Poseidon had burned and collapsed almost twenty years ago. Sand had long since covered the steps and floor. Weeds and even a few small trees grew amid the ruins. The temple seemed on the verge of being engulfed by nature, of disappearing into the landscape.

Even the gods, it appeared, were not immune to time.

Protos, his company of soldiers and the Spartan hostages would wait here for the arrival of Epaminondas and his escort. They would probably wait through this day and the next, for Isthmia was closer to Thebes than to Sparta. They would make camp and then eat and spend the rest of the night drinking and telling stories, all of them the best of friends. In a day or two the Spartans would ride south and the Thebans north, and when they met again it would be as enemies.

The world was a mad place.

What could be madder than sitting on a blanket with Eurytus, sharing a jug of beer? Yet that was what Protos found himself doing.

"The chamberlain took to his bed for a week after he opened your little gift," Eurytus said, laughing. "Our host Xabrinos could not be brought even to look at it."

"But they knew it was from me?"

"Well, *I* knew." Eurytus threw back his head and laughed. "I would have known even if I hadn't been there to watch you cut it off. Whenever I think of severed heads, I think of you."

Protos held out the beer jar and Eurytus took a long swallow. It was strong beer and they were both pleasantly drunk.

"We really are a race of savages, you know."

"We are not of the same race," Protos corrected him. "You are a Dorian and, admittedly, a savage. I am an Achaean."

He found he had to take particular pains not to stumble over the last word.

"But you too have done terrible things."

"Not so terrible as you." Protos took back the beer jar. He wasn't angry, just thirsty. "I have killed many men, but never a woman or a child. I have my bad dreams, but I wonder you can sleep at all."

"Our traditions and martial training dull the conscience," Eurytus answered glumly. "A sensitive nature is a luxury no Spartan can afford. They took me from my mother when I was seven years old. You were allowed to be human until you were . . . How old were you when . . . ?"

"I was fourteen."

"Fourteen, then. At fourteen I was already a monster."

"And you have lived to see your error? How old are you now?"

"Thirty-two."

"And now, at thirty-two, you realize what they have done to you?"

"Having you for an enemy makes a man reflective."

❧❦

Epaminondas arrived the next afternoon. He was unfailingly polite in his farewell to his escort and shook the hands of each of the Spartan hostages. He sat on his horse beside Protos, waving and smiling until the Spartans were well out of earshot.

"Let's go home," he said, irritably yanking his horse's bridle. He didn't speak again for perhaps half an hour.

"Well, you got your wish."

Protos was like one startled awake. He had accustomed himself to the silence and had no clear idea what the man meant.

"What wish, old man?"

"You will get your war. I know you never approved of this snuffling after treaties. The Spartans refused to let me sign for the Boeotian League, insisting that each city in the League had to sign separately while Sparta was allowed to sign for her allies. Naturally I refused, which is what they expected. I don't think they really wanted peace on any terms except our capitulation. So now we will have war, and this time it will be until either they are broken or we are."

35

King Kleombrotus was in Phocis when the messenger arrived with instructions from King Agesilaus and the Ephors to march against Thebes.

"So. The conference failed, did it?"

"Yes, my lord."

"How many days ago?"

The messenger, who was probably no older than fifteen and still as pretty as a girl, stared at the king in bafflement.

Kleombrotus tried to smile kindly, but the experiment was perhaps not a complete success. He desperately needed an answer.

"How many days have you been on your journey, lad?"

"Six days, my lord. Four by sea and two by land."

"Good lad. Now get some food and some rest. You'll come with us into Boeotia and watch us grind that army of goatherds into paste."

The boy grinned as if his heart's dearest wish had been met. He was gone as soon as the king made a little gesture of dismissal.

Six days. Epaminondas would be back in Thebes by now and doubtless knew that there was a Spartan army operating in Phocis. He would have already issued orders that the mountain passes between Phocis and Boeotia be manned. Kleombrotus had no intention of marching an army of ten thousand men into an ambush.

The only alternative was to lead the army north, skirting around the eastern side of Mount Parnassus, and then following the coastline east until they could drop down into the plains.

That would be the hardest part of the campaign, just getting there. Once in Boeotia, he would roll over the Theban army like a millstone.

It was strange, but days before Epaminondas returned to Thebes everyone seemed to know that the war with Sparta would go on. Protos knew it even before he left with the hostage escort.

"They don't really want peace," he told Nubit. "For them, peace means acceptance of Theban control of Boeotia, which amounts to admitting that they have been defeated. The Spartans will never be able to stomach that."

The next day he climbed on his horse and rode south. He was in very good spirits.

Six days later, when Epaminondas and his small company of officers rode under the Onkaiai Gate they were received like conquering heroes. The people of Thebes were weary of war, but they blamed the enemy.

So, it would go on and on. Seven years of war might stretch into another seven, or perhaps there would never be an end until every soldier in Greece lay rotting in the earth.

The night Protos returned, Nubit had a troubling dream—although at first she could not have said why she was troubled, since the dream was peaceful, even idyllic.

She saw Protos in a wheat field, the sun high overhead and hot and bright as iron ready for the blacksmith's hammer. He was sitting on the ground with other men, all of them in nothing but their loincloths, their bodies glistening with sweat. There was a copper scythe lying on the ground, so it was harvesttime. But they were resting from their labor, passing a clay jar of water from hand to hand.

Protos was speaking. She could not hear his words, and she knew from his gestures that he was in the grip of some enthusiasm.

Finally he stood up and pointed to himself, the tips of his fingers striking his chest so that she could almost hear the sound they made.

How many times had she heard him speak that way? His hands were as eloquent as his words. With a sweep of his arm he could make men follow him into the jaws of death.

And where else would he lead them? Protos was a warrior.

But this man, sitting in a wheat field, was not the Protos who had ridden into Thebes beside Epaminondas, resplendent in his blue uniform, a hero to thousands who had never even met him. This man was a peasant, talking to other peasants. What could he be urging them to do except to fight?

The war between Thebes and Sparta dragged along from year to year like a wounded snake, but someday it would no longer be Protos's war.

Who were these men, these peasants to whom Protos was speaking? Where was the wheat field? She had the feeling she would never know.

And that was what made the dream so troubling.

❧❦

"'They are like sleepwalkers, fighting the same battle over and over again. Hit them from an unexpected direction and they won't know what to do.' Do you remember telling me that?"

Protos shook his head. "No. Perhaps someone else said it. Nevertheless, it is the truth."

"You said it." Epaminondas leaned forward and stroked his horse's neck. "You were sixteen years old—even younger, perhaps. I have been a soldier since before you were born, yet never have I received better advice. I intend to follow it today."

They were on a small patch of rising ground, perhaps a quarter hour's walk from the village of Leuctra. It was a hot summer day. Spread out before them was the Spartan army: with its allies, perhaps ten thousand strong.

"Do you fancy our chances, Protos?"

The commander of the Theban skirmishers, numbering now some four hundred men, surveyed the enemy's battle lines through narrowed, speculative eyes. He was trying to identify the Spartan allies by their uniforms.

And not only their allies, but a body of perhaps eight hundred men, barefoot and dressed in homespun tunics, armed with nothing except the short iron spears that were useless for anything except defense. These men, positioned to the left of the Spartan phalanxes, were not in any recognizable formation.

It was with a shock that Protos realized they were Helots. They could be there for no purpose but to provide a distraction, with their numbers to tangle up the Thebans' attack and be slaughtered.

But perhaps some of them might survive . . .

"Do the Arkadians want this fight?" he asked, forcing his mind back to the problem at hand. "Do the Argolids?" He raised his arm and pointed to a compact body of infantry on the right side. "There, in the place of honor, are the only soldiers we need to beat today." Protos did a rough count. "There are seven hundred of them and six thousand of us. Those seem very good odds."

Epaminondas laughed.

"I think I could send you out there alone and you would kill half of them. But I want you and your men to hold back until I have fully engaged with the Spartans. Once that is done, you have my permission to make their lives as difficult and short as you can."

"You have something in mind, old man?"

"Yes." Epaminondas nodded vigorously. His knuckles were white where he gripped his horse's reins. "Yes, I've planned a surprise for them."

"What is it?"

"Think, Protos. What would you do if you were Kleombrotus? Or, more accurately, what would you do if you thought the way he thinks?"

"I would come straight at you."

"Precisely, and as you say we have only to beat the Spartans to win. So I will mass my best troops to the left, in a deep phalanx, directly opposite the Spartans, and I will wheel around so that my front line engages him not in front but at an angle. I will assault his corner. What do you think Kleombrotus will do then?"

"I don't think he will know what to do."

"Precisely."

※ ※

It was a good plan, possibly even a brilliant plan, but would it work?

Protos and his skirmishers were gathered on a piece of rising ground about two hundred paces behind the battle lines. They were enjoying the cavalry engagement that was a prelude to the main action.

In recent years, as the forces under his command grew, Protos had taken to riding a horse. A horse allowed him a better view of how the battle was unfolding and greatly increased his mobility. When it was time for the skirmishers to engage the enemy, he would get down on the ground and fight beside his men. He wore no body armor and did not even carry a shield. He relied on his feet and his cunning to keep him out of harm's way.

But that time was not yet. And from his horse he could see that the Theban cavalry, who were more numerous and simply better, were driving the Spartans back into their own infantry lines, creating a shambles that it would take Kleombrotus some time to sort out.

"I hate standing around like this," Agenor said, lifting his feet, one after the other, as if the ground had grown hot beneath them. "When can we hit them?"

Protos grinned at him. "Don't be greedy. In another quarter of an hour the Spartans will have more than enough misery to contend with."

The Spartan phalanxes were beautifully precise. They faced their enemy square on. The left side of the Theban line was beginning to fall back, without really engaging the enemy—letting the Spartans think they had the battle won. They were mainly allied forces, but Protos had fought with them before. They were not cowards, so they were obeying orders.

"They are falling into the trap," Protos told him, raising his arm to point to the Spartans. "A phalanx can only engage with what is directly in front of it, but Epaminondas is going to hit them at an angle, which they will be unable to counter unless they redress their battle lines. Seven hundred men—do you think they can manage it in time?"

Agenor's answer was to clap his hands and laugh.

And at that moment they saw the trap begin to close. The main Theban force, in a phalanx some fifty men deep, began to march. They had kept back, so they had plenty of room to maneuver, and they began an extended arc that would eventually bring them into collision with the right-hand front corner of the Spartan formation.

It was beautiful. For a long moment the Spartans didn't seem to know what was happening. They had no idea they were already doomed men.

❧❦

When Kleombrotus realized the main Theban force was on the move, he stepped outside the Spartan phalanx for a better look. He stared at the column of infantry for a long time, and gradually he saw that Epaminondas was using a deep phalanx, possibly fifty or sixty men deep.

That didn't matter. His own formation was nearly as deep, and his men were Spartans. And, besides, it was obvious that Epaminondas was a man who understood nothing about military logic.

What sort of a commander puts his best troops on the left? Didn't he know that one put them on the right to counter a phalanx's inevitable rightward drift? Didn't he care? Couldn't he see that his troops on the right were already in ignominious retreat?

Gradually, it began to dawn on him that the Theban column wasn't marching in a straight line but was following a wide curve. It was a thing that defied everything he had ever learned about how opposing armies engaged one another. Epaminondas must be mad.

And then he saw it. In possibly the worst moment of his life he saw that the Thebans meant to hit his forces at an angle. They would attack the corner.

Kleombrotus had to adjust his lines to meet the Thebans straight on. But there was no time, no time.

He gave the order, knowing it was already too late.

❧❦

"Now is our moment," Protos told his men. "They are disorganized and confused—let them die that way. If a man steps into the front rank, kill him. Rain down your javelins on the core of their formation. Teach them that to be brave is to die. Teach them to be afraid. For every one of them you kill, one of our brothers will live. Have no mercy! I will show you the way!"

Half mad with the joy of battle, he rushed onto the field. Then he stopped, not a hundred paces from the Spartan lines, and threw. His javelin arched through the air and then dropped like a falcon on its prey.

❧❦

The Spartans saw him. They knew who he was. They knew that his right arm was the very god of death. They watched the javelin leave his hand.

Kleombrotus saw and remembered the Barefoot One, this man who had killed so many, scattering death. *He has returned for me,* he thought. He watched the javelin as it reached the top of its arc and began to fall. He was glad. Better to be killed than survive the disaster this battle had become. He knew that this time the Barefoot One would not miss.

❧❦

The Spartans fought bravely. They fought to protect the corpse of their king, to at least carry him from the battlefield to be buried with his ancestors in Sparta. That was their only victory.

And for this they paid a heavy price. Over half of the Spartans lay dead on the field at Leuctra. Their allies, seeing how the battle went, fled back to their fortified camp. They would renounce their allegiance to Sparta, they said. All they wanted was a chance to live.

"There has never been anything like it," Pelopidas announced, almost beside himself with triumph. "The Spartans have never before fought an enemy on equal terms and been defeated. The myth of their invincibility is dead."

Protos, who was refreshing his soul with beer, could only smile.

"You did it." He held up his beer jar in salute. "You did it four years ago at Tegyra. You were evenly matched against the Spartans and you beat them. I know because I was there."

"Yes, but that was nothing like this. They will never recover from this."

Epaminondas was determined that it should be so. When the Spartans asked permission to collect and bury their dead, Epaminondas refused until the Spartan allies had removed their dead. He wanted everyone to see how many Spartans had died. He wanted everyone to witness the scale of their disaster.

And then there was the question of the exchange of prisoners. On this Epaminondas was prepared to be lenient, but there were a number of captured Helots whom the Spartans had used as lightly armed troops. The Spartans refused to offer ransom for them.

"They were born slaves, so let them die slaves," the Spartan negotiator said. "We care nothing about them."

Everyone knew the usual fate of prisoners whom no one ransomed. They would wear out their lives digging ditches and carrying stones. Most would be dead in six months.

When Protos heard of it he went to Epaminondas.

"Give them to me," he said. "I will know what to do with them."

Sitting on a camp chair in front of his tent, drinking a cup of wine and looking every bit the triumphant general, Epaminondas was in a mood to be magnanimous.

"And what is that?" he asked.

"I will turn them into a weapon."

The boeotarch, the hero of Leuctra, a man who had just won the great wager of his life, seemed to consider the idea for a moment and then smiled.

"Do as you think best, Protos."

※ ※

Protos found the Helot prisoners—his countrymen, his brothers—sitting on a barren patch of ground near the center of the battlefield. There were probably three hundred of them and only twelve or fourteen soldiers to guard them, but they made no effort to escape. They were defeated men, men who had lost a war they never sought, the abandoned refuse of a conflict they could not begin to understand.

The battle had ended two days before, but no one paid any attention to them. All they knew was that their fate was sealed, that they were as good as dead.

Protos came with a supply wagon containing four hundred loaves of bread and a hundred great jars of beer.

"Eat," he told them. "Satisfy your hunger and get a little drunk, and then we will talk."

It was amazing the transformation wrought by food and drink. Within an hour dead hulks had been transformed back into living men.

"And now listen to me," he said at last. "My name is Protos and I am one of you. I was born a slave, as you were. I had this war forced upon me when the Spartans butchered my family, and I have been fighting it ever since. I do not need to be told that you are not here out of love of your Spartan masters. I know you are here because you were driven out of your villages and forced to become soldiers.

"And believe me when I tell you that, had the Spartans won, you would all be as good as dead. Twice before, in long-ago wars, they have used Helot troops, promising them their freedom if they fought well. And twice before the Helots distinguished themselves and, after the battle, the Spartans massacred them. They cannot risk letting you live, not once you have learned to fight as an army.

"But here, on this battlefield, the Spartans lost, and now all of you are going home."

At first this was met with stunned silence, and then, one by one, they began to climb to their feet and cheer. The sound seemed to erupt from the ground. It was the mad sound of men forcing themselves to believe what they could not quite trust.

Finally Protos raised his hands and the cheering died away.

"You will be given food enough for your journey back to Laconia. The Spartans will not be allowed to bury their dead until tomorrow, so I advise you leave today lest they catch you on the road. But before you go I encourage you to do two things.

"First, go and look at the Spartan dead. By our count there are nearly four hundred of them. They would have you believe—they would have the world believe—that they are unconquerable. But here, at Leuctra, we proved that they can die like other men. Now go look at your masters, rotting in the sun.

"Second, follow my example."

Protos unsheathed his Spartan dagger and held it over his head for them to see.

"This is the knife a Spartan used to kill my mother," he shouted. "I took it from her murderer and used it to cut his throat. Since that night it has drunk deep of Spartan blood.

"The battlefield is strewn with the weapons of men who will never need them again. Take them and carry them home with you. Hide them away, and await the day when you can turn them against your oppressors.

"Await the day! And when it comes, if there is still breath under my ribs, I will be with you!"

They cheered and cheered. They cheered until their voices cracked, for now they believed. They believed they were going home. They believed in the possibility of freedom. And they believed in a slave named Protos, who had escaped and fought and conquered.

36

"There is to be another peace conference, inevitably in Athens." Protos cut open a fig and inspected its interior as if he feared the worst. Apparently satisfied, he offered half to Nubit. "Pelopidas wants me to come with him. He promises he will taste all my food."

Protos laughed at his own joke, although Nubit did not seem to find it in the least amusing.

"Why do you need a peace conference?" she asked. "Why can't you just march south and put an end to Sparta?"

"My very question, to which Epaminondas responded, 'Protos, my son, you are very naive.'"

He liked to make breakfast when he was home and the girls were still asleep. Today he was making wheat porridge. He offered a spoonful to Nubit to taste.

"The Athenians are less than pleased with our victory," he continued, turning back to his cooking pot to add more honey. "Pelopidas and Epaminondas proposed doing precisely what you suggest, but the Athenians and Thessalians objected—they want to preserve Sparta as a means of counterbalancing Thebes. So there will be a peace conference."

"Can I come with you?" Nubit touched his hand. "The girls are old enough to look after the house. I can follow in the wagon. No one will even know I am there."

Protos turned around and smiled at her.

"I think that's an excellent idea. The gods know I will have little enough work to do. Pelopidas has probably already got the treaty written."

"So he will have his way with the Spartans?"

"Oh, yes." Protos nodded, as if the conclusion was inescapable. "If I am any judge that old fox will leave Thebes in a position to do whatever she likes."

"How will that happen?"

"Wait and see."

✥

"Wait and see," Dienekes told his son. "Sparta will weather this storm."

"Sparta is nearly ruined and all because, after he was invited here for a peace conference, Epaminondas was not allowed to sign for the Boeotian League. King Agesilaus apparently chooses not to believe that the Boeotian League even exists. What a piece of folly."

"Agesilaus is my friend and your king, Eurytus. Show a bit more respect."

"Agesilaus thinks with his testicles. Agesilaus has brought Sparta to her knees. Because of him, King Kleombrotus and nearly four hundred Spartans are dead. Agesilaus is an idiot!"

At that, Eurytus pushed away from the breakfast table and stomped out of the room. His father could only sigh and shrug his shoulders, although there was now no one to witness either gesture. Eurytus, whose general mood had seemed to darken in recent years, had been excitable and irritable ever since the news of the defeat at Leuctra. He grew worse every day.

And now there was this Athenian proposal for a treaty, which, as Eurytus had pointed out, Sparta would be forced to sign no matter what it contained because it was the only thing that would keep Epaminondas out of the Peloponnese.

Time. Sparta needed time, to replenish her troops and to rebuild her system of alliances.

"After this disaster our allies won't have anything to do with us," Eurytus had said. "Why should they? If they choose to abandon us and form defensive leagues of their own, they know they can count on Theban support."

"Wait and see," Dienekes whispered under his breath.

✥

In token of Thebes's position as victor and arbiter, the treaty negotiations were conducted at the house of Dexileos, into which Protos was received with perhaps more honor than was strictly his due. Dexileos seemed to feel he had something for which he needed to apologize.

"I have given strict instructions to my cook that he and he alone is to prepare your meals, which will be served to you only by my oldest, most trusted servants. You will be perfectly—"

"What happened could have happened anywhere," Protos interrupted, placing a hand on his shoulder. "It could not have been foreseen and was no one's fault except the men who contrived it and the man who hired them."

On the second day of discussions, Protos saw Eurytus sitting with the Spartan delegation. A nod passed between them. When the meeting adjourned for dinner, Eurytus sought him out. They sat together outside, on a marble bench, balancing their trenchers on their laps.

"Do you think anything will come of this?" Eurytus asked.

"Oh, yes, there will be a treaty. It is upstairs in Pelopidas's luggage. I haven't seen it, so don't ask me what it says."

"Are they that confident?"

"As you would be had you won at Leuctra."

"Then there will be peace."

"Yes. For a time. How long depends on how much your kings can stomach," Protos answered, without looking up from his meal. "By the way, you ought to try the turbot. It's excellent."

"I've lost my appetite."

"Why? I haven't told you anything you hadn't already figured out for yourself."

"No, it isn't that." Eurytus set his trencher down beside him on the bench. "Something just occurred to me."

"What is that?"

"The fact that you are here means that the war will be renewed. Otherwise, you would never have come."

Protos looked at him and smiled. "Try the turbot," he said.

❧ ❦

The negotiations usually went on into the small hours of the morning, but Protos was never there after dinner. And, since no well-bred diplomat left his bed before noon, he and Nubit had plenty of time in the morning to wander about and fill their eyes with the wonder that was Athens.

"Didn't you see anything of the city the last time you were here?" Nubit asked him as they made their way up to the acropolis.

"I saw the insides of a few great houses. I saw the harbor district. For the rest I didn't care. If I go sightseeing, I like to have someone to share it with."

He smiled, taking her hand and bringing it up to his mouth. In that moment, the world seemed a wonderfully comfortable place.

The acropolis was a small space crowded with temples and dominated by the Parthenon. Protos could not take his eyes from it. Every few moments he would walk on two or three paces, but only to change his perspective or to have a better view of the statuary under the roof line. He seemed in a kind of trance.

Finally he turned to Nubit, shook his head and smiled.

"I've heard people say this is the most beautiful building in the world, and now I believe it."

"What god is worshiped here?"

"A goddess," Protos answered. "Athena, patroness of the city."

"I know her—her Egyptian name is Neith and she is a war goddess."

"Athena is the goddess of wisdom and crafts."

Inside, they found the statue of the goddess, almost eight times the height of a man.

"I told you she was a warrior," Nubit proclaimed triumphantly. "See the shield and the spear? This one, she is also a virgin?"

"Yes."

"And you say she is the goddess of wisdom?" Nubit shrugged. "The Greeks seem to think that war and wisdom are the same. But what is that perched on her right hand?"

"It is only an owl," Protos answered. "It is a symbol of wisdom."

Nubit's reaction was to wrap her arms around herself. She seemed to shudder, although it was a warm day.

"It is a symbol of death. Hear me, Protos my darling. Trust nothing that is done or said in Athens."

※※

"It is quite an elegant device," Pelopidas said. He was sitting in his bath while Protos read the text of the treaty. At home Pelopidas was ascetic in his habits, washing only in cold water, but in Athens, in the house of his friend Dexileos, he became a sybarite. This, he said, was wisdom because, while one should not seek pleasure and comfort, one should also not refuse them. "You can skip ahead," he continued. "The interesting passage is near the end, the list of the qualified signers."

Protos saw the point at once.

"You will sign for the Boeotian League, but each of the cities of the Peloponnese will sign separately. Sparta cannot sign for them and thus the treaty recognizes their independence. Sparta won't like it."

"They have no choice." Pelopidas smiled, the way he always did when he was being particularly guileful. "To refuse to sign is to invite us to invade."

"And if they do sign, and then try to enforce their leadership of the Peloponnese . . ."

"Their allies will revolt and request our aid. This is the price they pay for teaching their allies to hate them. Now, be a good boy and hand me that washcloth."

❧❧

When the treaty was signed there was nothing more to do in Athens, and Dienekes and his son took ship for Laconia. They had a miserable passage. A storm that came out of the west and lasted half a month forced them to lay up on the island of Kithnos, where there seemed to be nothing to eat except grilled octopus. When the winds finally changed direction they were nearly run aground off the coast of Argolis. They were glad when they could set foot on the solid earth.

Three days took them to Sparta, where they immediately found another crisis brewing.

"Do you have any idea what is happening in Mantinea?" King Agesilaus asked impatiently. "Where have you been, by the way?"

Dienekes had hardly had time to wipe the dust from his sandals when he'd received the king's summons. He hadn't eaten all day and he was prepared to spill blood for a cup of wine. But the king was the king.

"Traveling, my lord—by sea."

The king appeared to have forgotten his own question. He stared blankly at Dienekes and then dismissed the matter with a curt wave of his hand.

"The Mantineans, may the bright gods damn them for their impertinence, have unified their principal villages into a city and are preparing to fortify it. It seems they are foolish enough to take this treaty that you signed seriously."

"If you will remember your own instructions, my lord, I was obliged to sign anything that would bring peace."

"Well, we haven't got peace now, not with the Mantineans putting up walls!"

The king was now over seventy, and the limp caused by his left leg being shorter than his right had grown more pronounced over the years. It was apparent as he paced back and forth across his audience chamber. He was almost wild with anger.

Agesilaus thinks with his testicles, Eurytus had said. At this moment the justice of the observation struck his father with considerable force.

"We have peace, my lord, as long as we don't go to war. When we have regained our strength it will be a small enough matter to force the Mantineans to pull their walls down."

"Mantinea, I might remind my Lord Dienekes, is just across our border! If we do nothing, how long will we be able to control the rest of the Peloponnese?"

"Longer than if we give the Thebans an excuse to invade, my lord."

And thus Dienekes discovered that, for the first time in his life, he was angry with his king.

❧❧

At thirty Eurytus had been entitled to move out of the barrack and establish his own household. His father owned a house in the next street, which he made available to his son, and Helen arrived with a suitable amount of furniture and utensils. His father also provided Eurytus with household slaves, one of whom turned out to be an excellent cook. Eurytus did not miss the barracks. But for his wife, the house might have marked the beginning of a reasonably agreeable existence.

Helen was not without her virtues. She managed the household and the slaves well. She was careful about money. In many ways she embodied the virtuous Spartan wife.

It was simply that the woman was without tenderness. She did not love her husband—at least, not in the sense that Iphigenia had always appeared to love her lord. Perhaps Iphigenia had only feigned love, but, at least when he was with her, Eurytus had felt it as truth. Helen gave the impression that she valued her husband simply as a means of becoming impregnated.

As soon as they had their own bedroom, Eurytus began going into his wife as often as his stamina would allow. Yet after seven years of marriage, there were no children. He knew Helen blamed him.

From time to time, he entertained himself with the idea of divorce. Eurytus could not initiate such a step without creating political problems for his father—Nykander was a trusted friend and ally in the Council of

Elders—but there was nothing in the law to prevent a woman from divorcing her husband and finding someone new. Helen was only twenty-four and her property was her own. Yet she never mentioned the possibility.

Perhaps she was waiting for him to die. Perhaps she fancied the idea of being a widow. Certainly, as her hopes for children faded, there was nothing in her behavior to him to suggest that his life was in any way precious to her.

Thus, on an evening a few days after his return from Athens, the circumstances of Eurytus's domestic life provided no encouragement to resisting his father's invitation to dinner.

Except that Dienekes was apparently not interested in food. Eurytus found him in his garden, halfway through a jug of choice Lesbian wine, which he seemed to be drinking unmixed. This, Eurytus had learned, was always a bad sign.

"I apologize for the way I rebuked you over Agesilaus," he said, with a sullen gravity that confirmed how he had been spending his time. "You were perfectly right. Perhaps he's gotten too old. Perhaps *I've* gotten too old."

Eurytus sat down across from his father and poured himself a cup of wine, which he diluted with two measures of water.

"What happened?"

Dienekes explained the situation in Mantinea and Agesilaus's reaction. Then he shook his head and looked at his son.

"The question is, how do we restrain him?"

Eurytus shrugged and took a sip of wine. "I'm not sure we can. He is very popular and the people blame Leuctra on Kleombrotus. Even before Athens I had the sense that no one here has digested the magnitude of the disaster. But he won't attack Mantinea if the Council of Elders does not give its assent. He won't dare. So it is there you must make your case for restraint."

Dienekes considered this for a moment and then nodded. Then he put his hand on his son's arm.

"It shall be as you suggest," he said.

"But it may not be enough." Eurytus moved slightly, causing his father to withdraw his hand. "I keep remembering the prophecy about a lame king."

"That if the Spartans make a limping man king they will suffer through storms of war? Yes, perhaps the gods are punishing us for having disregarded their warning."

❧ ❧

"How would you like to go home, Protos?"

Epaminondas had come down to the athletic field, ostensibly to watch the skirmishers drill. He had been standing beside their commander for some time before he asked his question, as if it were a sudden inspiration.

"What has happened?"

"Happened?" Epaminondas's look of innocence collapsed into a cunning smile. "Well, yes, something has happened. Come to my house this evening and Pelopidas will explain it to you."

When the drill was over, Protos went home to bathe and change. He must have betrayed a certain excitement because Nubit cocked her head to one side and her eyes studied him speculatively.

"Are you going out this evening?" she asked.

"Yes, to see Epaminondas. Something is going on."

"And you have no idea what?"

"None, except that he said something about my going home."

"How can you do that?"

"I don't know."

Her face took on a stricken look, so that he gathered her into his arms.

"I won't do anything foolish," he said. "I promise."

"Yes, but *they* have not promised."

⁂

"The situation is very simple," Pelopidas explained. "Almost as soon as the ink was dry on the peace treaty, Mantinea proclaimed its independence of the Spartan League. The Arkadian cities, with the support of Mantinea, then entered into discussions to form a league of their own. To counter this, King Agesilaus, with, we are told, the reluctant support of the Council of Elders, has declared war on Mantinea, prompting all the cities of Arkadia to join the new league and to request our aid. For the Spartans, it is a fairly typical diplomatic performance—the way to win friends is to threaten them."

"It has been three months since the treaty was signed," Epaminondas interjected. "I am surprised they were able to restrain themselves so long."

"So what are we going to do?"

Protos's question hung in the air. They were having dinner on the roof to escape one of the last hot days of the season. The lights of Thebes twinkled around them, and beyond was the great black emptiness of the Boeotian plain.

He kept remembering what Nubit had said in the temple of Pallas Athena.

Trust nothing that is done or said in Athens.

"Would you like to invade Laconia, Protos?" Like a good host, Epaminondas refilled Protos's beer cup. "You know the area better than either of us. We will need you."

Protos experienced a strange flutter of emotion in his chest. He was going home. It was actually going to happen. He would feed his eyes once more on the place where he had been born.

"When can we leave?"

"Not until after the winter." Epaminondas shrugged, whether at the unavoidable delay or at Protos's impatience, it was impossible to tell. "Fortunately, Agesilaus is pursuing his war with uncharacteristic timidity, so there is no immediate hurry. If we are going to fight Sparta on her home ground, I would prefer to do it when we don't have to contend with the rains."

"What will you do in Laconia?"

"You mean what will we do to Sparta?" Without waiting for an answer, Pelopidas sighed dramatically. "Well, we can't murder the old girl—if we even threaten it, Athens would probably come in on her side. But we can strip her down to the skin and see how she likes shivering in the cold. Will that satisfy you?

"For the time being, it will have to," Protos replied. "But remember, my war won't stop when yours does."

❦ ❦

The night after Protos left for the Peloponnese, for the first time in years Nubit dreamed of her father. It was not the dream in which she watched him die. It was not a memory, or at least it was not wholly a memory. It was a true dream, born of the imagination—or of the gods.

She dreamed of the day her father killed her mother. Mother was worn out with what was called the Nile fever, which swept through the delta towns a few times every year. She had to carry an amphora heavy with warm water and she slipped and dropped it, cracking a tile in Father's bathroom.

"You clumsy whore," he shouted, climbing out of the tub. "See what you've done!"

When he saw the broken tile he went mad with rage. He kicked Mother's legs out from under her and kicked her in the belly, again and again, until she began to vomit blood.

Then suddenly, out of the empty air, came a man, a tall man, wearing nothing but a loincloth and carrying a sword.

"Murderer!" he shouted. "She was guiltless!"

He beat Father with the flat of his sword. He was merciless in his rage and Father howled in terror. Nubit could not see the man's face, but there were scars on his back and she knew his voice.

He was Protos.

37

A few hours after dawn, Dienekes and his son stood on a hilltop overlooking the Eurotas River and watched Epaminondas's vast army as it crossed. There were Thebans, along with her Boeotian allies, plus Mantineans and Arkadians, a force of at least sixty thousand men, and they were entering the Spartan homeland. Such a thing had never happened before.

"All we can do is try to defend the city," Dienekes said quietly. "We can't oppose such an army in the field. It would be suicide."

"Suicide now or suicide later—what difference can it make? In either case, this is the beginning of the end."

Eurytus smiled bitterly and Dienekes found himself wondering why, at this moment, he hated his son so much. And then he knew, and it made him feel ashamed. Eurytus was saying out loud what his own heart had been whispering for days.

"We can hold out. In the end they will go away."

"And then they will only come back."

"Eurytus, I forbid . . ."

But Eurytus was not listening. He held his arm out straight, pointing to the opposite bank of the river.

"There he is, Father," he said, almost gleefully. "It has been years since you've seen him, but you must recognize him. There—the one who wears no uniform and rides a black horse. That is Protos. The triumph he must feel at this moment!"

"Yes, it is he." Dienekes's face grew hard as iron. "That is the slave boy who murdered my son."

"He is not a slave and he is not a boy and he killed Teleklos in self-defense. If he had been born a Spartan, you would think him a great man."

"But he was not born a Spartan, and that makes all the difference."
"Does it?"

❧❦

The object of their scrutiny never noticed the two men on a hilltop and he felt no sense of triumph. The symbolism of the moment entirely escaped him. His mind was occupied with whether the countryside ahead held any danger of an ambush. The scouts said no, but they were Arkadians and Protos wasn't sure they knew their business.

"I am going to have a look," he told Agenor. "I'll be back by nightfall, sooner if I find a problem."

The road followed the river's left bank, but the river followed a plain that stretched all the way to the sea, so the army could spread out over both sides of the road. Given the slow pace at which so large a force was obliged to move, they were two days, probably three, from Sparta.

Protos crossed and re-crossed the plain looking for patches of dead ground where a significant number of soldiers might conceal themselves but found nothing. It seemed the Arkadians were right.

He drove his horse hard. By early afternoon he wasn't more than an hour's walk from Sparta.

About fifty paces ahead he saw a man carrying a mattock, which meant that he was a Helot and as such would assume that anyone who could afford to ride a horse had to be an enemy. Protos advanced slowly so that the man would not run.

He needn't have worried. The man turned to look at him and seemed to turn to stone.

When there were no more than a few paces separating them, Protos reined in his horse.

"Good day to you, friend," Protos began, "I wonder if you—"

"You're him," the man interrupted. "It's really you!"

Protos shook his head. "Have we met before?"

"Up north, last summer, there was a big battle."

"You mean Leuctra? You were there?"

"You gave us bread and told us to go home. You set us free!"

The man's name was Kibus, and on the walk back to his village, whither he insisted Protos accompany him—"Wait till I show you to the wife!"— they talked about what seemed to be going on in Sparta.

"We've known for the last several days that something was in the pot,"

Kibus told him. "We've seen a lot of soldiers on the road, and the Helots who work in Sparta haven't been allowed to leave. My uncle's daughter takes care of the little children for a family. Usually she comes back to the village to eat her dinner and sleep, but no one has seen her in five days."

"There is a Theban army on the march south."

"Who are the Thebans?"

"The people who broke the Spartans at Leuctra."

"Is that so? They never told us anything. We were only there to die." Kibus, who was about thirty, with a thin body and a round face, looked at Protos out of the corner of his eye. "Are they going to finish with the Spartans this time? I mean, will we be free?"

"Maybe not all the way, but closer."

❧❦

The village had lost ten men to the Spartan press gangs. Only four had come home. Those four remembered Protos as a deliverer, and their relatives, who appeared to include everyone, seemed prepared to take their word for it.

Protos bought five goats and the whole village feasted. There was even a tub of beer—Laconian beer, which Protos hadn't tasted since he was a boy.

All four of the men he had liberated dragged out Spartan weapons looted from the battlefield. They wanted him to see them, to understand that they were ready whenever he came back to lead them. They seemed disappointed that this was not to be the day.

"You must understand that they are weakened but still dangerous," Protos told them. "We have to break the sources of their power, and that may be the work of years. But it will happen."

"Now, tell me how the harvest has been."

It was a real indulgence for Protos to be among his own people again. For a few hours he allowed himself to forget he was a soldier and became once more the peasant who could feel with his toes the soil of his native place.

It was dark before he climbed back on his horse to return to the army. He did not encounter the first Theban sentry until after midnight.

"Where have you been?" Agenor demanded. "We thought the Spartans must have you."

"No, we have them." Protos shook his head and laughed. "They are preparing for the final battle."

❧❦

"No. It's madness."

"We can do it. Once and for all time, we can rid the world of this curse."

Epaminondas stared at his commander of skirmishers, precisely as if Protos had just suggested they could attack Sparta from the clouds.

"I saw Sparta once when I was a boy," Protos continued, his voice perfectly calm now, as if this were simply another tactical question. "It isn't even fortified. Apparently it has never occurred to them that anyone would ever come close enough to attack her."

They were across a table from each other in Epaminondas's tent. The table was covered with maps; the one on top was of Sparta. True enough, there were no walls.

"Doubtless by now they have put up earthworks, and our estimates are they have four to five thousand men under arms, all prepared to fight to the death for the mother city. It will not be as easy as picking up a coin someone has dropped in the street."

Epaminondas leaned forward until his face was no more than a span from Protos's.

"You have never taken part in a siege," he went on, gesturing with his hand as if to sweep away any objections. "It is a long, fearfully hazardous process. Until the final assault, numbers count for very little, and when we finally do go over their shattered defenses we can count on losing two or three men for every one of theirs.

"And long before that day comes we will have an Athenian army at our backs. Athens fears us as much as she ever did the Spartans. She will not sit still and allow us to become the sole arbiter of Greece."

"We have sixty thousand men. Why should we worry about the Athenians?"

Even as he said it, Protos knew he was talking nonsense. At least from the Theban point of view, Epaminondas was right. Sparta was finished as a power in Greek affairs. She would never come back. Thebes gained nothing by destroying her utterly.

Except, of course, that she was still the mistress of Laconia. She still kept the Helots in utter subjection. But what was that to Thebes?

"I will open my mind to you," Epaminondas said, pointedly ignoring Protos's childish dismissal of the Athenians. "I will tell you what I plan to accomplish during this campaign, and perhaps that will reconcile you to forfeiting your revenge."

When Protos at last found his bed, he was somewhat consoled. There would be no blood in the streets of Sparta. There would be no siege. Sparta would suffer a different fate, one which would not avenge his family nor the four hundred years of subjugation his people had suffered.

But it was close.

※ ※

With Pelopidas in command, a force of thirty thousand men, mostly Arkadians and Mantineans but with a large enough contingent of Thebans to stiffen their resolve, were left to guard Sparta. Merchants were allowed in and out, lest the Spartans be starved into desperation, but the city and the substantial number of soldiers it contained were otherwise sealed off.

Epaminondas led the rest of the army south to loot and burn the farm-houses of Spartan landowners and to confiscate their huge supplies of grain. The army took what it needed and left the rest to the Helots. There would be no famine in the villages that winter.

They went all the way down to the seaport of Gytheion, which they briefly held, burning many ships. Then they headed north again.

At Sparta, Epaminondas reunited his army and gave the order to retire back to their base in Arkadia.

38

On the second morning of their return journey, perhaps an hour's march north of the Eurotas River, the vanguard of the Boeotian army encountered a horse and wagon waiting by the side of the road. A woman sat in the front of the wagon, a woman with copper-colored skin and black hair that fell to her waist, a woman known to at least a few of the officers who first saw her.

"Send a runner to tell Protos that his lady is here!" one shouted, and then he rode over and the woman threw her arms around his neck and kissed him on his beard. It was the sort of gesture that would have been thought shocking in a Greek woman, but Nubit, as everyone knew, was an Egyptian and lived by no rules except her own.

When Protos arrived, on foot, he cocked his head a little to one side and frowned.

"I thought I left you in Thebes," he said.

"I grew tired of it, so I thought I would take to the road again." Nubit shrugged her shoulders and smiled. "What a coincidence that we should happen to run into each other like this."

"And you bought a new horse."

"The old one died—of boredom, I imagine."

He climbed up on the seat beside her, kissed her on the mouth and took the reins.

"I think you followed me," he said. "I shall have to find some way to punish you."

"I'm sure you'll think of something."

They watched the army pass by, and that evening no one could find Protos anywhere.

In the ensuing weeks the wagon followed the army, and the soldiers became used to the sight of it. At night it would be parked in some spot near water, the "witch woman's" campsite now an accepted feature of the landscape.

A creature of habit and a peasant in his bones, every morning Protos awoke two hours before sunrise and laid the campfire while Nubit slept. After they had had breakfast, he would return to the army.

One night, so late that the stars seemed close enough to touch, Protos lay with his head in Nubit's lap.

"Did you ever miss this life?" he asked. "I did. I hadn't realized how much until this moment."

"What did you miss about it?"

Protos was quiet for a moment.

"The sense that the future doesn't matter," he said at last.

"We have both lost that forever."

❧❦

A few days after they had settled in their Arkadian base camp, Pelopidas came by before dawn, just as Protos was teasing the fire into life.

"The Helots of Messenia have once more revolted against Sparta," he said. "Epaminondas says we should go and help them. What do you say?"

"I say, how soon can we leave?"

Within two days they were under way.

"This development is of considerable strategic importance to us," Epaminondas explained as he and Protos rode west and south, just behind the vanguard of the army. "Of course, as soon as we withdraw the Spartans will attempt to retake Messenia. They have controlled the region for two hundred years, so they won't surrender it willingly. But if we can leave the old capital sufficiently fortified the loss may very well be permanent and Sparta's sources of wealth will have been cut in half. The real strength of any state is not its army but its treasury.

"We will briefly take over Messenia's government—I rather suspect that right now there is no government—and we will invite what remains of the old aristocracy to return. The Helots may view both of these moves with suspicion, and that is where you find a place in this grand design. The explanation of what we are attempting to do will sound better coming from one of their own. Tell them that we will stay no longer than it takes to render Messenia defensible and that we will leave a democratic government behind. Tell them you have the word of Epaminondas that we entertain no designs of incorporating them into some Theban empire."

"And have I?"

Epaminondas nodded. "Yes, you have."

"Then that is what I will tell them."

❧❦

Three days later Protos began his career as a diplomat.

On the basis of a rumor that some sort of local government was centered in a seaport town no great distance from Mount Ithome, Protos set out to find it. Even before he saw the ship masts dancing in the harbor, he recognized the place

How long had it been? Twelve years? At least twelve years—almost half his life.

He reined in his horse and looked about. The empty road stretched before him over slightly rising ground, the sea about a quarter of an hour's walk to his right.

Drop the blade, boy. You're worth a good deal of money alive, but after this we're not disposed to take any risks.

There had been four of them, but one was already dead on the ground. It had been a choice between certain death that instant or the probability of crucifixion.

Drop the blade, boy, or you won't live to find out what awaits you in Sparta.

That had been the day Protos learned the Spartans weren't his only enemies.

He made a clicking sound with his tongue and the horse resumed its walking pace into the town.

It was two hours since dawn. The seaward wind had died away and it promised to be a warm day. Apparently it was a market day, since stalls were set up along both sides of the main street, but their numbers were fewer than the size of the town would have led one to expect, and the bustle and festive atmosphere of a small-town market was somehow missing.

"How can you ask so much for a few broken pieces of fish?" a woman asked, in a voice just below a scream. She was a harried little thing, hardly into her twenties but with the lines of endless struggle already etched into her face. "How can you stand to be such a robber? How can I feed my family at such prices?"

"And how can I afford to charge less?" the fishmonger replied, with almost as much heat. "I have my stall tax to pay!"

The woman dug into her purse and extracted a few coins, setting them down on the counter in the manner of one committing an act of contrition.

Stall tax? Protos could only shake his head. Who ever heard of such a thing?

Some of the seventy or eighty people at the market had noticed his arrival, which was not surprising. He was dressed in the blue uniform of Thebes and mounted on a horse. His weapons were in plain sight. To most people, soldiers meant nothing but trouble.

The building where he had stopped for a cup of beer all those years ago—and had acquired an understanding of treachery and the value of an Athenian drachma—was now a burnt-out ruin. The condition of the timbers suggested that the fire had been recent.

Protos dismounted and tethered his horse to a blackened post. Several people were watching him with sullen attention.

"What happened here?" he asked, addressing himself to no one in particular. "I remember when this was a wine shop."

He smiled, to indicate that his interest was in no way official.

At first there was no answer, and then a man took a step forward.

"It *was* a wine shop," he said. "It was owned by a rascal named Xabbos, an informer for years. When the garrison here heard about the revolution in Pylos, they fled and the people burned this place down with Xabbos inside."

His gaze dropped to the ground, seemingly to disown any personal responsibility. "The people" had done it, not he—as if "the people" in such a small place were as remote as the gods.

"I understand." Protos nodded. "A long time ago I spent a few days here as the guest of your garrison."

By then the crowd around him numbered perhaps twenty people. For a moment they remained silent and then, gradually, a murmur of voices made itself heard.

The man who had spoken of "the people's" vengeance raised his eyes and stood studying Protos's face, perhaps trying to place it.

"When I was twenty," he said, "the garrison was killed off, to the last man. They were holding a runaway slave, a Helot boy. People said the boy did it. People said he had killed some Spartans before he ever came here. I don't know about that, but five men, the whole garrison, were slaughtered like sheep in a single night—I saw the bodies. And I never heard that anybody ever caught the slave boy."

"Maybe they never did."

Protos smiled, like one entertaining himself with some innocent recollection, and the man, who looked in his early thirties, nodded his head.

"They were wicked men, those five," he said. "They were the Spartans' jackals. Nobody missed them."

"And now you have driven the Spartans themselves out," Protos answered, indicating that they had arrived at their actual subject, "but the real labor will be to keep them out."

It was an interesting moment. The whisper of voices died away, and Protos quickly became aware that no one, not even the man who had spoken of "the Spartans' jackals," seemed willing to meet his gaze. The little crowd seemed oddly hostile, as though Protos had stumbled against something they would have preferred to ignore.

But no, that wasn't it. It was something else. They were afraid.

"Who are you?" someone asked, when at last the silence itself had become oppressive. "What do you want here?"

"Who am I?" Protos shook his head. It seemed, even to him, a question without an answer. "At the moment I am an envoy of the Theban army, which is encamped only a few hours' ride from here. You would do better to ask me what *they* want. They, like you, want to keep the Spartans out of Messenia, and that is all they want. The Lord Epaminondas, commander of the army, has pledged his word that Thebes does not propose to supplant Sparta as master of the Peloponnese. When we withdraw, and that will be soon, we hope to leave you in a position to defend yourselves and to administer your own affairs as you see fit. We have a common enemy and therefore interests in common. We seek not subjects but allies, and allies must be free and equal."

"Free and equal—when has that ever been?"

At first Protos could not identify the speaker, but then the crowd shrank back to reveal three men with swords dangling from their belts. One of them, clearly the leader, stood with his arms folded across his chest, grinning as at a jest.

He looked to be about twenty and he was very dirty, yet not dirty the way anyone would be coming in from a day working in the fields. This man's dirt was habitual. His hair and beard were a greasy tangle and his face looked as if he hadn't washed it in months. A peasant was poor but not lacking in self-respect. No peasant would allow himself to become so degraded.

His companions were almost equally unsavory.

"Free and equal!" the man repeated, his voice full of contempt.

The townspeople were afraid and maintained a wary distance. Many kept their eyes on the ground, as if ashamed.

The situation was immediately clear. These were brigands who had set themselves up as masters of this little cluster of buildings by the sea. This was the "government" Protos had been sent to find. Their authority was the fear they inspired.

But Protos had no intention of treating with such as these, and thus the first task was to break the grip of that fear.

"You find that amusing, do you?" Protos asked, with provoking serenity. "Perhaps you think I lie."

"Or you are mad." The man made a gesture with his arm that seemed to take in the whole town. "These people may be cattle, but at least they understand that all power rests on the point of a sword."

"A very uncomfortable position for it, I have no doubt." Protos' smile was like a goad. "And who are you, except a runaway farm boy with a sword you probably use like a bread knife?"

The man's face became black with anger. His right hand rose to his belt and then clenched, but he was not yet ready to draw his weapon.

"I am Plakidos," he said, shouting the name itself like a challenge. "I am second in command to Karpos, who owns this town. Those who live here do so with his permission, for the very air they breathe is his."

Protos could not help but laugh.

"And, might I ask, how many men does this Karpos have under arms? Twenty? Thirty? More even than that?"

Plakidos, for the first time, began to look uncomfortable. He glanced at his companions, perhaps to assure himself they were still there.

"Let me tell you about the Theban army," Protos continued, like a man imparting welcome news. "It is very near, but within this month it was camped just across the Eurotas River from Sparta itself. Yet the Spartans, whom all the world has learned to fear, never dared to offer battle, for the Thebans and their allies number in the tens of thousands and when they march the earth trembles."

"Then, among so many, they will not miss one man."

Plakidos's hand was on the hilt of his sword. He was seething with blind rage, and Protos watched him with what almost amounted to pity. After a moment he shook his head.

"Don't be a fool," he said. "I have five hundred men under my command, and if I do not return tonight they will want to know why. I dare say they will hunt down every one of your little band of robbers, with results you will find unpleasant.

"Yet such efforts will not be necessary because you will not kill me. Think for a moment—do I seem afraid? You know nothing of me, but I have met you a hundred times before today."

Slowly, using only the tips of his fingers, Protos drew his Spartan dagger from its scabbard. He held it up for Plakidos to see.

"You are no longer the master here. If you want to live, you will flee Messenia. You will run from here and not stop until you find a place where you can earn your bread as an honest man. If you draw your sword, you will die here and now. This I promise you."

The two men were separated by no more than six or seven paces. Plakidos might have thought he could cover such a distance in an instant. He might have thought he had nothing to fear from a man holding only a dagger. Perhaps his mind was so clouded with anger that he did not think at all. In the end it made no difference.

He took a step forward, pulling his sword free as he came, but then he stopped, then took another stumbling step, then went down on his knees, then collapsed to one side. His left leg slowly straightened, but after that he never moved again. The blade of Protos's knife was buried in his heart.

This was all his two companions needed to see. They turned and fled.

Protos walked over to the corpse of Plakidos and twisted his knife free.

"I will tell you why the Thebans do not live in fear of such men," he said calmly, bending over to tear a strip from Plakidos's tunic with which to clean the blood from his knife. "In Thebes, every citizen between the ages of sixteen and sixty trains as a soldier. No tyrant can arise because a tyrant cannot rule except by force. Force resides with the army, and the army is the nation itself. Thus the nation is free."

He straightened up and looked about him, studying the faces of the crowd, which by this time had grown to perhaps fifty people.

"Now—who can direct me to this man Karpos, who fancies himself lord here?"

"He will be in the old garrison, it is—"

"Thank you," Protos interrupted, smiling. "I remember the way."

Not knowing what he might encounter in this lawless country, he had brought a quiver of javelins, slung over his horse's withers. He counted them now—there were eleven.

How many men would Karpos have behind him? He would find out soon enough.

He was afraid, but fear had become a familiar companion.

As Protos walked down the road that paralleled the sea, he was dimly aware that the crowd was following. He did not look back, for he did not wish to give rise to the idea that he was counting on them, but he had a sense—from the mutter of voices if nothing else—that their numbers were growing.

There was a small group of men, fifteen at the most, collected in front of the garrison. They were milling about, apparently aimlessly. It was no trick to discover which was their leader.

Karpos looked the oldest and also the strongest. His body bulged with muscle, so much so that his shoulders sloped and his neck almost disappeared into them. Yet there was something about his appearance that gave him a look of peculiar vulnerability, and it was with a slight shock that Protos realized what. The man was perfectly hairless, lacking even eyebrows.

Protos stopped about fifty paces down the main road. He drew six javelins from his quiver and struck them point first into the ground, making a little row in front of him.

"Karpos!" he shouted. "I call upon you to surrender. Your men may leave this place with their lives, but you must answer for your crimes."

The bandit chieftain wrapped his thick arms around his chest and rocked with laughter. It seemed the only answer Protos was likely to receive.

"Very well!"

There were three men standing close to the bandit leader. Protos pulled a javelin from the ground, balanced it in his hand and threw. It hit the man closest to Karpos square in the chest.

Before they could recover from their surprise, a second man pitched over dead. The third man tried to run, but Protos's javelin caught him between the shoulder blades.

"Karpos, if you draw your sword or utter so much as a word, I will kill you at once. As for the rest, will all who wish to die kindly step forward."

No one moved. They seemed frozen in place.

"Very well." Protos picked up another javelin.

In the next instant Karpos's men scattered like chaff in the wind. They simply ran away. Only Karpos remained.

Was it really going to be so easy? Was it really so simple a matter for one man to cow fifteen? "What a terrifying fellow I must be," Protos whispered to himself.

Slowly, he walked up to Karpos until only a few paces separated them. The man looked stricken. He was no longer dangerous. In the space of a quarter of an hour he had had everything taken from him, and now he was alone, staring into a future that seemed to hold only death.

But his gaze was not on Protos. His eyes were fixed on some far more terrible object, and a moment passed before Protos realized what it was.

It was the crowd.

Protos had almost forgotten them. He turned and looked over his shoulder, and there they were—men, women, even children. Possibly a hundred people in all. And their collective hatred had but a single object.

"Don't turn me over to them," Karpos said, in a voice that was almost a murmur. "Whatever you do, don't turn me over to them."

So much for glory, Protos reflected. The bandits had run away not out of fear of him, but of *them*. The people of this town had thus rendered his victory inevitable.

But at that moment they were little better than a mob, and Protos knew that if he gave them Karpos they might never rise to be anything else. They had to learn to be citizens, and it was time for the first lesson.

"Give me your sword," he said. "You will pay for your crimes, but not at their hands."

Karpos drew his weapon and presented it, hilt first.

"I accept your surrender."

⚜⚜

An hour later, Protos was sitting at a small table with three other men, representatives of the town, in the front room of the garrison. Karpos was in a cage, which, for his own protection, had been dragged inside and put in a corner of the room. The cage was small and badly rusted, and Protos suspected it was probably the same one in which he himself had been left out in the cold rain. The idea gave him no pleasure.

"You should turn him over to us," one of the townsmen said. "You could not sell a sack of grain without him demanding two parts in three of the price. He was more voracious even than the Spartans. Beyond that, his crimes include murder and rape. My own wife . . ."

For a moment he was rendered speechless by grief and rage.

"He attacked her in the marketplace—in front of everyone. She almost died and even now is fearful of leaving our house."

Protos glanced at Karpos, who, crouched uncomfortably in his tiny prison, was listening intently, and he smiled.

"Trust me," he said. "Justice will be done."

"He should die," another townsman said. "The worst death is too good for him."

"Trust me," Protos repeated. With a shrug he dismissed the subject. "And now let me tell you what the Thebans have in mind to do over the next few months, and what you should do to prepare for the changes that are coming."

※ ※

That afternoon Protos rode back to the Theban encampment. His progress was necessarily slow, for his prisoner followed him, his hands bound behind his back and a rope around his neck.

After two hours, Karpos begged to be allowed a little rest. Protos removed the rope from around the man's neck and let him sit in the shade of a plane tree. Karpos's hands were still tied, so Protos held his water skin for him to drink from.

He felt no hostility toward the man. He was a prisoner to be handed over to whatever justice Epaminondas decided upon, but he was still a human being.

"How did you come to be a bandit?"

Karpos closed his eyes for a moment, as if trying to remember.

"Hard times," he said at last. "I was a strongman in a traveling show. Our wagon lost a wheel in Sphacteria and we didn't have the money to fix it. We had been together for five years, but I saw this was the end. I turned thief. I was making a living so, when I had enough to buy a sword, becoming a brigand seemed the logical next step. Everyone wants to rise in the world."

He glanced at Protos and then turned his gaze away.

"What will happen to me?" he asked.

"The Thebans plan to rebuild the old capital of Messene. They will surround the city with a great wall to keep the Spartans out. I think they can find employment for you."

"I will work as a slave?"

"Yes."

"Well, it is better than dying."

"On that point there can be two opinions."

When he reached the Theban camp Protos turned his prisoner over to the guard and reported to Epaminondas what he had found in the town.

"The worst government is better than no government," was Epaminondas's judgment. "With the Spartans gone, every village in Messenia will be at the mercy of any cutthroat with a sword. I want you to take ten men and tour the country. You will still act as my ambassador, but you will have the additional charge of clearing out any brigands you find. If we bring these people peace and safety, they will trust us all the sooner."

With a detachment of ten of his skirmishers, Protos set off to visit the villages of southern Messenia. Nubit insisted on accompanying them.

"You will have need of me," she said. "You know what peasant villages are like. There will be sickness and these people have never seen a physician."

"You are not a physician," Protos answered with a smile.

"I am a better physician than any of your Greeks. All they know how to do is shake their heads and look grave. My mother taught me Egyptian medicine, and the Egyptians had physicians who could open skulls when the Greeks were still savages."

What could he say?

Upon entering a place, Protos would parley with the headman. Sometimes there was no headman, only a few brigands with swords.

"Who are you?" he asked one such in a large village they encountered on the third day of their journey.

The fellow merely smiled, displaying a mouthful of blackened teeth. He touched his sword hilt with the palm of his hand, as if this should be answer enough.

"Arrest him."

Inquiry among the villagers revealed that their prisoner was the local collector for a bandit lord who demanded "taxes" from several villages within a two days' walk in any direction. He commanded a force of ten men, all mounted and armed, and he would sweep in with no warning when he felt the need to assert himself. No one seemed to know where his base was.

His local representative was not popular. He had murdered at least three men who had objected to his attentions to their wives.

"I will give you a choice as to the manner of your death," Protos told him. "If you tell me where I can find your leader, I will simply cut your head off. If you don't, I will tie your hands and feet, dig a hole in the ground and bury you in it up to your neck. Then I will let the villagers take whatever revenge they care to. Which is it to be?"

The man was too frightened even to speak, so Protos gave him until dawn to consider his answer.

The next morning, after the man had wisely decided he preferred having his head struck off at once to having it torn apart by the fingernails of his victims, Protos and his men set off to find the bandit chieftain, who held court in a village only a few hours' ride to the south.

Thieves, even if they had swords and horses, were no match for trained soldiers, and they seemed to know it. They scattered as soon as they saw what was coming, and Protos's men ran them down individually and killed them. The chieftain was fool enough to allow himself to be taken alive and suffered the fate his underling had so wisely declined.

But usually there was a headman, and the visit of Epaminondas's ambassador proceeded in a manner much more agreeable to everyone. While Protos parlayed, Nubit would begin visiting the huts. She was good with infections, particularly eye infections.

"They are common in Egypt," she said, "so we have had centuries to refine the treatments." But many of the children were so run-down with hunger that they were almost without resistance to disease. "What they need is food. How can people be allowed to starve in the midst of such plenty?"

"That will change now," Protos told her.

"Your feasts do more good than my remedies."

And Protos would hold his feasts, which, as Nubit said, were probably the best medicine for people who sometimes hadn't tasted meat in years. He would buy four or five sheep and invite the whole village. And when everyone's hunger was sated, he would rise to his feet.

"My name is Protos," he would begin, "and I am one of you."

Then he would explain what the Thebans proposed to do and, because he had rendered them justice and feasted them and spoken to them in their own dialect, the villagers decided he was an excellent fellow and believed his words.

Usually they would spend one night camped outside a village, next to Nubit's wagon. Protos and his men would sit around her fire, and the men, most of whom had never been more than a day's walk from Thebes, would drink her beer and listen to her stories about Egypt and her travels.

"There are no rivers in Greece like the Nile," Nubit told them one night. "It is slow moving, like an old woman, and so wide one can stand on its banks and hardly see the other side. But one should not stand *too* close because of the crocodiles."

Babras refused to believe that such a monster existed.

"Believe it," she said with a little nod, as if revealing some great secret.

"I have seen them five or even six cubits long, and their jaws are powerful enough to snap a man in two. Sometimes they grab women who go down to the water to fill their jars. Great criminals are routinely fed to the crocodiles, so they have developed a taste for human flesh."

"I will never go swimming again," Babras announced, and everyone laughed.

But on one occasion Nubit did not return to the wagon. When the first stars began to appear, Protos grew worried and went to look for her.

"The witch woman is there," someone told him, pointing to a mud hut that was small even by village standards. "I think tonight she labors in vain."

The door was standing partially open, and he could see the flickering of a fire, so Protos went inside.

He saw Nubit crouched on the floor, beside the head of a woman lying on a dirty reed mat. Nubit was washing the woman's face with a damp rag.

At first Protos thought the woman was probably dead, but then he saw her eyes, wide and uncomprehending. She was alive but very little more.

"Is there anything left from the feast?" Nubit asked, her voice tense with anxiety. "She is starving to death and near her time."

It was only then that Protos noticed the woman's belly, which betrayed she was far gone with child.

"I'll find something," he said.

He returned almost immediately with a small clay pot, the contents of which were still warm. Nubit dipped her fingers into it and brought them to the woman's mouth.

"Her husband died half a month ago, and the villagers are poor enough that they left her to starve. She was so weak she couldn't even come out to the feast, and no one thought to bring her anything."

"Want makes people selfish," Protos said, keeping his voice to a murmur. "They can't help it."

Nubit merely glared at him and kept feeding the woman broth from the pot.

"I dare not feed her the meat," she said after a time. "In her condition she would never be able to digest it."

"What do you want me to do?" Protos asked her.

"Heat up some water."

After about an hour she sent him away. "This is woman's work," she said. "You will only be in the way."

But she smiled at him as she said it.

"Is there anything I can fetch for you?" he asked.

She only shook her head.

Two hours before dawn, Protos came back to the hut. The woman was lucid but in agony.

"Her water broke several hours ago, and she is in her birth pangs. I do not think it will be long now."

Nubit was kneeling between the woman's thighs and massaging her distended belly. It was possible to see the contractions, as rhythmic as waves on water.

"If the child is born alive, it will need milk," she went on. "Protos, could you find a goat with full udders?"

"I'll see."

He had to chase one down in an open field south of the village, but he caught it. When he came back, Nubit was already cradling the child in her arms.

"A boy," she said, her face glowing.

The mother was dead.

"I think her heart gave out—she hardly bled at all. Giving birth simply used her up."

Protos had to hold the goat down, but the child was able to suckle.

They stayed in the village through the rest of that day and into the next. Protos had an idea that perhaps Nubit would keep the child and raise it as her own, but in the end she surrendered him to a village woman who had lost a son the year before.

"We have hope now," the woman had told them. "You have made us believe things will be better after this."

"No one thinks of the dead mother," Nubit said bitterly, almost as soon as the baby was taken from her arms. "These people will leave her until she stinks. Protos, as a favor to me, will you bury her? Let her rest quietly in her grave, for my sake."

"Of course."

The next morning, before they left, he took the shovel from the side of Nubit's wagon and dug a grave beside a plane tree. He wrapped the woman's body in a soldier's cloak and put a coin in her mouth to pay the ferryman who would take her across the Styx to the Land of the Dead. He never learned her name, but she was buried with honor.

All during their journey to the next village, Nubit stayed in the wagon and wept.

❧ ❧

Protos was gone from Mount Ithome for a little more than two months. What greeted him upon his return seemed like a miracle. Where there had been ruin and desolation, there was now a city filled with people. Even the walls were nearly finished.

"We have built the best fortified city in Greece," Epaminondas said proudly as he took him for a tour of those walls. "The Spartans will never take it."

"But they will try."

39

The defenses of Messenia held. Defeat was something to which the Spartans had yet to grow accustomed, and it quickly made them bitter. And bitterness gave birth to a hunger for revenge.

One day Dienekes received King Agesilaus's invitation to a hunting party. It came as no surprise. It was a usual enough occurrence.

He was surprised, however, to discover that there was to be no retinue, no escort, no one except himself and Agesilaus.

And Agesilaus was in a filthy mood.

"Let's go find a patch of shade and get drunk." He stared at the back of his horse's head as if he hated the animal. "What do they say? 'In wine there is truth'? Well, my friend, at least I could always count on you for the truth."

When they found their shade, on gently sloping ground that stretched to the shore of the Eurotas River, Agesilaus used his thumb to break the seal on a wine jar, took a long swallow and passed the jar to Dienekes.

"Things are in a proper mess, aren't they," he said sullenly, running his fingernails through his beard. "I never thought I'd live to see a Theban army operating in Laconia. When it comes my time to die, I don't know how I will face my ancestors."

"It's not your fault. Kleombrotus made a mess of Leuctra."

"No. It is my fault." Agesilaus laughed bitterly and shook his head. "Kleombrotus was a dolt. I should never have sent him into Boeotia. And after he was killed I should have listened to you and avoided the trap of attacking Mantinea. It is my fault."

Rather than reply, Dienekes passed the wine jar back to Agesilaus.

"And now they've taken Messenia from us. Half our territory gone in an instant. They've fortified the old capital and that damned Helot . . . What's his name?"

"Protos," Dienekes answered. Whenever anyone talked about "that damned Helot" it was a safe wager they meant Protos.

"Yes, that damned Helot Protos goes about the countryside, telling the villagers they're free. It's nothing short of obscene."

"He killed my son."

"I know." The king turned his head and looked straight into Dienekes's eyes. "How long ago was that? Ten years?"

"Twelve."

Dienekes glanced away. He had the uncomfortable feeling that they had reached the real point of their hunting expedition and that their quarry was far away, in Boeotia.

"This Protos is the real danger," Agesilaus went on. "All slaves are self-ish, and the ambition of a clever slave is beyond imagining. I think he sees himself as the destined king of some Helot nation he plans to build on the ruins of Sparta. If we don't stop him, he may achieve that end. Just ten days ago a Spartan overseer was killed by a slave possessed of a sword—a Spartan sword. There is dangerous unrest among the Helots. We have to do some-thing."

Dienekes stared at the river, glistening in the sun like a snake in its new skin. He felt numb with dread. Although he knew that some response was expected, he could think of no words.

"I should have listened to your son during that first campaign." Agesi-laus's voice, like that of a tutor with a dull student, held a note of impatience. "Eurytus warned me about this Protos."

May the gods preserve my son, Dienekes whispered silently, in his own soul—and then, aloud, "Eurytus's mind, I suspect, is disturbed on the sub-ject of Protos the Helot. It was a great shock when—"

"Yes, of course," the king broke in. "I imagine he'll welcome the chance at revenge and, the gods know, there is no one among us who knows more about this slave than Eurytus. Who better to plan and carry out an assas-sination? Send him to me."

❧❦

A few months after their return from the Peloponnese, Nubit began to suspect she might be with child.

It had been many years since she had come to accept that she must be barren. Before she met Protos, when men wandered in and out of her life as carelessly as they might a wine shop, she had not cared. Indeed, she regarded it as a blessing. Wandering from place to place, giving shows in public squares, what would she have done with a helpless, squalling baby?

But then Protos had come, giving no sign that he did not plan to stay with her forever, and she had thought it hard that she could not give him a son.

Of course there were the girls, whom Nubit loved and who loved her as their true mother, but she had not suckled any of them at her breasts. She might have been more easily reconciled if at least they had been Protos's children, but they were not. Nubit had no one in the world who was either his flesh or her own.

And then, suddenly, in the thirty-seventh year of her life, when she had begun to think of herself as an old woman, she missed her monthly bleeding.

Well, there was nothing remarkable in that. It had happened before. She had grown unused to traveling, and her rhythm had become disturbed by hours in the wagon. It was a thing that happened to soldiers' women.

But several days later Nubit began to feel queasy—once she had to run into the back garden to vomit. This continued for nearly a month, during which she missed a second bleeding.

Finally she decided that she must be very ill or with child. Once the nausea stopped, she did not feel ill.

Nubit thought she would run mad with joy. A child, perhaps even a son—yes, certainly a son, whom she could watch growing up to be like his father. It was as if she herself were being born again.

But she did not tell anyone, not even the girls. Not even Protos. To speak of it would break the spell. To speak of it was to tempt the gods' wrath.

※ ※

No matter how politely phrased, one did not refuse an order from one's king. The last thing Eurytus wanted was to break the truce that existed between himself and Protos. He dreaded Protos the way a pious man dreads the wrath of the gods, yet even putting that aside he had no stomach for an assassination. They had been enemies for so long—with Protos dead, the world would seem emptier. To fail would be to die and to succeed, to kill some part of himself. Yet there was no choice.

And perhaps the time had come to pay the debt Eurytus owed his dead brother.

Thus that rainy autumn he once more took ship for Athens, this time alone. He was in possession of certain secret information, which he carried nowhere except in his memory. The king had allowed him considerable discretion in the means and timing of his mission.

"It would be as well if the thing could be managed before the end of winter," the king said. "But that gives you a few months."

From Athens, Eurytus traveled by horse to Plataea, where he had been told to stay at a certain inn and await instructions.

The next afternoon, five days after leaving Athens, Eurytus found himself in the kitchen of a farmhouse just outside of Plataea, in company with a certain Labotas, an officer of about forty whom hardly anyone ever saw and whom no one would have taken for a Spartan—he even spoke with an Attic accent. He had spent the last ten years of his life recruiting and running a vast network of spies throughout central Greece.

They were waiting for a man whose name Labotas rather pointedly neglected to mention.

Eventually the man came. He was small in stature and had a limp, which chiefly manifested itself in a faint scraping sound whenever he brought his left foot forward. His eyes, as black as his hair, betrayed a certain propensity for cunning. He did not look Greek, and when he spoke it was with an accent of indeterminate origin.

"Your Honors have need of me?" he asked with a smile that suggested a lewd jest.

"Just information," Labotas answered, the way he might have spoken to a slave. "You will answer some questions my associate will put to you."

Labotas glanced at Eurytus and, with an almost imperceptible shrug, turned the matter over to him.

"Essentially I have but one question," Eurytus said, trying to sound neither friendly nor otherwise. "What can you tell me about a certain Protos, once a slave in Laconia?"

The spy smiled again—or rather, as he had never stopped, his smile merely intensified.

"I know of only one Protos," he said, as if he had perceived some weakness he could exploit. "It is believed that he was once a slave, but whether in Laconia or elsewhere I could not say. He is a man of considerable daring and much in favor with the boeotarchs. May I assume he is the one you mean?"

"Yes. That is he."

For some reason the spy seemed to take this answer as bad news. He raised his hands in a gesture of disappointment.

"What is there to know?" he asked, and sighed delicately. "He is the man who killed the oligarchs. The assembly voted him a house and a sum of money, which he squandered on concubines. He lives with them and with an Egyptian woman, apparently a witch, who is several years older than he. Aside from a taste for harlots—perhaps forgivable in one so young—he leads a simple life and has no sense of himself as a great man. He will talk to the meanest laborer as an equal. Consequently, he is popular."

"Can you find out more?" Eurytus asked, struggling to keep the excitement out of his voice. "His habits, his movements, the names and histories of his associates? Such things I would wish to know."

"You mean to destroy him, then?" The smile on the spy's face died. "Come now, Your Honor, I am not a fool. Why else would you be making these inquiries?"

"Think what you like, but keep it to yourself," Labotas warned, the tip of his middle finger tapping the table.

"As you wish, Your Honor."

The spy, still sitting, made a slight bow.

"Leave us now," Labotas said. "You know how to contact me."

When they were alone Labotas rose and opened a small trapdoor in the kitchen floor. He began hauling in a rope tied to its underside. From the length of time he was at it, Eurytus guessed the shaft was astonishingly deep.

At last Labotas brought up an open wooden box filled with several small stone jars, all sweating with cold well water. Sitting down again, he broke the seal on one of the jars, set out cups and filled Eurytus's with dark, red wine.

"Distasteful, isn't he," he said. "If peace ever returns I may find it convenient to sell him to the Thebans, but until then he is not without his uses. Good spies are rarely good men."

"Will he be of use this time?" Eurytus asked.

Labotas nodded, as if agreeing to some obvious truth. "Oh, yes. Give him half a month and he will be able to tell you how often this fellow Protos changes his loincloth."

⁂

Eurytus waited in Megara. The city was a seaport and the people were accustomed to strangers. It was where he would meet his friends.

There were four of them, with Eurytus the fifth.

They came one at a time, overland or by sea, and stayed in different inns in different districts of the city. Each of these men he had known since the training grounds of boyhood. They had met when they were too young to hide their grief at being separated from their families and their fear of this threatening new life that was the road to manhood.

Eurytus and his comrades had traveled that road together, had shared its hardships, had accepted punishments that belonged to another's guilt, but each remembered seeing the others sobbing for their mothers, and thus among themselves none could pretend he was a perfect hero. And thus they trusted one another.

"It is an assassination," he had told them—he'd met with each separately, in Sparta. "I must warn you that it is possible, even likely, that none of us will survive. If we are caught we can expect no mercy, and the target himself is extremely dangerous."

"Who is he?"

"That you will learn in Megara."

All four had volunteered at once. That was what it was to be a Spartan.

The first to arrive was Dion, Eurytus's closest friend, who, characteristically, arrived as a crew member of a merchant ship out of Gytheion. He was tall, with yellow hair, and the only Spartan Eurytus had ever known who actually liked being on the water. He was an officer in the navy who happened to be home on leave when Eurytus was looking for volunteers.

"Yes, of course I'll come," he said. "The navy does little real fighting— I've almost forgotten what it is like to be a warrior. Thank you for thinking of me."

In Megara they found a dank tavern near the docks and spent what remained of the afternoon drinking a local wine that was dark as pitch and made one's face feel numb almost from the first swallow. Dion was very curious about the target.

"I'm hoping it's Epaminondas," he said. "I have a cousin who died at Leuctra."

"It's not. It's someone called the Barefoot One."

Dion's jaw dropped.

"We are going all the way to Thebes to put a *slave* to death? And five Spartans are required to do this? I can hardly believe it."

"Dion, this is the most dangerous man you will ever encounter. He kills as efficiently as a cook cuts vegetables, and with about as much compunction. I could tell you stories. . . . Suffice it to say he is someone to be feared."

The day before the last of the four was expected in Megara, Eurytus received a message that someone would be waiting for him the next afternoon at a certain farmhouse on the outskirts of Plataea.

The next morning he put on an ordinary tunic, purchased in Corinth, and took his horse from the stables. Plataea was no more than a day's walk and Eurytus disliked riding, but he did not feel safe venturing out into the Boeotian countryside alone and on foot. There was always the risk of being recognized.

The nameless spy sat on a bench outside the kitchen door, his eyes closed, his face turned up as if he wished to bathe in the light. Somehow he reminded Eurytus of a snake warming itself in the sun.

At last he opened his eyes and, upon seeing Eurytus, smiled his singularly repulsive smile.

"Your Honor does me the courtesy of arriving early," he said. "I suspect the mistress of the house will be as content if we finish our business sooner rather than later. I think she dislikes me."

Eurytus and the mistress of the house were of the same mind on that point.

"What do you have for me?" he asked.

The spy pulled himself up very straight.

"I have a list of the man Protos's associates, including notes on their family connections and where they live. I traced the former owner of the house—he resides in Athens now, in somewhat embarrassed circumstances, so for a small sum he consented to sketch the layout of the rooms. I know a good deal about Protos's personal habits, although his household servants have proved incorruptibly loyal."

"What of his friends?"

The spy seemed surprised. Perhaps he felt the question was irrelevant.

"I don't think he has any friends, Your Honor, at least not in the usual sense. He leads a military unit consisting of perhaps four or five hundred men who train with him on one of the athletic fields outside the city. It is odd but, like him, they all go about barefoot."

"Is there more?"

"I have written it all out for Your Honor," the spy announced, taking a papyrus scroll from the sleeve of his cloak. "You will find everything there."

On the ride back to the Megara, Eurytus's mind wandered through all that he had heard from Labatos's spy. The information confirmed what he already knew, for the spy could report nothing except the external facts of the life Protos lived within the walls of Thebes, within which he was somewhat bound by the circumstances of ordinary existence.

But outside those walls he was filled with stratagems and tricks, and he had the initiative.

Except by pure chance, Protos was never going to be captured or killed in the course of what he no doubt considered his personal war against Sparta. In that war he defined the terms of combat, about which he was both resourceful and clever.

Therefore, the only place to end that war was within Thebes itself, where he was a man like other men.

And had not Protos himself shown the way?

In the attack on the oligarchs, Eurytus remembered, Protos and his men had disguised themselves as whores, entered Lord Laius's mansion, and slaughtered him and his guests. Shouldn't it be easier for a small group of determined men to break into a private home and kill one man?

※ ※

The last of Eurytus's friends arrived the next day. That evening they assembled in his room to hear the plan.

"We will attack the house at night. We will need to be in and out as quickly and quietly as possible and be gone from Thebes before anyone knows what we have done. If we do not escape, we will all die there. Two of you will come with me. The other two will wait with a boat and horses with which to make our escape. You will draw lots."

Eurytus paused for a moment. He felt a curious reluctance, as if he were about to betray a friend.

"Protos lives in the northern quarter of the city, not far from the marketplace. It is a populous district, so we shall have to avoid calling attention to ourselves when we break in. We will have to escape to the west, since it is the shortest path out of the city and the only defenses are the river itself and some earthworks."

"How will we enter the city?"

Eurytus smiled. This was the part of the plan he liked best.

"Through the main gate, disguised as cattle drovers. Such traffic is quite ordinary. Thebes will not expect an attack by three men and twenty head of cattle, particularly since we will herd them the whole distance from

Megara. All of us will stay together until Plataea, where the two in charge of our escape will buy horses. When you reach Thebes you will buy or steal a boat.

"The remaining three will drive the cattle to the stockyards and leave them there—our gift to the people of Thebes."

40

A cattle drover usually wore nothing except a loincloth and was therefore burned almost black by the sun. Eurytus had worried that five men with pale torsos might attract attention, but the cattle raised so much dry summer dust that within two hours of departing from Megara they could have been white as buckskin underneath and no one would have noticed.

It was dull work, requiring no intelligence yet demanding careful attention. Cattle were stupid, perverse beasts, prone to wander off. A day of this would make any man glad to have been born a soldier.

Like drovers everywhere, they let the animals carry their gear. Among the various parcels and bags was a piece of sailcloth within which were wrapped, in careful folds lest they clink together, four swords—one for each of those who would enter Protos's house and one for luck.

They reached Plataea on the second day and made camp outside the city walls. In the morning, Proganos and Eukleidas, the two who would manage the escape, disappeared into the city.

Cattle are slow-moving and the sun was just touching the western horizon when the three remaining men reached the Proitides Gate. The guards took no notice of them. It was nearly dark before they had the cattle penned in the stockyard. Finding a stand that sold beer, they washed the dust from their throats. Then they inquired after the nearest public bath.

It was voluptuous to sprawl on the stone benches and feel the sweat dripping from one's body. Eurytus actually fell asleep. Then they cleaned themselves with warm oil and sank up to their necks in the baths.

As a precaution they had cut their hair, which Spartans traditionally wore long. Dressed in the change of clothes they had brought they could have been three young men from anywhere.

The spy had reported that Protos generally went to bed at the first hour of full darkness and rose two hours before sunrise—one wondered how he managed to discover such things. Eurytus judged the best time to reach the house would be when its occupants had been asleep for at least two hours, so he and his two friends had time for a leisurely dinner.

They found a small dining hall where they were able to hire a room. The proprietor seemed to take it as a personal insult that they ordered only a single jar of wine and avenged himself by raising the price. The men ate spiced duck, a local delicacy, artichokes, leeks, mushrooms and the bulbs of wild orchids.

Each of them knew that this might be his last meal.

"My father says that artichokes stimulate desire," Dion said.

"Desire for what?"

"For women, you idiot. What else?"

"It was a perfectly sensible question." The speaker was Theras, thickset and strong, who had wrestled in the last Pythian Games. "Who needs artichokes to make him desire women? Women manage that very well on their own. One might as well give something to a pig to stimulate his appetite for garbage."

They all laughed at this, more because it was a meal among friends than because it was outrageously funny. For the next hour or two, each man craved anything that would keep him from thinking of what was to come.

After they had tasted their second cup of wine—all the jar contained and all they dared allow themselves—they sang an obscene song about a whore and a traveling philosopher, of which there turned out to be multiple versions, each with its own champion.

Finally Eurytus went out to an alley to relieve his bladder, and as he did so he looked up at the night sky. Soon they would be paying their call on Protos. It was time for final things.

He went back inside and took his seat, silent, looking at nothing. It wasn't long before his silence descended upon the others.

"I have something to tell you," Eurytus said finally. "Something to confess. I trust each of you as I did my poor dead brother Teleklos, who died at this man's hands, so I know that what I am about to confide will never leave this room."

And then he told them about the four men with whom he had marched south to avenge his brother's death, about how Protos, still only a boy, lured them up that hillside, about how they had died, about how their severed heads bounced down the hill almost to Eurytus's feet.

"He could have killed me, but he did not. Instead he challenged me to a duel and I, coward that I am, refused. I refused because I knew that against this boy I stood no chance. Thus he shamed me, as he knew he would. He made life more bitter than death.

"We were five that day and we are only three now. The sole advantage we have is that he does not know we are coming. But I would rather walk into a den of wolves than into that house. I confess to you that I am very afraid, but fear will not stop me tonight.

"I tell you this that you may not underestimate him. I tell you this that you may fight him with all your courage and skill, for tonight it is not my honor which is at stake—my honor is perhaps lost forever—but Sparta's. This man has shamed us all. He has made us all afraid long enough."

※ ※

They found the house easily. It shared a wall with the next house, but the walls appeared to be plaster over brick, so it was unlikely the neighbors would be awakened. If they struck fast and hard, it would all be over in a few minutes and no one would know anything had happened until perhaps the next morning.

Everyone was familiar with the layout. On the outside, the house was like three-quarters of a square, with the last quarter being the garden. There were four rooms and a kitchen downstairs; upstairs were four bedrooms. The largest, presumably occupied by Protos and his sorceress, was in the back. Standing in the alley parallel to the main street, Eurytus could see the window.

There were two entrances, one from the street—where guests would enter—and another through the garden, which was walled and in the back. The garden was entered through a gate from the alley behind the house.

Eurytus and his friends would enter through the back door, since it would put them closer to the stairs. Control of the stairs was crucial because it would block all possibility of escape.

What to do about the women had been a vexing problem. There were the three slave girls, who might be sleeping in any of the upstairs rooms, and there was the witch. The simplest thing would be to kill them, but it was necessary to kill Protos first. He was the only one who presented real danger. Once he was dead, it hardly mattered what happened to the women.

Eurytus had decided that, provided they didn't make too much of a nuisance of themselves, he would tie them up and leave them. Let them shout their heads off once he and his friends were gone. It wouldn't matter.

He had told his friends that he would not tolerate any nonsense with the women. Somehow the idea of raping Protos's women after he was dead struck Eurytus as unseemly.

The back door presented the only remaining problem. If they simply battered it down, Protos would have too much warning. But, like every other household door in the world, the back door had a latch string. It would be pulled in for the night, but it was a simple enough matter to reach through the hole with a piece of wire, bent at the end like a fish hook, and pull it back out.

❧ ❧

Years of danger had made Protos a light sleeper. At first, in his new house, he had thought he would go mad as every creak of the timbers woke him. But he grew accustomed to them. It was as if in some dark, inaccessible corner of itself his mind had assembled an inventory of pops and crackles; even while he was deep asleep, his mind noted them and reassured itself, *Oh, yes, that is simply a nail pulling a little loose as the support beam contracts in the cold.*

But tonight something was different. Some sound Protos could not re-member hearing had chased away sleep. He lay in the darkness listening, his hand groping under the bed for Teleklos's knife.

There it was again—perhaps not a sound so much as a movement in the air. Somewhere a door was open.

Protos was already sitting up, his feet swinging over to touch the floor, the Spartan dagger in his hand, when he heard one of the stairs creak.

The air became still again, which meant that the door was closed. What was the distance between the back door and the stairs? Four, maybe five paces. The conclusion was obvious. There was more than one intruder in the house.

The rhythm of tiny sounds from the stairway indicated that two, per-haps three men were coming up. The one in front was big.

The knife was not going to be enough. There was a sword in the closet, but the closet was on the other side of the room. If he retrieved it they might know that he was awake.

And, besides, there was no time.

Well, these men probably had swords. To every problem there was a solution.

The doorway to the room was closed only by a curtain nailed to the lintel. Protos was on his feet and coming fast when the first man swept it aside.

What he saw was Protos's face—the last thing he ever saw.

Protos had the knife blade up under his ribs. The man stood there, already dead but not quite ready to concede the point. Protos could smell the man's breath on his face. He reached down and took his sword before it could fall from the man's lifeless fingers. When he pulled the knife free, the man collapsed instantly.

There was someone else behind him. This one was quick enough to learn from his comrade's mistake. The second man moved sideways down the corridor, probably trying to take himself out of range—but that was the way to the girls' room. Protos was not prepared to let him go there. He flipped the knife in his hand—it was still slippery with blood—and threw.

At that distance he could not miss. The second man pitched forward, the knife point in his heart.

But in that instant Protos realized that he had made a mistake. He had stepped out into the hall while a third man was coming up the stairs.

The sword was in his left hand. He made a clumsy parry against the thrust he knew was coming. He tried to twist out of the way and he heard the sound of metal grinding against metal, but it was too late. The point of a sword cut into his side, just below the rib cage. It went deep and then glided away, leaving a long slit.

And suddenly, in the darkness, Protos found himself staring into a face he knew better than his own. It was Eurytus. It was really he.

Eurytus opened his mouth, as if to say something, but Protos did not wait. He threw his weight against him, making him fall through the curtained doorway.

There was a scream. Nubit.

Two men were dead, but Eurytus was alive—and in the bedroom with Nubit.

Protos felt a spasm of pain shoot through him, from his wound straight up to his throat. He ignored it, grabbed the curtain and tore it away.

And there was Eurytus, his sword still in his hand, his face twisted into a strange grimace that mingled triumph and something almost like horror.

"I've killed you," he said. He held out his left hand to gesture toward the wound in Protos's side. "It's done. Look at how the blood is flowing. No one could survive that."

It was the wrong thing to say. The thought that came into Protos's mind was himself lying dead on the floor, and this man alone with Nubit. He could not abandon Nubit to his father's murderer.

He was not far from collapse and he knew it. The only thing within reach was Eurytus's extended left hand.

He swung down with his sword, catching Eurytus's hand at the wrist. It came straight off, like an apple cut from a tree.

For an instant Eurytus stared at the bloody stump. Then he screamed, more from surprise than pain, and Protos struck out at his sword—it fell from Eurytus's grasp. Protos tried to take another swing, but he was failing fast, fighting to stay conscious. Eurytus pushed him aside and ran for the stairs. Protos could hear him scrambling down the steps.

Protos turned to look at Nubit, who dissolved into blackness.

❧❦

Eurytus stumbled out of the house, into the dark sanctuary of the alley. His left arm felt as if someone were pulling out the nerves with a pair of forceps. He was bleeding badly. If he didn't do something quickly, he would be as dead as Protos.

Everyone was dead. His most bitter enemy, his closest friends—dead. Only he survived.

But the blood was pulsing out of his wound with each beat of his heart.

He tore at the neck of his tunic and managed to pull loose most of the front, which he wrapped around the stump of his wrist. The cloth was almost immediately saturated with blood. He stripped off the remainder of the tunic, but it was quickly soaked through.

He was wandering around the streets of Thebes in his loincloth and with his hand cut off. His life was ebbing away. How to stop the bleeding. How to . . .

At last he found himself near the marketplace, which was still crowded. At a stall a man was cooking long strips of meat over an open grill.

Eurytus pushed him aside and, to the man's horror, held the stump of his left arm over the flames, letting them sear the wound shut.

It was agony. He wanted so much to scream with the pain, but he couldn't. He felt he was about to collapse, but he couldn't.

Finally the flesh at his severed wrist was burned black. He pulled it from the fire. He walked away, sobbing with pain. People stared at him as if he were mad.

He had to get away. He *had* to get away. How far was the river?

How he made it he would never be able to remember, but finally he found himself sitting on the muddy riverbank. He wrapped the cold mud around his stump. It helped.

"Eurytus? Is that you?"

It was a man in a boat—Eukleidas. He was safe.

Eurytus splashed through the water to the boat. Eukleidas worked the oars and slowly they made their way across the river. On the other side would be Proganos, and horses. In three hours Eurytus would be back in Plataea, where a physician would attend to his wound and give him something for the pain.

He was alive. Dion and Theras were dead, but he couldn't think about that now.

And Protos was dead.

Eurytus felt an immense sense of relief. It had been worth it. It had been worth his friends' lives. It had been worth . . . Protos the Helot, the Barefoot One, was dead, by Eurytus's own hand. His brother Teleklos, son of Dienekes, was at last avenged. Perhaps now his ghost would find rest.

41

Except that Protos the Helot was not quite dead.

The noise of the fight and Eurytus's scream woke the girls. When they came out into the hall and saw the dead bodies they started screaming themselves.

"Stop it!" Nubit shouted. "They are dead. They can't hurt you. There is no time for this nonsense."

When something like calm had been restored, she motioned with her hand to the eldest.

"Come, Galene. Come now. Protos is injured."

At first all Galene could see was the blood and the severed hand lying on the floor. She seemed unable to move.

"Wake up, girl—do you want him to die? Help me turn him so I can get to his wound."

As gently as possible they rolled Protos to his right side, and Nubit wadded together some clothing to put behind his back. By then both women were covered in blood.

"We should fetch a physician," Galene said in a hoarse whisper.

"A Greek physician?" Nubit answered, her voice full of contempt. "We might as well let him bleed to death. Besides, there is no time. I will deal with this."

The other two girls stood peeking in through the doorway, apparently oblivious to the corpses in the hall and on the stairs. They stared in horror at Protos.

"Eupraxia, fetch me a bucket of clean water and all the towels you can find," Nubit ordered, without looking at them. "Hemera, put on some clothes and fetch Agenor. Do you know where he lives?"

There was a chest against the outside wall of the bedroom. When the lid was open the front detached to reveal drawers that contained a multitude of jars, some of bronze but most of clay, in different colors and sizes. Nubit selected a large jar with a red glaze.

"I only hope it is enough," she said, under her breath.

"And now you will learn something," she went on, speaking to Galene in the voice she used when she taught cooking—she knew she was talking only to keep Galene and herself calm. She broke the seal on the jar. "This red powder is a dried plant the Egyptians use as a spice, but my mother taught me that in the Eastern Lands it is used to staunch bleeding. I have used it on a cut thumb."

She coated her fingers with the powder and inserted them into Protos's wound. Even unconscious he must have felt the pain because his body stiffened and he groaned. When Nubit was finished her whole hand was thick with blood.

"Eupraxia!" she called. "Where are you, girl? Bring that water!"

"Will he die?" Galene asked, eyes full of tears, for she loved Protos. He was the hero of her sixteen-year-old soul. It was almost less love than worship.

"Do not even ask the question," Nubit answered, with more heat than she had intended. "He cannot die. He *will* not die. Neither I nor the immortal gods will allow it."

Eupraxia staggered in with her bucket of water and a few towels she kept pinned to her sides with her elbows. Nubit washed and dried her hands and again applied the red powder to Protos's wound.

"Get more water, girl. And another bucket into which we can pour it. We must keep the water clean."

Protos's breathing was ragged and tortured; the sound filled Nubit's soul with dread. She did not know if she was saving his life or killing him. She had only her mother's teachings to guide her, and if Protos died . . .

Perhaps only at a moment like this could she see with perfect clarity everything that this man's life meant to her. She loved him with the yearning love of the flesh and, like Galene, with her soul. Life without him would be empty. Life without him would be impossible.

The bleeding gradually slowed to a trickle and then stopped altogether. Nubit could not be sure that savage's blade had not cut into a kidney or a loop of gut. Sometimes those who suffered such injuries succumbed to terrible, killing fevers. But at least it appeared he would not bleed to death in the next hour.

By slow degrees Protos began to sleep more quietly. His skin was as yellow as candle wax, but he no longer seemed tormented. Nubit found a sticking plaster and closed the wound.

Half an hour later, Hemera returned with Agenor.

"Is he . . . ?"

"He is alive," Nubit answered. "That is all that can be said."

"What do you wish me to do?"

Nubit smiled weakly. She liked Agenor. She knew it made him suffer to see Protos like this.

"First, help me get him on the bed. Then get those corpses out of the house. Get them away from here. Finally, Protos must be guarded while the Lady Lachesis measures the thread of his life, lest his attackers return to cut it short. Perhaps it would be as well to circulate a report that he is dead."

"It shall be as you think best, but Epaminondas must be told the truth."

With a slight wave of her hand, Nubit conceded the wisdom of telling the first man in Thebes that Protos clung to life.

Once they had him on the bed, and the immediate danger seemed to be past, her nerves, so strong until then, took their revenge. She was covered in blood, weary and frightened. She hid her face with her hands and wept.

"I'm sorry," she gasped. "I'm sorry."

"Don't be. You have much to bear, and will have more still."

"He will live." Nubit spoke with a ferocity that even she knew was part bluff, as if she could bully the gods into sparing her lover's life. "He will not die. He has not yet done all that he must do in this life."

She turned her face from Agenor and sat down on the floor beside Protos's head. She touched his hair with the tips of her fingers, as if he were a sleeping child—*her* child, the child of her body.

"I will not let you die," she whispered. "You cannot leave me in this darkness. You cannot."

❧❧

For the next five days Nubit hardly left the bedroom. If she slept, it was only in a brief, absentminded stupor.

Through the first day, Protos did not open his eyes, and he was cold as a winter morning. Nubit lay beside him, covering them both with his Spartan cloak that she might keep him warm with her own body. She prayed to Mother Earth and the Egyptian gods of her childhood and, just to be sure, to the gods of the Greeks, in whom she had no confidence whatsoever. She wet her finger and drew it over Protos's lips that he might not thirst.

In the afternoon a Greek physician came, sent by Agenor. He touched Protos on the forehead and both cheeks and listened to his heartbeat by putting his ear against his chest. He shook his head and looked grave.

"I think he will not last the night," he said.

"You are a fool. Did you bring any maggots?"

"Maggots? What would I want with maggots, woman?"

"Go away."

The lower rooms were filled now with Protos's officers, speaking together in hushed voices. Nubit went down to speak to them.

"If you love him, find an animal that has been dead several days, cut it open and collect the maggots. Bring them to me."

Within two hours she had more maggots than she would ever need. Nubit put them in a jar and gave them a piece of rotten meat to feed on.

That night she drank a tea made from poppy seeds, lest she fall asleep as she kept Protos warm and hurt him with some unconscious movement. The tea made everything horribly vivid, so that even the very darkness assumed strange shapes. She heard voices in every whisper of air, voices full of terrifying prophecies.

In the morning Protos was still alive. Once, about two hours after sunrise, he briefly opened his eyes, but whether he saw anything or was even conscious was known only to the gods.

That afternoon, he turned his head, looked at Nubit and smiled.

"It seems I'm alive," he said.

"Yes, my love. You will live to be an old man."

She gave him a little water to drink and he was able to swallow it. Then he fell asleep again.

Nubit knelt by the bed and wept, blessing the immortal gods.

In the evening Epaminondas himself came. Nubit had only met him twice, on the night the Thebans took back their city and at Protos's eighteenth birthday celebration, so he was almost a stranger to her. She knew that Protos held him in the most profound respect, so she consented to come downstairs and speak with him.

"Will he live, Lady?" the great man asked her.

"He will live, Your Honor. He is strong."

Epaminondas nodded, apparently satisfied with the answer.

"He has cheated death so many times," he said, stroking his beard as if the white patch in it bothered him. "When he wakes, you might tell him that he has been voted a public funeral. It will be tomorrow. He will be amused."

When Nubit looked puzzled, Epaminondas shook his head.

"The body we will burn will be that of one of his attackers."

"Did the third man escape?"

"Yes.

"He saved my life," Epaminondas said as he prepared to leave. "And, more than that, he is like a son . . . I will take it as a kindness if you can save him."

❧❦

The next morning Protos opened his eyes and announced that he was hungry.

"I will allow you a thin gruel and I will feed it to you one spoonful at a time."

"I could eat a herd of sheep."

"Thin gruel. Yes?"

"Yes."

He only managed about half the gruel before falling back asleep. But this time it was true sleep, sleep that healed the soul as well as the body.

That afternoon he was awake for about two hours. He had a long conversation with Agenor, about the attack.

"If they would risk such a thing, it is clear that you have taken a bite out of their conceit," Agenor told him.

"I came over here directly from your funeral," he added. "It was beautiful. Everyone wept, even me." They could both laugh then.

But that night, Protos lapsed into a fever. By midnight he was delirious. Nubit cursed the treachery of the gods and wrapped him in a sheet soaked in cold water.

For three days Protos was out of his head, shouting one moment and talking the next to his dead mother. For three days Nubit wiped his face with a damp cloth and prayed. She moved the bed against the room's only window that the night air might cool him. For three days she hardly closed her eyes.

Sometime during the third night of his fever, Nubit felt a terrible cramping low in her belly. She knew what it was. At last, about two hours before dawn, her womb gave up its burden.

When she had recovered a little, she lit a lamp and looked at the bloody mess on the bedroom floor. Somewhere in that, she thought, was Protos's son. She had never doubted that she was carrying a boy.

But there was no time for mourning. She took off her skirt and used it to clean up every trace of her lost child. She took the skirt down to the kitchen and burned it to ashes on the hearth fire. No one must ever know.

And then, as the sun rose, Protos's fever broke as suddenly as it had come. When she was sure he was out of danger, Nubit lay on the floor next to him and wept.

After a time the fit passed, leaving her exhausted and shaky. When she went down to the kitchen to wash her face, she found Galene sitting beside the hearth, her eyes wide and frightened.

"It went out," she said. "The fire went out. I banked it myself last night. I can't understand it. Is it an omen? Does it mean than Protos will die?"

"No, it does not mean that. Protos is asleep. His fever is gone."

It was not an omen but a sign. The gods' message was clear. Nubit did not tell her daughter in all but blood that there had been a death in the family.

42

In Plataea the physician was astonished at how cleanly Eurytus's hand had
been severed. He had been told a story about how they were set upon by
robbers but had fought them off.

"Fortunately the cut line was straight on the joint. You lost the hand
but only the hand. Control of the arm will be unimpaired."

The physician, who had a white beard and the rosy cheeks of a child,
nodded vigorously. "But the burns must heal, and that will be a good few
months. I will give you a salve, which you are to apply twice a day. Keep
the site covered with gauze."

"I still feel pain in my hand. How is that possible if it lies back on the
road somewhere?"

"You feel what we call shadow pain. It happens sometimes when one
loses an appendage. No one knows why."

When the physician was paid and had bowed his way out, Proganos
poured Eurytus a cup of wine with his own hand.

"So—he is really dead?"

"No man could long survive such a wound. My sword went in right
under the rib cage. He was collapsing even before he took my hand off. He
must have bled to death in a short time."

"But you did not see him die."

"No, but he was obviously dying," Eurytus snapped impatiently. "My
hand was lying on the floor. Dion and Theras were dead. I was unarmed
and bleeding. It was time to leave."

"Then we accomplished our task."

Then why, Eurytus wondered, didn't he feel better about it? Was there
such a thing as shadow pain of the soul?

Knowing it was unlikely the Thebans would bury his friends with much honor, Eurytus offered sacrifice of wine and bread and cuttings of his beard for the repose of their spirits. It gave him no comfort.

As for his hand . . . There was a certain glamour to such a wound. It automatically made him something just short of a hero. In later years he would be telling the story to anyone who would listen.

No. It wasn't his hand, or his dead friends. This sorrow, this "shadow pain," was for Protos. Somehow Eurytus felt his very existence diminished by the slave boy's death.

It had been such a relief, and then somehow . . .

Or perhaps it was merely the pain of his burns that depressed him.

Yes, doubtless that was it.

※ ※

"They're disgusting."

"They are your friends."

"I don't have any friends who are maggots."

"They will clean out the dead flesh. Lie still and stop complaining."

Protos was too weak to argue, so he lay on his right side and let Nubit delicately arrange her maggots in the raw, puckered wound on his left. He was not sure, but he thought he could feel them moving about. He tried not to think about it.

Nubit fed him gruel and he slept a great deal. He was allowed beer, which made him sleepy—he suspected Nubit was putting something in it.

The girls came in every morning and kissed him. Nubit seemed to be encouraging them in this new intimacy. Perhaps she regarded it as some kind of compensation, for a strange sadness had enveloped her. In his weakened condition Protos did not object. He enjoyed the girls' visits.

As for Nubit, she said nothing and he did not ask, knowing she would not tell him. She had nearly worn herself out saving his life, so perhaps it was only that.

Nevertheless, it worried Protos. It was as if a kind of veil had come down between them.

Agenor was there every day with all the news of the city.

A month after the attack Protos could walk around, but he found he tired easily. Nubit had established a rule that his visitors, even Agenor— even Epaminondas—could only stay for a quarter of an hour because long conversations left him feeling exhausted. Even reading tired him. He could not seem to focus his attention on anything for very long.

He spent a good part of every day in his garden, even on days when the weather was cold.

He had been strong and active all his life, and now he was conscious of nothing so much as his own bodily weakness. It depressed him, and in his hours of solitude he tended to brood.

He thought a good deal about Eurytus.

It struck even him as strange that he harbored no ill will against Eurytus for what he had done. The attack had all the marks of a carefully planned operation—a military operation. It had been an assassination attempt, and Eurytus had already risked much to save him from another such attempt. Besides, he had brought two other men with him and none of them could have achieved their escape without help. Eurytus, on his own, would not have thought of such a thing. A duel, on equal terms, yes, but not a murder. Protos truly believed he would have to have been ordered to do it.

Eurytus was a soldier, as Protos was a soldier. They were both under discipline. Thus it was a thing impossible to resent.

In the meantime Eurytus thought he was dead. It made Protos smile to think how disappointed he would be. That would be his only revenge, not to have died.

But Protos wished he could be there when Eurytus found out. Imagining that moment was a sustaining pleasure.

There was little enough else to sustain him. Nubit said it would take him months to recover completely.

❦❦

It was nearly two months since the attack and Protos was mending, in body and in spirit.

Nubit had been out in the garden bringing him beer. When she returned to the kitchen she found Galene sitting at the table, her head resting on her hand. Around her wrist was a silver bracelet, a chain of delicate, glittering links. Nubit had never seen it before.

She went over and touched it. After a moment Galene pulled her hand away.

"It is a gift," she said.

"A very elegant gift."

With an expression that was almost defiant, Galene turned to face the woman she called her mother.

"He loves me."

"And who is 'he'?"

"He" was one Tagilos, a silversmith with a small shop just east of the marketplace. He was twenty-four and had come home after serving his apprenticeship in Athens.

"He seems a clever young man," Nubit said, fingering the bracelet, which Galene had taken off to show her. "This is a beautiful thing. And do you like him?"

"I love Protos best, but Tagilos will probably do."

They laughed.

"Well, then . . ."

"He wants to marry me, but he is afraid. He says that Protos is a great man and would spurn him for his presumption."

"Well, tell him from me that he is an idiot." Nubit could not decide if she was more amused or angry. "Let him come and present himself as your suitor. Protos is not 'great' in that way. Tell this lover of yours not to be such a coward."

☙❧

That night, having decided Protos was sufficiently recovered that it would do no harm to remind him that he was a man, Nubit smeared a few drops of scented oil between her breasts. After crawling into bed, she reached down to touch his manhood and discovered it was hard as stone. Apparently he did not need reminding.

When they were finished—they had to be careful because the wound in Protos's side was still tender—Nubit told him about Galene's lover.

Upon hearing of the silversmith's hesitation in approaching him, Protos laughed.

"He makes objects of use and beauty, and I send men's souls down to Hades. Which is likely to be more acceptable in the sight of the gods?"

The next morning the silversmith presented himself. Protos received him in the garden and could see at once that Tagilos, who was only a few years younger than himself, was very nervous.

"My lord—" he began.

"Don't call me that," Protos interrupted. "I am merely Protos, who, had the Fates been kinder, would today be a farmer in Laconia. Would you care for a cup of beer?"

Halfway through the first cup, Tagilos began visibly to relax. He was a slender man of middling height, but his hands were graceful and clever and there was that in his face which suggested intelligence.

"And so," Protos began, in an offhand manner, "I understand that you wish to marry Galene. Do you love her?"

"Yes." Tagilos suddenly pulled himself up straight on the stone bench. The question seemed to surprise him. "Yes, I love her. Who could help but . . . ? I cannot tell you . . ."

"Well then, you will probably be a happy man, for she is a sweet-natured girl. But since I stand in place of her father, I must consider practical matters as well as love. Tell me about your business."

The silversmith's answers were specific and to the point. He lived above his shop and was almost ready to buy the building. His main difficulty was the cost of purchasing silver, which, as his sales increased, and he needed more material, took an ever greater portion of his income.

But this was a problem of success and Protos was pleased with what he heard.

"Galene's dowry will be two hundred Athenian drachmas, to which I shall add some furniture and cooking utensils. I only wish it could be more."

"It is generous." From the expression on Tagilos's face, it was clear he had not expected so much. "I will work hard."

"Yes, I have no doubt." Protos stood. "And now I hope, since you are to be a member of the family, that you will join us for supper. Galene's cooking has improved since she was a child."

The meal was very pleasant, and Galene blushed with happiness. The only one who was not in a festive mood was Nubit.

This is how it begins, she thought. *The time of parting. First I will lose the girls, and then I will lose everything else.*

She kept remembering her dream—the dream she had dreamt countless times. Protos was walking away from her. Then he would turn and look back . . . and then leave her forever.

In the spring Protos gave Galene away in marriage.

"And not an instant too soon," Nubit confided to him the morning of the ceremony. "She is already two months gone with child. You will be a grandfather before you are thirty."

43

In the world of Spartan politics, no one under the age of forty counted for very much. Foreigners thus tended to assume that all Spartan diplomats were middle-aged men, and, if Eurytus did not call attention to his origins—as he did not among the Athenians collected in Xabrinos's house—he was largely ignored. He could listen to other people's conversations and be no more regarded than a servant.

His father continued to take advantage of this.

Tonight, Eurytus saw that the Athenians had no stomach for supporting Thebes with anything beyond their good wishes.

"Thebes and Sparta are like children who have fallen out over the possession of a toy. The quarrel is out of all proportion to its causes. Let them sort it out between themselves."

"Wars are expensive and their outcomes are never what one expects. Sensible people stay at home and concern themselves with their own business."

"Of course Sparta is to blame, but what is that to us?"

"Does anybody even know what Sparta *wants*?"

The one person who seemed to be firm in his support of Thebes was Dexileos, an old man with white hair and, from his dress and jewels, great wealth. If table arrangements meant anything, he was far from being a favorite with his host—the man was practically eating his dinner out in the hall.

Dexileos was also the only one of Xabrinos's guests who recognized Eurytus.

"You and your father were in my house once," he said. "For the peace conference after Leuctra. That must have been—what? Two years ago and more."

He glanced at the stump of Eurytus's left wrist and quickly looked away. "Not quite two years ago."

"Been pursuing a career as a soldier, have you?"

"Yes."

"And dabbling in politics as well, I'll venture."

"I am only here to assist my father," Eurytus answered, wondering why he sounded so defensive.

"Yes, of course." Dexileos smiled, giving the impression he was in on some secret. "And it seems to me I heard something about your adventures in Thebes. Quite a daring business, from all reports."

"I don't know what you—"

"Oh, come now. No need to be modest. It takes bowels to go after some-one like Protos, and in his own house! He is an acquaintance of mine, you know. Formidable fellow."

Dexileos winked, and his smile broadened slightly.

"They say he keeps your left hand in a box in his bedroom. Perhaps he hopes you'll come back for it—what do you think?"

Eurytus had no memory of how that conversation ended. He remem-bered almost nothing about the rest of that night except sitting on a back stairway, his head between his knees, trying desperately to catch his breath.

Protos was alive.

44

Protos's recovery was as slow as Nubit had predicted. When the next cam-
paigning season was upon them, Epaminondas ordered him to stay home.
Agenor took command of the skirmishers.

Protos spent the summer running, recovering his strength. He hated
the inactivity, but he knew Epaminondas was right.

When the army came home, Protos's officers gathered at his home to tell
him that Pelopidas had been captured in Thessaly by Alexander of Pherae.

"Alexander isn't going to do anything unconsidered," Agenor said.
"He knows the value of his prize, and he knows what will happen to him
if Pelopidas dies—he doesn't want the whole Theban army baying for his
blood. Already another expedition is being organized. We'll get Pelopidas
out or we'll leave Thessaly a wasteland."

"It might not have happened if you'd been there, Protos. Pelopidas is
sometimes too rash for his own good, but he listens to you."

The speaker was Ladamos, whose attention was distracted the next
instant by Eupraxia. She carried a tray of beer cups around the room, lest
any of the officers perish of thirst, and sometimes she let her eyes slide over
in Ladamos's direction.

She was tormenting him. She had been doing it for years, ever since
Protos's eighteenth birthday banquet, when, thinking she was Protos's concubine, Ladamos had tried to buy her.

In the years since, if he happened to be a guest at dinner—Protos, in defiance of aristocratic custom, always ate with his womenfolk at table—Eupraxia
would smile at Ladamos and look away, ignoring him, then glance at him
again and let him feel the heat of her green, almond-shaped eyes.

She was now seventeen, a bewitching little creature with hair the color of corn silk, and apparently she had made her choice of a husband long ago.

The next afternoon Ladamos came again and sat with Protos in the garden, drinking beer and discussing the bride price.

"Well, I have no intention of sending her off to you in her nightdress," Protos argued. "It would shame her to come to you without a dowry."

"I don't care about a dowry. I want only her."

"Nevertheless . . ."

In the end Ladamos agreed to accept two hundred silver shekels, which he did not need because he came from a wealthy family.

When she found out about it, Nubit spent the next day scolding Eupraxia. She was still in a black mood when she went to bed.

"Why are you acting like this?" Protos asked. "Do you object to her choice?"

"He is a soldier. What little fool marries a soldier in the middle of a war?"

"You have been living with a soldier for over ten years."

"You weren't a soldier when I met you."

"No. I was a hunted fugitive."

Even lying beside him, Nubit seemed far away. Without warning, she buried her face in Protos's arm and wept.

"I hope she leads him a wretched life," she said through her tears.

And then, of course, Protos understood.

"You will miss her," he said.

Nubit didn't answer. She only wept.

❦

After two expeditions to retrieve him, Pelopidas was finally rescued. He received a hero's welcome when he returned to Thebes, but he seemed embarrassed by the whole business.

"I was a proper fool to let myself be captured like that, but I will make Alexander pay for it before I am done."

"I agree that you were a fool," Epaminondas said. "And I agree that Alexander will have to be dealt with, but you take all these things too personally, my friend."

It was the middle of the morning and they were both somewhat overstrained with wine, which was itself a measure of Epaminondas's relief at his friend's safe return.

"What do you say, Protos?" Pelopidas asked. "Shouldn't I cut the dog's throat?"

Protos laughed.

"I say you are too old for that kind of nonsense, but that if you want his throat cut I'll be happy to cut it for you."

The two boeotarchs found this astonishingly witty and laughed accordingly.

❧❧

The last of the girls, little Hemera, found favor with a cattle dealer. Nubit accepted it with a stony resolve. She did not weep. She seemed even to welcome it, as if it ended some long ordeal.

Protos did not know what to make of her.

For the rest, men struggled and died, apparently to no purpose, and only time itself seemed to move forward.

The next year saw the death of Pelopidas. He won his war against the Thessalians but, wishing the personal satisfaction of killing Alexander of Pherae, he was instead cut down by that despot's guards.

Epaminondas was on campaign in Achaea when he received the news.

"Thebes has lost one of its principal supports and I, a dear friend," he said, handing the letter to Protos. "We played together as boys. We were in the army together, and together we planned and carried out the liberation of our city. What have we not shared?"

He buried his face in his hands and wept convulsively, his fingers seeming to claw at his flesh. It was a sight Protos had never seen or expected to see. He began to rise that the man might have privacy to grieve, but Epaminondas, still blinded with tears, reached out his hand to him.

"Stay with me," he said.

They were up most of the night and got very drunk together. Epaminondas seemed to need to talk. He told stories about his youth, about his parents, who had had no other children, and gradually Protos began to understand the sense of isolation that surrounded the man.

He had sacrificed almost every human attachment to his love for Thebes. He had studied war and politics and these had nearly consumed him. Born to wealth, he had given it all away. He was a philosopher, which in his view involved the embrace of an almost inhuman standard of virtue.

And now the friend of his youth was dead. It was no miracle he was devastated.

"I have had but two close friends in my life," he said, "and now you, Protos, are all that is left to me."

Perhaps an hour before dawn, Epaminondas finally found his bed. Protos left orders that the boeotarch was not to be disturbed.

※ ※

Three days later, a Theban patrol was ambushed and all six men were killed. No one knew anything about it until that evening, when two of the horses wandered into camp. Protos recognized one of them as belonging to Agenor.

It was almost dark, but Protos set out with twenty of his skirmishers for a reconnaissance in force. They followed the usual patrol route, and they were obliged to find their way by torchlight by the time they discovered the bodies. Agenor had wounds in four places, and the one that killed him had almost taken his head off.

For a long time Protos stood staring at the corpse of his friend—who had spoken out for him while they planned the massacre of the oligarchs, who had fought beside him ever since.

"You shouldn't have come," he said, almost in a whisper. "There was no need. . . ."

But Agenor had always been like that. He was a skirmisher—there was no reason why he should have gone out with the patrol, except that he had always sought excitement. His death was pointless.

Finally Protos knelt down, took off his cloak and wrapped Agenor in it. He slung the bundle over the back of his horse, took the reins in his hands and walked all the way back to camp. It was already morning before he and his men returned.

That afternoon, every man of the skirmishers, five hundred in all, came to the funeral. Agenor's body was purified with wine and Protos lit the pyre with his own hand. When the fire had died away, he collected the bones and sealed them in a bronze jar. They would go home to Thebes.

For three days Protos shut himself up in his tent and grieved in solitude.

A month later the army returned from its campaign, having achieved nothing.

※ ※

One night Nubit awakened to find herself alone. She thought at first that Protos had gone off to relieve himself, but when he did not come back she got out of bed and went looking for him.

She found him sitting on the stone steps that led down from the kitchen into their little garden. A jar of beer was beside him on the step.

"Couldn't you sleep?" she asked.

"No." He picked up the beer jar and took a swallow. He sat holding it in both hands and staring into the darkness. "Go back to bed."

Instead, she sat down beside him and took the beer jar from his hand. She tasted it and gave it back to him.

"What troubles you?"

For a long time he did not answer. He sipped his beer and seemed to forget her presence. Then at last he put his arm over her shoulders.

"Are you cold?" he asked.

"I am an Egyptian, you fool," Nubit answered with a hint of laughter in her voice. "And here I am in the middle of Greece, surrounded by mountains. Of course I am cold."

His response was to draw her closer.

"I will ask again: What troubles you?"

"Nothing." He shook his head. "Life."

She knew she had only to wait.

"I just wish . . . I wish the gods had left me as I was. Then I could have grown up to be a farmer like my father, who lived his life untainted by the spilling of blood."

"And in the end they murdered him," Nubit said quietly. "The gods have chosen you to avenge him. And so many others. You will end the slavery under which your people labor."

"I may never have the chance."

"Why do you say that?"

There followed another silence, but she knew from the tension she could feel in his arm that he was trying to find the right words to make her understand.

"The world is a mad place," he said finally. "We fight battles in which men die by the hundreds, and somehow we delude ourselves that each battle will be the last, that we can go back to being men instead of butchers. But the battle is fought, and then another and another, until we stop only because we are too exhausted to go on. And in those intervals of quiet everything returns to the way it was before. We are in a maze. We will never find our way out."

"What has happened?"

"Sparta has rebuilt her system of alliances in the Peloponnese. Even Athens has aligned herself with them. Of course, that is just like the Athenians. First they are on one side, then another. They fear the growing might of Thebes, so they kiss and make up with the Spartans. We will go on fighting until we are all bled white. The Greeks are a race of madmen."

"So what will happen?"

"There will be another invasion of the Peloponnese. Mantinea has broken with the Arkadian League and has attacked Arkadia because of some
foolish business about the shrine of Zeus. The Spartans and Athenians
have joined her, so we have to defend Arkadia." Protos sighed. "They are
all like children who can't play together without quarreling."

"But you will go?"

"I don't know. I don't want to. I want to stay with you." He smiled,
although perhaps he was not even aware of it. "Perhaps we could find
somewhere I could be a farmer and grow wheat—somewhere the world
would leave us alone."

"You must go," she said quietly, as if explaining a mystery. "While
Thebes fights Sparta, you must fight for Thebes. You are Protos, 'destined.'
The Great Mother set your feet upon this path and you cannot alter it.
It is the debt you owe your murdered family. It is the debt you owe to me."

He turned his face to her, and his expression said, *You are someone
I don't know.*

"I had thought you would want me to stay," he said.

"Would I like to grow old with you in some quiet place? Yes." She nodded. The gesture was emphatic. "I wanted nothing else, but the gods punished me for my presumption and now I know it is not to be. I have learned
that. You must fight."

"I am thirty-two years old. I have been fighting since I was fourteen.
I am sick of killing. I feel that my soul is forever stained with the blood I
have shed."

"Perhaps, although you have done no more than the will of heaven. But
you must fight that your children may live innocent lives."

"Children? I thought . . ."

"They will not be mine, Protos, my darling, but you will father children."
She took his head in her hands and smiled sadly. "Perhaps, if you have a
daughter, you will remember me and call her Nubit."

They sat together for a long time, silently mourning the children they
had never had together.

"I will tell you something," she said at last. "I will tell you something
about myself that you never knew, and then perhaps you will understand
that when you fight, you fight for me as well. Like you, I was born a slave."

"You . . . ?"

"Yes. My mother was a slave in a rich man's house. He was my father, but to him I was just another slave—he used me the way any man uses a woman he owns.

"One day he kicked my mother to death because she spilled his bathwater. I waited my time. I waited nearly two years. Then I poisoned him. I watched him die.

"That was why I fled Egypt.

"But the gods abhor the murder of a parent, and they have cursed me. That is why I have never borne children. That is why I know that my time is running out. Yet I cannot regret what I did. Slavery degrades slave and master alike. When you fight to free your own people, you fight for us all."

45

"I am going with you," Nubit said. "You will not leave me behind."

There was something in her face, something Protos had seen many times before, that told him she would have her will in this. Still, he had to ask.

"Why?"

"Because this will be the last time you fight for Thebes."

That appeared to be as much of an answer as she was prepared to give him.

But Nubit was wise. He had learned to trust her judgment and believe in her dreams and visions. He would trust her now.

"You must promise me, then, that you will stay beyond the reach of harm," Protos said. "If we lose, the Spartans' revenge will be terrible. I must know that you are safe from that."

"I will be safe. I will stay away from the battle, and an old witch woman in a wagon will not excite much interest."

"You are not old."

"Today, this moment, I feel old."

The day before the army was to head south, while she knew that Protos would be out all the afternoon, Nubit summoned her girls, now married women, to say goodbye.

"I think that Protos's work for Thebes is nearly finished," she told them as they sat about in the main room. Galene had brought her little son, who could stand if his mother held his hands. "I think it likely that neither of us will ever return from this campaign."

This announcement was greeted with a flood of lamentation—even the baby cried, but eventually, after many tears, Nubit was able to proceed.

"If such should be the will of the Great Mother, that neither Protos nor I return with the army, then this house and all it contains will be yours. Let there be no squabbling. Divide the furnishings as seems fair to all of you, then sell the house and divide the money equally. I trust you in this and you must trust one another."

"But you are our mother," Eupraxia cried. "Won't you come back to us?"

For a moment, Nubit could only shake her head. This was the hardest thing, she thought. She had not, as she feared, lost the girls to their husbands. They still loved her. But she was losing them now, this moment. It was bitter.

"I think not," she said quietly. "I think my time is short."

"And Protos?"

"Protos's work will not be done even when Thebes and Sparta have ended their war. He may not know it yet, but his war will last many years more."

❧❧

Half a day after they crossed into Arkadia, there was a fork in the road.

"If you go to the left," Protos told her, "eventually you will reach a village called Nestina, which is close to the border with Argolis. Wait for me there. If the battle goes against us, cross into Argolis and keep going until you are out of the Peloponnese. Do this for me."

He kissed her, climbed on his horse and rode off.

When Protos was gone, Nubit was alone with her visions. During the day her mind was clear enough, but as soon as the sun began to fade she would mix a little of her powder into a jug of beer, rest her back against a wagon wheel and let the visions overtake her.

Protos was away fighting his war. She never worried about him because she knew the Mother of All Life, She who spun the thread of destiny and was the author of dreams, had promised that he would outlive her by many years.

It was not that parting she dreaded but the one that must come, and soon. For her dreams had told her that she could never enter the place where Protos would one day lay down his bones.

She knew that Protos's war could only end one way. She knew that in this coming battle, or the one after that, or the one after that, Spartan power would break beyond repair. The Spartans were bleeding to death, and like a wounded lion Sparta would soon have the jackals tearing at her flesh. The Helots would revolt and with them would be one whom some men called Death's beloved son.

It was for this purpose that Fate cradled him in her hand.

So the end was approaching—their end. Their end would be her death. Could she face that? She would not lose him, but he would lose her. Or would he?

What awaited her in death? Nubit believed, had always believed, that this life was the true death and death opened the way to the world she saw in her dreams. She did not fear death.

But Protos relied on her. Perhaps he could rely on her still. As a mother holds her child's hands, lest he fall as he takes his first steps, perhaps she could still be there for him.

Perhaps she would live in his dreams.

46

＋≈•≈＋

Within an hour Protos had caught up with the army of the Boeotian League, which was already south of where he had expected to find them. When he reached the vanguard and saw Epaminondas he dismounted and gave his horse to a groom. Epaminondas, who was nearing sixty and whose hair and beard were now completely white, still marched with his men.

As soon as Protos fell in beside him, the boeotarch turned his head and grinned. "You're probably wondering why we're still on the road and not encamped outside of Mantinea."

"It had crossed my mind. I thought you wanted to meet Agesilaus there."

"I did, but my spies say he's coming north with his whole force, so it occurred to me that he's left Sparta unprotected. I thought I'd snatch up the city behind his back."

"So when he reaches Mantinea and sees you're not there, he'll guess what you've done . . ."

"And he won't have any choice but to turn right around and come back, by which time we'll have taken Sparta and had a bit of rest."

"And they'll be exhausted by the march back and forth and in no condition to fight."

"Precisely."

"You're clever, old man. You're almost devious enough to have made a passable Helot."

Epaminondas erupted into laughter and clapped Protos on the back.

❧❦

But the goddess Chance did not smile on the Thebans that day. Within six hours a deserter from their army was brought before King Agesilaus.

"He says that Epaminondas is moving south on the river road," reported the officer to whom a cavalry patrol had first brought the deserter. "He says they plan to attack Sparta while it is undefended. He also claims to be a Cretan."

Agesilaus had dismounted his horse and stepped a little away from the crowd of officers who always surrounded him. He studied their prisoner through narrowed eyes. This one was hardly more than a boy and seemed to have turned sulky. Probably he had expected to be received as a hero.

The king smiled at him.

"Tell me the truth now, lad, and I'll let you live. But if I take this army all the way back to Sparta and discover that you've lied to me, I promise you'll find out what your testicles taste like before you die."

"I've told the truth," the deserter said, still unwilling to raise his eyes from the ground.

"I hope so." The king glanced at a guard and made a curt gesture with his left hand. "Take him out of my sight."

"Your orders, my lord," the officer said, as the deserter was being led away, but Agesilaus could not seem to withdraw his attention from the Cretan boy, who was not receiving very courteous attention from his guards. He seemed to be trying to make up his mind about something.

"I loathe deserters," he said, as if to himself. He shook his head. "But I suppose we have no choice." And then, in the voice his army was used to hearing: "Reverse the column. We'll return to Sparta."

※ ※

An army of thirty thousand men cannot move in total secrecy. So many men and horses make a fearful noise, and the dust they raise is visible over a considerable distance. Thus the citizens of Sparta had something like an hour's warning that they were about to be attacked by the soldiers of the Boeotian League and their allies.

In this interval they had time to consider the utter hopelessness of their position. Sparta was no more than a grouping of villages, without even a wall, only earthworks that had lain neglected since the first Theban invasion of the Peloponnese. Riders had immediately been dispatched to find King Agesilaus and his army, but effective defense was impossible. It would probably take the enemy less than half an hour to overrun the town. The only choice lay between surrender and annihilation.

Eurytus had already made his choice. When his father came by his house, he found him in the anteroom beginning to strap on his breastplate.

"You aren't thinking of offering resistance," Dienekes said, in a voice of subdued horror. "There aren't fifty men of military age within an hour's march of here. You will achieve nothing except your own death."

"Is death so negligible a thing when compared with the alternative?" Eurytus allowed himself a few syllables of bitter laughter. "At least I will show the Thebans that the blood of Spartans is still red."

"It is madness."

"Was it madness at Thermopylae? You were the one who told me how your grandfather's father, for whom you named me, was blinded with an eye infection and yet had his servant lead him into the line of battle that on the final day he might have the honor of dying with his men."

Dienekes shook his head. It was a gesture more of grief than of denial.

"The men at Thermopylae died to save the army," he said quietly. "They gave up their lives to achieve a military objective. What you propose is the emptiest of gestures." He paused for a moment and his face hardened into something like contempt. "I think you are simply afraid that filthy Helot will imagine you are a coward."

They both turned, suddenly aware that they were not alone, and saw Helen, standing in the doorway. She greeted her father-in-law with a smile of perfect unconcern.

"You will leave your wife a childless widow."

Eurytus was already in the act of opening the front door to leave. He paused for just a moment, glanced at his wife, and said, "Somehow I think she will endure it."

Then he was gone.

※ ※

Epaminondas already knew from his cavalry patrols that Agesilaus's army had reversed itself and would arrive back in Sparta before he could have his forces positioned for an attack.

Still, he could not resist the temptation to borrow a horse and ride ahead with Protos to within sight of the town. They crested a small hill and gazed down at a network of narrow streets and small, dun-colored houses.

"It doesn't look like much, does it," Epaminondas said, trying to soften the sharp edge of Protos's disappointment. "Probably it was a bad idea from the start."

"We could still fight them here. One place is as good as another."

It was nonsense, and Epaminondas knew that Protos knew it was

nonsense. It was simply hard for this Helot slave to surrender the idea of
Sparta, that hated place, at once a smoking ruin and the graveyard of its army.

"No. We will fight them where we have the advantage. Here the advantages are all with them. Sparta, in itself, matters little."

"I know."

They rode back to the army, which was already in the process of swinging itself around for the march north.

"What will you do now?" Protos asked. The question meant that he was
trying to free himself from his obsession. Epaminondas smiled.

"We will go back to Mantinea. We will fight them there."

"And of course they will follow us, and by the time we reach Mantinea
both armies will be exhausted."

Epaminondas turned his face to his young friend and favored him with
a sly grin.

"That is precisely what I am hoping for."

"You're clever, old man," Protos said, nodding slowly to indicate he
understood.

Protos threw back his head and laughed.

❧❦

When Agesilaus reached Sparta he found no more than a handful of men
in arms and had to make inquiries to be sure the Boeotians had ever been
near the place.

"We never saw them, but they were here," one of the defenders told
him. He was apparently the leader and seemed embittered, as if the enemy
had somehow cheated him. "They must have gotten word that the army
was returning."

"And what would you have done, six or seven men in your dress uniforms, if we hadn't returned? Would you have held the town against them?"

There was a ripple of laughter among the king's officers, and the man
glared at them and waited for the laughter to subside.

"No, my lord," the man answered, in the coldest voice Agesilaus had
ever heard. "We would have fought and died here that our ancestors might
not be ashamed to receive us."

At a loss for a reply—there was no reply—the king reached down to offer
his hand.

"Eurytus, son of Dienekes," he said. "Many might call you a fool, but
no one will ever be able to call you a coward. You and your friends have
upheld the honor of Sparta this day."

Eurytus took the king's hand and held it perhaps longer than the salute strictly required.

"Then may I beg a favor of my king?"

"What is it?" Agesilaus, asked, releasing Eurytus's hand.

"I assume you will now head back north to engage the Thebans?"

"Yes."

"Allow me to march with the army." Eurytus's eyes were pleading, though his voice was level. "This may be the battle that decides everything, and I still have one hand left with which to hold a sword."

The king nodded. "So be it," he said.

And then he glanced about him, like a man who has misplaced something.

"Somebody find that Cretan deserter," he shouted, and then, more quietly, "I suppose we owe him some money."

❧❧

As they rode back to the vanguard together, Epaminondas described the broad outline of his plan.

"We're a few hours ahead of the Spartans, although that lead will dwindle by the time we reach Mantinea. There's a place where the valley narrows down to something a man might walk across in less than half an hour, and the foothills on both sides provide a good defensive position. We won't reach it until the early hours of the morning, but once we're there, what do you think Agesilaus would expect us to do?"

"To rest until the next day, when the battle will start," Protos replied.

"Precisely. And I propose to give Agesilaus every reason to suppose that is our intention. His own men will be tired. He will *want* to believe it."

"And, besides, it is a basic Spartan assumption that where he is only tired any other man is probably half dead."

"Precisely. How could we be ready for battle when he is weary? Everybody knows that the Boeotians are an army of old women."

"I'll tell the men that you said so."

It was a jest, but Epaminondas appeared not to have heard. Protos thought perhaps he was offended and was about to apologize when Epaminondas forestalled him.

"We will win in any case," he said. "We have the weight of numbers, but winning is not enough. I don't want a victory where we hold the field but it is covered with our dead. I want to catch the Spartans off their guard and to crush them like wheat in a hailstorm. I want this war with Sparta to end."

❧❧

A night march was always an ordeal, especially when it covered the same ground an army had crossed only a few days or even hours before. Soldiers would endure much if they felt it was to some purpose, but a sense of futility was dangerous.

Thus Protos spent the night of the march back to Mantinea riding up and down the columns, talking to commanders and common soldiers alike, bringing them all the same message. "This is not for nothing," he would tell them. "Epaminondas means to end this campaign with a stroke from which the Spartans will never recover. For the rest of your lives, you will tell your children and grandchildren about your victory at Mantinea, but for now stay strong and trust in the boeotarch."

They had taken the main road, which forced the Spartans over to the western edge of the valley and slowed them down accordingly. But the very size of the Boeotian army reduced their speed and, besides, they were in enemy territory, far from their bases of supply. The Spartans could travel without so ponderous a baggage train.

All through the night, as the two armies moved north, they remained in fragile contact. Theban and Spartan outriders, whose only duty was to provide intelligence about the enemy's movements, occasionally crossed each other's paths, but no one wanted to die in the dark and they maintained a wary truce.

In the first gray light before dawn, Epaminondas borrowed Protos's horse and rode it into the open prairie beyond the road. One by one his principal officers mounted their horses and gathered around him to hear the plan he carried in his mind and receive their orders. The soldiers, as they marched by, turned their heads to watch them, knowing that their fates depended on the words of one man.

The conference took a little longer than a quarter of an hour, then Epaminondas rode back and rejoined his soldiers.

"What did they think?" Protos asked him.

"I wasn't riven through with a sword or relieved of my command, so perhaps they can see how it might work. What do *you* think?"

"I think it's something a lunatic might have dreamed up. But that's why you keep winning battles, because you're a crazy old man who lives under the special protection of the gods."

"From you, I'll accept that as an endorsement."

❧❧

At first light Epaminondas and his forces came down into the valley, and for the first time the two armies could see each other. They marched in parallel, the Boeotians to the right and a little ahead, but what the Spartans could not see was that the rear of the Boeotian column, what would be the left side in their line of battle, was already strengthened to a considerable depth and consisted entirely of Theban infantrymen. Among them was Epaminondas himself.

At the head of the Boeotian column, among other officers but riding his black horse all the way to the outside, was Protos, the soldier the Spartans feared most. But Protos was merely a distraction. The Spartans would expect him to be in the front of the Boeotians' main assault. He would keep their attention away from the rear, the hammer that would break the Spartan right.

For two hours the enemy armies proceeded up the valley together, almost within shouting distance. And then, at a place where the foothills on either side were within an easy walk of one another, the Boeotian vanguard, which was well ahead of the Spartans, nosed to the left and crossed the valley, blocking the Spartans off.

They had reached the point where Epaminondas had decided the battle would be fought—both sides knew it. The only question was when.

The armies had been on the march through a day and a night. Everyone was weary beyond endurance, in need of food and rest. It was a reasonable assumption that no one would think of offering battle this day.

And the Boeotians had assumed what the Spartans would have to interpret as a defensive posture.

The Spartans were watching. They were wary, but they would expect no fight today.

Protos climbed down from his horse and gave it over to a groom. Like the Spartans he was watching, and what he saw was that the Spartans were beginning to relax.

Protos gave the order to lay down weapons. The Spartans could not hear him, but they could see the result.

What happened next was like a dance. The rear lines, hidden from Spartan eyes, stayed in place, but the men in the front lines began to move about, apparently aimless, the way men do when their only thought is of a hot meal and bed.

Protos kept his vigil. The Spartans were being taken in. They were beginning to accept as a fact what they desperately wanted to believe, that the Boeotians were standing down, that no one would have to fight and die today. The ruse was working.

"You crazy old man," Protos said under his breath, "you've done it again."

※ ※

Eurytus had declined a horse, preferring to march in the ranks. Yet he had only covered the distance between Mantinea and Sparta once, so by the time the order was given to halt he was tired but not exhausted. Perhaps that fact left him more alert.

Like everyone else, he was relieved when he saw the Boeotians put down their weapons. And then he happened to notice a particular officer at the extreme right of their line. It was Protos.

Well, he thought, *there you are. And I am here and perhaps it may even happen that we can at last settle this long quarrel between us.*

It was almost comforting to see Protos there. It provided a satisfying closure, like the last lines of a tragedy.

They would hunt each other out, Eurytus supposed. Did he have any chance at all against this slave? He supposed not. It didn't seem to matter. Only the fact of its being over mattered.

And then he noticed how still Protos was, how watchful.

And then he looked about him and saw how the battle lines of the Spartans were decaying into the shapeless confusion of a camp.

The idea only gradually took shape in his mind. It couldn't be true. It was too horrible to be true.

But it was true. The Boeotians had tricked them. The Spartans would be caught disorganized and defenseless.

He must find the king. He must—

But it was too late. In the next instant he heard what had to be the most terrible sound in the world, a battle cry erupting from ten thousand throats.

There was nothing to do now but fight and die. Eurytus drew his sword and rushed forward.

Then suddenly there was a blinding light, as if he had stepped inside the *halos* of a god. He was on his knees before he was even aware of falling. In the last instant of consciousness, he realized something had hit him in the head.

Is this what it is to die? he thought.

47

The Spartans were beaten. Never, never had they suffered so humiliating a defeat. Their dead were strewn over the field like leaves in autumn. One could almost cross the battlefield walking on the faces of dead Spartan warriors.

But Epaminondas was wounded. Fighting in the front line, he had been struck in the chest by a javelin. The shaft had broken off, but the iron point buried itself on the left side, two finger widths below the collarbone. Everyone, including Epaminondas, knew that the wound was mortal.

There was a brief but fierce struggle to keep the Spartans from gaining possession of his body, and then he was carried back to the rear. A tent was quickly set up over him that he might be out of the sun.

"How does the battle go?" he asked.

"We have beaten them," someone answered.

"Then I have lived long enough, for I die unconquered."

By this time Protos had received word. He arrived almost out of breath and knelt beside his friend, who took his hand.

Great as was his pain, Epaminondas turned his head so that his gaze rested on Protos's face.

"I never married," he said, in a voice that was little more than a whisper. "My bride was Thebes. But I have left two daughters, my battles Leuctra and Mantinea, and perhaps one son."

He lived about half an hour longer. He spoke to his officers, and when he learned that his two principal lieutenants had also fallen, he recommended peace with Sparta, for there was no one left whom he trusted to continue the war.

"And now, physician, remove the spear tip from my breast, for it pains me and I must be on my way."

All the time he held Protos's hand. At the last he looked up at him and said, "When I am dead, my son, you are free."

The great man was no more. After a while Protos delicately extracted his hand from Epaminondas's lifeless grasp, rose to his feet, and walked away.

He had no tears. Rage swept through his soul like a dark and terrible wind. Someone must pay for this.

❧❦

The Spartans who fell in battle were the lucky ones. The survivors, their honor lost as the price of survival, crouched on the ground, waiting to find out what their conquerors would do with them.

For Protos, riding in front of this neat square of cowed and broken men, the fury of his grief still swirling within him, these were the final enemy, the killers of his friend, the murderers of his family, the power that had held his people in helpless subjection for four hundred years—evil, arrogant, and at last in his grasp.

He would have his revenge. Some inner voice told him he would live to regret this hollow victory, but he did not care. He would have his revenge.

He dismounted from his horse and stood before them.

"What is it that Spartan mothers say when their sons go to war?" he shouted. "'Come home with your shield or on it'? It seems you have missed your chance at both. You chose to live, at any cost.

"Still, I offer you this last opportunity. I, Protos the Helot, a slave in Laconia, but the victor on this field, I, who saw my mother and father butchered before my eyes that boys could think themselves men for having spilled innocent blood, I will show you this much mercy. Any one of you who has the stomach to face me in equal combat, if you win, you will walk away from this place a free man. Go home and tell what lies you like. If you lose, you will find a common grave with braver men than you. Otherwise, perhaps your families will ransom you—if they can bring themselves to share your shame—if not, may you wear out your lives in chains.

"I am waiting. Show me your Spartan courage."

There was silence, a pause in which the defeated Spartans chose between honorable death and at least the possibility of life. They had all heard the stories of Protos the Helot, this invincible warrior whom Death loved and whose very name turned men's bowels to water.

Finally one stood up. He was a big man, heavy with muscle. He smiled, as if he fancied his chances.

"I will fight you," he said. He stood with his feet apart, his very attitude a challenge.

"Good." Protos grinned at him. "Tell me, do you still have your sword or, in your haste to surrender, did you throw it away? If you did, I have a spare."

The man's face went dark with rage.

"I have my sword," he answered, spitting out the words.

"Then step forward." Protos made a summoning gesture with his left hand.

The big Spartan drew his sword and, as he emerged from among the square of sitting men, made a few threatening passes through the air with it.

Their duel was short. The Spartan made a lunge, which Protos parried, staggering back as if momentarily overwhelmed. The Spartan fell into the trap. He lunged again, overextending himself, and Protos had only to step forward and drive his sword into the man's right armpit, killing him with almost contemptuous ease.

The big Spartan went down on his knees and Protos kicked him over. For a moment the Spartan's legs moved and he clawed at the earth, as if trying to rise. Then he was still.

"There is one who will sleep tonight with the honored dead." Protos turned back to the men squatting on the ground. "Is there no other? *IS THERE NO OTHER?*"

"There is one," a man said as he struggled to regain his feet—an operation made somewhat more difficult by the absence of his left hand. There was an untended wound across his left temple, crusted with blood. "There is one more, and then have done with this folly, Protos."

It was Eurytus.

"In light of our long . . . 'association,' shall I call it, will you grant me a private word before I draw my sword?"

Protos was too appalled to do more than nod, but it was invitation enough. For a moment they stood facing each other in silence.

"What are you doing here?" Protos shrugged in a kind of dismay. "With only one hand, no one—"

"This time we were fighting for our homeland. And, besides, I knew you would be here. I had no choice.

"I want you to know," Eurytus murmured, his eyes on the ground, "that I did not surrender. Something, I know not what, struck me in the head. I woke up to find myself a prisoner."

"I believe you. I can see the wound."

Eurytus shook his head.

"You called me a coward once. Do you remember?"

When Protos made no answer, Eurytus moved his shoulders in a faint shrug and smiled mirthlessly.

"You were right," he went on. "But I have never truly been afraid, except in front of you."

"It was a long time ago."

"No so long. I was terrified then. I wonder why I am not afraid now."

"We are not the same as we were then, either of us."

For more than half his life Protos had waited for this moment, and now it seemed empty. Had Eurytus had a choice, all those years ago? Had *he* had a choice? The world into which they had been born guided them through the steps of this strange dance of murder and revenge, and now it was nearly over.

Or perhaps not.

"Go home, Eurytus," Protos murmured, so that no one else could hear. "Let it be over between us. Take your life and go home."

Eurytus laughed and shook his head.

"Do you mock me?"

"No."

"No? Then are we to forgive each other, as if the things we have done mean nothing?"

His face seemed to compress, as if he was on the verge of tears. It was neither fear nor anger that oppressed him, but some anguish perhaps even Eurytus himself could not have defined.

"I killed your father," he said, his voice heavy with emotion. "You killed my brother. We each have a debt to pay—not to each other but to the ones we lost. For both of us it is a choice between death and shame, and I will not be shamed again. Here and now, either I must take your life or you must take mine."

"So be it."

There was no other answer to make. Protos understood what he meant. It seemed at last that the only victory for either of them was to end it with each respecting the other, as between equals.

Protos opened his hand and let his sword, still stained with blood, drop to the ground. He drew his knife.

Suddenly Eurytus laughed.

"My brother's dagger," he said, shaking his head as if at some private joke. "You offered me the same terms the first time."

Eurytus drew his sword and then, without making a show of it, Protos put his left hand behind his back, slipping it under his belt and closing it into a fist.

The points of the two weapons touched. The duel was on.

At first neither man seemed willing to attack. They circled around each other warily, as if each hoped that the other would strike first.

At last Protos made a feint, but Eurytus was not such a fool as to counter. Their blades never touched.

Then, suddenly, Eurytus went over to the offensive. He slashed with a wild determination, as if his opponent were some barrier he had to cut through to escape. His sword, having not only greater length but more weight, was difficult to turn, and it was harmless once one stepped inside its arc. Protos threw himself against Eurytus and knocked him off balance.

All at once Eurytus was on his back. He looked up at Protos with what might have been defiance but was something else. He wanted his enemy to know he was not afraid. He was waiting for the stroke that would kill him.

"Get up," Protos said quietly. "Come—this is no way for a brave man to die."

He brought his left hand around from his back and offered it to Eurytus, who held up his right hand, still holding the sword. Protos grabbed him by the wrist and pulled him to his feet.

"You should have killed me," Eurytus almost whispered. "Now I know to keep you at a distance."

"But you don't know how."

They exchanged a glance. They understood each other perfectly. There would be no more quarter given.

It was hard to attack when one's opponent had a longer blade. One could only wait for him to go over to the offensive and hope for an error. But Eurytus was very obliging. He seemed intent upon drawing first blood.

At the same time, however, he was a good swordsman and made few mistakes.

But at last he seemed to grow tired. He overreached himself and Protos was able to step in and drag the point of his dagger up the inside of Eurytus's right arm.

Eurytus dropped his gaze and stared at the blood pouring out over his arm. For that instant he had forgotten that he was fighting for his life, and in that instant he doomed himself.

Protos did not hesitate. He lunged and caught Eurytus low in the belly.

He pulled the dagger free with a twist that must have been exquisitely painful. Eurytus dropped his sword. It was over.

Eurytus began to sink and Protos caught him in his arms, lowering him gently to the ground. There was no more hatred. Vengeance was only a word. They were simply two men who had known each other almost since boyhood.

"I can't feel my legs," Eurytus gasped. "I suppose that means I'm dying." His hand was covered with his own blood. He laid it on Protos's arm.

"I'm sorry," Protos murmured. "I'm sorry."

"Don't be. You would have done worse to let me live. I have no desire to see what must come hereafter." And then he smiled. "Is your revenge complete now?"

"It's not about revenge anymore. It's about learning to be free."

Perhaps those were the last words Eurytus heard, or perhaps even they were lost to him. He looked up into Protos's face and in the next instant he was dead.

※※

In the evening Gaiomaxos came by Protos's tent and they sat outside, drinking beer.

"The war is over," he said, as if he could hardly believe his own words. "The Spartans have already arrived to discuss terms with our principal officers. There seems to be some confusion over who precisely is in command among us."

"I'm sure they'll sort it out."

"But you don't care, do you."

"No." Protos turned to Gaiomaxos and smiled. "Would you like me to recommend you?"

They laughed briefly and then lapsed into sullen silence.

"Will you leave the army?" Gaiomaxos asked.

"I have no idea what I'll do."

※※

The next morning there was a truce on the battlefield as the two sides began the process of burying their dead. At sunrise Epaminondas's body was consigned to the earth. His grave was separate and a little ahead of the trench that would hold the Thebans who had been killed. Protos watched as the rites were performed.

Epaminondas had been a great man, which in practical terms meant that he had used others to attain his ends. However, there had been nothing selfish about him. Thebes itself was the great love of his life.

But Protos did not love Thebes. To him, Thebes was no more than an instrument, a means of carrying on his war with Sparta. So perhaps he had used Epaminondas as ruthlessly as Epaminondas had used him.

But Epaminondas had been his friend and Protos was grieved to know that he was no more. It was almost like the end of his own life.

The Spartan dead would take days to bury.

The prisoners had been given their freedom—it was a gesture of conciliation and no doubt wise. Besides, the presence of these men in their midst would only further demoralize the Spartans. If only a few men had surrendered, those would probably have felt obliged to commit suicide, but so many . . .

Yes, let them go home. It was an indignity that Eurytus had been spared.

❦❦

What to do.

All the next day Protos sat in front of his tent contemplating what had suddenly become the central dilemma of his life. Every path forward seemed to be blocked.

What if he simply gave it all up? He had some money. He could buy a farm somewhere and become what he would have been if the Spartans had not twisted his life out of all recognition. He could stay in Boeotia and grow wheat. Nubit would probably like that—she had taken a fancy to the settled life.

Or he could go on living in the house in Thebes, drawing his army pay as a ranking officer. He was a respected man in Thebes.

Except what was there in the world more useless than a soldier without a war to fight?

So farming was a better plan. He would be happy and prosperous—this while the people of his native village labored under the lash and starved in hard years.

Could he live with that? No.

What he wanted was to go back to Laconia and fight to free his own people. The Helots of Messenia were free and his own people were slaves.

But what about Nubit? Could he ask her to follow him? Would he *want* her to follow him, to lead the life that awaited him in Laconia? To be a soldier's woman was bad enough. In Laconia he would be an outlaw. If she were caught . . .

It didn't bear thinking about.

But to be separated from her, after all these years?

He needed to talk to Nubit. Nubit was wise. Nubit would know what to do.

❧❦

The next morning he climbed on his horse and rode to Nestina. Nubit waited there. Probably she had not even heard of their victory.

It really was only a village. Perhaps no more than two hundred people lived there, and the first person he spoke to told him where he would find the "witch woman" who lived in a wagon.

She didn't seem surprised to see him.

"So," she said. "You were victorious."

"Yes, but there are problems."

She didn't want to hear about his problems. She wanted him to climb on her belly. She was hardly even willing to wait until he had tethered his horse. She almost dragged him into the wagon.

Half an hour later, naked and glowing and still gasping for air, she was prepared to listen.

"Epaminondas is dead. Before he died he instructed that the Thebans should make peace with Sparta. Probably it is their best choice, but it is not my choice. Tell me what to do."

"What do you want to do?"

She sat there, her skin rose-colored from just below her eyes to her navel. She loved him, and she was asking what he wanted to do. In that instant he did not know himself.

"I will save you the trouble," she said. "You want to go back to Laconia and kill Spartans until they leave your people in peace."

He said nothing. He felt ashamed.

"And that is precisely what you must do," Nubit said. "What you do is not your own choice but the gods'. You were born to be a warrior and your enemy was chosen for you."

"Will you go with me? I want you to, but how can I ask such a thing? I want you to be safe."

"There is no safety. There is only the will of heaven. I will go with you. I will stay with you as long as there is breath in my body.

"Now come and let me feel your weight again. It has been a long time."

❧❦

They left early the next morning. Protos drove the wagon with his horse tethered behind. They would go first to Mantinea, since the road south from there avoided the mountains. And besides, Protos had his goodbyes to say.

"So, you killed this fellow Eurytus. How did it feel?"

It was one of the little shocks of living with Nubit that he had never become accustomed to. He had not even mentioned Eurytus and yet apparently she knew all about it. He did not have to ask how.

"Empty. It made me feel empty."

"Good. That means at last revenge has died in you."

She smiled at him.

48

On the journey south, Nubit's hair began to turn white. Protos noticed it on the first evening, when he returned to their campsite with an armload of wood for the fire. The moon was full and seemed to shine down on her head. At first he thought the few strands were nothing more than the white sheen of the moonlight.

Then, when the fire was burning, he noticed them again and reached out to touch them.

"What is it?" she asked, as if she had been awakened from a trance.

"Just a little white in your hair," he said. "It's beautiful."

"It isn't beautiful. It's age. I am getting old."

"You look the same as the first time I ever saw you."

She turned her eyes to him and smiled sadly.

"Except that now my hair is going white."

She didn't want to make love that night. She said she was tired, but she seemed to be holding herself in, as one might in preparation for some ordeal that could not be avoided. She asked him if he would sleep under the wagon.

"As I have many times in the field." He kissed her and whispered, "I love you."

In the darkest part of the night he was awakened by some sound. He lay wrapped in a blanket, trying to identify it.

And then he heard it again. It was Nubit, quietly sobbing.

"I had troubling dreams," she told him in the morning. "Could I sleep in the wagon while you drive?"

"Yes. Of course."

He noticed that the streak of white in her hair was a shade wider.

When he stopped the wagon to water the horse, he went back to see how she was feeling. She was sitting with her back against a pile of blankets, drinking a cup of beer.

He could tell from her expression that she did not see him, that she was in another place and time, alone with her visions.

She looked older.

That night Nubit came down from the wagon and watched silently as he stirred the cooking pot. She didn't want to eat. She only drank beer.

"I will stay with you until I die," she said finally. "And beyond. But one day you will meet another woman, one who will bear your children and close your eyes when you die. Know that I will bless her with my last breath."

Protos found that he could make no answer, that his voice had died in his throat. His eyes filled with tears.

It had been many years since he had wept, but he wept then.

She took him in her arms and comforted his grief, as one does a child.

"I know you love me," she murmured into his ear. "That is the last comfort the gods allow me."

"Won't you come with me?" he was finally able to ask.

"As far as I can. As long as my life lasts."

❦❦

They followed the main road to Sparta almost to the border with Laconia and then branched east toward the mountains. Protos wished to avoid the Spartan patrols since, once his presence was known, he would have an army to deal with.

The road was good enough for the wagon and Nubit rested comfortably in the back, although it was not clear what she experienced of the journey. Most of the time she was not in her body but somewhere else.

At night, alone with the campfire, Protos tried to understand what was happening. Nubit was not sick in any way that a physician would have understood. She was not in pain, but she was growing old before his eyes. It was as if she had decided that her life had gone on long enough and she was hurrying toward its end.

How would he live when she was gone? He could hardly imagine. He had been not much more than a child when he met her and now he was in the middle of life. He loved her and relied on her wisdom. How would he manage when she was gone from him?

What did death mean for her? She had said once that her dreams were more real than the world and that at last she would live in them forever. Did she believe that still? He hoped so. He did not want her to die in fear.

That she was dying he never doubted. She had said as much.

The road led over the foothills and ran south. On the fourth day he suddenly became quite sure he was back in Laconia. He could not have said how he knew. He simply knew.

He stopped the wagon and went back to tell Nubit, but she was already dead. The instant he touched her he knew she had been dead for at least an hour.

In death she was an old woman.

Protos sat down on the ground beside the wagon and wept bitterly. His very eyes seemed to be dissolving into tears. He remembered the night his parents had died and how he had crawled into a cave and wept for them. It was like that all over again. He felt abandoned.

When his grief had abated a little, he stood up and fetched the shovel that was strapped to the side of the wagon. He dug Nubit's grave, and he made it deep.

Then he went back to the wagon and wrapped her body in his Spartan cloak.

Nubit had never mentioned the burial customs of her country. For a slave the dead were merely dead—one dug a hole and left the rest to the gods. That did not seem enough for Nubit.

Protos searched through his purse and found a gold coin, which he put in her mouth to pay the ferryman who would take her across the River Styx to the Land of the Dead. Then he drew his Spartan dagger from its leather sheath and put it in her right hand. At last he climbed down into the grave and pulled her in, that he might be sure she rested comfortably.

As an afterthought he dropped her medicine bag into the grave with her.

By then it was nearly dark. He did not want to bury her at night, like a suicide, so he sat beside her open grave straight through until dawn, hardly closing his eyes.

At first light he filled in the grave. When he had patted it smooth with his shovel, he took the horse by its bridle and led it forward until the wagon was directly over Nubit's final home.

"Your work is done," he said to the horse as he freed it from its bridle and harness. When he was finished he slapped it on the rump and it trotted forward a few steps and then turned its head back to him as if it could not understand what to do next.

"Go, girl. Go," he said. "You are free."

At last the horse began to wander away.

There was only one thing left to do. He retrieved his weapons, wrapped in a blanket, and then built a fire under the wagon. It blazed for a long time before the wagon collapsed into a heap of smoldering ashes. It had burned the ground around it black. No one would ever suspect that Nubit was buried here.

He picked up his weapons and began to walk away. Then, all at once, he had the sense that someone was watching him. He turned back to look, but there was no one.

❦ ❦

The journey was long and the way hard. It was like his first escape, only backward. He kept to the mountains, living off the land, drinking from the cold, clear streams.

Gradually, he knew where he was. The shapes of the mountaintops were familiar to him, as if he had spent his life looking at them.

Sometimes he felt as if he was being reborn, as if everything that had happened to him was no more than preparation for this. The past years were receding to some infinite distance.

One day Protos found a mountain pool that must have been fed by a spring, since there was no visible source. At one end a small stream raced away down the mountain, but the pool itself was deep and tranquil, so calm its movement hardly disturbed the reflections of the trees that gathered in clumps around it.

The bottom of the pool was lost in shadow. It might have reached down into the Underworld.

It was a hot day and the pool was inviting, so Protos sat down on its bank and scooped up water in his hands, which quickly began to feel numb with cold. The water was delicious.

Wisps of cloud were sliding by overhead, but he did not have to look up to see them. He saw them on the pond's surface, as if the water had become a window into the heavens.

To erase the impression he threw a pebble into the pond, and the clouds broke up in an ever-widening circle of ripples.

And then, for an instant, he thought he saw Nubit's face—or part of her face, her eyes and a strand of her hair—reflected back at him from the gentle swell of the water. It was only a glimpse. It couldn't have been real. It was a trick of the mind, the momentary victory of longing over death. He would banish the idea from his mind.

And yet, a moment later, he picked up another pebble and threw it into the pond, and again he was rewarded with a hint that died in the instant of its birth.

Her shoulder, the way it looked when she raised her arms to comb her hair.

Stop this, he thought to himself. *This is folly.* And a vast sadness filled his soul, so that he almost broke down weeping.

And yet he did not. There was a kind of comfort even in grief. He could not rid himself of the impression that she was somewhere near. It was almost as if he had merely to turn his head to see her.

He stayed by the pool the rest of the afternoon, until the sun disappeared behind the trees, leaving the water murky and blind, an image of death.

And when at last he rose to leave, his heart was calm, like the pool itself, for he had the sense that Nubit would always be with him, always there, a presence he could feel but never grasp. She would never really leave him.

❧❧

One day he looked down from the mountains and saw a road that ran between two villages, and he knew he was home.

It took him most of the day to reach the plain. He stood on the road, on the spot where his father and mother had died, and he could almost hear his father's voice.

Run, Protos! Now!

They were dead, his mother and father both. The men who had killed them were dead, and at their son's hand. What had it all meant?

He had learned that revenge was empty, that some debts could never be paid. He had learned that men can do wrong and believe it right. We were all, it seemed, prisoners.

Or perhaps not. What would he be now if Eurytus and his brother had never appeared on this road? A farmer, innocent of blood. A slave, under the lash of those who thought his life had no value. Now, standing where his parents had died, what was he?

That question was still to be answered.

❧❧

It was nearly sunset when Protos reached the village where he had been born. The harvest was at its height and the men would not be coming in until dark. Naked children were playing in the dirt. The house where he had lived with his parents was occupied by another, luckier family.

He saw no one he recognized.

He sat down under a tree in the center of the village and watched the smoke from the cooking fires slowly dissipate into the darkening sky. Now and then women, on their way to and from the village well, would glance at him. He was an object of suspicion, a stranger.

At last the men began to return. They were weary and hungry and paid him no heed.

Then he saw a face he thought he knew. It belonged to a man in the late afternoon of life, but still strong. He carried a bronze sickle in his right hand.

Protos rose to his feet.

"Friend," he said, in a voice just loud enough to be heard by this one man. "Will you afford me dinner and a little beer and a bed for the night? I can pay in silver."

The man stopped and looked at him, seeming to weigh the sickle he held as if he thought he might have to defend himself. Then, with his left hand, he waved Protos over.

"Let me see the silver."

Protos dug in his purse and brought out a single Theban drachma.

"I have never before seen a silver coin," the man said, in a voice hushed with awe. "How much is it worth?"

"In the cities of the north one could live on it for four or five days."

"Then I will tell my wife to kill a chicken that you may have flesh with your meal. There is a jar of beer we were saving for the end of the harvest, but this, it appears, is a greater occasion. Come. My name is Rakios."

They sat outside drinking beer while Rakios's wife killed and cooked a chicken. Protos remembered him now.

"You sound like a villager," the old man said after a short pause. "But that tunic is not village work. Have you come far?"

"I have been many years away, though I was born not far from here."

"Have you come back to stay?"

"Yes."

Rakios's eyes narrowed with suspicion.

"If you were born near here, you must be a Helot. Are you a Helot?"

"Yes."

"Then you are a slave like us," Rakios announced, nodding to emphasize his obvious logic. "You must have escaped."

"I did."

"Then why would a man who has lived in freedom, who has silver in his purse, come back to this place? When they hear of it, they will make you a slave again—or crucify you."

The bundle Protos had carried was beside him, leaning against the wall of Rakios's house. Protos laid it on the ground, undid the strap that held it together and opened the blanket. Inside were five javelins and four swords.

"They have tried before," he said quietly. "They are welcome to try again."

"Who are you?"

"My name is Protos."

Rakios seemed to go blank for a moment, and then his eyes settled on a house just beyond the tree that marked the center of the village. It was the house where Protos had been born.

"A friend of mine called Midios named his son that," he said. "He and his wife were killed by the Spartans. A few days later, his brother's wife and children were killed in their home. That was a long time ago. No one knows what happened to Midios's son."

"Perhaps he escaped."

"Perhaps he did."

The two men exchanged a glance. They understood each other perfectly now.

"Then I wonder what would bring him back. A sensible man, if lucky enough to escape, would know to stay away."

Protos, his gaze fixed on nothing, smiled.

"Perhaps he is not a sensible man."

�֍ ֍

The next morning Protos went out with Rakios to help with the harvest. Like all the other men he wore nothing but a loincloth, and anyone who troubled to look could see the scars on the stranger's back that marked him as a slave.

He enjoyed the work, the gathering in of great armfuls of wheat the very smell of which was almost enough to sate a man's hunger. He had worked this same field with his father, not a month before his parents' murder.

And he enjoyed the company of men who had never in their lives held a sword or known what it was to stain their souls with blood.

When the sun was at its height they stopped for an hour to rest and drink water. Everyone was in a cheerful mood because this year's harvest was good.

"It is possible we may make it through the spring without tasting a single turnip," someone said. "Wouldn't that be nice."

"They're not so bad when they're boiled soft. And the greens, with a little oil, make a nice salad."

"Without a little oil, they wouldn't do for goat fodder."

Protos could only smile, remembering the time in Thebes, at the house of a friend, when he had been served turnips as a delicacy.

He looked about him at the fields thick with grain and wondered that it was possible for people to be poor surrounded by such plenty.

"What share of the harvest do the Spartans take?" he asked.

Some of them looked at him strangely. How could he not know such a thing?

"Two bushels in three," someone said.

Protos was reasonably sure that in his father's day it had been three bushels in five. The Spartans, obviously, were feeling squeezed.

The problem was simple. A farmer was left with one bushel in three and must save out a third of that for seed. The remaining grain wouldn't feed his family through the year, so he was thrown back on his kitchen garden and roots. In a good year he would survive, but in a bad year famine would haunt the villages. If there was a turnip blight he would die.

The solution was also simple.

"I wonder why you tolerate it," Protos said. "The Spartans do not work the land and therefore they are not entitled to its produce. Give them nothing."

This produced astonishment and laughter, in about equal proportions.

"They would kill us."

"They cannot kill all of us without starving themselves. They are not farmers or craftsmen or traders, only soldiers."

"They are the best soldiers in the world. Surely they would kill us."

Now it was Protos's turn to laugh.

"I saw them defeated at Leuctra, nine years ago," he said. "The following year, the Thebans came into the south and drove them out of Messenia, freeing the Helots there. Within this month they were defeated again at a place called Mantinea in Arkadia, and this time with great slaughter. The Spartans are a broken reed."

"They can still kill us."

"Some of us, yes." Protos nodded in agreement. "But not as many as will die in the next famine. And if we drive them out, they will no longer be free to take our women for concubines, and their young men will not come to wet their swords with the blood of our fathers and mothers."

He had to stop. Suddenly his throat seemed to close.

"It can be done," he said at last. "I have *seen* it done."

"We have no weapons."

"Make them. Steal them. Take them from the dead bodies of your enemies. If you fight, soon you will have weapons enough."

"We are farmers. We know nothing of war."

"Then learn."

"Who is to teach us? Who would lead us?"

Finally Protos had had enough. He picked himself up from the ground and stood facing them.

"I will teach you. I will lead you. That is why I am here."

"Who are you? We don't know you. You are a stranger."

"My name is Protos, and I am one of you."